KINGDOM OF TODAY

OTHER BOOKS BY GENA SHOWALTER

Book of Arden Series

Kingdom of Tomorrow

Stand-Alone Title

The Great and Terrible

Kings of Fury Series, with Jill Monroe

The Wrong Bride

The Stolen Bride

A Jane Ladling Mystery Series, with Jill Monroe

Romancing the Gravestone

No Gravestone Left Unturned

Game of Gravestones

Twelve Graves of Christmas

Conrad: Falling for the Gravekeeper

Grave Wars

Grave New World

KINGDOM OF TODAY

BOOK OF ARDEN

GENA SHOWALTER

Published by Montlake, Seattle
www.apub.com

EU product safety contact:
Amazon Media EU S. à r.l.
38, avenue John F. Kennedy, L-1855 Luxembourg
amazonpublishing-gpsr@amazon.com

ISBN-13: 9781662530531 (paperback)
ISBN-13: 9781662530548 (digital)

Cover design by Faceout Studio, Molly von Borstel
Cover image: © alblec / Getty; © GB_Art, © alias612, © Tattoboo, © Miroslav Becvar, © All for you friend / Shutterstock

Printed in the United States of America

***To Vicki Tolbert**, my extraordinary, beautiful, faith-filled mother. I've dedicated books to you twice before—in the first inadvertently calling you "kiss-a" instead of "kick-a," and in the second misspelling your name entirely for reasons I have yet to even comprehend. Third time's the charm, right? (But let's be honest. Considering none of my siblings have ever put you in a book dedication, I still hold the title of favorite.)*

***To Mike Tolbert**, my wonderful, strong, and unstoppable father. Your life is a living testimony to God's goodness. While I wrote this book, you faced a heart attack, a stroke, and pneumonia, among other things—and you overcame them all. Your resilience humbles me, and your determination inspires me. I will always be in awe of you. (And your favorite.)*

***And to you, my beloved readers**, who have embraced the Book of Arden. Thank you for loving this passion project and walking this epic road with me. Your enthusiasm and support mean so much.*

It was the best of times, it was the worst of times, it was the age of wisdom, it was the age of foolishness, it was the epoch of belief, it was the epoch of incredulity, it was the season of Light, it was the season of Darkness, it was the spring of hope, it was the winter of despair.

—Charles Dickens, *A Tale of Two Cities*

PROLOGUE

A grinning Cyrus clutches two scarlet-stained daggers.

We stand in a stalemate, the battlefield between us a nightmare of lifeless bodies and scattered limbs bathed in the unflinching light of Theirland's twin suns. Lavender and gold streak the sky, casting an eerie glow over the blood-soaked earth, where rivers of crimson carve fresh paths through the flatland. Overhead, a restless flock of scavenger birds circles, their shrill cries piercing the thick, heavy silence as they await their feast.

A fresh wave of CURED soldiers floods in, surging from behind the former high prince and hurrying to kill the array of glowers trapped around me. Men and women I admire. Many more will die today if I don't stop Cyrus. But how do I strike down the man I love?

Is he still the man I love, though?

In the morning's brightness, I notice his missing facial brand. No sign of it remains, and my guts twist. More evidence of the monster he's becoming.

"It doesn't have to end this way, Arden," he calls.

"You're right." I huff and puff my breaths. "Walk away now, and I'll spare you."

His grin turns wry as he spreads his arms. Thin, snakelike shadows seep from his fingertips, coil up, and band around his neck. "I admit, your new confidence is adorable."

"Isn't it?" I rock on my heels and white-knuckle my sword hilt as I scrutinize my newest enemy. Cyrus is a god of a man in more ways than one. Beautiful, tall, and powerfully built, with features somehow both surprisingly soft and far too harsh. The contradiction fits. He's always been a paradox. Demanding yet indulgent. Mysterious but open. Perfect in his imperfections. An opponent feared by the world and yet my greatest ally. From the first moment I laid eyes on him, he fascinated me. And now here we are, soldiers on opposite sides of a war I only just realized I've been fighting my entire life.

A chorus of grunts, groans, clinking metal, and gunfire rises as his army attacks my allies.

"You won't kill me." Urgency whips at my back. "But I will hurt you if you continue on this path."

He tsks. "You give me too little credit and yourself too much. I will do whatever proves necessary to secure my rule." A promise he made at the start of this journey. "Join my team. Merciful leader that I am, I'll give you one more chance. Refuse, and my desire for you will no longer factor into my decisions."

There is no need to ponder my response. I lift my sword. "I will never help you destroy Soal."

Cyrus shrugs. "That's disappointing but not shocking. Just know you chose this, sweetness."

I jut my chin. "No, *sweetie*. You chose it."

He draws in a deep breath, then releases a short, sharp exhalation. "Let's get to it, then."

"Yes. Let's." Heart a war drum, I run at him.

He runs at me.

We meet in the middle . . .

—*The Book of Arden*, volume 20, section 18, paragraph 3, verses 5–26

Chapter One

The past cannot be undone, but you can begin again right where you are.

—*The Book of Soal* 1.23.43.18

"I won't do it." The words echoed in the empty train cart as it rattled along a winding track. I stood with my back pressed against a cold metal pole, its unforgiving chill seeping through my shirt. High Prince Cyrus Dolion occupied the space just in front of me, his massive frame a tower of strength. He gripped the bar just above my head, his arms forming an unbreakable cage around me.

"Yes, kitten. You will." Each gravelly syllable contained the full authority inherent in his title. He searched my eyes, intense to the max, before leaning closer to set his mouth near my ear. "We both know I didn't issue a request, but a demand."

My pulse jumped wildly until I felt a heartbeat in every part of my body. "You aren't the boss of me?" A breathless question when it should have been a firm statement.

"I am indeed the boss of you." He recaptured my gaze. "I outrank you by miles."

An undeniable fact. "Fine." I exaggerated a put-upon sigh. "You've convinced me. I'll do it. I'll obey the oh-so-important order of a superior officer." Gliding my palms up his powerful torso to toy with the ends of his silken hair, I confessed, "I will miss you today."

"You had better, because I'll be missing you." He brushed the tip of his nose against mine. "Thinking about you. *Craving* you."

The air between us crackled, filling my nostrils with his intoxicating, ambrosial scent. There was no man more striking than Cyrus Dolion, especially when he cranked up his smolder like this. From the dark shadow dusting his firm jaw, to the large handprint branded on the side of his face, to his heavily lashed eyes, aquiline nose, and soft lips, he exuded pure confidence. But then, he was a warrior to his core. Absolute control radiated from every inch of his lean, muscular form, now decked out in fatigues.

"You'll be safe," I said, a demand and a request rolled into a plea. Behind him, windows revealed a whizzing underground tunnel illuminated by pritis light. Every few seconds, a clock flashed the time remaining until we reached Fort Bala. A familiar destination amid unfamiliar circumstances. Our first time back since the Incident. "Yes?"

"I'll be as safe as you'll let me be," he vowed.

Not the response I'd expected. "I have no intention of endangering you."

"Are you sure?" He leaned in, erasing what remained of my personal space, ensuring I burned in the flames of his searing heat. "Let me start by saying I'm not attempting to manipulate you. I'm being honest about what will happen if you stir up trouble during the investigation into my father's death. I'll do anything to keep you safe, even risk my life."

My bones melted to the consistency of warm butter, which I'd recently sampled and loved far too much. "I'm going to be a model student. You'll see." At Fort Bala Royal Academy, I studied as a lady-in-training, the lowest rung of CURED's military forces. But I was now a double agent, no longer loyal to the Citizens for Unified Reform, Education, and Defense. I worked for Soal, their greatest enemy. Best not draw any attention to myself. Well, other than what I would garner when news of my romantic relationship with a certain high prince leaked. "Guess that means you'll be extra safe."

"A nice change of pace since meeting you," he teased.

I snorted and gripped his shirt, wrinkling the material. The train and its bumpy track rocked us closer together. "Now that we've got that covered, put me out of my misery and kiss me, Cyrus."

"Oh, I will kiss you." Agonizingly slow, he lowered his mouth to mine. A torment and a temptation all at once. But he didn't claim my lips with his. Instead, he rasped, "Just not now. I prefer to take my time."

"I'm not rushing you, honest!"

"No, *you* aren't."

"Two minutes out," an automated voice announced over the intercom.

"Ah. Okay." Regret set in, but I rallied fast. I had tons to do today, and pouting didn't even make the podium.

Cyrus gave my brow a sweet peck before shoving a hand in his pocket and withdrawing a small velvet box. My breath caught. Um . . .

He lifted the lid, the case's hinges opening with a soft whine to reveal a barely there necklace with small, clear stones that reminded me of waterdrops. His knuckles brushed my skin as he secured the piece around my neck, sending delightful shivers raining over the ridges of my spine. "This blends into your skin, preventing theft. Never take it off. It will distort your voice whenever you're being recorded."

Very cool. But. "Won't that be suspicious?"

"It would be suspicious if you *didn't* wear it. All royals and their closest associates take such precautions." He tapped one of five rings displayed on his fingers. "This is my distorter."

Okay. All right. "Thank you for looking out for me."

"Always." That said, he severed contact, pivoted, and stared straight ahead. All hint of softness vanished from him, leaving a hard, shudder-inducing expression behind. Truly the stuff of nightmares. "We're ready for what's coming. We'll be fine."

"You're right," I agreed with a nod. Last night, we'd discussed and compared our stories, then practiced being interrogated.

"We'll be *fine*," he repeated, as if I'd protested.

My sweet, protective Cyrus. I shifted to his side, offering what comfort I could. Difficult to do when our lives depended on our coming performances.

In only twenty-four hours, both our worlds had turned upside down and inside out. From cementing our unlikely romantic relationship to killing his father, the king. Yeah. The Incident. We were the ones responsible for the death of Tagin Dolion, and there was no going back, only forward.

The awful action had saved me from certain death, yes, but it had also ushered in a whole new host of troubles. And not just Cyrus's conflicted emotions regarding the loss of his father. Now, CURED must crown a new king of the United Provinces of Ourland. A position of unequaled authority and power, answerable only to the emperor, who answered only to a god named Astan. Not that the public knew of the otherworldly immortal operating behind the scenes.

Cyrus was one of seven high princes eligible for becoming king. Considering he was a double agent like me, locked in a secret war between Astan and Soal, the god of all gods, Cyrus's victory would absolutely, beyond any doubt, facilitate necessary change worldwide. But his loss could spell our ruin.

"I sense your growing anxiety, Pink." He kept his attention on the clock. "Remember the expert teachings of your extraordinary instructor."

"That's a task easier thought than implemented. Last night, I read the royal handbook," I admitted. "If you opt not to throw your hat into the king ring, you'll remain a high prince, able to help Soal in ways no other person can, but you'll fall under the authority of an unknown, possibly bigger threat than your father. If you do it and win, we can defeat Astan at last. But if you lose, you'll be stripped of your royal title and kicked out of the army. We'll forfeit the unfettered access we require for victory." He couldn't even hobble the competition. To strike against another candidate without the emperor's permission meant certain disqualification. "But no pressure," I rushed to add with a wince.

"High stakes ensure nonserious contenders are weeded out."

"Can we afford to take the risk? Everything has changed." Our circumstances. My allegiance. My outlook. All of my goals, hopes, and dreams. My very *purpose*. Three days ago, I'd left the base as Lady-in-Training Arden Roosa, mostly loyal citizen and dedicated cadet, but I was returning as a determined spy and willing traitor. While my mistakes in the days to come wouldn't cost us the war, they *could* usher in my death. Or his.

"Great risk, great reward." He notched his chin. "Consider the possibilities, not the complications, or you'll crumble before things get difficult."

"They aren't difficult now?" I squeaked. Then I muttered, "Leave me, fear." Watch Arden put one of those expert teachings to work: speaking to fear when it speaks to her and reminding it of who's boss. Because once again, Cyrus wasn't wrong. If I didn't put what I'd learned to work, I would absolutely crumble. "I'm strong and brave, and I can overcome anything."

"Yes, you are, and you can. Never forget."

Right. I *must* keep my eyes on the prize: Breaking through mass terror stoked by CURED and proving everything we'd been taught the whole of our lives was a lie. Stopping the purposeful spread of a terrible disease known as the Madness and defeating Astan before his human-animal acolytes wake from their centuries-long slumber and slaughter us all. Talk about treasure upon treasure. And yet, the obstacles.

We were up against a war machine with well-oiled cogs. CURED had an unfathomable number of supporters who believed Soalians like us were a threat to civilization. Once, I'd been among their numbers.

"When I'm king, as I was born to be," Cyrus said with steel, menace, and relish, "I will dismantle CURED and free every imprisoned Soalian."

Goose bumps spread over my limbs. "King Cyrus Dolion. I like it."

"Not as much as you like calling me sugar bear, I hope." Some of his previous playfulness returned.

I rolled my eyes, but I also smiled. Despite the seriousness of our circumstances, he still showcased a sense of humor reserved for me alone, and I couldn't help but tease him about it. "You are so into me."

"I am. I'm all in with you, Arden." The sudden gravity of his tone affected me as strongly as his nearness. "Whatever happens in the coming days, remember that."

"I'm all in with you too," I whispered, taking his wonderful confession and planting it in the Beloved Moments section of my memory garden. Since my childhood, I'd longed to work in agriculture. I'd been forced to join the military instead. Now, I gardened the only way I could—inside my mind. What better way to keep track of my double life?

Less than a minute remained until we arrived.

Doom prickled me, a seed born of mysterious origins, and my stomach curdled. Why feel this way? Inhale, exhale. No reason to discuss it right now, adding to our plate of problems. I'd wait until I'd dug deeper and discovered the source. For the time being, I buried the doom in my least favorite section of the memory garden: Problems for Later.

"I can't tell you everything that will happen today," Cyrus said, "but I can tell you this. We'll be separated. You'll be shut in a room, tested for Madness, and questioned."

I swiped my tongue over suddenly dry lips. "Got any hot, new tips for thriving during a CURED interrogation? Something you may have forgotten while we practiced?"

"Just remember what I told you. The interrogator's comments and questions might seem innocuous, but they are designed to trigger your defenses so that you'll elaborate and explain why you did certain things, what you thought or intended. Don't fall into the trap. Answer only what is asked, never elaborate."

"No elaborating." I tapped my temple, pretending this was all no big deal and I wasn't a weak link in our partnership.

He wasn't done. "Don't lie or exaggerate. Every word will be used against you at some point."

"Noted. I'll take a page from your book and misdirect."

He might have winced. Since his misdirection had led me to shoot him with a netter gun and flee his presence as if my life depended on it, it wasn't exactly our preferred topic. "Never deviate from our agreed story."

"No deviating." I gave an almost-confident nod. "Is there anything I *can* do?"

"We've already discussed how much you'll miss me." Cyrus captured one of my fingers between two of his, gentle, so gentle. A slight touch I felt in the deepest depths of my soul. "For the next few weeks, I'll be traveling to and from Theirland to meet with the emperor. I won't have many opportunities to see you."

I'd thought I wouldn't see him for a day, maybe two. Now I might have to go weeks? *Do not whimper.*

"We'll tackle this one day at a time," he assured me. "As soon as possible, I'll establish a mode of communication between us."

The train slowed before coming to a squealing halt. Once again Cyrus severed all contact. He rolled back his shoulders.

My heart raced as the door opened, revealing the cluster of armed knights and barons awaiting us. As predicted, they immediately oversaw our separation. Most accompanied the future king, marching him one way, while ten soldiers herded me the opposite direction, each keeping a hand on the hilt of a netter.

I struggled to mask my tremors. This was my first time being back at the base since my big change. While I knew I was free of the Madness, the coming test marked my debut screening as an active member of the Tome Society. A.k.a. a Soalian. A.k.a. a glower. Someone CURED touted as the worst of the infected. For people like me, "treatment" wasn't optional. Or humane.

Breathe in. Out. Taking in the acrid bite of scorched earth and aged leather, I wrinkled my nose. Thanks to my connection to Soal, invisible scales had fallen from my senses. The truth was so clear now. Oozing shadows as thick as paint coated limestone and granite walls. The same gloom coiled around every jewel-studded marble statue we passed. Images of old gods. Giants who were half human, half animal. They produced a low, almost-imperceptible hum, like some kind of machinery worked beneath the surface of the stone. A vibration I felt in my bones. But. Hmm. Their eyes, once lifeless, now seemed to follow us, their gemstone irises catching the light like watchful predators in the dark.

I must be mistaken, my imagination going haywire. Yes, yes. High-stress situations had never brought out the best in me.

Our procession ended at a small, sterile exam room with gray walls, zero windows, and a metal shackle attached to a gurney. I swallowed a denial and clutched my new necklace—my connection to Cyrus—allowing the soldiers to push me onto the stiff mattress and bind me to the bed. *Eye on the prize. Long game, long game.*

Out went all guards but two, and in came a medic. He didn't seek permission before pricking my finger with a needle and scanning the chip embedded in my hand. But then, he didn't need it. CURED controlled all within these walls, even the treatment of my body.

A beep sounded, the results in. Per custom, I wasn't told the results before he exited. As minutes passed with agonizing slowness, more and more perspiration dotted my palms.

CURED might not know I'd switched sides, but they absolutely suspected I'd had dealings with Soalians. Even if a suspect was innocent of wrongdoing, such transactions almost always led to accusations of illness. So. This could go one of two ways. Either CURED lied, labeling me "infected" so they could "treat" me, or they told the truth and allowed me to go so they could secretly observe me in my natural habitat.

Dr. Korey, the physician who'd overseen my "care" since my first day at the base, entered with a sure stride. "You're about to meet Emperor Dolion's right-hand man," she announced. "I suggest you behave."

Showtime.

A handsome gentleman with cold eyes strode in next. Though we lowly peons wore uniforms, he dazzled in a black-and-white pinstripe suit. His slick, put-together appearance should've inspired calm. I only wanted to vomit as he looked me over, silent.

"Congratulations, Lady Roosa." Dr. Korey pulled different things from her lab coat pockets and placed them on a rolling table. "You are negative for Madness."

Relief deluged my muscles, unraveling knots of tension. Observation in my natural habitat for the win.

"Your identity chip is now registered with a special designation reserved for the royal family." She grated the words as if they tasted foul. "From now on, medical personnel must explain what we do."

Thank you, Cyrus, for logging me in as a royal.

As she shifted my shirt this way and that to adhere small, round transmitters on my neck, collarbone, and above my heart, she said, "I'll be monitoring your vitals while you chat with Mr. Vyle."

Great. A man with no royal title but a higher clearance than Cyrus would catalog every blip of my tumultuous emotions.

Normally I might have replied "I've got nothing to hide, carry on," but that would've been an elaboration, so I stayed quiet.

Mr. Vyle dragged a metal stool in front of the gurney, unfastened a button on his suit jacket, and eased down. In his early thirties, he projected enough confidence to fill the entire base.

"I'm pleased to meet you, Lady Roosa." His rich baritone stroked my ears, conveying only charm. "My dear friend Count Folley tells me High Prince Dolion is quite smitten with you. That he encouraged you to question officials about our protocols."

Uh-oh. We were starting off with a bang. Mr. Vyle had just let me know he'd investigated my actions at a high society event where I'd quizzed the former head of Ourland Medicine about forbidden things. Designed to make me defensive indeed.

"I'm romantically involved with Cyrus, yes." Excellent. Short, sweet, and as unembellished as it was true. Now, for the rest. "I did ask Count Folley and others about the mass outbreak of Madness that had just transpired among civilians, but I did it of my volition. As a lady-in-training, I'm eager to learn prevention rather than intervention." Oops. I'd explained my reasons.

Mr. Vyle's lips quirked at the corners. "Such a diplomatic answer. Cyrus has coached you well."

A lump grew in my throat. I couldn't deny the claim without jumping headfirst into an obvious trap, exactly as the high prince had, well, coached me. I merely offered a fleeting smile.

"Didn't Cyrus coach her well, Dr. Korey," Mr. Vyle stated without glancing her way.

"He did, sir," she replied, bowing her head in deference. Something she hadn't done even for the high prince.

Mr. Vyle tapped his fingers over his knee. "Let's get business out of the way. Not too long ago, Cyrus consumed a berry grown only in Theirland. You are the budding horticulturist assigned to map his reaction. How do you think this berry affected him?"

Hold up. "You aren't here to ask me about Tagin Dolion's death?"

He arched a brow. "Is there something you'd like to share about Tagin Dolion's death?"

Okay, so, I'd expounded when I shouldn't have. "I can only tell you what happened."

"All right. Please do so."

Hmm. He'd urged me along a specific route, yet now we were traveling another. Either he'd played me, or I'd played myself. Nothing I could do but forge ahead. "Cyrus and I argued about our relationship. I left. He hunted me down with his father's help." As I spoke, I divided my attention between Dr. Korey and Mr. Vyle, gauging their reactions. She grew tenser. He displayed only polite interest. "The three of us headed to the base. In the vehicle, mid-drive, Tagin broke with Madness and killed an entire contingent of soldiers. To save myself and Cyrus, I confiscated one of Cyrus's weapons and killed Tagin." There it was, everything and nothing, all rolled into an accurate but misleading story.

Mr. Vyle didn't take notes or ask a follow-up. He merely adjusted a cuff of his jacket. "Thank you for the information. Now, let's return to our discussion about the berry."

I gulped. The fact that the fruit mattered more than a king's death couldn't be good. Did Mr. Vyle envision pinning Tagin's death on Cyrus, courtesy of the little fruit? "I know Cyrus was assigned to bring a berry back to the base. In order to succeed, he was forced to eat it. I've since noticed no differences in him. He is the same today as he was before." Truth.

"Then describe him."

"Excuse me?"

"If he is the same, describe who he was then and who he is now."

Sweet goodness, I'd walked myself into a trap, hadn't I? "He's . . . honorable." Another truth.

"A great thing to be," Mr. Vyle replied, obviously expecting me to say more.

No, thank you. A full minute passed in silence. Toward the end, Dr. Korey huffed with aggravation.

Mr. Vyle cast her a quick frown, nothing more, yet it seared deep pink into her cheeks. She bowed her head and withered, making herself smaller. With a wave in my direction, he continued. "You saw the berry. Describe it to me."

Easy. "Small, round, and glowing red."

He nodded and stood. "Thank you for your time, Lady Roosa."

My eyes widened. That was it?

"That's it," he said, as if he'd read my mind. He refastened the button on his jacket. "You may go to class. I'm sure I don't need to tell you not to discuss this with anyone save Cyrus."

"Understood, sir."

"If you recall any other details, inform Archduke Heta or Dr. Korey that you wish to speak with me." With a graceful pivot, Mr. Vyle motioned for Dr. Korey to leave, which she did after removing the electrodes.

But. Where were the intimidation tactics? The accusations that I must be hiding something? The threats of being punished if I'd uttered a single lie?

"I don't understand," I breathed out before I gave my mind permission to speak.

Mr. Vyle stopped in the open doorway and turned just enough to meet my gaze. An almost smile tinged his perfect features. "The only thing you need to understand is this. I'm certain there's a glower in our midst, playing both sides of the war, and I will stop at nothing to find them."

Chapter Two

He who knows the end from the beginning need not fear the fires along the path, for My words shall forever stand.

—*The Book of Soal* 1.23.46.10

In a daze, I trailed an unfamiliar knight through the winding corridors of the base. Thoughts tangled, creating a chaotic mess. Mr. Vyle suspected Cyrus of being a traitor. Probably me too. Okay, definitely me. Why else kick off the interrogation by highlighting my romantic involvement with he who'd once eaten a forbidden berry?

I should alert Cyrus. Hunt him down and explain all. Unless that was what the emperor's right-hand man hoped I'd do.

Yeah, better to wait until Cyrus sought me out. In the meantime, I should act as if nothing was amiss. Besides, he probably expected the suspicion. He wasn't a newbie double agent. Far from it. He had years of experience.

But dang it, foreboding slithered back in, constricting my airway in a viselike grip. We wouldn't win this. We *couldn't.* CURED was too powerful, too entrenched in every aspect of our worlds, and we were too weak.

What are you doing? Stop! I buried the newest doom seed in my memory garden, beside the last. For too long, I had believed CURED was the superior force, while Soal and his Soalians were lesser. We weren't. Not even close. We *could* win this.

Calm came as my guide navigated the twisty hallways, leading me from the unfamiliar palace half of the building to the all-too-familiar prison half. The second we rounded a corner, everything altered, warm air turning stale and cold. Glistening crystal walls gave way to rough, pitted concrete. There were no statues here, but something equally ominous: a row of cells, each with a slightly rusted wall of iron bars. A distant drip echoed through the silence, each drop landing with a hollow *plink*, marking time.

The stark differences struck me as never before, and I wondered if the history I'd been told was accurate. CURED had lied about so many things, so why not this?

The most accepted theory: Over two hundred years ago, Ourland, my world, had fused with another world, Theirland, when someone sprayed certain chemicals into the air, burning through an invisible veil. In an instant, both territories became a mishmash of each other. Half and half. We retained a portion of our architecture and acquired a portion of theirs. Even our soil combined with theirs, causing the Great Soil and Seed Anomaly, with little able to grow. Not to mention we exchanged our good health for their Madness, a terrible disease that turned its victims into vicious killers.

The guard stopped at the women's locker room. "You have five minutes to prepare."

I didn't bother responding. Entering the open space, I took in the banks of cubbies, the benches, and the individual shower stalls with smoked, armored glass. Empty. Everyone else must be in class. Morning warm-up, to be specific.

As quickly as possible, I changed into a clean uniform—which was no longer blue but green, the color for Archduke Baracas Heta's students. Despite being only halfway into my first phase of training, I had a new lead instructor. I'd anticipated that, but being without Cyrus was going to suck. The fact that the archduke disliked me only added to the suckage.

Sighing, I adjusted my new necklace beneath the shirt's neckline, then braided my hair and plotted my next move. Like Cyrus suggested, I must do this one day at a time. Today's goals: Forget that the emperor's right-hand man walked among us, determined to oust the double agent in his midst; keep my ears open for any tidbit that might help Cyrus become king; and avoid any hint of panic, all while proving to Mr. Vyle there was no reason to suspect us of being double agents. No big deal.

Tremors plagued me as I trudged from the locker room to the designated gym. My steps faltered when I realized my original escort had been replaced by two higher-ranking barons. One soldier moved in front of me while the other trailed us. Both remained silent. They were either here to act as my protectors or my wardens. Since I knew my words would be reported, I remained silent.

This was fine. I was fine. *Breathe. Just breathe.*

A bell rang, signaling the end of warm-up. Well. Looked like I'd start with Realms and Travel, the second class of the day, taught by Archduke Heta himself.

I soared through the open door just as the bell rang. Hmm. A mere fourteen lords- and ladies-in-training occupied the seats, and I recognized only four of them. Roman, a friend, plus Miller, Cash, and a girl named Merlot, mere acquaintances. They sat with lords- and ladies-in-training I'd never met, whispering together. If CURED had split Cyrus's class down the middle, giving an equal number to both Heta and Duchess Mimidae, the other instructor, I should see three other familiar faces in here. Either the powers that be had brought in a new instructor, or something had happened to my former teammates.

Someone noticed me and alerted others. All conversations tapered to silence as every eye swung my way. Expressions shifted to display one of four emotions in various degrees. Curiosity, confusion, envy, and disdain. What had they heard?

Heart thudding, I claimed the lone available seat. Front row center, with a direct sight line to the archduke's desk, where the man in question currently sat, organizing his notes. At least Roman was my neighbor. But, um, what was the strange sensation currently uncoiling beneath my sternum?

It wasn't unpleasant but warm, sweet, and strong enough to dissolve a new rush of foreboding. Nerve endings whirred, igniting a sense that a long-lost friend waited nearby, eager to speak with me.

The sensation disbanded when I noticed my guards. They remained at the door, one on each side. Uh . . .

The archduke extended his arm and made a shooing motion without glancing in their direction. "Wait in the hall." A little person in his late forties, he exuded strict control and unwavering assurance.

Though the soldiers were of a lower rank, neither obeyed him. "We come with a message from Emperor Dolion, sir," the one with a buzz cut stated.

Heta worked his jaw, clearly irritated, but he also offered a clipped nod. Rather than invite the men closer, he stood and strode over, using a cane he hadn't needed three days ago. He exited the room, and the guards followed, shutting the door behind them, leaving me alone with my classmates.

I sank down in my seat, wondering if anyone suspected that a traitor lurked in their midst. A glower, at that. Their greatest enemy. Someone they would kill without hesitation or remorse.

Roman gripped the side of his desk and leaned my way to quietly say, "Did you hear? King Tagin is dead." More anger than sadness lit his eyes. "An entire unit got mowed down with him." He listed a bunch of names, more than the number of soldiers I'd watched Tagin murder.

A loud *boom! boom! boom!* of gunfire echoed inside my head. In a flash of vivid color, I relived the executions as if I stood in the clearing once again, bordered by a road and old, dead trees. The bodies of my friends and those with them jerked as bullets sliced into their brains.

Their knees buckled, and they crashed into the dirt, motionless, staring at nothing.

"I'd known about Titus, Juniper, Lark, and only a handful of others," I croaked. Tears stung my eyes, and I tried to blink them away. It didn't work. Using mental gardening shears, I snipped the blooms now growing from one of many bushes in the Grief and Despair section of my memory garden. Finally, success. The moisture dried. This wasn't the time or place to mourn.

Roman reached over to pat my hand. "People die in this world, Ardie. You'll get used to it."

"I really hope I don't." The bulk of my life, I'd kept people at a distance, afraid to make friends, certain they'd all break with Madness. I spent years lonely and isolated, counseled strictly by anxiety. With Cyrus and the Soalians, I'd experienced the joys of relationship. I cared now, and there was no going back.

Roman nudged my shoulder. "Whatever you do, get your mind right fast. Things are about to get wild. From what I've heard, only two high princes opted not to go for the title of king. The remaining five will converge at Fort Bala soon. Word is, the emperor favors Cyrus's half brother, High Prince Felix, as well as High Princess Lolli."

I'd heard of both royals, of course. Who hadn't? The princess was Cyrus's sister-in-law, a widow once married to another of his half brothers, a high prince who'd died in battle. Many called her a force of nature. HP Felix was famous for his merciless infiltration of glower strongholds. If they could be recruited to our cause, great. But if not . . . we must deal with them.

"What about Cyrus?" I asked. "His capture-kill rates can't be beat."

Roman leaned closer still. "My source says his chances are low. That the emperor—"

"Quiet down," Archduke Heta commanded as he reentered the room.

Argh! The emperor *what*?

To my dismay, the barons followed the archduke inside and repositioned at the door.

"Ignore Lady Roosa's bodyguards," Heta announced. "They were assigned by Emperor Piven himself."

My eyes widened. No, impossible. Except, Mr. Vyle. The one who currently wielded the same authority as the emperor. He wouldn't hesitate to do this.

A barbed lump congealed in my throat as everyone but Heta and the guards reassessed me. No doubt they speculated about how someone like me had garnered such keen interest from our illustrious leader. Because there was no way Emperor Dolion would ever concern himself with a random, low-ranking girlfriend of a royal high prince, even if said high prince was his grandson.

Roman frowned at me as I slinked lower still in my seat. So. One question had an answer, at least. They were surveilling me. An intimidation tactic meant to scare me into a confession of guilt.

Miller gave me a look of disgust and muttered, "The high prince wasn't good enough for you, eh? You had to go and sleep your way to the very tippity top."

My cheeks heated. For the most part, he'd ignored me before this. The emperor's guards must have put me on his radar.

I held his gaze and followed Cyrus's example for dealing with unruly trainees. "Are you sure you want to travel this route with me, Mills? Right or not, I obviously have connections you don't."

He paled and backed off. And yeah, okay, satisfaction bloomed.

"All right, let's get started." Archduke Heta spread his arms. "With the mass loss of cadets who were on special assignment with King Tagin, and the restructuring of the teams, I'm now your be-all and end-all. No matter who you are, or how high your connections"—he hit me with a pointed glance—"I will not tolerate a break in the chain of command. If you have a problem, come to me. Are we clear?"

My cheeks burned a thousand degrees hotter, but I nodded for his benefit.

"A few updates," he continued, casual now. "We won't be traveling to Theirland on Friday. You require more training. Also, the competition for top soldier has been postponed."

His last bombshell inspired groans of disappointment and gasps of shock.

Heta held up his hands in a demand for silence, which he received. He might be small in stature, but he projected a big presence. "Since the Soalians have increased the ferocity of their attacks against CURED, we're accelerating your training this month. We want you focused on learning, not on winning a prize. Though I'd dare to say knowledge is the ultimate reward."

Done with that subject, he lifted his infamous clicker. "Since you'll never outgrow warfare, you must learn to fight." With the press of a button, he caused the wall behind him to light up with images.

I saw a night-darkened sky lit by blasts of lightning and broken circus rides spotlighted by pritis stones. Those small golden orbs topped poles in clusters, resembling grapes on a vine. My fingers curled over the edge of my seat, righteous anger sweeping through me. Now that I knew how those glowing "stones" were harvested, I wanted only to tear down the posts and spit in the holes.

"By now you've visited Theirland on numerous occasions," Heta said. "You've walked through the rifts between our two realms. Have experienced the other world's eternal darkness and inverted vision, and have participated in a mock patrol, slaying feeders too far gone for treatment."

Feeders. Of the two types of maddened—according to CURED—feeders were the most common. In truth, they were the only ones actually infected. Driven by hunger, they craved the second type: glowers. Glowers weren't infected; they were Soalian. When feeders couldn't get to them, they settled for whatever flesh and blood they could find.

Heta continued, "When I feel the team is ready, you'll each accompany a superior officer on an actual patrol. Stakes have never been higher, so I suggest you pay special attention when I speak."

Once again, perspiration glazed my palms. Me. On patrol. In the dark. The moment someone pegged me as a glower, I was as good as dead. And how could anyone *not* discover it? True to the description, I now glowed in the dark. Well, sometimes I glowed. Mostly. I did it on command but also spontaneously. Kind of. Maybe. Ugh! I just didn't know. I was too new to this. As a two-day-old Soalian, I had more questions than answers.

And I was missing the archduke's lecture, dang it. *Inner shake.*

"—left behind for whatever reason, hide there," he was saying. "A knight will come for you at some point."

Ack! Hide where?

"There will be more maddened than you can fathom, and you'll be fighting for your life nonstop. Amid the pandemonium, you must work with your teammates, learning when to strike, when to dodge, and when to back off. To help you navigate this, you'll be chained to a different trainee each day for the next five days, from warm-up until free time. Grab a tether on your way out. Today, you're paired with whoever is sitting next to you."

Roman reached out, gripped the edge of my desk, and tugged me closer still. Great. I now had three guard dogs observing my every move. At least none of them were the meta, short for "metal." The robotic dogs patrolled the cities, recording everything.

I stayed pressed together with my partner as the archduke played footage where swarms of mindless maddened surged forward, their irises eclipsed by blazing crimson. Small, pale worms writhed from their scalps, squiggled in place of their lashes, and slithered from their ears and noses. A froth of white foam leaked from the corners of their mouths in a continuous stream.

Revulsion rocked me. How I hated the idea of entering Theirland, the abandoned world where this type of feeder congregated. But I must.

I had orders from my *real* boss. According to Ember Cruz, I must remain immersed in CURED's training program.

Budding anxiety distracted me as Heta spoke about the different places the maddened preferred to hide to ambush patrolmen. By the time the bell rang, I was certain I had retained none of it.

"Don't forget your chain," he commanded. "Make sure you and your partner are secured for weapons class. Today, Duchess Mimidae is teaching you how to properly wield a spear, my favorite weapon." As we stood and filed out, he called, "Lady Roosa. A word."

I winced and glanced at Roman. "I'll meet you in the hallway."

"Nope," he said with a shake of his head, his usual smug but lovable self. "We're bound together, baby. Where you go, I go. Instructor's orders."

Wonderful. Tremors overtook me as we approached Heta's desk.

The archduke leaned back in his chair, linked his fingers over his middle, and peered up at us. "If your personal life continues to disrupt my classes, I won't be pleased. I don't care who you're dating. I will excuse no tardies, tolerate no disrespect, and show no preferential treatment. Do you understand?"

"Sir, yes, sir. Thank you, sir," I replied, and I meant it.

"Dismissed." He turned his focus to his files, saying nothing else.

Roman grabbed a thin metal cord and guided me out of the room. My guards followed. In the hall, the trainee slung his arms around my shoulders, saying quietly, "I haven't forgotten your super-secret, special mission before all this started. I'm sure you can't speak about what's going on . . ."

"Correct. I can't," I confirmed.

"Just be careful. I've heard things."

As the son of a marquis, Roman had grown up among the gentry. "Don't stop there. Tell me what you've heard." I kept my volume as low as his, ensuring the guards heard nothing. "And while you're at it, finish what you were saying earlier, about Cyrus. Why is his shot at king low?"

"Hang on." Roman led me into the commons, a spacious room divided into a trio of sections designated for entertainment, studying, and dining. But he didn't stop. On we went, entering another hallway before descending a flight of stairs. Rather than huddling up in our next classroom, he kept me in the thick of a crowd, dozens of conversations taking place around us as trainees and soldiers rushed here and there. He bent his head and told me, "I heard the HP and his grandfather are feuding. Started recently. I don't know all the details . . ." He paused, giving me a chance to respond.

"I don't either." At Roman's look of disbelief, I added, "Honestly, I know nothing about a feud." Cyrus hadn't mentioned it. I wondered, though. Did it revolve around me, the nobody girlfriend? I mean, our relationship was a recent development as well.

For victory, I would absolutely, unequivocally end the relationship. At least publicly. And temporarily. *Don't vomit.* "You mentioned High Prince Felix is the front-runner. Do you know why?"

"A year ago, a glower killed his wife. He's been on a revenge tour ever since. Across the board, his stats are mind-blowing."

Okay, forget recruiting him. He wouldn't be interested in becoming a glower like me and Cyrus. Although, there must be more to the story of his wife's death. A mistake of some sort. Murder wasn't the Soalian way. That much, I knew.

"Look," Roman said. "Whatever caused the quarrel between grandfather and grandson, Cyrus will have to patch things up if he wants to win the crown."

I raised my chin, determined. "Mark my words. Cyrus will be the next king of Ourland." Quarrel or not, we would find a way. Nothing would stop us now.

Chapter Three

In fear, there is no safety, solace, or stillness, only a path to ruin.

—*The Book of Soal* 1.18.3.26

How I survived weapons training with Roman tethered to my side, I may never fully understand. Before class began, we secured the nexus of chain to our waists, both of us grimacing as we realized only a few inches separated our bodies—and there was no way to undo it. The fasteners cinched tight.

As we trained with weapons, he operated with total abandon and zero qualms. He spun this way and that, taking me along for the ride as he wielded his spear with expert precision, protecting us both from the hologram we fought. Anyone who got in our way got mowed down. By the end, bruises marred my legs, but I didn't mind. Roman took the time to help me learn from my mistakes, surprisingly patient and endearingly amusing.

At lunch, he ate his meal bar and half of mine. He also drank most of my hy-water. A blessing, honestly. I was resolute: no bathroom breaks today. Standing at his side during *his* breaks was bad enough.

I even survived running a complicated obstacle course during drills, chased by a horde of holographic feeders. Actually, I excelled at the course; mostly because Roman tossed me over walls whenever necessary.

We didn't collide until self-defense class, now taught by some unknown baron rather than Cyrus. My partner zigged when I zagged, and I ended up with a ton more bruises and several cuts. Completely my fault! I remained distracted, continuing to mull the possibility of a breakup with Cyrus.

Again and again, I told myself the separation wouldn't be permanent. Once the heat with Mr. Vyle died down, we could get back together. And yet, even the thought of a temporary split-up hurt worse than these physical wounds.

A bell rang, signaling the start of free time. The chain opened without prompting, falling.

"Thank goodness." I rushed to the bathroom, where I peed for an eternity. After washing my hands, I headed to the commons to swipe a meal bar and extra hy-water, which I guzzled like a madwoman. Well, not *mad* mad. To my surprise, my energy didn't rally as I emptied the third carton but tanked.

Though my team congregated in the entertainment portion of the room, eager to socialize, I trudged to my old cell. My shadows remained outside it, in front of the bars, flanking the open doorway. I tumbled into my hard, uncomfortable bed, done with the day.

Hmm. The mattress. It was much softer than I recalled. And there wasn't a chain attached to the wall to ensure I couldn't harm anyone if I broke with Madness in the middle of the night.

But. What would happen when I got a new roommate?

Spotting a digital reader on my pillow, I reached out to press the chip in my palm against the ID pad at the bottom-right side of the device's hard outer shell. Maybe I'd find a note from my sweet prince.

Or not. A schedule appeared.

LADY A.R.

Tuesday–Thursday

0500–0530: Wake up/Breakfast

0530–0730: Warm up/Work out (Gym A)

0800–1000: Realms and Travel (Room 2)

1010–1230: Weapons (Room 6)

1230–1300: Lunch

1300–1500: Self-Defense (Gym A)

1500–1550: Battlefield First Aid (Room 1)

1600–1930: Drills (The Dome)

1930–2000: Dinner

2000–2200: Free time

2200–0500: Lights out

Friday–Saturday

0500–0530: Wake up/Breakfast

0530–0600: *Travel to Theirland

0600–1600: **Patrol

1600–0500: Free time

Sunday

0500–0530: Wake up/Breakfast

0530–0600: Travel to Ourland

0600–0730: Warm up/Work out (Gym A)

0800–1000: Evaluation (Room 1)

1010–1230: Testing (Room 4)

1230–1300: Lunch

1300–1500: Madness Basics (Room 3)

1500–1550: Driving (TBA)

1600–1930: Drills (The Dome)

1930–2000: Dinner

2000–2059: Free time

2200–0500: Lights out

Monday

Free day

*Friday only

**Breaks scheduled by superior

A list of cellmate pairings followed.

Only my day off and a few room assignments had changed. The best part? I hadn't been assigned a new roommate. Mykal, my previous roomie, had quit the program after a mutual friend broke with Madness and attacked us. I couldn't blame her. The break had come courtesy of CURED, the government we'd trusted to protect us. Not that she knew the truth. Still. I wish she'd stayed.

Learning to fight and defend myself had helped me in ways I hadn't known I'd needed. Maybe Mykal would return. Of course, I would lose the desk that had replaced her bed, but better to have a friend than a workstation.

Hold up. My new desk chair was *cushioned*?

Thank you, Cyrus. I eased into an upright position, reviving, and noticed a second reader on the desk, next to a pot of pure, untainted soil with a single mystery seed germinating beneath the surface. Also a gift from Cyrus, which I'd left at his apartment in Bala City.

Ignoring my aches and pains, I climbed to my feet and crossed over. The reader lit up thanks to a motion sensor, the desired note from Cyrus dominating the screen, inspiring a wide smile.

TURN ME ON

With a snort, I plopped onto the ultra-luxurious cushion and did as commanded: pressed my chip against the ID panel. The screen lit up again, brighter, revealing another message.

> Lady Pink,
> Remember my command, and your agreement. Also 1) this reader isn't for class. I promised I'd find a way for us to communicate, and this is it. Be aware—a dozen analysts will read every word. And 2) The upper right drawer of your new desk serves as a safe for any treasures I give you. The lock code is a number you recognize. I won't get to see you tonight, but I'll be thinking of you . . .
> Yours,
> Cyrus
> PS. When you're alone, don't be afraid to get dirty and find out what I gifted to you.

Both confused and excited, I clutched the reader to my chest. While I fully understood the reference to the code, Cyrus could've meant several different things by "get dirty," considering he'd gifted me many things. I thought, maybe, probably, he referenced the pot of soil with that mystery seed planted within its depths. Per his instructions, I'd watered it every day, yet nothing had sprouted.

Considering I was a wannabe horticulturist who'd spent her life studying to unravel the Great Soil and Seed Anomaly caused by the fusion of two vastly different worlds, I practically frothed at the mouth for a chance to discover what I was growing. But disturbing the soil and digging up a seed to "get dirty" was foolish. I could interrupt and damage the germinating process. Unless . . .

Chewing on my bottom lip, I set the reader aside and examined the dark soil. Thoughts tumbled over each other. Perhaps the seed had already grown and now thrived beneath the surface. There *was* such a thing as a hydrothermal vent ecosystem, where plants grew without the need of light. Although it was a unique process usually found at volcanic fissures along the ocean floor, and this wasn't that. But. I couldn't not do it.

My guards remained at their posts, their focus straight ahead. As alone as I'd ever be . . .

Even as I trembled, I put my back to them and plunged a hand in the soft, sweetly fragrant dirt, digging until my fingertips brushed—I blinked. The seed had tripled in size and developed a smooth velvet casing. But. Um. I felt no protrusions. No roots or sprouts.

Frowning, I slowly, gently worked the precious seed from its bed of soil and . . .

That moment. That very second. I registered what I held, and my jaw went slack. Heart thudding, I hurried to close my fingers around the orb. Surely Cyrus hadn't . . . this wasn't . . . it couldn't be . . .

But he had, it was, and it could.

"Is everything all right, Lady Roosa?" a guard asked.

Oops. I'd been making little strangling noises. Schooling my features into a semblance of calm, I glanced over my shoulder to meet his gaze. "Yep. All good. Thanks for checking. Just doing a bit of gardening." With a chin wag to the pot, I added, "My preferred method of stress relief." Was I babbling? Elaborating, as Cyrus told me not to do?

The pounding of my heart worsened as I returned my attention to the pot and smoothed the soil, being sure to keep my treasure hidden. If I got caught with this, I'd be jailed. Perhaps executed. Or worse! And yet, elation poured through me at record levels, drowning any fear.

I held a fragment of the Rock, the sole entrance into the Kingdom of Yesterday, Today, and Tomorrow. Also the home of an invisible library filled with coded books that detailed our past, present, and future. There were other names for the structure too. Door to Shaddai, the utopia beyond the Library of Soal, was one, and oh, sweet goodness, this might be the greatest gift anyone anywhere had received ever. And I wasn't being dramatic. The beautiful, priceless fragment had a translucent, mirror-esque exterior that revealed an intricate network of internal veins flowing with scarlet liquid. The cure to Madness.

My cells sang with joy. Cyrus had given me a prize beyond imagining. Maybe, just maybe, I could share this with a friend.

I would never forget the moment I had ingested a crumble just like it. A seed teeming with the essence of life. That was the moment the invisible scales had fallen off my eyes, and I'd finally seen the world unfiltered. Light versus night. Good against evil.

A loud commotion erupted beyond my cell, jolting me to my feet. Some kind of fight had just broken out. My guards abandoned their posts as my barred door slammed shut, sealing me inside the cell.

"You summoned?" The strong, authoritative voice hit my ears, and I spun.

My gaze landed on a striking, bearded man I recognized, and my jaw slackened. Domino Crane. A powerful member of the Tome Society, Soal's elite force. Domino wore the same crimson robe he'd sported the other two times I'd encountered him. Like Cyrus, he was tall, muscular, and intense, but that was where their similarities ended. The high prince might be icy with anyone other than me, but this guy embodied the arctic. So much so, I felt a chill of his presence deep in my bones. Didn't help that his arresting, rugged features appeared molded from steel, and his fathomless eyes examined me with unrelenting, unabashed curiosity.

"I know you," I rasped at low volume, doing my best to hide my unease.

"That statement is inaccurate. You've met and spoken with me. You do not know me." He offered the rebuke without any inflection of emotion.

Well, here's what I did know. He wasn't just a member of the Tome Society. He was a librarian. The elite of the elite. And he now stood only a few feet away, here but also not here in some kind of holographic form. Which was a major problem. Cameras were everywhere, and they recorded projections the same as bodies.

He'd just blown my cover.

"Help me get out of here," I demanded in a rush. Expecting an army to arrive any moment, I pocketed the Rock and palmed a dagger I hadn't yet stored. A special weapon with a hole in the upper part of the blade and a small canister of CO2 hidden in the hilt. With the press of a button, I could turn a stab wound into a fatal explosion. And I would do it, too, if I had to fight my way out of Fort Bala.

"No need to worry." Domino spoke at full volume, unconcerned by the consequences. "I created a distraction to buy us a few minutes alone. You are the only one able to see and hear me. Not even the cameras detect my presence." He partially turned and perused the room. From the carvings on the walls, left by past trainees, to the stained concrete floor and flat ceiling. His features pinched. "I know mice with better living accommodations."

I sheathed my weapon, relaxed my stance, and arched a brow at the librarian, a silent command for more information. His voice might not reach others, but mine certainly could, scrambled or not.

He motioned to the fragment stashed in my pocket. "With that little piece of the Rock, I have access to you, and you have access to me. In this skin, at least."

And what was "this skin," exactly? There was no way a hologram could gobble up so much oxygen. "I don't understand how this is possible," I muttered.

"You don't understand many things," he remarked.

I attempted to stare him down and wring a better answer out of him. He stared back. The longer we peered at each other, each too stubborn to look away, the more I felt as if I stood too close to a live wire.

Okay, so, forget winning this contest of wills. I required a reprieve. Wrenching my gaze free, I said, "I have comments and questions." So many questions. I launched into a back-and-forth pace, just in case anyone passed by my cell. Maybe they'd think I was mumbling to myself. "How did I . . . you know?"

"Summon me?" Domino queried, and I nodded. Yep. That. "You clutched the Rock and yearned for me. I came."

I stopped abruptly, a million butterflies taking flight in my belly. Now hold on just a sec. "I didn't . . . I would never . . ."

"Yearned for Soal's help," he clarified. "He dispatched me to . . ." Domino drew in a deep breath, as if seeking a nice way to present a hated curse. "Oversee your needs."

Like, he had to do whatever I commanded? Well, well. What a brilliant development. I mean, what even was my life right now? I'd gone from being ready to die for CURED to being a traitor to the crown to dating Ourland's future king, with my own personal, invisible butler-type who answered only to the god of gods.

"But why you?" I whispered, pressing for more. My specialty, thank you.

"Punishment, perhaps?" A faint, bemused glaze spread over his eyes. "To be candid, I'm not sure what I did to deserve this."

Ouch. "That isn't what I—never mind." For some reason, Soal had decided I was worthy of utilizing such a rare, special resource. Gift accepted. Even though said gift wasn't exactly thrilled.

Domino sighed as if he were the last sane man in the universe. "Tell me what it is you want, Arden." He didn't bother with a title. An insignificant fact I didn't find so insignificant, but I didn't know why.

I glanced at the cell doors, on the lookout for my guards, and whispered, "I'm desperate to read." I really hoped he filled in the words I didn't dare speak, even at low volume. My tale. *The Book of Arden*, written by Soal himself. I *craved* a glimpse of my future. Instructions for the upcoming trip to Theirland. A tidbit to assist Cyrus in his dealings with Mr. Vyle. Coordinates for where an imprisoned Soalian named John Victors was being held. Something!

Victors had helped guide me to Soal's road, and I owed him.

"I'm allowed to do many things to aid you," Domino said, voice flat, "but that isn't one of them. Reading sacred, coded tomes can only be done inside the library." He anchored his arms behind his back, a teacher with an unruly student. "You must visit the Rock."

"That's not possible at the moment." I couldn't get to the Rock until my day off. Not without Cyrus at my side. While he had a legitimate reason to leave the base outside of free time, I did not.

"Another inaccurate statement. Anything is possible," Domino corrected. "You mean it's difficult."

I gave him *the look*. The universal expression for *why are you like this*. "You're going to annoy me every time we're together, butler man," I muttered. "I can already tell."

"The feeling is mutual, soldier girl, I assure you." He pursed his lips. "For the record, I correct you not to scold but to serve you. Words are like your cherished seeds. Living containers able to grow and produce after themselves. Once spoken, they take root in the soil of your heart and get watered by your thoughts. What develops is a tree of life or death. The semantics you lament decide the fruit that grows—fruit you *will* eat."

He made a good point. One I'd delivered to others upon occasion. One I cultivated in my memory garden, for goodness' sake. Today, the reminder only annoyed me further.

"In the meantime," he continued. "There's another glower on your team. A soldier who's been one of us since birth, hidden within the ranks of CURED, able to help you if such a choice is made."

I nearly tripped over my own feet mid-pace. A glower on my team, yet I hadn't even suspected. "Who is it?" *Please be Roman, please be Roman.* He would be a tremendous asset. He was also someone I admired.

"That," Domino said, "I can't tell you without permission, which I do not have and will not request. But such interference isn't necessary. Look inward. You are connected to the Rock, just as I am, and you now possess an inward sense. If you quiet your mind and follow the leadings of your heart, you'll sense those who are with Soal and those who are with Astan. I'd be willing to bet you've already sensed the glower's presence."

My eyes widened as a plant in my memory garden flowered with a reminder. Earlier, in Heta's Realms and Travel class, I'd experienced that amazingly sweet sensation that had dissolved my foreboding, making me feel as if a long-lost friend waited nearby.

"Judging by your expression," Domino said, a little smug, "I won the bet."

Who was the Soalian? I *must* know.

The librarian glanced behind him, as if someone was speaking to him. Maybe they were. The corners of his mouth turned down. When next he faced me, he projected anger. "You were questioned by Mr. Vyle?"

I went statue still, though my heart kicked into a race. Uh-oh. Had I already made a mistake? "I was," I admitted. "It went well." Kind of. Mostly. "Maybe."

"No, Arden. I assure you, it did not go well." Domino stepped into my personal space, hijacking my next thought. "Mr. Vyle isn't just the emperor's right-hand man. He's the royal executioner."

Oh. Oh no. I gulped.

"If Mr. Vyle is here, it means the emperor, and Astan, already suspects that someone in authority is a traitor. Considering how heavily you're being guarded, we must conclude that someone is Cyrus."

"Well, that little gem was obvious before the interrogation," I said, going on the defensive.

"Ah. But did you know Cyrus's execution is already scheduled?" Domino dropped the bomb and vanished a second later.

I could only stand there, spinning out, as my guards returned to their posts, and the door to my cell opened.

Fighting for my next breath, I closed my eyes and forced myself inward. Okay. All right. This wasn't insurmountable. So I hadn't known anything about a scheduled execution. Now I did. I could get the heat off Cyrus before anyone struck. If the high prince outed me as a Soalian, all suspicion toward him would be erased in an instant and total blame would fall on my head. I could escape to the Rock, aiding our team from the sidelines, and the future king would be cleared of all wrongdoing.

Or he would look foolish for trusting me.

Ugh. There must be another way.

Quaking, I scrubbed a hand over my face. Rather than cave to fear, my usual inclination, I forced myself to inhale a slow, measured breath and concentrate on the only action available to me right now: get a message to Cyrus.

Chapter Four

Pursue wisdom and stand unashamed, forever bound to truth.

—*The Book of Soal* 2.16.2.15

Determined, I secured my piece of the Rock in my new desk safe. The recognized lock code? A long series of numbers Soal had given me, once used by Tagin. That done, I sank into my comfy chair, mentally drafting a message to Cyrus to outline everything I'd learned. But before typing a single word, I erased it all with a frustrated shake of my head. As he'd warned earlier, our messages would be scrutinized—read, reread, and dissected by die-hard CUREDians. Astanians? Whatever. I had to be careful not to raise any alarms while still informing Cyrus about the threat to his life.

Taking a deep breath, I began to type.

> Dear High Prince Dolion,
>
> I received your gift. Thank you. I CANNOT wait until we're together again. I'm certain my thoughts will surprise you. Also, you'll be happy to learn I followed your orders.
>
> Yours,
>
> Lady-in-training Arden Roosa

I hoped 1) my formality portrayed the seriousness and urgency of the situation; 2) he understood I desired to meet with him face-to-face as soon as possible; and 3) I reminded him how much I cared.

His response came quickly, words flashing over the screen.

I'll arrange a meeting.

I closed my eyes for a moment, relieved, then prepared to shoot him another message.

"Officer on deck," a voice called.

Groaning, I leaped to my feet. What now?

Cyrus strode into my cell and winked at me. "Is this a good time?"

"You're here!" With a cry of delight, I tossed the reader aside and threw myself at him. "You said I wouldn't see you today."

He caught me in his arms, holding tight, and buried his face in my hair. "I can't stay long, but I couldn't leave without seeing you."

Both elated and disappointed, I pulled back to cup his cheeks. "There's something you need to hear." Might as well jump right in.

"No business, Pink, only pleasure." With a smile on the wolfish side, he cupped my cheeks in kind, tracing the pads of his thumbs over each rise. "I'm delaying a transport team to Theirland, and I'd rather spend our remaining seconds hearing about your day."

"I can do both," I assured him, moving my grip to his chest. "Tell the guards to get lost."

"Go," Cyrus barked at the men without looking away from me.

They marched off without complaint. Good riddance.

Alone, I spewed words. "I did pretty okay in the interview, didn't freak out more than three dozen times during classes, got paired with Roman, will be paired with someone else tomorrow, and learned your execution is already planned," I whisper-rasped. "I heard about your feud with the emperor. What if he's decided to end it *permanently*?"

"The scheduled execution isn't for me, not anymore, and I'm not feuding with my grandfather. We have a difference of opinion, nothing more." Cyrus smoothed a lock of hair behind my ear and bent to nuzzle his cheek into mine, not the least bit dismayed. "He says the consumption of the berry tainted me, whether there are outward signs or not. I disagree."

No wonder Mr. Vyle had focused on the berry. But how had Domino, a librarian in the know, missed the canceling of the execution order? "You have to convince your grandfather you're not tainted," I said, failing to hide my worry.

Cyrus's stunning eyes glittered with amusement. "I will. In fact, I'll do it the same way I convinced you to date me. With patience, wisdom, and great restraint."

I snorted. "I wasn't that bad."

"Bubble Gum, you were worse. But I'm safe for the time being, I promise you. I've read Mr. Vyle's orders. He's greatly limited in his dealings with me. Despite the berry and my grandfather's reaction to it, I've always been the royal favorite. That hasn't changed."

Okay. I trusted Cyrus more than a librarian I hardly knew. "Thank you for gifting me with these stolen minutes." I thrilled as his pounding heartbeat ignited an answering pulse in different parts of me.

"Staying away from you has never been my strength. But now, I must go." Regret radiated from him. He brushed his lips against mine. "I wasn't going to kiss you until we had a proper amount of time, but the separation is killing me, and I need a fix." He showered me with more kisses between words.

Chuckling, I fisted his shirt and kissed him back.

"I'll see you tomorrow, I hope." Cyrus pressed his brow against mine. "Be safe, Arden."

Serious now, clinging, I rasped, "Be safe, Cyrus."

After giving me another swift kiss, he released me and strode from the cell. "Lord Roman," he greeted as he disappeared around the corner.

"High Prince Dolion," the lord-in-training returned from beyond the wall. Only seconds later, he rushed into my cell. The guards weren't far behind him, though they remained outside the enclosure. "I hope this means you'll stop pretending you're not sleeping with him." He sounded more amused than anything.

No reason to deny the relationship and every reason to admit the truth. One day, I hoped to recruit Roman to my side. If he wasn't already Soalian, of course. Better I stayed honest. Lies tainted connections, always. "I'm *dating* Cyrus."

"Dating," Roman echoed with a wince. "That won't end well for you, Ardie. I've been part of the gentry my entire life. If you want to bang a royal, fine. But coupling up *never* ends well for the other party."

I waved his warning away. "You don't have to worry about me. Cyrus is a good man." The best I'd ever met. He wasn't going to change his mind about us.

A bell rang, warning of the coming curfew, now two minutes out.

Roman backed up, hands lifted in a sign of surrender. "He's a good man, sure. But even the good ones make bad decisions." The newest warning hung in the air after he exited, inviting more doom.

Grinding my teeth, I buried a third seed in the Problems for Later section of my memory garden. I should probably unearth and sort through them before they sprouted, but I had another matter to consider first. Pinpointing the Soalian in my midst. As I'd learned during my battle with Tagin Dolion, a teammate could mean the difference between victory and defeat.

A second bell rang, and my cell door slid shut again. I prepared for bed, then climbed onto the mattress . . . where I tossed and turned all night, replaying every interaction I'd ever had with each member of my team. Nothing screamed "I'm a Soalian," but nothing screamed "I'm not a Soalian" either. Guess I'd have to do some stealthy interrogating while being investigated myself.

Not exactly my specialty. Frustrated, I banged a fist into my pillow, then rolled to my back and pinched the bridge of my nose. Complications should be shrinking, not increasing.

At the ringing of the morning bell, I groaned, fluttered open burning eyes, and eased upright.

My door opened with a whine, new guards already in place. As I rose, my gaze strayed to the drawer in my desk, where I'd stored my little piece of the Rock. First decision of the day: Carry the fragment around in my pocket, risking its discovery, or leave it behind. If Mr. Vyle opted to search my cell and bypassed the lock . . .

"Yo, Arden—" Miller ground to a halt outside my space, blocked by my guards, who stepped in front of him. Only after he explained his purpose did they part. He padded in while grumbling under his breath and holding a familiar link of metal. "Are you as excited to buddy up as I am?"

"Sure sounds like it," I offered dryly.

He was a little taller than me, and lean, with wavy hair and a barrage of tattoos that covered most available skin below his face. Uh, there was a lot of available skin right now. He wore boxer briefs and a grin. My cheeks heated when I realized I'd been checking out his ink. But ten points for that perfectly etched bouquet of roses.

"I refuse to secure the cord until I've used the facilities." I had to *go*.

"Might as well get used to having me at your side." He wiggled his brows. "Don't worry, I'm not dumb enough to make a move on the emperor's new bump buddy."

I bit my tongue. Minus twenty thousand points. "Let's not speak." No way this guy was the ally I sought. Just no way. Something had to go right for me; I was due. And yet . . .

I swallowed a groan. He was the other Soalian, wasn't he?

No, no. I experienced no repeat of the warm, sweet uncoiling of friendliness. Therefore, he couldn't be. Thank goodness!

I walked with Miller to the men's locker room, the now unisex space a stark, functional area designed for security and efficiency, with two rows of metal cubbies, two benches, and open shelving that displayed clean, folded uniforms. Concrete walls bore a smattering of stains from who knew what. Surveillance cameras occupied nearly every corner, ensuring everyone behaved. An automated device periodically emitted a disinfectant spray, keeping the air (almost) scent-free.

In a private stall, I peed and changed into my uniform.

Holding my stare as I emerged, daring me to look away, Miller stripped out of his underwear and donned a clean pair of fatigues, forgoing a new undergarment altogether.

"Could you be any more inappropriate?" I muttered. How I hated this.

"Definitely. But go ahead, pretend you're not impressed." He secured one end of the metal around his waist. "Are you bummed High Princess Lolli Dolion arrives today? 'Cause I would be."

"I'm not bummed about anything." Because I was currently bummed about *everything*.

"Sure, sure." Miller made an obscene gesture with his hand before handing me the other end of the chain. "I believe you."

Ignore him. I secured the metal, as well, connecting us.

We sat on a bench and tied our boots, knocking elbows and growing more irritated. The teammates around us, each bound to another, were no happier. Only Roman and Merlot worked well together, totally in sync.

"Lolli was only, like, the love of High Prince Cyrus's life, once upon a time," my partner said, diving back into the conversation as if there'd never been a lag.

Nope. No way. "That's a lie. She was married to his brother."

"Yeah, but only after she dated Cyrus. They lived together for a year, I think. And now that she's a widow, Cyrus has another chance to win her."

That . . . no. Maybe Cyrus had dated his sister-in-law before she got hitched to his brother, maybe he hadn't. Either way, he didn't desire her now. For whatever reason, Miller was attempting to razz me up with jealousy.

"I said let's not speak," I snapped. Cyrus had chosen me. Our relationship was new but solid, and nothing a guy with questionable motives suggested would alter my certainty of that.

"Your loss." Miller blew me a kiss, attempting charm. "But I was gonna tell you about all the other women he's dated and how he dumped them as soon as they fell in love with him."

Promised to lay low. Can't throat punch him. An urge I hadn't entertained until today.

Domino's warning replayed. *Words are like your cherished seeds. Living containers able to grow and produce after themselves. Once spoken, they take root in the soil of your heart and get watered by your thoughts. What develops is a tree of life or death. The semantics you lament decide the fruit that grows—fruit you will eat.*

Here was a perfect example of that. Miller had just planted a seed of fear. What if I fell in love with Cyrus, and he ended things?

Argh! No. Enough of that. "Let's go."

Miller and I headed to the gym and took our place in line beside Roman and Merlot. The pair teased each other and laughed as if they were on a date. Because of course they did. Roman was a man of many interests, and most of them involved bed hopping. Other trainees streamed in after us.

The room itself was large, with a small set of bleachers for spectators, different pieces of equipment pushed against a cement wall, and a hardwood floor marked up for various activities. In the back was a small office encased in glass, leaving a desk and two chairs on exhibit. *The* spot for getting reamed by our instructors.

Heta marched past the double doors. "There's been a change of plans today," the archduke called as soon as the bell quieted. "We're taking a tour. Some of you need a reminder of what we're fighting against." He didn't glance at me, yet I felt singled out.

I shifted from one boot to the other and tried not to worry. Deviating from schedule didn't strike me as a good thing.

The archduke led us through the winding hallways and down different flights of stairs, into a windowless basement more heavily guarded than any other part of the building I'd visited. We scanned our ID chips at the final door and entered a sleek chamber illuminated by soft white and blue lighting. There, we were given protective gear: a mask and a papery neck-to-foot body suit that zipped over our clothing. Garments we were required to don while fastened together, an impossible task made possible only with creative alterations.

I looked ahead. Transparent screens projected vitals and diagnostics. Doctors and technicians clad in lab coats embossed with CURED's emblem moved about. The air vibrated with quiet efficiency, coated with the same chemical scent found in the locker room.

"This," Heta said, leading us down a long series of intersecting corridors with small, glass-walled rooms on either side, each housing a patient, "is where we treat soldiers infected with Madness."

What! I lagged behind Roman and Merlot at the rear of the line, forcing Miller to slow his steps as I looked over every patient. Many paced. Some sat upon a cot, the only piece of furniture, but all exhibited signs of great physical and emotional distress. From vomiting to slamming their fists into their temples to banging their heads against the walls.

Many moved their mouths, as if they were talking, but the words remained trapped with them inside the rooms.

Compassion gripped me, a soft, aching pressure against my heart. I recalled my mom's recovery. How she'd grown weaker, becoming a shell of her former self. How she'd been unable to keep down food and required daily handfuls of medication just to survive. The worst part—no one needed to suffer this way. Soal's cure was painless, instant, and lifelong. And yes, okay, that did sound kind of cult-y, exactly as CURED claimed. Even I could see that. But I'd lived it, and truth was truth.

"Everyone you see here has a greater chance of recovery because we struck hard and fast at the first suspicion of illness," Heta said from the head of the line.

"That's how you work best, eh, Roosa?" Miller quipped, earning chuckles from other teammates. "Hard and fast."

I bit my tongue again, and this time I tasted blood.

Heta continued as if the lord-in-training hadn't spoken, but the muscles between his shoulders bunched, a clear sign Miller's name was just scribbled on the archduke's naughty list. "This is why we travel to Theirland, risking our lives to gather the resources and medications that were used by the civilization before us. Why we show no mercy to Soalians, who work to exacerbate the spread of the illness."

Okay, the last statement irritated me more than Miller's taunt. Heta might believe what he said, but that didn't make it true. The Madness came from Astan. A poison intended to turn mortals into controllable immortals. Lesser gods on a string. The problem was, the formula wasn't perfected. To retain power and ensure people willingly participated in their experiences, CURED continued to stoke fear of the true cure.

"This is *awful*," someone at the middle groused.

"Have you listened to nothing I've said?" Heta snapped. "This is *necessary*. Suffering now facilitates recovery later." He waved to a cell on his left. "Like this poor girl, a former trainee. She would've died without our interference."

As we motored forward, I searched every face until I identified the individual Heta singled out. My heart nearly stopped. I did a double take. Rapid blinked. The horrifying sight never improved.

Reeling, I stepped out of line, dragging Miller with me. "Mykal." I flattened my palm against the glass. "Mykal!"

"Hey," my partner grated, trying to jerk me into motion.

I dug in my heels, refusing to budge. My former roommate and forever friend perched at the foot of her cot, staring at the floor. Draped in a paper-thin hospital gown, she appeared weak and fragile, with uneven tufts of hair sticking out at odd angles, as if she'd given herself a trim with a rusty axe. The already slender girl had lost much-needed weight. Cuts and bruises marred her face and hands.

Tears blurred my vision before streaking down my cheeks. "Mykal," I breathed out.

"This is unfortunate." Roman crowded in at my side and winced. "Poor kid." He and Mykal had grown up in the same apartment complex and were as close as blood siblings.

"We have to help her," I said, and I didn't care if it got me into trouble.

"She's being helped right now, getting treatment. A shame she got infected, though." Clicking his tongue, Roman turned on his heel and motored on, as if there were no need for further discussion.

"Let's go," Miller growled, clamping my wrist and tugging.

Still I resisted, knocking on the glass until an angry voice bellowed, "No touching."

Mykal never looked up.

Thoughts hit me with the force of punches as Miller dragged me away. Forget chain of command. I'd go straight to the top. Surely Cyrus could do something. When Mykal was freed, and she would be, I'd tell her about Soal, and she would listen, then eat my piece of the Rock. What she wouldn't do? Turn me in at a critical point in the war with CURED. A time when the lives of my loved ones hung in the balance.

Unless she did.

In my worried daze, I almost overlooked the person imprisoned in a cell near hers. The second my mind caught up with my eyes, I ground to a halt. John Victors, the formidable glower who'd allowed himself to be captured to help me see a truth I'd denied my entire life. Now, he lay motionless on his back, his eyes swollen shut, his wrists cuffed to metal rails, his skin pallid, and his body hooked to multiple machines. Tubes protruded here, there, everywhere. A thin blanket draped his lower half.

A ragged cry lodged in my throat, releasing a bitter burn.

Miller pulled me along the hallway, and I let him do it without resistance. Forget going straight to the top. At the first opportunity, I would sneak back to this area. I had royal clearance. I could bypass security. I'd be careful. Wouldn't alert Mr. Vyle. Wouldn't even tell Cyrus, allowing him to maintain genuine deniability. But one way or another, I had to act. My friends were being *tortured.*

Heta concluded the tour and ushered us from the basement of nightmares back to class. I searched for Cyrus but didn't see him. Nor did I pay attention in class. Or eat lunch. Or converse with anyone.

I even lost sight of Miller, who remained at my side, chatting about nothing during every break, unconcerned by my silence.

My mind remained trapped in a loop. *Mykal. Victors. Mykal. Victors.* The horrors they must have endured—*must be* enduring. The danger of my plan. I'd have to leave the base for good. There'd be no coming back from this.

"Hey!" Miller tapped my cheek. "Get your head in the game, Roosa."

I focused to find his scowling face inches from me. We occupied the gym with the whole team and a trio of barons barking orders at us. Self-defense class, I realized. I'd missed most of the day.

Heat bloomed in my cheeks. "Apologies," I muttered. "What are we doing?" Whatever it was, I could do it. For a couple of hours, I would set my worries aside and pretend I wasn't planning to betray all of CURED.

"We're learning to move together, what else?" He wiggled his brows. "Though if we're gonna improve, we should probably do extra credit after hours, like Roman and Merlot."

I recoiled and shuddered. "Not happening. Not ever." Not even if he tattooed Cyrus's face over his.

Miller shrugged, unabashed. "I didn't say we had to be naked."

I punched the bag he pushed at me.

"Better," he said, as if he'd purposely incited my wrath.

For the next however long, we acted as if a pair of punching bags were feeders determined to kill us. Too often Miller angled into my personal space, hindering my motions as well as his own. Or maybe I angled into his. Whoever was at fault, it sucked, and both our tempers sharpened to razor points.

The only bright side was the slight vibration dinging on the inside of me, alerting me to the presence of my fellow Soalian. But who was it? *Who?*

"Roosa. Bosworth. Get over your dislike of each other and get in sync," a baron snapped. "Stay aware. Notice the other's slightest fluctuations."

Miller and I exchanged fresh scowls and geared up to go again. An ear-shattering scream tore through the gym, and everyone stilled. Either someone had just broken with Madness, or this was a hologram-type pop quiz meant to prepare us for the mean streets of Theirland.

We waited, collectively on edge. When aggression electrified the air, zapping my nerve endings, I knew. This was no simulation. Someone had indeed broken.

I reached for a dagger only to realize I had no weapons. Other screams rang out, blending with grunts of pain, hard thumps and thuds, and pounding footsteps. The infected person headed this way.

So I was unarmed. So what. My determination strengthened until it produced a heartbeat of its own. *Stop the maddened before anyone gets hurt.*

"Open our chains," someone shouted.

"Formation," a baron called. The chains remained fastened.

Miller and I rushed to join the defensive line forming behind our instructors, almost tripping over each other. Not exactly a boost to my confidence. The other trainees were without weapons as well. Well, other than our fists, feet, and skills.

My personal guards moved to shield me from the front and the rear, one providing me with a dagger, the other giving Miller a netter. Just in time. A man in a hospital gown blazed into the room and climbed the walls, moving so quickly he was fuzzy. Eyes wild with glee, he cried, "Love Soal! My Soal!"

The barons rushed for him, everyone else remaining in formation, ready. Good thing. Other maddened in hospital gowns rushed in next, a chaotic procession as they too screamed about Soal, climbed the walls, and attacked trainees. There were at least twenty, many faces familiar because I'd just seen them in the treatment ward.

Battles broke out all around. Horror returned, choking me. Worse, heat sparked in my cells, as if I were seconds away from glowing, announcing my status to one and all. I fought to subdue it. Fought so hard.

But when two maddened launched my way, I couldn't tamp it down . . .

Chapter Five

That which you see shall pass like shadows at dusk; set your eyes upon the unseen, for therein dwells those things that endure beyond time.

—*The Book of Soal* 2.8.4.18

I glowed, radiant and unstoppable, my skin emitting golden rays as intense as the sun. There, amid combat, surrounded by teammates, with hidden cameras capturing each second, I silently declared my true allegiance, and I could do nothing about it.

Fear and panic collided, icy shards slicing through every other emotion, leaving me momentarily frozen in place. But.

None of the barons or trainees noticed. Not even when a handful of maddened rotated in my direction, abandoning their opponents to concentrate on me. But I thought Cyrus once told me the infected avoided the light?

Either way, my limbs suddenly came back online. With a previously untapped grace and speed, I took down my attackers, then shielded a guard from a biting maddened. To my shock, I absolutely, utterly *dominated.* For a little while, at least.

"On your left, on your left," Miller shouted, netting the maddened until he ran out of ammo.

I angled in that direction, swinging at a new challenger. Success! Miller didn't screw with my rhythm, and I didn't screw with his. We flowed in harmony. Maybe it was my new aptitude or the adrenaline rushing through my veins. Perhaps the fact that we were more concerned with staying alive than annoying each other. One after the other, we took down our targets without incident.

If only our synchronicity and my newfound expertise lasted.

More maddened flooded into the room, each stronger and faster than the last. The newest cluster came at us, growling and drooling, snapping their teeth and swiping their fingers. Unlike the feeders in Theirland, with advanced cases of Madness, these "newly" infected lacked claws, thank goodness. I tried not to cause fatal damage as I defended myself, a mercy that allowed many to land their strikes.

The chain around my waist jerked when Miller sprang at an opponent. He yanked me from my defensive stance and into the kick of a maddened. An elbow to the chin followed, knocking air from my lungs. I lost my hold on the dagger. My glow snuffed out until the only light I detected came from the pinpricks winking through my vision. I wobbled on my feet, weaker than before and ready to topple.

The guard behind me noticed and attempted to help, but three maddened glommed on to him, taking him down.

My partner surprised me, pivoting to serve as my buffer, taking the next blow himself and giving me a moment to regain my bearings. The moment I straightened, Miller returned to my side.

I worked on freeing my guard, punting a maddened in the face and throwing a hard one-two punch at another. Unfortunately, a new group swarmed us. Too many! Though overwhelmed, I punched, blocked, and ducked, exactly as trained. If we could just neutralize this throng, we could exit the gym and search for Mykal. I didn't expect to encounter Victors; he'd been too injured to leave his bed.

Chaos mounted as students fell. Grunts, groans, and curses created an erratic chorus accompanied by constant shouts of "Love Soal!" and "Find Soal!"

The instructors and my guards did their best to protect the fallen as the battle raged on. Miller and I made more mistakes and got in each other's way again and again. Every time, we paid a high price. Aches and pains assured me I would feel every injury later.

"I'm not sure how much more I can take," someone panted, his voice ragged.

"Keep fighting," a baron bellowed.

An army of knights and other barons rushed into the room, firing netter guns, catching maddened inside thin metal nets. Just like that, the threat downgraded, and my adrenaline crashed.

Both Miller and I hunched over, struggling for breath. He dropped to his knees and dragged me with him. I took in the carnage around us, dismay swelling to new heights with each trainee I spied strewn across the floor, writhing in pain and bleeding.

A thin line of crimson trickled from Roman's nose, and bruises were already forming under his swollen eyes. Merlot clutched a broken wrist between her breasts. Cash and another teammate remained motionless, as if . . .

I swallowed a barbed lump in my throat. Unconscious. Only unconscious.

"Talk to me."

The authoritative voice cut through the noise, my head, and my very being. My heart leaped with recognition and relief. Cyrus. He strode inside the gym, radiating fury and full authority.

Behind him were Mr. Vyle and four others. The ultra-stunning High Princess Lolli Dolion and three men I recognized as high princes, each dressed in decorated uniforms reserved for royals.

A gaggle of medics rushed into the gym after them, approaching those with the worst injuries first.

"Royals on deck," someone called.

Everyone awake lumbered to their feet as Cyrus and his entourage looked us over, their eyes sharp and unreadable. My heart pounded with the urge to run to him, but I held myself still. Now wasn't the time. Or the place.

The future king of Ourland looked me over and stiffened. When his gaze met mine, he arched a brow in question.

I nodded to convey the fact that I had no mortal wounds, and he nodded back. A quick, clipped incline of his chin before he shifted his attention.

"I can feel his chill from here." Miller sucked air between his teeth with an exaggerated wince. "Guess things are over with the HP, huh? Makes sense. I wouldn't want to be with the girl banging my grandpa either."

I lifted my nose in the air and said nothing.

Cyrus called, "If nothing is broken, line up."

Trainees rushed to stand shoulder to shoulder. My body protested the action with sharper aches and pains, but not by word nor deed did I display it. I kept my gaze on Cyrus, my safe place.

Mr. Vyle walked before us, his arms behind his back. "My name is Mr. Vyle. I'm here on behalf of the emperor. We've come to believe there's a traitor in our midst. In this very room."

My stomach twisted into a thousand knots. No one dared speak, but many gasped.

"One of you planted a device in the treatment facility and opened patient rooms at a specified time." The royal executioner focused on me a second longer than necessary. "I will find out who did it, and they will learn the error of their ways."

I didn't allow myself the luxury of cringing outwardly, but there was no stopping my inner flinch. How did he know what happened so quickly, without an investigation? Experience told me CURED released the infected, intending to blame an innocent they targeted.

"We are already gathering evidence. It won't be long until we have answers." Mr. Vyle adjusted the cuff of his suit jacket. "For now, I'm sending you to medical for testing, but expect a summons sometime soon. I'll be speaking with each of you individually." He nodded to a baron.

"Out," that man commanded. "Go, go, go."

Trainees rushed for the door, Miller among them. He dragged me along until Cyrus snapped, "A word, Lady Roosa."

Miller and I stopped in unison, grinding to a halt mere feet from the royals. I felt the gaze of everyone who remained in the room.

Though my cheeks flushed, I kept my head high. "Yes, sir."

A muscle jumped in my boyfriend's jaw. Motions liquid smooth, he wrapped his fingers around the chain that bound me to Miller. The metal unfastened, freeing me. "Go," he commanded my partner.

Miller didn't stick around to protest. He raced out as if his feet were on fire. Realized I had a thriving relationship with a future king, and I might tattle about his awful behavior, earning him a good spanking, had he?

Cyrus didn't say anything else, just stalked into the gym's corner office, clearly expecting me to follow. Which, of course, I did. The transparent glass smoked over, shielding us from prying eyes.

As soon as the door closed behind me, he spun and enfolded me in the safety of his arms. I hugged him back, letting his ambrosial scent wash over me. His heat warmed all my cold spots.

He straightened, cupped my cheeks, and searched my face. "You're okay?"

"I am now," I replied, clasping his wrists. "I'm glad your trip to Theirland was so short."

"I was there, in a meeting with the emperor, Vyle, and the other royals when word of the attack reached us."

The attack. Something we needed to discuss in detail. But first things first. "How'd it go with your grandfather?"

A muscle jumped in his jaw. "I'm not sure. I remember arriving in Theirland but nothing else until today's meeting." He rubbed his sternum. "Now there's an itch right here I can't explain."

Alarm bells erupted inside my head. I fought to control my expression and reveal only reassurance. "The memories will come back to you." They must. But something had happened to him, and it did not sound good.

"Yes," he agreed. "They'll come back."

"In the meantime, we've got several problems." I'd start with the most recent. "During a tour of the treatment ward, I saw Mykal and Victors in cells. I'm not sure if they escaped with the others." No longer high on adrenaline, I realized I couldn't free them without help.

Stiffness invaded Cyrus's limbs, and he released me to massage his nape. "CURED suspects you of being the spy. My guess is, they released the patients to gauge your reaction and give themselves an excuse to question your friends. They'll also pick a random trainee to blame and punish. An often-used strategy for a multitude of reasons."

Ding, ding, ding. "If they believe I'm committed to luring you to the other side, they might seize the opportunity to blame *me*."

His features softened. "Don't worry. This kind of suspicion isn't uncommon, and our connection explains the enormity of the test. But I'm working behind the scenes to dismantle Mr. Vyle's assumptions. The tour proves my efforts are having a positive effect."

Positive? Seriously? "Explain, please."

"Tours aren't given to first-year trainees, which means he wanted you to see Mykal and Victors and tell me about it. He isn't sure about either of us, and he's watching to see how we react. What we do. If he didn't think he could use you and was certain of your guilt, he would have tried to take you out already."

Ugh. I read between the lines and heard loud and clear what Cyrus didn't say. Breaking my friends from their prisons would only make things worse for us all. I didn't like it, but I understood. But there must be *something* we could do to help them.

"I'll find and free Mykal and Victors," he vowed, smoothing a curl behind my ear. "I'll do it without incriminating us. There's no need for you to endanger yourself."

"Okay. All right." I trusted him. But there was more to discuss. Gripping his shirt, I pondered the best way to present my forthcoming suggestion. "My day off is Monday. I intend to visit the library." As Domino had reminded me, only in the Kingdom of Yesterday, Today, and Tomorrow could I read books detailing my future. "Maybe I should stay there and not return to the base."

Concern pulled taut the puckered skin of Cyrus's facial brand. "I'd rather you *remain* at the base."

"That's not happening." Here, now, there was a tug deep inside me. A desperate need I wouldn't deny. I couldn't not visit the library.

I couldn't not revisit a certain idea either. "I think we should stage a breakup." I'd do anything to keep Cyrus safe, even this. "Just for a little while."

Scowling, he gave a clipped shake of his head. "Absolutely not. I'm your best line of defense."

"True, but I'm clearly a hindrance to *yours*." I cherished his refusal, but more was at stake than my life. "On my day off, while I'm safe in the Rock, claim you've discovered I'm a Soalian spy. I'll take responsibility for whatever Mr. Vyle knows or finds."

A harder shake of his head. "Ember ordered you to continue your training as if nothing has changed. I promise you, there's always a reason to obey her."

I heaved a sigh and released him. "There's a high likelihood I'll be outed as a Soalian while I'm in Theirland anyway. I glowed during the fight with those feeders. No one seemed to notice except the infected, who glommed me, but what will happen when I'm in the other world, in the dark?"

Again, his features softened. "Do you remember when you ingested the piece of the Rock and felt as if an invisible filter fell from your eyes?" He waited for my nod. "It wasn't a filter, but a frequency modulation produced by the Madness."

Frequencies. Yes. I didn't know much about them, but many believed the Rock produced a particular pitch, and that was what screwed with people's minds, causing them to break, becoming crazed.

"There are different levels of infection, and our light affects each differently," he said. "Before you became Soalian, I glowed many times in your presence, and you never noticed."

"Nice!" I mean, I remembered he'd once mentioned that there were soldiers who hadn't noticed his light, but I hadn't realized the same phenomena applied to me, the novice. Now, on to the next topic while we had this rare moment of privacy. "The librarian, Domino Crane, told me there's a Soalian on my team." Speaking of, I hadn't yet acknowledged Cyrus's incredible gift in person. "Thank you for the best present I've ever received. Not that I understand how a seed grew into a piece of the Rock or how it summons a librarian."

A veritable parade of confusion, dismay, irritation, and resolve dashed over Cyrus's face. "You summoned the librarian? And he just appeared?"

"Yes." My brows knit together. "Isn't that what my piece of the Rock does?"

Cyrus worked his jaw. "It's supposed to give you added strength when you ingest it, not act as a crooking finger for Domino Crane."

Something about his tone grabbed my attention. "You don't like him."

"I don't not like him. We . . . have history." He rubbed two fingers over his brow. "Let's not talk about him right now. He probably won't appear again, making him a moot point. The other Soalian on your team is a nonstarter. Unless one of your books leads you otherwise, do not admit what you are. The fewer people who know the truth, even among supposed allies, the better. Not everyone is good at keeping secrets."

As he spoke, he looked as if he carried the weight of the world on his shoulders. I intended to comfort him, to hug him and fill his ears with reassurance, planting and watering good seeds in his heart, but a sprout of doom broke through the soil in my memory garden.

Something terrible was soon to happen. Something worse than anything we'd ever experienced. I *knew* it.

The blood in my veins flash froze. "Cyrus," I croaked.

His gaze snapped to mine. He stepped closer to me. Opened his mouth.

A whoosh sounded as the office door opened, welcoming in Mr. Vyle and the other royals.

Cyrus compressed his lips into a thin line. He didn't move away from me but wound his arm around my waist, resting his fingers on the curve of my hip. "Arden, you've met Mr. Vyle."

"Good to see you again, Lady Roosa." The executioner offered a pleasant smile as I hurried to uproot the doom and forage for calm. He wore a black suit without stripes today, this one as perfect as the last, made from the softest-looking cloth I'd ever seen. Not a hair was out of place. He exuded undeniable magnetism.

I managed a lame nod of greeting. What I didn't do? Respond verbally. It *wasn't* good to see him, and I wouldn't lie about it.

"Arden, meet High Princess Lollipop Dolion." Cyrus's tone became as sharp as glass. "My sister-in-law."

Um, I'd only ever heard her referred to as Lolli. Was Lollipop her full name or a personal endearment?

She glared at him and grated, "*Lolli.* Ex-sister-in-law. Ex in general."

Unconcerned by the corrections, he waved to the men. "High Prince Summit Bardin, High Prince Mallow Merrick, and High Prince Felix Dolion."

"Hello," I said, doing my best not to wither with intimidation. Especially when Lolli looked me over with obvious contempt.

The high princes looked me over as well. While Summit sneered a bit, Mallow appeared curious, and Felix amused.

"So you're the one who put stars in my brother's eyes," Felix remarked, and I blushed.

In appearance, the half siblings shared many similarities. Both men were striking and self-assured, harsh in their intensity, but Felix projected a slightly easier aura, as if you could approach him without permission and not lose your head for it. Well, not right away.

"I'd heard the rumors but didn't believe them until now. Slumming it with a lady-in-training. Really, Cy?" Summit rolled his eyes. "And at such a critical time."

"If he wants to blow his chance at ruling the kingdom, let him," Lolli quipped. "I support his foolishness, and you should too."

Undeniable digs at me. Though my confidence took a beating, I maintained my polite mask.

"When I'm crowned king," Cyrus stated, utterly at ease, "I will remind you of these insults, and you will beg for Arden's forgiveness."

I mean, I wouldn't say no to an apology.

While Lolli and Summit bristled, Mallow smiled at me. "I'm pleased to meet you, Lady Roosa. I hope you realize their slights reveal their character flaws, not yours."

"I'm pleased to meet you as well, High Prince Mallow." I returned the smile. "And yes, I do."

"I'll take your statement, Lady Arden," Mr. Vyle said, moving the conversation along.

"Of course." *Here goes.* "I noticed nothing out of the ordinary during the tour of the treatment ward. We returned to class, began training, and the maddened attacked." The facts, no elaboration.

"Thank you." He asked no follow-ups but shifted his attention to Cyrus. "Your presence is required elsewhere."

My cue to go. "I'll be on my way." I looked to Cyrus.

"We'll talk soon," he promised.

"Yes, please." Maybe I'd made a mistake, not telling him about the doom while I'd had the chance. He deserved a warning.

But then, wouldn't I be giving him a seed of doom? A fear as much of an enemy as CURED.

Cyrus dipped his chin and pressed a soft, swift kiss into my lips before releasing me.

Lolli made a huffing noise. I lifted my head high and strolled from the room, certain CURED and fear weren't my only enemies.

Chapter Six

For as long as you live, troubles and trials will arise, but understand this: Outside pressures lose their power when they are not allowed to dwell within.

—*The Book of Soal* 2.4.16.33

I didn't see Cyrus for the remainder of the week, but we did message via my special reader.

Cyrus: Mykal and another patient escaped the base.
I've got trusted scouts searching.

He meant Victors. Were the "trusted scouts" CURED soldiers as well as Soalians? I certainly hoped so. My friends needed help only we could give them.

I knew better than to ask follow-up questions, even in a roundabout way. Or to inquire if Cyrus had remembered what had occurred in Theirland with his grandfather. Something we absolutely needed to dissect sooner rather than later.

Arden: Thank you for letting me know. PS: I miss you.

Every day, in every way, and I didn't care who knew.

My heart leaped when his response came seconds later.

> **Cyrus:** Prepare yourself. Soon I won't settle for another rushed peck.

Anticipation prickled my skin. I craved his kiss more than my next breath. It was necessary, and the longer I went without it, the more I ached for it. For *him*. My brightest light in a world of darkness.

I still hadn't tended to the Problems for Later section of my memory garden, but I hadn't had time. If I wasn't updating Cyrus, I was training. If I wasn't training, I was studying or observing my teammates, searching for my fellow Soalian.

Yes, Cyrus warned me not to trust anyone else, even another Soalian, and I understood his reasons. But this was a mystery I must solve. This particular Soalian had kept the secret for years. A skill I wished to acquire. Plus, I really needed a friend right now. A mentor. I wouldn't admit what I was.

Mr. Vyle had made sure of that. He did indeed punish a trainee for the treatment facility incident. The culprit was hung in the courtyard and left to rot for days. I hadn't known the chosen soldier, but the loss stayed with me.

Though I'd "summoned" Domino, he hadn't visited me, proving Cyrus's assertion that my piece of the Rock was meant to provide a burst of strength after ingestion, nothing more. And yet, I sometimes thought I detected a low hum of the librarian's relentless intensity. But if he was nearby, why not appear? I didn't expect to have a long, drawn-out back-and-forth with the guy, but come on. At least let me lie down, close my eyes, and pretend to sleep while he explained more about Soal, the Rock, and the books.

When my day off finally dawned, I was beyond ready.

The morning began as any other, a bell buzzing and cell doors opening. The only difference? Trainees cheered. As I sat up in bed, I noticed my guards no longer stood at the entrance. Guaranteed, they lurked somewhere in the shadows, intending to follow me as I made my way through Bala City.

I hadn't forgotten Cyrus's request that I remain at the base. While his happiness mattered, I ached to be inside the Rock. I couldn't stay here. I just couldn't. Answers awaited me, the tug stronger by the second. No way I could pass up this opportunity.

After a beat of hesitation, I freed my seed from the safe and stuffed it in my pocket. Just in case I needed a boost . . . or didn't return. Like my team, I hustled into the hall and made my way to the locker rooms. While others chatted about their plans, jubilant, I did my best to hide my nervousness. Today I was going to break countless CURED laws. If caught, I'd lose everything I valued, perhaps even my life.

I hurried through a shower and changed into regular clothes. The infamous pink tank and shorts I'd worn my first day on the base. The very reason Cyrus called me Lady Pink. I relocated my Rock to my shorts pocket.

My stomach churned as I speed-walked toward the underground train station on the other side of this building.

Halfway there, a trainee named Winslet caught up and draped her arm over my shoulders. "Hey."

"Hey," I echoed, confused. This was the first time she'd approached me. "Everything okay?"

"Everything's great." She had spiky hair, multiple piercings, and strength many envied. And she was funny. A trash-talker who let nothing intimidate her. If she was the Soalian I sought, even better.

"Let's hang today," she suggested with a bright smile.

I almost blurted out, "No, I'm meeting someone." Such a rejection opened the door for more questions. "Maybe next time."

"I don't mind tagging along, whatever you've got planned." She hit me with a sad expression. "I could really use the company right now."

Hmm. Was she too eager to stick with someone she'd never interacted with? Perhaps she was assigned the duty of spying on me up close and personal. With CURED, the possibility always existed.

I made a noncommittal noise to buy myself a little time to cobble together an appropriate but firm response. We reached the steps leading to the underground station, where hundreds of soldiers congregated. A cornucopia of conversations filled the air.

Down we went. As usual, a musty odor greeted me, and I wrinkled my nose. Pritis clusters illuminated the congested expanse. Secured to the rocky ceiling, they chased away shadows. In an instant, my blood boiled. CURED had removed every orb from a Soalian's heart. *We* produced the light able to repel feeders.

An answering light heated my chest until a luminous glow burst from my pores. As promised, no one noticed. Hands balled into fists, I trekked farther into the underground corridor. Winslet kept pace.

Soldiers in and out of uniform swallowed us. Brakes squealed in the distance, the train coming to a stop near the platform. A door on every cart opened, allowing the throng to swarm inside. My companion released me to push someone out of our path, and I seized my chance, purposely surging into a crowd at warp speed and slipping into an already filled cart. The doors closed, leaving Winslet outside.

Disaster averted with zero casualties. I searched for Cyrus among the faces, hoping, hoping. Boo, hiss. No sign of him.

The cart wobbled and the train shot forward, zipping along the narrow tunnel at a faster and faster clip. Though no one paid me any heed, I felt spotlighted as I gripped the bit of the Rock in my pocket. My link to Domino. To help. The sensation of being watched lingered the entire ride and only increased when I disembarked onto an overcrowded platform.

As I climbed a flight of stairs and emerged into a sunny, bustling cityscape, mouthwatering scents replaced the subtle but awful stench of a leaking battery. To my shock and delight, I caught sight of Cyrus.

I hurried closer. Hmm. Disappointment killed the thrill of excitement. Not the real Cyrus, after all, but a hologram. The display showcased all five royals in the running for king, their images flashing over a building's wall.

A question scrolled over their heads. **WHO WILL BE CROWNED?**

"Come, taste the nectar of the gods," called a woman costumed as a mermaid. She lounged on a large square pedestal that served as the base for a colossal statue of a fish-man, petting him with one hand and beckoning to pedestrians with the other. "Our sea cakes are the land's sweetest treat, and only half a trill."

Citizens paused to pet him too. Someone kissed his tail. My entire life, most people had treated these statues as mere decorations while only whispering accounts of sleeping gods in secret. Witnessing this open adoration surprised me. Something had shifted among the masses.

Another problem for later. The Rock called to me, urging me on.

My eyes raked the background, my nerves taut as I hunted for any sign of trouble. The area buzzed with life, vehicles whizzing along paved roads and people rushing down winding sidewalks. Buildings of varying shapes, sizes, and materials flanked the streets. Glass monoliths gleamed under a too-bright sun, their sleek surfaces reflecting the city's constant flow of movement, while weathered shelters with peeling paint stood in stark contrast. Lavish crystal palaces sparkled atop hills, as lovely as frozen waterfalls as their faceted walls glittered. Alongside the magnificent structures, odd, angular buildings made of a polished golden alloy shimmered, seamlessly fused to sturdy brick buildings.

Intermixed throughout, multicolored lights flashed from signs advertising a plethora of services. Everything from spending an hour with a robotic lover to punching a living (supposedly willing) person to blow off steam. Screeching, fast-paced music resounded, the notes setting my nerves on edge. A feathery breeze carried a blend of new scents, and I caught myself wrinkling my nose again. Fried foods, the metallic tinge of metal, and clashing body odors. The overpowering smells left an unpleasant residue in my nostrils.

Other statues formed by a shimmery silver material that rippled slightly with each caress of wind topped marble bases where people danced, celebrating the deities the images represented. I usually looked past such displays, yet today, they held my attention. I thought, maybe, something was different about them, but what? I pinpointed nothing out of the ordinary.

Except. There. A bronze statue that hadn't been here during my last visit. My steps faltered. The sculpture depicted Astan, former ruler of Theirland. He was the biggest of the gods and the only one to possess both horns and wings. In this portrayal, he stood tall, one arm half raised, his wings spread wide.

But his horns. I'd seen many renderings of him inside a Theirland temple devoted to his worship. In each, those sharp horn tips had pointed down. In this version, however, the thick, ribbed projections thrust almost midway.

The small change shouldn't have mattered, and yet it acted as fertilizer to my sense of doom.

Someone bumped into me, and I tripped forward. Okay, time to shelve statue deliberations and move on. Besides, the Rock loomed just ahead. A spectacle of grandeur eight feet tall and eight feet long with translucent stone and circles carved throughout the outer surface. An intricate interweb of crimson veins ran through the center. My heart picked up speed.

Though I longed to rush, I maintained an easy pace. Small metal dogs—the meta—walked along the structure's top, disturbing the lush garden of flowers flourishing there. Those dogs observed and recorded all who passed, growling at anyone who lingered.

I didn't let myself stare as I considered what to do next. I needed to pause and study the Rock before I could step inside it, something I couldn't do without garnering attention.

Also, was I being followed? Trepidation tempted me to cast a suspicious gaze over one shoulder.

Resist. Act normal. I racked my brain but came up with a grand total of zero ideas to accomplish my goal. Then I was there, walking along the sidewalk behind a couple who trailed a small group, all of us beside the glorious edifice. A yearning to look and touch consumed me, but I wouldn't risk it.

The Rock's surface thinned, appearing as mist. I swallowed a yelp when Domino appeared, a solid oak of a man, strong and unbending.

He'd trimmed his beard.

A silly observation. Since no one cried out or screamed, I guessed only I could see him.

He stood inside the doorway, his gaze trained on me. "Keep going. You're being watched from above and followed from behind."

Knew it. When no one reacted to the sound of his voice, I breathed easier.

As if to prove his claim, the meta atop the Rock glued their sights to me, acting as if no one else existed. I tried not to make it obvious that I noticed or cared. Perspiration dampened my palms.

"I've arranged cover for you at the next section," Domino announced. "You can enter there."

Okay. I could do this. I cleared the Rock, the tug stronger than ever, keeping me marching forward. By an act of my will, I maintained my leisurely pace. Finally, my patience paid off, and I neared the next section.

Anticipation tangled with frustration. The area swarmed with people moving in both directions, their shifting bodies creating a living wall that hindered my view. What kind of "cover" had the librarian arranged?

Suddenly, a thick white fog seeped from the stone, sweeping out to envelop the crowd and beyond. I almost tripped over myself, but again, no one else seemed to notice. They continued without a break in their conversations.

The fog collected and concentrated around me, warm and scented with fresh rain and rich earth, my two all-time-favorite fragrances. That sweet perfume erased the stench of Bala City and brought a perfect calm I'd sought my entire life. In that moment, I had no fears.

A tinkling laugh escaped me. I expected my vision to haze, but it didn't. Everything stayed razor sharp, colors bright, edges defined. A man on his phone almost plowed into me, stealing my amusement, but I jerked aside just in time. One side step turned into a scramble as I twisted and dodged through the crowd, not a single person reacting to my presence. That's when it hit me: I wasn't being ignored. I was invisible. The "distraction."

With full confidence and awe, I stopped to focus on a carved circle, exactly as Ember once instructed. The fog did its thing, ensuring no one protested or shouted accusations. Inside the ring, broken lines drew together. The second they fully aligned, the circle began to spin. My cue. Overjoyed, I walked forward, leaving the cityscape behind.

My surroundings altered in a snap, the outside world replaced by a spacious room complete with polished wood, hanging flowers, and trees heavy with colorful fruit. The fog receded, taking its great peace with it, but I didn't mind. I was too busy marveling at the beauty around me. Precious gems studded the walls, and gold bars paved the floor. Trees grew through them, their thick branches curling out in every direction. Someone had fashioned shelves into the trunks, each stacked with books. Cozy chairs offered places to read in comfort. Some had occupants, many didn't.

I rotated, taking everything in. I'd never been in this part of the library. Crystal chandeliers hung from a tiered ceiling, casting soft rainbow flecks across the room. Delicate vines wove over the bookshelves, with tiny glowing blossoms pulsing like captured stardust. Ornate lanterns floated gently in the air, producing a quiet hum and illuminating the waterfall trickling down a crystal wall. Elegant tables bore a selection of porcelain teapots, their contents steaming.

"Magnificent," I said out loud. Despite the lack of fog, the scent of fresh rain and rich earth remained strong, but now it infused with a perfume of parchment, honeyed fruit, and something indefinably ancient. Absolute heaven.

"Welcome to the Kingdom of Yesterday, Today, and Tomorrow."

The familiar voice drew my gaze. A flesh-and-blood Domino stepped from air, suddenly only a few feet away. He wore the same red robe as before, hood down, and hadn't changed in the slightest, yet he looked different somehow. Honor stamped every inch of his being, the perfect complement to the little specks of light dotting his irises, like pinpricks in a night sky. And look at those thick, long lashes. Three freckles formed a half circle on his right temple, framing his eye. Well, a half circle if you were to trace the marks with your fingertip. Which I would never do. Like, ever.

Inner shake. But his intensity, wow. He radiated it. More than I'd ever thought possible, and it possessed a powerful pull, yanking thoughts from my head until I was completely grounded in the moment. A weird sensation I wasn't sure I liked because I liked it far too much.

"Thank you for the assist out there," I said.

"There's no need to thank me for doing my job."

Oookay. I recalled the oddity I'd encountered along the way. "CURED moved a statue of Astan into Bala City."

"Yes." Domino started forward, saying nothing more. "They did."

"His horns are different," I added, rushing to catch up.

"Yes. And we will discuss it. Later."

"That's fine." Later was better than never. Might as well dive into other matters. "There's a problem. Cyrus has lost memories of time he spent in Theirland with his grandfather. Also, you told me he was scheduled for execution, but he says it's someone else."

"I'm aware of both. The high prince visits us when he can, and we're working on the first."

Well, that was something.

"As for the execution, Cyrus was wrong. He wasn't removed until days later."

But he was off it, and that was what mattered. "I summoned you a couple times, yet you never showed."

Domino gave no reaction. "I was there."

A simple statement, his disappointment in me bubbling inside it. I winced. Had I insulted him? "I wondered if I sensed you. Why didn't you reveal yourself?"

"You were not in danger, but you were more heavily guarded than before. I weighed the pros and cons of appearing and decided to aid you from the shadows. Among other reasons."

Well. "I apologize for complaining," I said with a sigh.

"I take no offense. You are still learning me, Arden. Once I prove myself, you won't have reason to doubt me."

The gracious, unexpected show of kindness won me over in ways nothing else could have. As we walked on, I asked, "How did you become a librarian?"

"I bonded to the Rock on a deeper level, becoming part of the doorway itself."

Interesting. Worthy of further questioning, but I noticed a reader watching me with unabashed curiosity and frowned. "You won't tell me the identity of the Soalian on my team, yet these people are logging my identity left and right. Any one of them can turn me in."

Domino shook his head. "These are permanent residents of the library but not librarians. They're not able to communicate with anyone other than fellow residents." He stopped and motioned to a full, lush tree, its branches heavy with palm-size fruits of the deepest, richest purple. "Go ahead. Taste and see."

Don't mind if I do. I tabled the urge to question him further and plucked a bulb. A new fruit instantly matured in its place, spurring a delighted laugh from me. Amazing.

"This is the first plum tree to grow in Ourland."

I'd heard of plums. Supposedly sour and mushy, with a hint of fermentation. "Our vegetation came from here?" I asked, giving the soft flesh a light squeeze.

"The Library of Soal birthed all that is good," he replied, as if that explained everything. "The reports you've read about plums are not accurate. Go ahead. Try it." With eager curiosity, he urged my hand to my mouth.

I sank my teeth into the fruit, unsure, only to groan, my eyelids sinking shut. Sweet and tart. After devouring the rest, even the soft pit, I reached for a second. When I finished it, I licked my fingers, greedy for every drop of juice.

For a moment, I just stood there, basking in the energy now flooding my veins.

"Good, yes?" Domino asked.

"So good."

"Finally!" another familiar voice called. "You deign to visit."

I twisted to meet the gaze of Ember Cruz, the powerful glower only a few years my senior. The woman who'd helped Cyrus recruit me. As she strode over, everyone she passed jumped to their feet to salute her. She remained focused on me. "Big things are underfoot, Roosa. Huge. Colossal."

"As if I don't know that, Cruz," I quipped. "I'm currently under investigation for being a Soalian spy who murdered King Tagin and now hopes to lure his son to the enemy's side."

"Well, you *are* a Soalian spy who murdered King Tagin. It doesn't matter that he attempted to kill you first. To CURED, you are at fault. But no matter. We're dealing. The good news is, Victors is free."

My heart leaped. He was the second escaped patient Cyrus had mentioned, as I'd suspected. "How is he? Can I see him?"

"Fine. And nope. He's not here. But you didn't let me finish," Ember said, and I heard the heavy sigh hidden in her words. "We're going to have some trouble with Cyrus. Okay, a lot of trouble. Tons."

"What kind of trouble?" I demanded. Foreboding flared anew, setting off a chain reaction. Ice sprouted over my spine, acid churned in my stomach, and tremors consumed my limbs. "Tell me."

"That's to be determined." As I wrestled with brewing panic, she told Domino, "Your petition has been approved. Congrats."

He blinked slower than usual. "I filed no petition."

"Ah, but you will, and soon," she replied, then dashed off, as if the conversation was over.

"Hey," I called. "Elaborate on your bombshell. Tell me everything you know about this supposed trouble with Cyrus. Leave nothing out. No detail is too small."

"You'll have to read your book and tell *me*," she called back. "But first, go to class. I scheduled it to begin upon your arrival, and you're about to be late."

Chapter Seven

Consider the source.

—*The Book of Soal* 1.20.1.7

"This way," Domino said, heading in the opposite direction.

"Class?" I grated as I caught up. "I'm all for learning, but I'm here to read my book." My blueprint of the future. Truth amid a world of lies. Victory in the face of defeat. The only way to help Cyrus.

"If Ember has delayed a class for your arrival, it's because you won't be able to decode your book until you ascertain a specific truth."

Concentrating on anything other than Cyrus was gonna be tough. I mean, was I putting him in danger by being here?

Wait. Was I? "CURED tracks the chip embedded in my hand." They tracked everyone. "Do they know I'm here, in the library?"

"The library sits upon Ourland and is also within Ourland. If you keep within certain perimeters, CURED will record only locations you can walk while in Bala City. Soal has thought of everything."

Okay. All right. But still.

Domino led me into an empty room with an open door of light centered on the far wall. A sign over it read **The Beginning For Beginners**. We crossed through, entering . . .

With my head tilted back, I stopped and spun in a slow circle, examining every inch of the space. An impossibility. We were inside the library, yet also outside, standing in an endless garden fantasyland both with and without walls.

A large golden orb beamed the most incredible warmth and glorious golden light from an endless expanse. And the fragrance. A luscious cornucopia of floral delights, featuring everything from roses to wildflowers to honeysuckle. How I distinguished the individual notes when I'd never encountered them, I didn't know. Petals of every color bloomed in every direction, even the sky. Little drops of dew glistened on a carpet of lush grass.

A gentle breeze caressed my skin as I toed off my boots and socks and sank my bare feet into the softness that pulsed with the very beat of life. Stones of varying sizes carved out a winding pathway, humming a perfect accompaniment to the sounds of a distant, rushing river. The two created a celestial melody I hoped to hear every day forever.

At the center of it all stood a tree like no other. A wide, twisty trunk made of three separate parts. The bark on each resembled a filigree as intricate and lovely as lace. White flames flickered over leaves of sapphire blue, crimson red, and vibrant purple, offering a visual feast.

The tranquil garden quashed any sense of urgency I'd previously entertained. For a moment, I could only close my eyes and savor a grandeur too glorious to take in all at once.

"I've lived here over three centuries, yet the beauty never ceases to amaze me," Domino quietly stated.

Excuse me? The astronomical, impossible age nearly broke my brain. "Three centuries?" I echoed. Despite the thick stubble on his jaw and eyes as fathomless and deep as an ocean, he appeared less than a decade older than me.

"It's not as shocking as you think. In certain places of the library, such as this garden, time passes differently," he replied with a shrug. "In some ways, I am both older and younger than you."

There was so much I had to learn.

Around twenty people filtered in through a side entrance. I probed each face, searching for Shiloh, the guy I'd dated before Cyrus, who'd first set me on the path to Soal. Problem: Everyone looked blurry. I shook my head, rubbed my eyes. No change. Then, one face cleared as if the air had been sprayed with cleaner and wiped with a rag. I squealed, delighted. Mom!

She wore the same nanny uniform as usual, but today it emphasized a pink flush of health. Something I hadn't seen since her treatment for Madness. Even her hair gleamed.

"Arden?" she cried with surprise, as if a haze had cleared from *me*.

We lunged toward each other and hugged so tight we might leave bruises. Domino stepped back, providing distance and privacy, while also surveying the reunion with curiosity.

"You're here." I laughed as I pulled back. "You're Soalian."

"I am." A huge smile stretched from ear to ear. "I joined Soal's army three days after you whisked me from my apartment."

Then she'd joined three days after Tagin Dolion died.

"Tell me everything," she urged. "What's new with my sweet baby girl?"

No way I would burden her with the details. "Here's a late, breaking headline. I need to get my eyes checked. Everyone but you is blurry," I said, waving to the other occupants now settling in front of the majestic tree.

"That's for everyone's safety." Mom chuckled. "Trust must be given to erase the shields."

Um, I'd become a Soalian four days before her, yet she knew more than me.

"So you're good?" she asked, clasping my shoulders and giving me a motherly once-over.

"I really am. And you?"

Another huge smile broke out. "Better than ever. Oh! There's my friend, *Beeeep*," my mother cried with all the happiness of a schoolgirl. "You're gonna love her. Come on, I'll introduce you."

"Did you say . . . *Beeeep*?" I asked, but she'd already rushed off.

I hung back, wanting to laugh and cry, and needing a moment to collect myself. Mom was here, and she was well, and she had a friend she trusted enough to share identities with. It was everything I'd hoped for her, and my heart overflowed.

"This is usually the moment I experience a new deluge of doom," I confided in Domino as he returned to my side. And I should have. The thing with Cyrus . . . But no. My delight remained. A miracle had occurred with my mother. A miracle could occur with the high prince too. Whatever was needed.

The librarian might have smiled, but the microamusement vanished so quickly, I convinced myself he'd experienced an involuntary muscle twitch. "There isn't room for doom right now. You're too happy." Domino faced me, as if to bid me goodbye, but seconds passed, and he remained rooted. "What is it you so greatly admire about Cyrus?"

"Many things." Remembering the feud Cyrus had mentioned, I asked, "What is it you so greatly *dislike* about him?"

"I don't dislike him," the librarian said, frowning. "Why would you think so?"

"Well . . ." What did these two formidable men not wish to discuss? They'd both denied animosity while projecting a boatload of it. "For starters, I've met you both."

His frown deepened, but he motioned to the other students with a tilt of his chin. "Go. Learn. The faster you do, the safer you'll be. The world as you know it is soon to change."

"More cryptic words. Great." There'd been so many already. "Quick question first. Is my mom's friend really named *Beeeep*?"

For the second time, I was pretty sure he almost smiled. "Just as you see blurry faces, you will hear a sound rather than names, unless told by the person in question. Another security measure."

Ah. Made sense. Mostly.

"Hey, new girl. Your instructor is here, and we're about to start. Join us."

The familiar voice drew my gaze, and I snorted. Ember herself stood at the tree, ready to begin. Like Domino, she wore a crimson robe made of the finest fabric trimmed in gold.

"Thank you," I told Dom, reaching out to clasp and squeeze his hand. "For everything."

Manner suddenly as sharp as ice, he slid his eyes to our joined hands, silent and still. Oops. I'd made an obvious blunder. Touched an elite without permission.

"Apologies," I muttered, severing contact and turning sharply. I forced the librarian from my thoughts and bounded over to stand beside my mother.

Leaning into me, she said, "Baby, this is *Beeeep*." She motioned to the woman on her left. "*Beeeep*, this is Arden."

"Hello," we both said. *Beeeep's* face remained blurry, and I believed mine remained blurred to her. What sound did she hear in place of *my* name?

"Nice to meet you," she said, and I thought I heard kindness in her voice.

"You as well."

Ember clapped, gaining everyone's attention. "Before anyone decides to rush me, I'm happy to report this garden is time adjacent. We can stay here for years and return to our lives without missing more than a few minutes. Now zip it. Everything I'm about to tell you comes from *The Book of Soal*." Reverence dripped from her tone. She anchored her arms behind her back, saying, "Sometimes, words must be lived to be seen. Follow me, please." One step forward. That was all she took, and a cobblestone path appeared out of nowhere.

With Ember at the helm, we walked the path, single file, the air around us shimmering with images. A fantastical world of unimaginable wealth and opulence, with castles made of crystals, gardens teeming with life and color, and roads paved with gold bricks. Trees abounded, birds with glimmering feathers flying from branch to branch. I gasped with delight. Look there! Bees and butterflies!

"This is the Theirland of yesteryear," Ember announced. "A land Astan the Destroyer would come to infect with his Madness. Perhaps you noticed the statue of him in Bala City. He's preparing the masses for his next grand entrance. The beginning of the end."

I pressed a hand over my belly.

The teacher began to teach. "The more you know of the one you battle, the better prepared you'll be. First fact. Astan wields only two weapons. Lies and fear."

No one spoke, the students riveted by flashing images of Astan in flight and battle, a thick, black smoke curling from his mouth. I was eager to see and hear more, to learn everything.

"He lives for one purpose," Ember said. "The devastation of Tsuri, Soal's son."

Excuse me? Soal had a *child*?

Another image appeared, this one featuring a thirtysomething man with a snow-white tunic, scuffed leathers, and a stunning purple robe.

"Astan once served as Tsuri's second-in-command. Tsuri was married to Rose, whom he adores."

A woman in a ball gown made of ethereal light appeared next. The closest example of perfection I'd ever seen. She looked as if she'd been spun in moonlight and woven with threads of stardust, a vision too radiant for this world or any other. Petals fell from a crown of roses, catching in her glorious mane of hair. Her eyes reminded me of wishing wells, deep chasms filled with countless dreams.

"Rose and Astan had an affair, and Tsuri retaliated, pouring his wrath upon his former second. Fearing her own retribution, Rose fled, and in her haste, she tumbled to her death."

The scene showed the perfect fairy-tale beauty tumbling through the night sky, whizzing through clouds and ultimately slamming into land, leaving a large crater that quickly filled with tears.

"Tsuri, who loved her still, poured his life into her, bringing her back from the abyss. He died, and she lived again, as Briar Rose." Ember spread her arms. "The Rock grew where Tsuri's body sank, and now Briar Rose and Astan seek to finish him."

So much to take in. The scene switched, showing the water level sinking while the Rock grew and rose. It had been, was—*is*—a living entity, and I now walked within him. Wow, wow, wow.

"Know that you cannot outreason Astan," Ember continued. "He has lived millennia and understands the human mind in ways you do not. There's no better manipulator. And when that doesn't work, he uses intimidation. If that fails, he promises you worlds. He'll even follow through . . . at first." A perfect breeze made her long tresses dance over her shoulders. "His council aids him, all former guards in Tsuri's army."

A parade of deities appeared in flashes.

"After soundly defeating Astan and his ilk, and razing Theirland, Soal trapped the lot within their own monuments. They would have remained imprisoned, leaking their hatred, the Madness, until the end of the age if humans hadn't burned through the invisible veil separating the two worlds."

War scenes flashed next, the council of gods fighting an invisible force—and losing. Amid the battles, buildings fell, and smoke billowed. And when that smoke cleared, those same deities stood frozen in stone casings, shadows oozing from tiny cracks . . . until the sky split with a line of crimson fire and half of the statues vanished. Confused, terrified people appeared in every direction. The Rock, gone.

"As more and more of us became infected, the gods strengthened within their prisons, doing everything in their power to prevent Soal from aiding us," Ember said. "And yet, he made a way, through Tsuri, weaving the Rock into Ourland."

She stopped, giving us a moment to absorb her newest revelations. I tried my best. Tsuri. Rose. Excuse me, Briar Rose. Astan. An affair. Life for death and death for life.

"Many of you have heard the gods are waking," she said, and I realized we were back where we'd started. "The truth is, they are already awake. In fact, some of the lesser gods escaped years and months ago.

Something Soal arranged, allowing us to learn and practice on the weakest of the bunch before we face the big bads, who remain trapped within their monuments, disembodied." Her gaze swung to me, rocking me on my feet. "When they break free, and they will, they'll require hosts. Humans able to survive the power surge that comes with them."

I shot a hand into the air, and she nodded at me. "You're talking about possession," I said, half question, half statement.

"Yes and no. I've seen it happen with the lesser gods I mentioned. They merge their essence with a human's and fight to take over. Things became distorted for the human. Time, light, shadows, reality. The human then descends into a madness far worse than anything you've previously encountered. On the flip side, Soalians are conduits for Soal's power. It is *his* light that glows within us. As we read our books, his words, we fuel it, which makes us stronger conduits."

She canted her head to the side, frowned, and nodded, as if she listened to someone we couldn't hear. "All right. I've got somewhere to be. Class dismissed." Her gaze landed on me once again, and I shook under the weight of it. "Think about all I've said and how it might apply to you. Okay?"

"Yes."

Both instructor and students dispersed, but Mom hung back with *Beeeep* and me, as I put on my shoes. We had only just started discussing the shocking history lesson when Domino approached.

"You may read your book," he said, attention fixed on me, "or remain with your mother, but you cannot do both. The choice is yours."

"Book, book, book," I rushed out, clasping his hand and darting forward, intending to drag him if necessary. "Bye, Mom. Love you." I would find a passage featuring the problem with Cyrus, and that was that.

Domino didn't budge, which meant I didn't budge. Oh, sweet goodness. I'd grabbed him without permission again. For the second time, I released him in a hurry and muttered an apology.

He faced my mom, unconcerned. "You are Elise Roosa, mother to Lady Arden."

"I am. And you are Domino Crane, famed librarian."

He inclined his head. "I'm pleased to meet you," he said, and I wondered where this polite version of my librarian had been hiding.

I may or may not have muttered the question out loud, and he may or may not have smirked at me.

She glanced between us and grinned. "Go on, you two. Do your thing," she urged, shooing us away. "There's plenty of time for chitchat later. Just know I'm always available to help."

"You shape the lives of the children you tend," Domino said, still not budging. "You help us every day."

He'd meant those words. They hadn't been a polite rejoinder, but a considerate observation from a powerful man.

Mom flushed with pride. "I see why all the girls are crazy for you," she said, beaming at him.

No question about it: He blushed. I pressed my lips together to stop a laugh.

She didn't seem to notice his unexpected reaction as she kissed my cheek and hugged me once more. "I love you, baby."

"I love you too."

Off she and *Beeeep* went, conversing happily all the way.

"So all the girls have a crush on you, huh?" I teased.

"Not all." Blushing again, Domino finally budged of his own free will, walking off. "Come." He returned me to the space with the cozy chairs and trees growing through the gold-paved floor. The other occupants were gone. We were alone.

He motioned to a square table, and I eased into one of the two chairs stationed there, ready. As he eased into the chair across from me, his scent registered, and I frowned. The same delightful fragrance I'd detected in the fog. Fresh rain and rich earth.

Had *he* produced the fog?

Before I could delve deeper, he passed me a book I hadn't known he'd held.

Instant obsession, all other thoughts fleeing. Tingles spread up my arm as I glided my fingers along the smooth brown leather. Over the title. "*The Book of Arden*, Volume 20." The same tome I'd read before. Lovely flowers were etched over some of the letters. In the center was a circle with seven lines of different sizes inside it. According to Ember, that circle contained the mysteries of *The Book of Soal.*

"Why did you select this particular volume?" I asked. Why not nineteen or twenty-one? For that matter, how many volumes told my story?

"On most occasions," Domino replied, "you'll select the book you wish to read. This time, I made the selection. It has called to me for days. Whatever waits inside the pages occurs in the future, and I'm part of it."

I tried to look up at him, but I couldn't drag my attention from the cover. It called to me too. *Open . . .*

Yes. I must. And there was only one way. I concentrated with all my might, willing the lines inside the circle to move. And move they did, but slowly. The barest twitch. Not good enough.

The harder I stared, the stronger the twitches became, until . . . yes! The lines drew together and snapped in place, pushing the outer ring into a spin, exactly what occurred to open the Rock. Bubbling over with eagerness, I cracked open the spine. A yellowed title page led to a letter from the author. No coded text, all readable.

Excited, I devoured the passage.

> My dearest Arden,
> I have written for you a beautiful love story. Yes, there is pain within your pages. Yes, there are tests and trials too. We have a determined enemy. Let me assure you, the end is worth every hardship. I can help you, no matter what snares he constructs, so let me. Read my

thoughts, see what comes. Trust me or not. Every day, in every way, you decide.

Yours,

Soal

A lovely note, but also nerve-racking. Pain. Tests and trials. A determined enemy. "Soal says he wrote my book, a romance, as if he *authored* my future."

"He did. He's able to see the end from the beginning and shape events to get there. But Astan sees a different end and writes books as well. I promise you, his tale of your life is horror."

"I've already lived a horror novel," I mumbled. Never again. Trembling, I flipped to the next page and found the coded text I'd expected. A sigh slipped out. This was going to be a long day.

Letting the world fade from my awareness, I worked and worked . . .

And worked . . .

And worked.

Finally, the little symbols unraveled, more letters forming right before my eyes. A single paragraph became clear.

Astan has claimed Cyrus as his chosen. It's obvious. Tick tock goes the clock. The beginning of the end is here.

My stomach dropped. Astan would select Cyrus as his host? The knowledge settled hard, but okay. So it wasn't great news. It wasn't the worst either. Cyrus would say no, and we'd move on.

On the next page, a larger passage cleared, and I hurried to read.

We stand in a stalemate, the battlefield between us a nightmare of lifeless bodies and scattered limbs bathed in the unflinching light of Theirland's twin suns. Lavender and gold streak the sky, casting an eerie glow over the blood-soaked earth, where rivers of crimson carve fresh paths through the flatland. Overhead, a restless flock of scavenger birds circles, their shrill cries piercing the thick, heavy silence as they await their feast.

A fresh wave of CURED soldiers floods in, surging from behind the former high prince and hurrying to kill the array of glowers trapped around me. Men and women I admire. Many more will die today if I don't stop Cyrus. But how do I strike down the man I love?

No. No, no, no. Cyrus would say no. He wouldn't accept . . . couldn't . . .

But he might.

"No!" I burst out. Soal had promised me a love story.

And pain.

And tests and trials.

I swallowed. This must be a mistake. Cyrus would never accept Astan. Not ever.

But if he did . . .

We would absolutely go to war.

I swallowed harder. I must have misunderstood what I'd read. Yes, that was the simplest explanation. I just had to read on, and I would learn what came next. Perhaps a celebration because we'd so thoroughly fooled all of CURED, pretending to do battle. Yes, yes. I must only read on.

On edge, I buried my face in the tome and labored to decode the next passage.

Chapter Eight

Every path Astan offers ends in destruction.

—*The Book of Soal* 1.20.14.12

"Time to go."

Domino's voice penetrated my haze of concentration, yanking me kicking and screaming from my study.

I had yet to decipher another word, much less a second passage. *Just need to try harder.*

"Arden!"

Jolting, I clutched the tome close and met the librarian's determined gaze. "I'm not going anywhere, Dom. Astan targets Cyrus, and at some point, we fight, which means he might say yes to possession, so I need to read more and find a way to stop it. Okay? Okay." Had I really called him Dom?

Domino plucked the book from my intractable clasp with humiliating ease. "Fear impedes your ability to decode. You know this."

Ha! "The joke's on you, because I don't know anything anymore. Maybe the battle is pretend. A trick meant to confuse Astan. That's possible, right?"

"If you don't exit the library now, you will miss the final train back to the base."

"But—"

"You can argue with me, or you can return to Cyrus. You cannot do both."

Return to Cyrus. Yes. Purpose rampaged through my veins, and I popped to my feet. "Let's go." I would warn him of the god's plan, and he would mount an unbeatable defense. Because Cyrus wanted nothing to do with Astan; he'd already chosen Soal.

Guess I did know something, after all.

Domino led me through a maze of hallways scattered with private reading nooks. "Remember there's always a path to victory, no matter what you read. The answer is here, and we'll find it."

Great. Wonderful. "I'm not sure I can trust you with this particular mission. Your dislike of Cyrus clouds your judgment."

"I told you, I don't dislike him. And it wouldn't matter if I did. He's one of us. I'm willing to die to protect him, just as I'm willing to die for you."

His ferocity turned his words into a vow. As he steered me forward, I was struck anew by his quiet strength. If he was even half as loyal as he seemed, he might just be the friend I'd been searching for—someone worth trusting, after all. "Thank you, Domino," I said softly.

"There's no need to thank me for—"

"Doing your job. I know. But it's your choice to do it with honor and kindness, and I appreciate that."

His gaze cut to me for a split second, like he was trying to determine if I was a figment of his imagination.

"I call that look the Arden Effect," I bragged, earning another of those maybe smiles.

We cut through different exhibits featuring holographic displays of phenomena from around the world, throughout history. He stopped in front of a particular wall with no decorations. The stone—Tsuri—thinned, allowing me to see Ourland beyond it. Bala City, to be exact. Citizens went about their evening, unaware they were being watched from within the Rock as well as outside it.

"I'll count down the seconds," Domino said. "You will simply walk out of this room and keep going without pause. I have a hologram of you strolling along a path to this location. That image will vanish as soon as you make contact. You are safe." He pointed to someone approaching the sidewalk in front of our section of the Rock.

I gasped. Me. It was me. I wore the same pink tank and shorts, my hair braided.

No time to process anything.

"Five. Four. Three. Two." He gave me a gentle shove, his touch warm and firm, and I stumbled outside.

The hologram walked into me, disappearing for good, igniting a tingling whoosh all over my body. As instructed, I kept moving, awed. I didn't let myself look back at the Rock as I headed toward the train station.

I descended the steps and joined a growing crowd on the dock. Though I had to force my way through, I made it inside a cart and whisked back to the base, where I holed up in my cell to unpack what I'd learned in the library.

Cyrus. In danger. Perhaps my enemy.

The doom I'd buried overwhelmed my memory garden, as if its roots had invaded every section. It had always pointed to this, hadn't it? Astan might choose Cyrus as his host . . . and Cyrus might say yes.

When was this supposed to happen? And what about the war itself? Finally, I'd learned the truth about what had spurred it, but so many questions remained. At the top of the list: All this for jealousy? *Seriously?*

What was Astan's goal, anyway? He must want more than just the destruction of the Rock.

Quaking, I shot the high prince a message.

I need to speak with you ASAP.

I awaited his reply, hoping he'd come visit me. Minutes ticked by. An hour. Curfew arrived, and I was sealed inside my cell.

I tossed and turned all night.

The next morning, I checked my reader, but there was no response. Looked like I'd have to go about my day as if nothing was wrong.

My guards followed as I stomped from my cell. They even accompanied me inside the locker room. "Hey," I snapped and shooed them off. "Go."

"We have new orders from High Prince Cyrus," one said. "Stay with you at all times, no matter where you go or who you're with."

Defiant, I tugged on my fatigues. Orders from Cyrus, not the emperor or Mr. Vyle? But why? Confusion set in, and I steeped in it.

Winslet stomped over. "I lost you in the crowd yesterday."

"Yeah," I said with a wince. "Apologies. It was packed in there."

She leaned against a cubby and crossed her arms. "What did you end up doing?"

"This and that." What else could I say without lying? I sat on the bench and tied my boots. "How about you?"

"Same. Look," she said, plopping beside me. "If you don't want to be friends, just say so. You're dating a high prince, and I'm a nobody. I get it." Resentment replaced her tinge of anger.

An urge to soothe bloomed from a seed of guilt. At the same time, part of me wondered if she purposely sought to rouse such an emotion. She might be a CURED spy . . . or the Soalian I searched for. "I'll pretend you didn't just insult me. You don't know me, and I don't know you, so let's pair up and change that."

"Fine," she replied, as if she didn't care, but I noted the glint of satisfaction in her eyes.

We spent the day tied together by the chain I despised, but I admit, I enjoyed her more every hour. Her quick wit kept my mind off my problems and grounded me in the moment.

Was she the Soalian or not? And if not, how could I recruit her?

"You know Roman better than anyone," she said at the end of the day as we changed in the locker room, readying for our free time. Well, she changed, uncaring that my guard stood in the doorway. I just removed my fatigues, leaving me clad in the pj's I hadn't shed this morning. "You got any tips for snagging his attention?"

Oooh. Was he responsible for her sudden interest in hanging out with me? "I don't know him well. Just well enough to understand a girl only needs to keep breathing for a shot. He likes variety."

She snorted and finished up. "Yeah. That tracks. Anyway, you should come to the commons for once. We always have fun."

"Maybe one day," I hedged. Just not today. I bid her goodbye and hustled to my cell to check my special reader.

Grrr! Still no response from Cyrus.

Nor was there a message the next morning. Or the next. Thanks to my guards, I couldn't sneak off to hunt him down and demand an answer face-to-face. My optimism plummeted, which soured my mood. Though I held my piece of the Rock close each night, while alone in my cell, Domino never appeared either.

A sense of abandonment spiced my growing dismay, creating a toxic brew of anxiety. Perhaps a little anger too. Had I been forgotten? Was I unwanted?

What was I supposed to do? How was I supposed to warn Cyrus about Astan if I couldn't speak to him?

Finally, on the morning I was to travel to Theirland, I received a response.

I'll make arrangements.

Relief and anticipation pummeled my other emotions. I expected a summons at any second. Before I reached transport, at the very least. Except, I never made it to transport.

"No need for a chain or partner today," Roman called. "Report to classroom three."

Questions sprinkled the air, all revolving around why.

"I don't know," he groused. "I just know what I was commanded to tell you."

Everyone switched direction. We made our way to the appropriate classroom, where we each claimed a seat. I waited, hoping against hope this had something to do with my meeting with Cyrus.

Before long, Heta strode into the room and announced, "You're not going to Theirland today. You're not ready. Instead, you're taking a surprise field trip to Bala City. Line up at the door and follow the baron to the bus."

Curiosity and dread colored the expression of my fellow trainees. No one protested, though. We jumped to our feet and hustled out the door. Roman and Merlot took the lead, the cast on her wrist not disqualifying her from service, while Winslet and Miller flanked me, and my guards remained glued to my heels.

In a lobby, we neared a group of royals, and I spotted Cyrus. Relief, so much relief.

Except, he stood off to the side with High Princess Lolli, who laughed at something he said. The exes looked so comfortable together, especially when she angled her body closer to his and whispered.

He didn't welcome the action, but he didn't protest it either. I huffed. I'd been a mess of emotions, concerned for his safety, not to mention our future, and he'd spent the time hobnobbing with a former flame?

Okay, so, I knew Cyrus, and my trust in him was absolute. He wasn't a liar or a cheater. He'd said he wished to be with me, and only me; therefore he wished to be with me, and only me. If ever he changed his mind, he'd tell me. He wouldn't string me along. He wasn't a coward.

What's more, he wouldn't pretend to desire someone, even to recruit her to our side. His stalwart integrity wouldn't allow him to cross a line, destroying our relationship right from the start. But then, he might not be himself right now.

The blood rushed from my head. I hadn't forgotten what *he'd* forgotten: Something had happened at the emperor's palace, but Cyrus couldn't remember what. What if Astan had gotten to him already?

"Sucks to be you, eh, Ardie?" Miller cackled. He bumped my shoulder with his own. "On and off again."

Cyrus stiffened and straightened his spine, his gaze zooming to me, as if he'd sensed my presence. Awareness buzzed between us, and Miller shut up.

The high prince left the princess while she was in the middle of a sentence. He closed in on me. Most of my teammates peeled away like layers in an onion, giving us space. Those who didn't were nudged by my guards.

I didn't stop, but then, I didn't need to; Cyrus didn't miss a beat, keeping pace beside me. Wanting to both kiss him and shake him, I snapped, "You and your Lollipop sure looked cozy."

Dang it, I instantly hated myself for going there. Either I trusted him, or I didn't. If I didn't, I shouldn't be with him. "Whatever. Never mind. I learned something that concerns you, and you need to hear it as soon as possible."

"I see." He said nothing else. We exited the building, entering a sunlit parking lot where a silver bus idled. Before I could board, Cyrus snaked his arm around my waist and hauled me off to the side. He peered down at me, and I peered up at him, tension quickly dissolving into affection.

We linked fingers. The sunlight adored him, paying his beautiful, harsh features perfect tribute. But those bright rays also highlighted deep lines of stress he'd not previously sported. "Cyrus," I croaked, worried for him.

"There's no one for me but you," he told me quietly. Intently. "Lollipop is her given name, and I use it to knock her off balance, not as an endearment. I'm playing a game because I must, but you can rest assured, I'll never do anything that threatens our relationship. That, I swear. Recall my pledge on the train."

His words played inside my head, a verbal caress. *I'm all in with you, Arden. Whatever happens in the coming days, remember that.*

I ran my bottom lip between my teeth, nodded, and stepped closer to whisper, "You're in danger." I pressed my palm against the scarred handprint covering the right side of his face, and he leaned into the touch. A privilege reserved solely for me. "At the first opportunity, go to . . . where you wanted to take me when you were first assigned to recruit me." The Rock. "Talk to the . . . my new friend." Domino. "Cancel whatever you must, but go there today. Please. Do it for me." For us.

He gave a clipped shake of his head. "There's no need. I've already done what you've asked, and I know what you're referencing." His hold on me tightened. "Please don't worry, kitten. I'll never war with you. We're rock solid."

A play on words that roused a toothy grin in me while his confidence soothed the worst of my fears. I was obviously misinterpreting the passage. "I believe you." But. Um. "Why didn't you respond to my message before today?" I tried not to pout, I really, really did.

"I only returned to the base this morning."

Okay, so, that wasn't an explanation because contact could be made between worlds, but I let it slide. "Did you remember anything?"

"No." His tension cranked up again. "I lost more days."

Now *that* was an explanation. One that disturbed me greatly. "There's a classroom beyond time. Let's go together. We can stay until you decode those days in your book."

"There's a downside to those timeless rooms, and I'd rather avoid it." A muscle jumped beneath his eye. "About Domino. I don't want you to see him anymore. Command him to stay away, and he will."

What? I hadn't known Domino long, but he'd been nothing but helpful. Not to mention he was a major asset to our team. "I get that he's not your favorite, but he's a great resource."

"I don't care."

But I did. "This is a big ask. You gotta give me more than an entreaty. Tell me why."

"I just need you to trust me." Cyrus dipped his head to press his brow against mine. "At least promise me you'll think about it."

Though the very idea pricked like a thorn, I nodded. Nothing wrong with musing something over. "I will, I promise." I'd probably think of little else.

His gaze jumped behind me, to the bus, and narrowed. "You better go. Be safe, Pink."

"You, too, sugar bear. By the way, I miss you already," I added because I couldn't not.

"Good. Because I love you, and I'll never let you go." He pressed one of those too-swift kisses into my lips before striding away.

My mouth floundered open and closed. What? He hadn't just . . . he couldn't have . . . *What?!*

I trudged to the bus and boarded, still floundering. Forget what he'd requested regarding Domino. I'd figure that out later. Cyrus Dolion did not just confess to being in love with me. I'd misheard. Or . . . or . . .

He might actually love me?

My guards entered the vehicle behind me. I didn't let myself consider Cyrus's declaration a second more—I'd only melt. That must come after this field trip.

Winslet pointed to the bucket seat in front of her. "I saved you a spot."

A whirlwind of emotions churned as I gathered the scattered pieces of armor and an assortment of weapons piled on the seat. Steeling myself, I slid into place. One guard stood watch up front, rigid and alert, while the other silently took position in the back, ready for whatever lay ahead.

Duchess Mimidae stood at the front as well. "You've learned to work together in pairs. Now, you'll practice in a small group of five. Suit up."

I obeyed, donning the armor. Pieces I'd worn before, each made of a lightweight substance with malleable seams. The arsenal consisted of a netter gun, a retractable spear, two regular daggers, one CO2 special, a gun known as the harbinger, and a pair of metal cuffs interlaced with stun pins. Hmm. I'd never worked with cuffs.

"Your individual goal is simple," the duchess stated. "Without issuing a field test, identify and detain someone you suspect of being at the breaking point of Madness. Your group goal is to protect innocent civilians while securing each candidate."

"How will we know who's infected if we can't run tests?" Cash asked. "Feeders without worms can pass as clean."

Features pinched with disapproval, the duchess snapped, "At this point, if you need worms to identify those who exhibit symptoms of the Madness, you shouldn't be a member of the gentry. Quit the program and go home."

Silence swept over the bus. Any hint of excitement withered, replaced by unease that magnified as the vehicle ate up the miles. By the time we reached our destination in the heart of the city, many soldiers-in-training looked ready to shatter. Even Roman. I think we all understood the ramifications if we got this wrong. Innocent people would suffer.

"Stick together with your team, aid each other," the duchess said. "Feel free to traverse the entire city. You may detain and interrogate anyone of your choosing. Your chips will open most doors, and there's a badge on your vest the citizens of Bala City will recognize and respect. Return with someone in your custody or a very good reason why you're empty handed."

I glanced down at said vest and sure enough, an emblem decorated a spot above the left breast. A jagged circle with broken lines inside it, like Soal's yet quite different.

"Do us proud." Duchess Mimidae stepped aside and waved to the door. "The group that returns first wins the greatest prize of all: bragging rights. Pick your own teams. The countdown starts now. Go, go, go."

We spilled from the bus at warp speed. Roman, Winslet, Merlot, and Miller invited me onto their team.

"Let's go somewhere private so we can strategize." Roman didn't wait for our acquiescence but led the charge.

We marched down a busy sidewalk, my heart thudding all the while. The Rock called to me, urging me closer. Closer still, drawing me like a magnet. Longing choked me. What I wouldn't give for five more minutes inside the library. Or even just a peek at one of the symbols on the surface. Just for a second.

The urge magnified when I spotted the statue of Astan. The horns seemed to have risen another two inches.

I rubbed the sudden burn in the center of my chest. What did that even mean? Domino had said we'd discuss it "later," but we'd gotten busy with other things. And now, I might have to cut him from my life for reasons I didn't fully understand.

Focus. Surely the most difficult task of my life. But I did it, visually x-raying everyone around me, ready to spring into action at the first sign of an impending break. Agitation. Wild eyes. Cold grins.

An unsettling wind kicked up in my head, swirling with debris. Something about this task wasn't right.

Thoughts took shape. My first day at the base, Cyrus had voiced a profound yet often forgotten piece of wisdom. *Everything* was a test. So, what was the point of this one?

What had the duchess said? *Without issuing a field test, identify and detain someone you suspect of being at the breaking point of Madness.*

CURED could make anyone break, or seem positive, which meant absolutely everyone we encountered was a candidate. We could bring in anyone and pass.

Too easy!

Could we pinpoint outward signs of a coming break to support our choice? Yes. But many of those signs also pointed to anxiety. I should know. And who wouldn't feel anxious with a bunch of armed lords- and ladies-in-training marching about, determined to arrest someone. The victim would lose a full day's pay. And what if they had a dire medical appointment they were forced to reschedule, which could take months or a year? What if they missed a child's birthday party?

After pressing the heel of his palm into an ID pad, Roman entered the lobby of an apartment complex. We followed. The concierge vaulted to his feet, noticed our vests, and paled. He eased back into his seat, trying to make himself invisible.

"Okay," Roman said as we huddled together. "Here's how this is going down."

The inner wind quickened. "I don't think we should arrest anyone," I blurted out before he could begin. Wait. I didn't?

Noises of refusal exploded from my peers.

"Just listen." I clapped my hands, earning silence, and the wind stilled. My thoughts settled. "Usually CURED issues explicit instructions, no exceptions, no excuses. They don't give us an out. Yet the duchess did. Come back with a victim or a reason. So let's give her a reason. Without a proper test, we can't identify an infected person." Yes. That was it. That was the purpose of this activity.

More protests sounded from my teammates. Miller said, "Unless you got a hot tip from the high prince, I'm bagging me a feeder."

"No hot tips. Just an inner knowing."

Roman pursed his lips. "You're outvoted, Ardie. If you want to risk it, that's fine. But we're going to stick close to the Rock. Anyone who even glances at it, we'll question. We should have our suspects within the hour."

Chapter Nine

A war is waged in the corridors of your mind, and only you can crown the victor.

—*The Book of Soal* 2.11.4.8

Minutes seemed to last days as I stood with Roman and the others near a section of the Rock. The yearning inside me swelled, reaching new heights, nearly overpowering me with a desire to enter the library. It was so close, mere feet away. Almost within reach. *Right there.*

"Got one," Roman muttered, and stopped a big, burly man with a limp.

Poor guy.

As the two barked words at each other, my teammates geared up to step in and aid Roman. I shoved a hand in my pocket and gripped *my* Rock. The essence of Tsuri. Rather than appeasing my yearning, however, the action galvanized it. I caught myself peering at a symbol and taking a step closer. Thankfully, no one noticed me—or the robe-clad, transparent Domino who stepped from the structure. Another robe-clad, transparent man accompanied him. Someone I'd never met, probably the same age, with rough features.

Air stalled in my lungs, every particle a needle's kiss as both men fastened their gazes on me, cold and merciless. They closed the distance, side by side, warriors on a mission. What . . . why . . .

Domino wasted no time. "Tell your teammates you're going to the bathroom. Sprint north, turn right. Enter the Lumen Bay Apartments. Speak to no one. In the lobby bathroom, tell the girl to trust she who comes after you."

What the—

"I'll handle your guards," the other man said, his voice a growl.

He and Domino vanished.

I didn't give myself a chance to debate all the reasons I should refuse. "I'm going to the bathroom. I'll be back." I darted off in the correct direction as if my feet were on fire, not giving anyone an opportunity to protest or ask questions.

I dashed through clusters of people and dodged every obstacle. Running was my thing. I pumped my arms in sync with my stride. "Apologies," I called after knocking a guy with my shoulder.

Distinct footsteps echoed behind me, a war drum in my ears. My guards, no doubt. I didn't risk a glance over my shoulder and possibly a crash caused by distraction. Instead, I let Domino's friend "handle" them.

Turning the corner on Lumen Avenue, I spotted the correct apartment building. Wondering what I'd find, I flew inside. Nice place. Modern furnishings, mirrored walls, fancy fixtures.

A woman behind the reception counter shouted, "Hey!" Like the man who'd backed off earlier, she spotted my badge, clamped her mouth shut, and sat.

Bathroom, bathroom, where was the bathroom? I raced here, there. Yes! I shouldered past the door, entering a utilitarian space with two full-length mirrors, two sinks, and two stalls, one on each side. Someone stood at a sink, washing her face. We froze in unison.

Realization slapped me. "Mykal," I burst out, throwing my arms around her. I owed Domino so big. He'd known how desperately I wished to help her, and he'd made it happen. He was a good man.

"Be quiet." Frantic and panicked, she unsheathed a makeshift dagger. "How did CURED find me? I removed my ID chip."

Oh, wow, she looked worse than before. Too thin, fragile, her eyes sunken and her cheekbones sharper than broken glass. Her hair stuck out in dirt-streaked spikes. Torn, stained clothing hung on her slender frame.

Staving off tears, I held up my hands, palms out, to let her know I intended her no harm. Mykal was my friend. Maybe my best friend. Considering she had turned against CURED, as evidenced by her words, she might be ready to hear the truth. Which meant, I now had a choice. Give her the truth, straight up, or don't. If I did it, and she got caught after we parted, she might tattle on me, putting me more firmly in Mr. Vyle's crosshairs.

Honestly, though, Domino had sent me here with a specific mission. He'd all but ordered me to take the risk.

Very well. At least I wouldn't be recorded, my necklace scrambling our conversation. "We don't have a lot of time," I rushed out, fierce but quiet. "I'm a Soalian. Part of the Tome Society. A glower. CURED has lied to us our entire lives. You are infected—"

Making a noise of distress, she jabbed the knife in my direction. The action lacked skill and grace. "I'm not infected!"

I twisted out of the way, avoiding injury, and resumed my all-innocence stance.

"I'm not infected!" she repeated, looking ready to sob.

"I won't turn you in to CURED," I assured her. "Everyone is infected. I was too. But Soal is real, and he's got a cure. Someone I trust is going to explain further."

Hinges squeaked as a humming woman strode into the enclosure. Both Mykal and I froze again. The moment the newcomer's identity pinged, I relaxed.

"Mykal, you remember Shiloh's sister, Ember." They used to live in the same building.

"Hello, Mykal." Ember removed big, dark sunglasses. Dressed in a stark-white dress, with a scooped bodice and a hem that stopped just below her knees, she dazzled. She'd anchored her mass of hair in a sleek bun. A large hat cast shadows over her bold features.

I wanted to stay and help so badly. Mykal kept the dagger raised, her eyes as wild as a maddened amid a full breakage. But I had to go back.

"Please listen to her, Mykal. She'll hide you from CURED. Keep you safe. Reveal the truth and expose lies." Without another word, I raced out and retraced my steps.

By the time I reached my teammates, Miller was cuffing a pale, trembling citizen. The other three stood nearby, holding their own captives and cheering him on. My guards waited among them, tense.

Roman noticed me and scowled. "Pick someone," he commanded. "I won't lose this challenge because you couldn't pee somewhere close."

"No need." I notched my chin. "I told you. I have a reason, so I don't need a captive."

He worked his jaw, clearly wishing to argue. In the end, he moved on. "Fine. I won't force you. But if I'm punished because you refused to do your job, we're gonna have a problem."

"I'm good with those terms," I said, and I meant it.

We made our way toward the bus. While we weren't the first group to return, we were the second. Now, there were two vehicles parked at the curb, and armed guards flanked the doors of both. Three soldiers-in-training waited in a single-file line at the first, each holding a cuffed civilian.

One soldier came stomping out of the vehicle alone, discharging fury as if it was a round of bullets. He didn't speak but made a beeline for the other bus. The next soldier entered with his captive. We took our places behind the last.

The line dwindled as trainees entered one after the other. Different groups arrived with cuffed citizens.

My turn. I lifted my chin and climbed the steps, my guards following. Duchess Mimidae reclined in a seat up front, with Dr. Korey beside her.

The duchess motioned to the spot across from her. "No offering for us?"

I eased down and shook my head. Carefully selecting my words to speak truthfully without elaborating, I said, "I bring you a reason. Without the proper tools, we cannot accurately judge who is and isn't infected."

The doctor narrowed her eyes. "Well, well, well. Cyrus must have tipped you off."

"He didn't." So I'd gotten it right. I should celebrate, but I knew my teammates weren't going to be happy for me. Considering Miller's earlier taunt, they would believe as Dr. Korey did: that I'd had royal help.

"But that isn't something we can prove, now, is it?" Duchess Mimidae dropped her gaze to my neck, as if she could see the flesh-colored necklace. "You may go, Lady Roosa."

I joined the others on the original bus, and just as I'd suspected, no one applauded my win. In fact, no one glanced my way. Everyone ignored me.

Fine. That was fine. I chose a seat in the back and used the time to consider Mykal. Had she accepted Ember's aid?

And what of Cyrus, who admitted he loved me? Loved. L.O.V.E. A smile of delight spread. Except, he probably expected me to return the sentiment. And I should. I wanted to, but . . . I didn't think I was ready. Which had nothing to do with Miller's claim that Cyrus dumped women as soon as they fell.

Bye-bye, smile. Falling in love wasn't something I'd contemplated. I'd feared the Madness too much to risk hooking my wagon to someone else's. While I didn't fear the Madness anymore, love meant forever. Becoming a family. Which was welcome, yes. Forever actually sounded good. Great! But love also meant risk in ways I'd not considered. What if I let myself fall, and he later tired of me the way my dad had tired of my mom? What if Cyrus died? I mean, we were traitors to CURED and in constant danger. Death wasn't just possible, it was probable.

What if I couldn't edit my book?

Worry trapped me in a bubble, leaving the world a distant blur. That bubble popped when the bus pulled from the curb and eased down the road, with Duchess Mimidae announcing, "Congratulations to Lady Arden Roosa, our sole winner." I hadn't even heard her board.

Weak cheers greeted the pronouncement. Shoving my hands in my pockets, I slunk down. As my fingers curled around the Rock, Domino materialized, seated beside me. He didn't say anything, didn't even glance in my direction, but calm washed over me. Until Cyrus's request boomed, a harbinger I could no longer ignore.

He wanted me to cut the librarian from my life. Sever my connection to a good man who'd just done a very good thing. An ally who'd never lied to me. A mentor who shared the same goals as us.

"Mykal listened to Ember for several minutes before she ran from the bathroom," Domino said. "She's panicked, but she'll continue to consider everything she heard. We'll keep tabs on her, and at the right time, Ember will approach her again."

I knew the process—I had *lived* the process. It had taken Ember multiple encounters to reach me. But Domino was right. I had continued to consider her words, never able to escape them.

"Thank you," I breathed.

He hesitated before reaching over to give my hand an awkward pat. His fingers misted through mine, but the gesture wasn't lost on me. "There's still no need to thank me for doing my job," he said, then paused. "But you are most welcome, Arden."

Only six words, yet a strange little blip went off in my heart, as if our friendship had just deepened.

Cyrus wasn't going to like this, but I didn't send Domino away.

❧

The remainder of the week passed without incident or a new message from Cyrus. Not even a visit. My teammates acted as if I no longer existed. A development that stung, I admit. But Domino came to see me often.

Every time we were together, I reconsidered Cyrus's request. But even the thought of disassociating with Domino caused a terrible anxiety to seize me, and I never spoke the words. The high prince had to be wrong about this. Soldiers in a war shouldn't treat their allies like enemies.

Right now, Domino sat at the edge of my bed, lost in his head, his quiet presence a welcome peace in my small cell. Though he was as insubstantial as mist, I swore I detected that incredible rain-and-soil scent, as if he'd sprung from the land itself.

I perched at my desk. "Hey, Winslet," I called as she strode past.

She gave a half-hearted wave and hurried on.

Miller wasn't far behind her. I called out a greeting to him too. He, at least, stopped. "You should have expected this, Roosa. You had insider information, and you denied it. If you'd just told us the truth, we would've heeded you."

"I—"

"Nope, I'm not interested in a conversation." Off he stalked.

I worked my jaw and moved to the bed to sit beside the librarian, my second reader in hand. I started to type, then worried someone might read the words even if I didn't push send, and set the reader aside. How to ask him questions while my guards maintained their posts outside my door?

"CURED only logs what you send," Domino assured me, understanding my hesitation.

Thank goodness. I reclaimed the reader and typed a message.

My teammates treat me as if I'm infected.

"They envy you," Domino said. "Your star is on the rise. You have what they want, yet they can see no way to get it, so they lash out."

Delete. Type.

That doesn't make it hurt any less.

"True, but their approval isn't a requirement for your happiness. You are making a difference in the world. You helped Mykal more than you know. She approached the Rock of her own volition yesterday and asked for Ember. Don't worry, we hid her from CURED's cameras," he added when my spine jerked ramrod straight. "I apologize for not telling you sooner. I've been . . . gathering my thoughts."

No need to apologize. I understand. And thank you. I appreciate all you're doing. Made any headway recovering Cyrus's missing memories?

"Not yet. The answers are in his books, but he's having trouble decoding." Domino stood and moved to the cell bars, halfway in, halfway out, and peered straight ahead. "Your trip to Theirland approaches."

Yes, tomorrow I would travel to Astan's homeland. I intended to find a way to sabotage the god's access to Cyrus once and for all. We could have our happily ever after.

And just like that, my mind circled me back to the high prince's confession. How he loved me. Loved, meaning felt deep affection for. Total devotion. Could I risk everything and let myself fall for him?

Despite being ghosted, I adored him, craved his nearness, and admired his strength and confidence. I believed we had a future. In fact, not too long ago, Victors had told me I would marry Cyrus. A revelation I'd never forgotten but had rarely allowed myself to consider.

The Soalian leader had proclaimed, *Who wouldn't want to speak with the much-desired wife of the high prince? Though I suppose you are merely his future much-desired wife at this point.*

If I married Cyrus, we wouldn't war with each other. Crisis averted.

I winced. Well, of course we could marry and war. Couples did it all the time.

"There's something you should know," Domino said, the seriousness of his tone pinging my nerves.

"Yes?" I croaked, uncaring if the guards heard a lone, random word.

"One of the signs that the gods are rising nears its completion."

Excuse me? Signs? What signs? I tossed the reader and gripped the edge of the bed, projecting urgency. *Go on.*

"There are three." He kept his back to me, his hands fisting and opening at his sides. "The first has already come to pass. A man able to contain the full brunt of Astan's power has been born."

Outside, I went still. Inside, apprehension flogged me. Off to a terrible start.

"Second, Astan's horns will straighten. When they reach maximum height, they will release a blast across both realms."

I'd *known* those moving horns represented something nefarious. I almost shouted, "What will happen then?"

Domino heard the unasked question. "We can discuss the third sign at a later date."

"No," I burst out. That was his standard response, and I wasn't okay with it. "Now."

This time, the guards snapped to attention, gazing my way. "Lady Roosa?"

"Just thinking out loud," I muttered, sinking into myself. When they returned their attention straight ahead, I glared at Domino, my message clear. *Tell me now.*

He didn't. "The gods search for their hosts. Astan and all his council. Some have already chosen. Others will pick from those closest to Cyrus."

A sudden clarity gripped me, and I pressed a trembling palm to my churning belly.

Me. I would be chosen.

"I tell you this not to frighten you," Domino said, facing me, "but to prepare you. In Theirland, the selection process escalates. Be on guard. Trust only me. Avoid Cyrus. He'll be there, and when you see him, you'll wish to aid him. Do not."

I must have misheard. Avoid Cyrus—not aid him? Nope, not happening. The high prince needed me now more than ever, and I *would* help him, however possible. Nothing and no one would stop me, not even Domino.

"You understand that I'm privy to information you are not, yes?" he asked, tone flat.

I swiped up the reader and jabbed my fingers at the keyboard, then showed him the screen.

Cyrus told me to avoid you, but I didn't do that, either.

Domino compressed his lips into a thin line. "I'm aware he asked you to dismiss me. He doesn't want me to tell you what he *has* read in his book."

Type, type, type.

What did he read? You can't mention it and not share. That's just cruel.

"That is a question for Cyrus."

The bell announcing curfew sounded, and my cell door slammed shut, the metal bars slipping through Domino. Amid the commotion of trainees preparing for the night, he held my stare, his grim expression hitting like a punch to the gut.

"Some things you must do because you trust the one we serve, and me, not because you understand why." The librarian's fathomless eyes glittered with determination. "But you can know this. I will never ask you to do something meant for your harm or the harm of others."

Between one heartbeat and the next, Domino vanished.

I threw the reader at my pillows and slammed my fist against the mattress. Jumped up and paced. Stewed. Dissected the librarian's appeal and Cyrus's request, and finally stretched out on the bed, energy depleted. Yet again, I tossed and turned most of the night, dozing lightly on and off.

All my life, I'd had trouble sleeping. Then Cyrus had come along and taught me the joy of being enveloped in the safety of his arms, the only place I slept well. And now, Domino expected me to give that up in Theirland, if given the chance to enjoy it. Not happening.

Whatever the librarian knew didn't matter. I refused to be the rope in a tug-of-war between him and Cyrus. This came down to who I trusted most, and the answer was simple. Myself.

I refused to do something so potentially detrimental without a solid reason. Besides, I could guess Domino's motivation. No doubt he hoped to prevent one of the gods from choosing me. Well, too bad, so sad. I didn't care if I was chosen or not. I had free will; I'd say no. Not for any reason would I bail on the man who'd just admitted he loved me.

Decided, I let a wave of fatigue drag me into a turbulent sea of darkness.

I woke before the wake-up bell, beyond tired but cognizant of a strange sensation in my chest. As my brain kicked online, I sensed a presence . . .

My eyelids popped open, and I reached for the knife stored under my pillow. When strong fingers clamped around my wrist, I jolted upright and swung my free hand, intending to punch first and ask questions after. Mid-strike, I detected a familiar ambrosial scent.

Cyrus.

He caught my other wrist before the blow landed, and I gasped with surprise and pleasure.

"What are you doing here?" I asked, grinning.

Shadows couched him, giving his face a sinister sharpness. He didn't speak but gently, insistently, urged me to lie down. Though confused, I offered no resistance. With my head on the pillow, I frowned up at him. He stared at me, somehow too harsh and too soft at once.

Hmm. His expression . . . How best to describe it? Crazed determination? Tender adoration? Mild irritation? Perhaps a tinge of all three.

"Cyrus, I hate to say it," I muttered, "but this is kind of creepy."

"Have you spoken with Domino?" he demanded in a quiet tone.

At the librarian's name, I jerked my gaze behind the high prince. My guards were gone. "I have, yes." It was the truth, though not the truth he sought. I didn't offer any other information, and he didn't ask.

But he did narrow his eyes. "Do you love me?"

Okay, I should've expected such bluntness from him. Never mind Domino's orders and my concerns for the future. Here, with Cyrus, there was only this moment. "I think I do," I admitted, speaking just as softly. "I must." I felt more for him than I'd ever felt for another. "But I'm afraid to say the words."

Far from upset, he flashed a sultry smile and caressed my cheek. "That's okay. You're falling. You'll never leave me."

Heat bloomed where his fingers brushed. I flattened my hand over his and leaned into his touch, the creepiness factor fading. "Will you leave *me*?"

"Not in a thousand years. Not in eternity," he vowed. "Stay in my suite while we're in Theirland."

My heart skipped, and I opened my mouth to accept.

Be on guard. Trust only me. Avoid Cyrus. He'll be there, and when you see him, you'll wish to aid him. Do not.

I will never ask you to do something that will lead to your harm or the harm of others.

Ignoring the whisper of Domino's words, I kissed the heel of Cyrus's palm. "Yes. I will."

"Good." He cradled the back of my head, the firmness of his touch sending shivers down my spine. The air charged with anticipation as he lifted me and leaned in, rasping, "Every second I didn't kiss you was a second wasted. I don't plan to waste another."

CHAPTER TEN

Listen, and you will hear the victory plan.

—*The Book of Soal* 1.20.4.20

Our lips met in a fervent press. I wound my arms around Cyrus's sculpted form, drawn to the furnace of heat that poured from his body. That heat seeped through the thin barrier of my clothes, and it was as if sunlight melted frost. He claimed my mouth with aching reverence, sweeping his tongue past my teeth, enthralling me with a kiss both a promise and a possession. His rich, familiar taste struck a chord buried deep, where reason couldn't reach. Something primal answered.

I matched the rhythm of his next thrust with a desperation that rivaled his, every lick an unspoken vow between us. He seduced me with devastating precision, stoking a slow burn of longing until it roared. My senses fractured and re-formed around him, sharper, hungry, and undeniably transformed.

Time blurred. Thoughts dissolved. There was no room for doubt. No escape from the intoxication. He was mine, and I was his, and we belonged together. Never should we part.

"You want more of me, sweetness?" He rumbled the words between ragged breaths. "Perhaps just a little?"

A new endearment. One I wished to hear again and again and again. And yet, a whisper of denial bubbled up. *Not here. Not now. Not like this.*

What was wrong with here, now, and like this? I'd longed for this moment, and I wouldn't give it up.

I brushed the tip of my nose against his and with a throaty voice, beseeched him. "Yes, please, and thank you."

"Then more you shall have." He nipped my bottom lip and soothed it with a slow drag of his teeth, more reverent, more possessive. "I'll give you everything, but I'll demand nothing less in return."

"Then take it." I toyed with the ends of his hair. "I'm yours. I've always been yours."

Satisfaction glinted in his eyes. "I'm the man for you, not Domino. Say it."

He thought I might be falling for the librarian? "You're the man for me, Cyrus Dolion. Only you."

With a husky groan, he clasped my hips, lifted me to his lap, and kissed me again. Everything else fell away as I straddled him, pressing closer. Closer still. He breathed my name. I mewled his.

What began as a slow, awed exploration soon unraveled into a frenzied devouring. His hands roamed, kneading my waist, my backside, my thighs before threading into my hair to tilt my head just so. The kiss deepened, quickened, but I couldn't get close enough. Couldn't touch enough. His heat called to me, demanding skin to skin. I fumbled at his shirt, eager for the barricade to be gone.

"Well, of course you're here, doing her."

The dry tone struck my ears, and I jolted. Wrenching from Cyrus, I leaped to my feet.

High Princess Lolli stood in the open doorway, clicking a blunt-tipped nail against a bar. *Tap, tap, tap.*

I panted while Cyrus remained seated on the bed, calm as could be. She wore a black tank top, camo pants, and combat boots. A sleek bun highlighted sharp, lovely features. Annoyance oozed from her pores.

My cheeks blazed, realization slapping me hard. Public make-outs weren't my style, yet I'd done just that. How many of my classmates had heard us?

Although, the ward wasn't exactly silent. Several trainees were moaning and groaning, creating a chorus. Unless they'd been released from their chains, they were pleasuring themselves. Others whispered together. Some snored.

"We need to go," the princess stated. "Something's happening in Theirland, and I know you sense it too. Vyle says he'll brief us as soon as we arrive."

They sensed things that were happening in Astan's world? And what was happening there?

Domino's voice whispered once again. *A man able to contain the full brunt of Astan's power has been born.*

Astan's horns will straighten. When they reach maximum height, they will release a blast across both realms.

I went cold. Were the gods closer to being freed? Had Astan's horns fully straightened?

Cyrus worked his jaw before slowly unfolding to his feet. A mere handful of inches separated us, ensuring we exchanged breaths. Vibrating with banked ferocity, he lowered his chin and pinned me with his stare. "I would die for you." He canted his head slightly to peer at Lolli while still speaking to me. "I would kill for you too."

She blanched but tried to mask it by blowing him a kiss with bite. "You're whipped. I get it. Can we go now?"

Maintaining his languid pace, he leaned down and nuzzled my cheek with his own. "I'll see you on the other side, Pink." He strode off with the high princess.

Suddenly alone, I felt as though I'd tumbled down a hill, slamming into rocks. The man who'd threatened the other woman wasn't the Cyrus I knew and adored. And yet he was the exact same, merely amplified. But at what cost?

The door closed behind him, but my guards didn't return. As I struggled to order my thoughts, I sensed another presence. Familiar. "Show yourself," I rasped, not sure what emotion he elicited right now.

A robe-clad Domino stepped from the corner shadows. "Astan already influences him."

Ice crystalized in my veins. "Then I need to be a stronger influence, *not* avoid him." I would remind Cyrus what we were fighting for. *Who* we were fighting for.

The librarian didn't try to hide his disappointment in me. "I can't and won't try to stop you."

"Good." Smart, even. So why was my chest clenching?

"What I *will* do is offer advice." He moved to my side, his bigger body eclipsing mine. Today he smelled sweet verging on heady, like the flowers that grew on top of the Rock. I didn't like it. Not one bit. "Listen, and your heart will tell you things your mind hasn't yet grasped."

I recalled the whisper of denial I'd perceived while kissing Cyrus and gulped. "Any, um, news on my friend?" I asked, changing the subject to Mykal.

Domino studied me for a long while, silent as I shifted from one bare foot to the other. "Nothing new," he finally replied.

"And my mom?" I shuffled to my bed and eased onto the edge of the mattress. "She's well?"

"She is."

I wrung my hands together. "And you still can't tell me who my, um, new friend is?" The other Soalian.

"Correct."

"So why are you here?" I demanded, suddenly mad at him, Cyrus, myself, and the world. And I didn't even know why.

No answer came, and when I looked up, I discovered Domino had gone. His absence only added fuel to the fires of my irritation.

Hoping to better understand my reaction, I focused inward, spotlighting my memory garden. *What in the world?* So. Many. Weeds. Too many to pinpoint a specific section.

The sight roused tears I couldn't bank. What even was my life anymore? I had the truth but little else. Cyrus was my boyfriend, and he claimed to love me, but I rarely saw or spoke to him. I was supposed to help him become king and overcome the courting of a god but also stay away from him for reasons. I'd kissed him, but he'd walked away with a past girlfriend. I'd become a Soalian, a citizen of the Kingdom of Yesterday, Today, and Tomorrow, and a member of the much-feared Tome Society, and I should be shouting the truth from rooftops. Except, I couldn't mention CURED's lies without the threat of death. Though I'd always yearned to grow my own garden, I'd failed to tend the one in my head. Right now, my best friend was a projection of a man no one else could see or hear, yet I'd sent him away. Hopefully only temporarily.

My shoulders rolled in but squared in a snap. This wasn't a time to indulge in self-pity. I had work to do.

Determined to start fresh, I torched the memory garden, letting righteous flames of fury eat up the weeds. A simple action, and yet a weight I hadn't known I'd been carrying lifted from my shoulders. Much better.

The morning bell spilled over the airwaves, and my door opened again. I flowed from the bed, collected my fragment of the Rock, and stuffed it in my pocket.

Today, I traveled to Theirland.

Head high, I stalked forward. Still no sign of my guards. Though the hallway overflowed with trainees, none of them paid me any heed, per usual. No matter. I continued with purpose, every step fueled by intent. I would apologize to Domino at the first opportunity and help Cyrus as I saw fit. I wouldn't put anyone in added danger, not even myself.

After I showered and dressed in clean fatigues, I double-checked that I still wore my necklace—yes—and transferred my piece of the Rock into my new pocket. With nothing else to do, I headed for the rift room, where one of three doorways to Theirland would instantly transport me to a CURED-owned military base. Hmm. Knights and barons rushed through the crowd in a steady stream, all heading in the same direction, leaving a trail of stinging anxiety in their wake.

Whatever the high princess had referenced must have escalated.

I picked up the pace, lagging a few steps behind Cash and Miller. They muttered together, speculating about what could be going on.

Miller glanced back at me. When he did it again with a frown, I thought a spark of recognition arced between us. I frowned too. Surely that didn't mean . . . he wasn't . . . couldn't be . . .

But maybe. I would find out.

We entered the rift room with other trainees in tangled lines. The atmosphere changed immediately, becoming denser, humming with an eerie static that prickled my skin. The trio of rifts loomed in the center of the spacious chamber. They resembled giant slashes, as if some monster had clawed and split the very air itself, leaving jagged doorways to the abyss beyond. Wisps of darkness curled at their edges, writhing like smoke trapped in a vacuum. Inside, the gashes pulsed faintly, an unnatural glow casting warped shadows across the concrete walls. A low, distorted murmur leached from the openings, sending a shudder down my spine. The scent of scorched metal and something sickly sweet filled my lungs as I took my next step forward.

Usually we traveled in an orderly fashion. Today, chaos reigned. Men and women from every level rushed through the gloom, vanishing.

At the front of the room, strapping on pieces of golden armor, was Mr. Vyle.

I pressed a hand to my churning stomach. Everyone in his vicinity appeared stressed to the max, except him. He remained as cool as ever, even when he swung his gaze to me, as if he'd sensed my attention. He inclined his head in acknowledgment, and I did the same.

Miller moved between me and the royal executioner, obstructing my view. He wiggled his brows. "Heard you trying to win back your sweet, sweet prince this morning, Roosa."

My cheeks burned anew. He couldn't be the Soalian. He just couldn't be.

"Focus up." Roman stepped in and elbowed Miller in the gut, surprising me with the show of support. "Something big is happening, and we get to be a part of it. We'll give our best today. Got it?"

Hunching over, Miller gasped for breath he couldn't catch. He offered a thumbs-up.

"Classes, follow me through," Mr. Vyle called. "The royals and upper gentry are awaiting our arrival." He took position at the front and entered the darkness.

My group joined the clusters of soldiers-in-training surging toward the seams. Winslet entered first, then Cash and Miller. I followed Roman and Merlot, bracing for an onslaught of agony as I entered the gloom.

Just as it had done every time before, the foundation crumbled under my feet. I tumbled into an endless void, yet the agony never came. I experienced not even one flicker of pain. Didn't feel as though my limbs were being ripped from their sockets and used to beat me over the head.

I marveled, unsure what to make of the change. Although, the reason for it struck me as obvious. I was a Soalian now. A glower. Did travel only hurt the CURED?

In a blink, the foundation returned, and the gloom fled, replaced by a large gymnasium like the one I'd just left. This one came with a magnificent view. Out of habit, I glanced up, drinking in the glass ceiling that revealed a star-studded night sky. Something I'd never seen until joining the military.

"You're good?" Roman asked, confused as he looked me over. Sweat trickled from his brow, and he panted.

I had zero perspiration and normal breathing. Uh-oh. That might be a problem. A dead giveaway. My temperature cooled fast, and I trembled. "Y-yeah. I'm okay."

Thankfully, he moved on without further comment.

My gaze shifted to Miller, who helped a pale Merlot to her feet, careful of her healing wrist. He evinced few signs of distress, but he didn't appear unaffected. Actually, no one appeared unaffected.

I forced myself to turn and help the soldier who exited the seam after me. Like Merlot, he collapsed. I eased his fall to the best of my ability and helped him to his feet.

"Let's go," Cyrus called from somewhere in the room.

Ah, there he was. He and the other royals stood with Heta and Mimidae. Honestly, as happy as I was to have him near, I wished he'd stayed in Ourland. He kept losing his memories in Theirland.

Clearly seething beneath the surface, he snapped something at his half brother, High Prince Felix, who laughed and patted his shoulder, defusing the situation.

Each of the royals wore a camouflage jacket, the left breast decorated with the CURED emblem.

As if he'd been attuned to my presence despite the chaos of the crowd, Cyrus caught my gaze with his own. The noise around me faded until only he existed. He raised an eyebrow, his question clear: *Are you all right?*

A shiver rocked me, and I nodded. *You?*

He returned the nod.

As soon as Mr. Vyle joined them, the royals led us into a larger room, where we shuffled from one booth to another, collecting armor and weapons. Netter guns, whips, daggers, and swords. My nerve endings buzzed. As usual, we were going to dive into combat without taking a break. Now, though, I understood why we'd always done so. In emergencies, there was no time to prepare.

"Line up and listen," Heta called, and the room went silent. "There's a field twelve miles from the base. Numerous toxic berries are growing there. Troops are attempting to torch the fields, but glowers are stopping them. Feeders are arriving in droves."

Berries like the one Cyrus had eaten and the emperor lamented? The reason the emperor might have sent Mr. Vyle to Fort Bala?

Each breath became a blade, each exhale a wound. We were going to be sent into the fray, weren't we?

Worry lines branched from Heta's eyes. "Our forces need all the help they can get, even from trainees. I know you're scared, but you won't be alone. We have paired you with a high-ranking officer."

Anticipation infiltrated the barrage of other emotions swimming through me. Knowing Cyrus, he'd arranged for us to do this mission together. If I made a mistake, revealing my true allegiance, he'd cover for me. And together, we could help our fellow glowers save the berries without drawing unwanted suspicion.

"Everyone will go out together but arrive at the field from different points. When I call your name, step forward," Heta commanded. "Roman Alexander, you're with High Prince Summit."

Summit kissed his middle finger and blew it at the rest of us as Roman joined him, pumping a fist into the air. The HP led him from the chamber.

"Merlot Doogle, you're with High Prince Mallow. Arden Roosa."

I snapped to attention, my excitement on par with Roman's.

"You're with High Princess Lolli Dolion."

What? My steps faltered, and so did my heartbeat. With sheer will alone, I restarted, stalking through the door on the heels of Cyrus's ex-girlfriend.

Don't panic, don't panic. But.

But.

Really?

High Princess Lolli led me through a maze of dimly lit hallways accented with polished stone. Each security checkpoint bustled with quiet efficiency—scanners beeped, armored guards checked our IDs, and the faint crackle of radios filled the silence between commands. When we finally stepped into the garage, a cloud of heavy air hit, the odor of motor oil, singed metal, and the bite of gunpowder overpowering. The space lived and breathed urgency, the rhythmic whirring of drills blending with the sharp clank of wrenches being used to tighten bolts. Metal scraped against metal, and the unmistakable sound of magazines snapping into place echoed like a drumbeat of war.

Three massive trucks loomed in the center, their exteriors dull with dust and wear. Crates of ammunition and tactical gear covered nearby shelves, an armory on standby. Soldiers worked with methodical precision, their uniforms rustling as they adjusted straps and checked weapons.

As soon as they noticed High Princess Lolli, the men snapped to attention, their boots striking the concrete. They saluted, then returned to their tasks, hands steady, focus unwavering.

"There are soldiers out there now, creating paths for us," the princess told me. "When they're done, we'll head out. Could be five minutes, could be five hours." She stopped at an open section with a bank of lockers, straddled a bench, and faced me. "Let's chat while we've got the chance."

I eased down across from her, struggling to hide my growing apprehension.

She jumped right in. "You are dating our Cyrus."

I bit my tongue. "I'd argue your use of the word *our*, but yes, I'm dating him." The snippy tone slipped out before I could run it through my Is This Smart filter.

Rather than take offense, she grinned, showcasing perfect pearly whites. Although, it wasn't amusement I detected in her but, hmm. Nothing. I detected no emotion. "Good to see he still likes his women feisty."

Okay, that irritated. "Cyrus isn't a topic I'm willing to chat about."

"I'm sure you're disappointed not to be paired with him," she continued as if I hadn't spoken, "but he chose to be with Lord Miller. I wouldn't worry, though. It probably means nothing." She flashed another cold smile. "I decided to seize my chance to learn more about you."

I gnashed my teeth. If I knew Cyrus, and I did, he thought he was protecting me in some way. Something we'd be discussing.

"I'll be straight with you." She dropped her chin but kept her gaze on me. "I know what you are."

My stomach twisted into more of those awful knots, but not by word or deed did I reveal it. "Okay. I'll bite. What am I?"

"What Cyrus is." She hiked her shoulders in a shrug. "What I am. Which is a recent development, but a development all the same."

"Okay." An internal alarm erupted as I tried to process her confession. She couldn't mean what I thought she meant. That she was a new Soalian and an ally. I would sense it, just as I sensed the other Soalian. While I only distinguished the other sometimes, there was always an underlying knowledge. But here, now, I felt no tug of connection. No beat of familiarity.

This must be a trick. Or another test.

This woman vied for the same exalted position as the high prince. If she could convince me she was on my side, get me to confess to a crime, then pin me as a traitor, she could damage Cyrus's chance of success.

"You'll have to elaborate if you'd like me to understand what you're saying," I grated.

She canted her head, examining me further. "We are people with an agenda. You seek Cyrus, Cyrus seeks the crown, and I seek what Cyrus can give me. I'll win him back, I assure you."

Bile churned in my throat, frothing. "He's your competition."

"I have no competition." She spread her arms, all *look at me*. "He respects strength, and I have that in spades. We can rule the kingdoms together. But you . . . you are a lamb among wolves. You'll make a pitiful queen. I just thought you should know so you don't waste your prime on unattainable dreams."

More teeth gnashing. "Thanks for the heads-up."

A grim-faced Domino appeared behind her, stepping from thin air. "There's a problem," he said, and I jolted. "The fires Heta mentioned are producing smoke laced with some kind of sedative that affects only recently turned Soalians. As soon as one falls, feeders converge."

Panic delivered a one-two strike, stealing my breath. "Is there a way to combat it?" I burst out without thought.

Lolli narrowed her eyes. "You did not just bark a question at me." A pause. She grated, "Combat what?"

I opened my mouth, unsure what to say. A loud buzzer went off, spilling from the intercom system, saving me from having to eke out some kind of apology or explanation.

The princess popped to her feet. I did the same, my heart racing. The other soldiers quickened their pace, rushing to finish loading a truck.

"They're calling for us," she said, stalking to a table littered with equipment. "We'll deal with your insubordination later." After sheathing a handful of daggers, she jumped up and down, shook out her hands, and touched two fingers to her lips three times before pointing those fingers into the air.

Some kind of good-luck ritual?

I looked to Domino, wide eyed. How was I supposed to avoid an airborne sedative? I couldn't not breathe.

"A battalion is en route," he informed me, resolved. Perhaps even concerned? "They'll clear the air. The problem is, they are twelve minutes and eighteen seconds out."

Guess I'd have to find a way to stay awake, no matter the provocation, for twelve minutes. "I've got this," I muttered, and he gave a stiff nod.

Lolli handed me a familiar metal band. An RVM corrector. I anchored the piece around my head and programmed the eye lens to drop. In Theirland, once you exited the base, you experienced upside-down vision. The lens righted everything, but not without consequences. Sharp pains sliced into my brain, and they were worse than any time previous. Usually those pains faded, leaving a dull ache behind. This time, the sharpness remained. Nothing I could do about it now. Eleven minutes, forty-five seconds.

I followed the princess to the truck, expecting the librarian to follow. Before vanishing, he merely called, "Stick to Lolli as if you are glued."

Great. Just when I needed him most. Trembling, I climbed inside the vehicle. The men jumped in after me. The princess and I sat in the back, settling upon the bench that rimmed the cab, with the others sitting in front of us.

Another thirty seconds down.

High Princess Lolli reached out to slap the side of the truck. "Let's go."

CHAPTER ELEVEN

Wounds given by a friend are better than the kisses given by a foe.

—*The Book of Soal* 1.20.27.6

The twisting in my stomach only worsened as our truck approached the open garage doors. I palmed a netter and a harbinger. The second we cleared the entryway, entering the night, everything changed. From a well-lit interior to a darkness so thick I felt the ooze of it against my skin. A fetid stench stung my nostrils—one I knew well. The rot of the maddened. Though we hadn't yet reached the smoke, I made each inhale brief, drawing in as little oxygen as possible. Just ten minutes to go.

We cleared the fenced area around the base, and I heard the maddened too. A symphony of screeches, calls of "Love Soal," and eerie clicks and hisses. They blended with an ebb and flow of gunfire.

A sharp grinding sound blasted at my left. I lifted my weapons into firing position, preparing for an attack. But where was the threat? My RVM lens only let me see within a five-foot radius.

"Hold your fire, newbie. Pritis poles are rising throughout the terrain," Lolli explained, and a second later, light exploded from above us, chasing away a measure of the gloom.

Instant fury. So badly I wanted to leap out of the car and tear down each pole.

Misinterpreting my anger, she said, "You may not like me, but you have a job to do. If I receive a single scratch, it will be your fault, and you'll pay for it."

"If you're good enough to rule the realms, you shouldn't need a quote, unquote newbie to protect you from scratches." The words escaped before I pondered the wisdom of them.

Her eyes narrowed, and I knew I'd pay for this insubordination too.

No regrets.

We zoomed and bumped along cracked and weathered roads, our tires skidding on loose gravel, sending up tiny, stinging flecks of dust. The acrid scent of burning rubber and more rot tormented my nostrils. In the distance, hordes of feeders cloaked in thick, greasy smoke noticed us and let out guttural, wheezing shrieks before rushing our way. Their bare feet slapped wetly against the pavement, leaving behind dark, viscous smears.

Tremors settled in my hands when the horde cleared the hazy veil. They were nothing like those we'd fought at Fort Bala. Their eyes, devoid of pupils or irises, shone like crimson, radioactive marbles. Wriggling worms, slick with mucus, protruded from their scalps and noses. Even their eyelashes had been replaced with the writhing parasites. White foam bubbled and popped at the corners of their mouths. Putrid green teeth snapped, and nails sharpened to razor points clicked together, eager to tear into flesh. The stench of bile and decay joined the assault against my senses.

I tried to see these creatures as they once were—people, friends, family—and my heart ached. CURED claimed they were beyond help, but I knew better. The berries contained the cure. But right now, mass numbers of soldiers were doing their best to incinerate the field, the fruit juices sizzling and blackening in the flames.

I clenched my jaw. To CURED, feeders were better off dead than saved. Alive and well, they could reveal the mountain of lies fed to the world.

Our driver executed a swift turn, and thumps rang out. The vehicle bounced, bodies crushed under our tires. I pressed my tongue to the roof of my mouth. The smoke rolled ever closer.

"I'd hate for you to get injured out there, Lady Roosa," Lolli called over the noise, filling an ammo clip with glowing green bullets. "Whatever you do, stay out of my way."

I recognized a threat when I heard one. "What are those?" I motioned to the bullets. I'd never seen anything like them.

"An experiment," she replied with another cold grin, loading and sheathing the gun. "Respond to what I said previously."

"I will guard your back, and I won't get in your way." An easy promise to give since I meant it. *Stick to Lolli like glue, Domino?* Very well.

"Two minutes out," the driver hollered. Bounce, bounce, bounce.

The smoke reached us at last. I held my breath as long as possible, the burn in my lungs intensifying fast. Though I snuck an inhalation here and there, I never felt in danger of passing out, so, win.

I cobbled together a plan to help any fellow Soalians who succumbed to the sedative. My only play? Accidentally-on-purpose disrupt Lolli's aim if she took a shot at them, then hobble any feeders who approached.

I would look incompetent, but honestly, I no longer cared.

"One minute."

Lolli unhooked a whip from a metal loop at her waist and extracted a sword anchored to her back. Her armor, like mine, glowed in the dark thanks to a dusting of pritis stone powder, allowing fellow soldiers to more easily spot us in the gloom while repelling feeders. The emblem on her jacket proved brightest.

I counted down the seconds inside my head, my tremors worsening. The same sensation I'd encountered during the last attack gathered in the center of my chest, readying to flare. A heat that had nothing to do with the fires and everything to do with my glow. This time, I would let it happen, certain no one would notice.

"Thirty seconds."

Eight minutes until Domino's reinforcements arrived.

The men lurched from their seats, grabbed a large wooden box, and crouched at the edge of the vehicle, one in front of the other. Lolli got in line without a box, and I did the same.

"Five. Four. Three."

I braced. The truck ground to a screeching, spinning halt, and the soldiers poured out. I stuck to the princess's heels, springing into a thicker veil of smoke, which I inhaled, because I couldn't not. And yet, still nothing bad happened. We raced forward without problem, dodging carnival rides I'd only ever seen in holograms and history books, skirting walls of flickering flames, bypassing soldiers and feeders: those engaged in combat and those who'd already fallen, all highlighted by bright beams spilling from a plethora of pritis poles.

Feeders mobbed a trio of soldiers who wobbled on their feet, doing their best to not pass out. A red-robed guy whose skin possessed a soft, golden radiance appeared unaffected by the smoke as he sliced and diced the feeders who focused on the threesome.

A desire to rush over nearly overpowered me. *They'll be okay, they'll be okay.*

I held my breath until I grew dizzy as I tracked Lolli. When I could stand it no longer, I sucked in oxygen, expecting a stream of lethargy to finally hit. But one second passed. Two, three. Six. Still nothing happened.

Was I not really Soalian?

Panic rose, but it didn't have a chance to flourish. I grazed a feeder as I passed him, drawing his notice. He gave chase, and my instincts kicked in. Without slowing, I spun, netted him, and resumed chasing after the high princess.

So many sights vied for my attention. So many sounds. Total chaos all around. The uninfected and the infected waged a vicious war for victory. Tonight, there would be only one winner and zero second chances. I must get this right.

Incoming! I contorted, barely missing a collision with a group of feeders. *Focus.*

Lolli kept running. At least the smoke thinned as we approached the field populated with berries. The seven colors of the rainbow glowed brighter and brighter within the fruit, reminding me of pritis and serving as lamps, filling the area with illumination. A majestic sight, to be sure.

The soldiers we'd come with dropped their wooden box and formed a circle around it. Two guys worked to put together large . . . drills? The others stood guard, stopping feeders from impeding their progress.

What confused me more was the fires. CURED soldiers weren't attempting to torch the berries, as Heta had claimed, but the areas beyond them. The berries they fought to protect.

Lolli's grunt returned my attention to her, and my eyes widened. With the whip and the sword, she was a master class of lethal elegance, destroying the feeders around her. And her speed! The emblem on her jacket blurred with the swiftness of her motions.

The coiled heat in the center of my chest unfurled. Adrenaline ripped through my veins, a searing pulse of energy I unleashed as I leaped into the fray, ready to put my plan into action. I netted feeder after feeder, faster than usual. When I ran out of ammunition, I replaced my clips with only a slight pause in my shots.

Short though it was, the pause cost us, allowing a throng to surge too close for comfort.

"Another horde," I shouted, and Lolli shifted her focus. Together, we downed them all.

The smoke thickened, clinging to my skin and clothing. The more I fought, the faster I panted and the itchier my throat became, but at least I didn't weaken. In fact, I only got stronger, the heat spreading, spreading, bringing renewed vitality to my limbs.

Click, click. Another clip depleted. Dang, that had been my last. No matter. I stashed the netter and the dagger, and palmed my short swords.

A feeder swiped at me with razor-sharp claws. Contact. He cut through a seam in my armor. Skin split. Bone might have cracked. Pain exploded in my arm but dulled quickly. I punted him in the abdomen. As he skidded backward, I followed, driving a blade into his torso.

His knees collapsed, and I removed his head. I hadn't trained with the swords for long, but I'd trained hard, and instincts I hadn't realized I'd honed guided my motions. I felled another opponent, then another.

"Glowers," Lolli hissed, exchanging the clip in her gun for the one with green bullets.

My heart skipped a beat when she ran from the field, leaving behind the soldiers we'd come with as they continued messing with whatever they'd brought. I followed her, sticking as close as possible.

My mind blipped when over twenty of my allies appeared in the skyline. They flew through the clouds, their golden robes somehow acting as wings as they arrowed down upon the battlefield. They were at one with the wind and as majestic as the berries.

Landing with ease, they sprinted across the ground, never missing a beat. Their robes appeared liquid as the material settled in place, the light radiating from their skin shimmering through the fabric. The only weapons they brandished were swords. But then, they didn't need anything else. As they swung, the blades caught fire.

I struggled not to stare. One day, I would learn how to create a fire-sword, and I couldn't wait.

Feeders converged upon them en masse, even leaving behind fallen CURED soldiers in favor of attacking the glowers. Like flies drawn to light.

CURED's forces focused on the glowers too. Gunshots exploded through the night.

The glowers ducked and dodged, expertly swinging those flaming swords.

Lolli fought her way through the throng, hacking at feeders left and right, aiming for the glowers. I pumped my arms faster, coming up behind her. When she reached the front lines, she lifted her gun.

Determined, I bumped her shoulder with my own. She stumbled as she squeezed the trigger, the green bullet grazing a glower's side. Phew! Not a kill shot.

Before I could interrupt, Lolli fired off another round. This one the glower avoided on his own, jumping out of the way. But only a second later, he went statue still, as if frozen in place. Because of the bullet?

Feeders rushed to him, eager to dine, but other glowers served as shields. The remaining glowers attacked the soldiers nearest the berries. Or tried to. They slammed into an invisible barrier and bounced back, toppling to the ground and writhing.

Perplexed and concerned, I cut down a feeder and followed Lolli toward another glower. Grunts and groans provided a chorus for more rounds of gunfire. Something exploded in the distance, a waft of thicker smoke sweeping over the terrain.

In the ensuing pandemonium, I spotted Archduke Heta. He wielded a spear with incredible speed, unrelenting elegance, and zero mercy. Feeders fell around him in piles. A trainee trailed him, finishing off those he injured.

There was Roman and High Prince Summit, moving in sync as if they'd been partners for years. Both men grinned, gleeful as they slayed their enemy.

My stomach and heart traded places when I spotted Cyrus. There he was, living poetry as he sliced through feeders with lethal grace. He was a Grim Reaper without equal . . . until Miller got in his way. Cyrus jumped to avoid a collision and rammed into a feeder, who swiped its claws across his throat.

"No!" Forgetting everything else, I sprinted over.

A hard weight slammed into me from behind, shoving me down. Air abandoned my lungs in a rush, my goggles flew off my face, and I lost my grip on a sword.

Too-bright light blinded me. A high-pitched ring filled my ears, drowning out all other noise.

The feeder who'd tackled me didn't suffer from any of the same problems. She clawed at my back. Searing agony overwhelmed me, but I twisted. As I held her off with one hand, I unsheathed a dagger with the other. Though my world spun, I stab, stab, stabbed until she went limp. Cold fluid wet my hand.

Huffing and puffing, I pushed the motionless body off and scrambled to my feet. A mistake. I tripped over a severed limb and fell again, crashing into a pool of blood. Wanting to vomit, I lumbered into an upright position and blinked.

The too-bright light faded at last. I expected the darkness to return. Instead, I saw colors.

No, I saw everything.

My breath caught. I did. I saw the world around me with perfect clarity. Miles of dirt, littered with both fallen and standing statues. Winding roads made of crumbling gold bricks. The mass of feeders, with heads full of slithering worms. The glowers fighting them off. The CURED soldiers who now focused solely on felling the glowers. The field of berries. The invisible but shimmering wall the glowers hadn't yet breached. Carnival rides in the distance one way, a massive crystal castle in the other—the home of Cyrus's grandfather, as well as Astan, the true leader of CURED. I inwardly cringed. The same shadows I'd noticed at Fort Bala slithered around its steepled roof.

I didn't understand this. How . . . why . . . Domino appeared a few feet away from me, there but not there, a vein bulging in his forehead as he seemed to shout with all his might.

The ring in my ears dulled at last, new sounds hitting my awareness. All the grunts, groans, and shrill screams. Every pop of gunfire. Laughter from Mallow, who led Merlot through the fray while spraying bullets with his automatic assault rifle.

Domino's furious voice rose above the noise. "You were told. Do not leave Lolli. You were told," he repeated, practically spitting fire.

Cringing, I covered my ears. As panting breaths sawed between my lips, I scanned the battlefield. Cyrus, Cyrus, where was Cyrus?

I'd already messed up and disobeyed the librarian's command. Now, I wanted only to find the future king and make sure he was okay.

Felix and Winslet worked together against a glower—Ember! They brawled with Ember. As she swung her flaming sword, Felix spun behind a feeder, using the infected one as a shield. Ember's fiery weapon cut through him, and his knees buckled. The high prince seized his opportunity, shoving the slain one into her, knocking her down. He readied to deliver an ending strike.

Nearby, Merlot miscalculated a blow and paid the ultimate price, quickly taken down by three feeders. Mallow didn't notice, but Felix did. With a scowl, he left the fallen Ember behind in favor of rushing to the trainee, but he was too late. The maddened had already ripped out many of her vital organs.

No, no, no. I climbed to my feet, ready to fly into action. To do something. Anything. But. My neck. My face. The burn of my injuries contrasted with the ice forming in my veins. My limbs trembled, growing heavier.

Felix returned to battle, but Ember was long gone. He took out his annoyance on a different glower. A man not quite as skilled but faster. Lolli fired a green bullet at the guy and missed.

"Where's Cyrus?" I demanded of Domino.

"You were told," he repeated. "Do not go near the high prince."

"I get it. This is my fault. Where's Cyrus?" I caught sight of Miller, drilling through feeders, and my pulse leaped. Cyrus must be nearby. I started forward, but every step proved a greater lesson in agony.

Raucous sounds drew my attention to the left. Four feeders advanced on me, closing in. They ghosted through Domino, not even realizing he was there, and I palmed a dagger. The moment they were in striking distance, I slashed, slashed, slashed. Ducked, twisted, and slashed some more. Ducked, kicked. Spun. Two went down. Two to go. Oops. Wrong. Five others rushed over.

I took down another, then hobbled a fourth. A fifth. My breaths turned choppy, and my motions slowed. Energy waned, new cuts draining me faster. Weakness spread until remaining on my feet required every bit of strength I possessed. Still I fought. *Must find Cyrus.*

"A high prince is dead, fall back, fall back." The cry came from Summit as he herded soldiers toward a fleet of waiting vans.

No! He couldn't mean Cyrus. He couldn't. But there was no sign of my boyfriend anywhere. "Cyrus," I screamed.

Another contingent of glowers arrived on the battlefield. Domino waved them closer with almost frantic insistence.

Boom!

Sharp pain sliced through my midsection, and my entire body jerked. Blood rushed up my throat, choking me. Shocked, I pressed my palm to my abdomen, right against the source of my anguish. A gaping, gushing hole.

Lolli stood across the way, a gun in hand, the barrel aimed at me. Streaked with scarlet, she peered at me.

She had . . . shot me?

As she rushed off, I gasped for air I couldn't quite capture and looked down. Wet crimson soaked my armor, leaking through the hole in the material. Oh, yes. She'd most definitely shot me.

My knees buckled, and down I went. Upon impact, my brain rattled, and my vision blurred.

"Cyrus survived," I heard the librarian snarl, "but you might not. If you die—do not die, Arden. Do you understand me?"

"Help him, please," I commanded. Or tried to. My voice frayed at the edges as blood continued to flood my throat. The ring in my ears started up again, dull at first but building to a piercing shriek. Panic sparked again, and this time, I couldn't tamp it down. It became a wildfire that consumed my every thought. I couldn't breathe. I needed to breathe.

I thought I heard the librarian shouting orders to help me as icy cold invaded my fingers and toes, swiftly spreading up my limbs. Something slapped at my body, and I laughed without humor. Had feeders come to finish me off?

Suddenly, Cyrus appeared in my line of vision. Concern dominated his features, and blood streaked his skin. His lips moved, but I heard nothing he said. When he vanished, I whimpered. *Come back!* Then hands slapped at me again, and I realized he was ripping off my shirt and pulling first aid supplies from my plethora of pockets. Domino loomed behind him.

Cyrus pried my lips apart and shoved something metal into my mouth. A terrible pressure sucked the liquid from my throat. Suddenly I could breathe again, the ring fading.

"—live, do you hear me?" he was shouting.

My vision cleared just in time to watch a feeder swipe at him. He paused his ministrations only long enough to shoot the intruder in the face. A quick slash of his sword finished the creature off, then he was back to administering medical aid.

"You're going to be okay." He worked hard and fast, forced to pause a few more times to kill an enemy. "You had better be okay."

I drifted in and out of consciousness, each time drawn back by . . . something. A faceless someone. A presence who wouldn't let me step over into the abyss. At some point, I noticed the glowers fighting around us, keeping crowds of the infected at bay. Though Cyrus finished cleaning and sealing my wound, he didn't leave me to rejoin the fray.

"She lost too much blood," he bellowed. "Get Ember. Ember!"

Domino vanished, and time ceased to matter. Minutes, hours, and years passed, yet Ember arrived only seconds later. She, too, was streaked with blood. Cuts marred her face, and one of her eyes was swollen shut.

"Heal her," Cyrus demanded as Ember knelt at my side to look me over.

The librarian reappeared, and I would swear the freckles near his eye glittered, creating the half circle I'd mentally drawn the first time I noticed the marks.

"She was warned—" Ember began.

"You will do this, Ember," Domino commanded at the same time Cyrus roared, "I told her she'd be okay out here. Will you make me a liar?"

My pain was dulling fast, thoughts floating away on a sea of nothingness. The gloom returned to cover my mind, creeping into my awareness.

The glower flattened her palm where my heartbeat fluttered too fast and too light. Heat seeped from her. A speck at first, but it quickly grew. Hotter and hotter, soon dispersing. Pain returned with a vengeance, and a scream burst from me. My spine arched, then flattened, the pain gone as quickly as it had begun. I sagged over the ground, panting.

"I'm good, I'm good," I croaked.

Ember sagged over me, and Domino snarled, "Ember is drained. She'll be out of commission for weeks when we need her most. All you had to do was listen to me."

Guilt pricked me, sharp and sure. I'd never seen the librarian so furious.

Another glower rushed over to gather Ember in his arms and hold her protectively against his chest. The same glower who'd accompanied Domino the day I'd interacted with Mykal. "Do not ask her to do this again," he growled at both Domino and Cyrus. He didn't wait for a response but carried the unconscious glower away. Many others followed them.

With a hand under my nape, Cyrus helped me sit up. "You able to stand, Pink?"

"I think so." My gaze flicked to Domino, but the librarian had already disappeared. I winced. Bet he couldn't stand to look at me. I'd done the one thing he'd asked me not to.

"Good. Because we have a journey ahead of us. We've got to get to the castle on foot as fast as possible. It's closer than the base. CURED released more feeders to combat the glowers. It's about to be hundreds against two."

My stomach churned. "We can't go to the castle." Astan was there. I gripped his armor. "Please, Cyrus."

He pursed his lips. "Very well. We'll head to the base. Let's go."

Chapter Twelve

Those who think they can and those who think they can't are both right.

—*The Book of Soal* 1.20.23.7

As I ran behind Cyrus, I inspected my stomach. Shock almost knocked me flat. Nothing. No bullet wound. No scar. Not even a bruise or a hint of pain. Just smooth, unbroken skin.

When Ember healed me, she *really* healed me. I owed her everything. Cyrus and Domino too.

But we weren't out of danger yet. Far from it. My actions had opened an entire train cart of problems. "By the way, I lost my goggles, yet I can see. Nothing is upside down or dark. Everything is upright and well lit."

"That's because Soalians see past the darkness and automatically correct the RVM. For us, the lens is the problem." Cyrus shouldered his way past a cracked door hanging by its hinges on a brick building threatening to topple at any moment. "That's why CURED keeps a log of all goggles worn into the field, and by whom. If anyone deactivates a pair and survives an outing, they know why."

Uh-oh. "Maybe I should go back and find mine."

We'd passed the door, entering an outside courtyard overrun with thorny vines.

"No need. I picked yours up while Ember worked on you." He spun and tapped the metal band secured around his neck, different from the one over his eyes. "The lens remains activated. You can put it on when we're closer to the base."

"Thank you." He always thought ahead. But. Um. "Maybe I should take the lead. I can see without hindrance. You can't."

"The goggles I'm wearing are inactive. I store their chip in the heel of my boot and swapped the lens for a fake that doesn't restrict my vision."

Smart.

Cyrus led me across another portion of the battlefield. We jumped over bodies, picking up discarded weapons along the way, all while skirting around the feeders ignoring us in favor of dining on slain glowers, all-you-can-eat-buffet style. The grotesque sight left me gagging. Didn't help that a fetid stench of rot coated the air, carried by wafts of smoke.

Speaking of. "Why didn't the smoke affect me?" I rested my finger on the trigger of a harbinger, ready to punch holes in anyone who approached me. "I'm a new Soalian. I should've gone down."

He kicked a severed limb out of our path with more force than necessary. "My guess is your link to Domino impacted your reaction."

I winced. "About that." But "link" wasn't the right word. Unless he knew something I didn't?

"Later," he stated, as if he didn't trust himself to have the discussion now. "What I don't know is why certain glowers froze."

That, I could explain. "Lolli shot them with strange green bullets."

Cyrus hissed something under his breath. "She's determined to deliver Ember to the emperor. A gift to garner his favor."

Evil, awful woman. "Lolli is the one who shot me."

A moment of stunned silence. "What makes you think so?"

"Not think. Know. For starters, she told me she wants something only you can give her, and that she'll do anything to win you."

He snorted. "Lollipop loves herself and power. There isn't room for anything else, least of all a former boyfriend. Our relationship never developed beyond a surface level and isn't worth repeating. Whatever she said, she only hoped to intimidate you and distract me."

No. I didn't believe that. How could she not want him for her own? He was the epitome of power, with a brand on his face to prove it. I mean, look at all he'd survived. He was honest and faithful, the two best traits. His intensity never slackened. Whatever life threw at him, he handled with confidence. He was rugged and smart. And his dry wit. He was always so serious yet somehow also witty. Not now, of course, but usually.

"I was told you dumped her when she fell for you."

The muscles between his shoulders bunched. "Is that why you—rumors are wrong," he grated. "She never loved me, and I never loved her."

Maybe he hadn't. But. "She *is* the one who shot me. Before I collapsed, I saw her standing a few feet away with a smoking gun aimed in my direction."

Another beat of silence. Then, "I'll handle her."

An undercurrent of rage accompanied each word, and I shuddered. *Lolli's gonna get it.* "I watched a feeder claw your throat, but you are uninjured."

"I wore a protective covering," he said, an odd note in his voice. A note I didn't understand.

But I didn't press. Not here, not now. "Your brother seems nice-ish," I said, making small talk as we raced on.

"He isn't. Since the death of his wife, he's been . . . not right."

I had a million other questions, but a few dozen feeders raced our way. As I aimed, intent, they stopped short. Hmm. They didn't attack but stared at us while huffing and puffing, as if they'd never wanted anything as much as they wanted to eat us.

Cyrus helped me spring over a stack of dead bodies made of soldiers and feeders alike. *Don't look, don't look.* The vans were long gone, no living lords, ladies, knights, barons, or royals left behind.

My gaze landed on one of the slain, and my chest squeezed. Cash. His blank eyes peered at nothing.

He'd survived the attack at the base only to die in the field. Tears welled, but still I motored on.

We cleared the rubble and came across more staring feeders. They kept their distance, observing us, all but drooling for a taste.

"What's going on?" I threw a glance over one shoulder, then the other. "Why are they avoiding us?"

"They sense the healing power flowing through your veins. It's strong enough to kill them."

"I don't understand." Although, yes, I did feel different. Not just stronger, but clearer, more confident and driven, with a frenzy of heat burning soul deep. "If Ember is the source of this healing power, she carried it inside herself before passing it on to me, yet the feeders weren't afraid to approach her."

"The power isn't hers. She's merely a conduit for Soal's power, the same as we are. Some are better conduits than others, able to contain more. She's one of the best, and yet she only contains the barest taste."

Well, well. Becoming a better conduit suddenly topped my to-do list. But, um, exactly how powerful was Soal? Because wow. If this was simply a taste . . .

"Having experienced the healing power for myself, at Victors's hands, I can tell you the bonus effect will last about an hour. The problem is, we're at least three hours from the base." He picked up a fallen CO2 dagger and rotated without missing a beat, shoving the weapon into an empty sheath at my waist.

"Thank you," I said, already dreading the loss of this wondrous power.

We turned the corner of a cracked wall made of some kind of glistening crystal, and Cyrus ground to a halt. What the—ah. A statue of Astan loomed to the left, his wings stretched wide. The head was gold, the midsection and arms silver, the legs iron, and the feet a mix of metals caked in mud. Most other sculptures were made of marble, bronze, limestone, or terra-cotta. I'd never encountered one like this. His thick horns had raised another inch.

I licked chapped lips. With arms spread wide and a smirk lifting the corners of his mouth, he appeared to survey the battlefield beyond us.

Astan's horns will straighten. When they reach maximum height, they will release a blast across both realms.

Tick tock.

Dread attempted to infiltrate my mind. *Focus.* There was nothing I could do about the horns right now. They weren't even the most imminent threat.

I gave Cyrus a little nudge. "Let's go."

As soon as we cleared the depiction of Theirland's leader, Cyrus looked back. Confusion and longing etched in his features. "I remember . . ." He pursed his lips and cursed. "Nothing. Memories form only to slip away just before I grasp them."

The same used to happen to me when I wrestled with anxiety. Calm would help, but considering the look he'd just given the statue, I didn't have any to spare. "Astan has chosen you," I stated. We might as well put everything out in the open.

"He has, yes." The high prince drew in a fortifying breath. "That doesn't mean I've accepted his offer."

Wait. If he'd already made an offer . . . "He's spoken to you."

"More than once," Cyrus confirmed.

My grip on the gun tightened. "Don't make me drag details out of you. Start talking."

Aggression crackled around him, an invisible barrier that dared anyone to step too close. "I've not seen him, but there have been times I've heard his voice inside my head, mingled with mine, as if I'm thinking his thoughts."

Acid singed the edges of my composed facade. "Go on."

"He likes to remind me of my last visit to the library, when I read a portion of my book. A snippet of the future. It claimed I must . . . let you go. Astan alleges I can keep you, if I serve as his host."

"For starters, Astan lies, always, without exception." Using Cyrus's revelation as a key, I must assume the god intended to tear us apart. But. My book predicted the same. Astan and Soal never shared the same goal, and yet, they seemed to do so now. "I was supposed to stay away from you while we're in Theirland," I admitted.

Cyrus spun, and I crashed into him. He clasped my hips, holding me steady as he seethed. "Did you read it in a book, or did the order come verbally from the librarian?"

"Both," I said, and winced. "He inferred you had been chosen by Astan, and I would be chosen by another. That you would say yes, and I would say no, which supports the snippet where we seemed to be enemies."

"The war. Yes, I remember that part." His nostrils flared. "I will continue to refuse Astan. I will *never* harm you, Arden. Tell me you know that."

I didn't need to consider my response. "I do know that. I trust you. As you can see, I didn't stay away." The reason we were now in trouble. Inner flinch. "You don't need Astan to keep me."

He flicked the tip of his tongue against an incisor before muttering, "You should put on a new shirt and armor. CURED will note your lack of a wound and want to know why you stripped."

"Good thinking," I replied, letting the subject change slide without comment. We both needed time to think.

We searched the fallen until we found someone my size, without blood. Once he liberated the desired garments, we set off and I dressed. Feeders followed us, their wiggling worms hissing.

"You good?" Cyrus glanced at me over his shoulder.

"Yes, sir." The usually raised, puckered flesh of his facial brand had flattened a bit, and I gulped. Did this mean anything? "Why did Victors mark your face?"

"I asked him to do it. I wanted a vivid reminder of my true allegiance every time I glimpsed my reflection."

"No wonder I'm so enamored of it. And you!"

He turned and gave me a playful wink. A moment of levity I treasured.

"I think we should visit the Rock together," I suggested. "Find out why Soal is urging us to remain apart." Something big *must* be happening behind the scenes.

A glowering Domino appeared, walking at my side, matching my speed. The hem of his robe flapped around his ankles with an elegant flurry of ripples. "Ember imparted so much of her own energy to you, she required a healing of her own."

"I'm sorry, okay," I cried. "I screwed up, and I take full responsibility." As Tsuri had done for his Rose, Ember had poured her life into me. I would be forever grateful. "The lesson is learned, I promise."

The librarian had warned me. Had asked for my trust, and I'd chosen to rely on myself, allowing fleeting, fickle emotions to lead me. Turned out Cyrus hadn't even needed my help to survive the battle. I'd seen him fall, yes, but my eyes had deceived me. He'd recovered without injury or aid. By leaving my post as Lolli's bodyguard, I'd put myself in her line of fire, giving her a green light to attack while she had the chance.

"Domino is with us, I take it." Cyrus swooped down to collect a fallen clip of ammo.

Right. Only I could see and hear the librarian. "He's not happy with me."

"I'm furious with you," the librarian agreed easily enough. "But you need me if you're going to reach the base in one piece, and that matters more. See for yourself." He motioned up ahead.

I cast my gaze forward and groaned. More and more feeders gathered along the sidelines of our path, observing us with narrowed eyes while pawing a foot over the ground. This wasn't good.

"You decided not to dismiss him," Cyrus said, a flat statement.

Guilt hardened into a wall laden with traps and defenses. "Domino found Mykal. Concealed and protected me when I visited the Rock. Kept me company when my teammates turned against me. Provided me with information I needed." Comforted me in ways I couldn't explain. "He's been a good friend. I won't be a bad one."

Domino rolled back his shoulders, not quite as annoyed as before.

"I suppose I owe him a debt of gratitude, then." Kind words that Cyrus pushed through clenched teeth. "Did he see the high princess shoot you?"

"First, he owes me nothing," Domino said, almost offended. "I did it for you. Tell him that. Second, I flashed in and out of the battle to issue orders to soldiers inside the Rock. I didn't witness the discharge of the gun, nor have I read about it." He pulled ahead and searched the nooks and crannies of a huge pile of rubble. "I sense souls in need."

I clasped Cyrus's hand to slow him down, giving the librarian a chance to investigate. "He's on the hunt for survivors."

Cyrus squeezed my fingers, and I welcomed the prolonged connection. Had missed being close to him. And his heat. And his calluses; they tickled my palm. Here, now, I'd take any intimacy with him I could get.

"Clear," Domino announced before sweeping even farther ahead. In fact, he moved ahead at such a fast clip, I lost sight of him.

"One day you'll have to explain your dislike of each other," I told Cyrus.

"I'm stunned he hasn't explained." The high prince snaked an arm around my waist and pulled me closer under the guise of helping me avoid a pothole rippling with a thick, oily substance. "He wants you for his own."

What? No. *What?* "You're wrong." Very wrong. But the razor-sharp steel in Cyrus's voice remained with me, shattering my focus, scattering my thoughts like glass across a stone floor. I jumped between astonishment and denial. "That's why you asked me to end my friendship with him." Which meant I'd almost ended a budding friendship for ridiculous, misconstrued jealousy.

"It may have played a part," he muttered.

"Well, you're wrong," I repeated.

Domino reappeared, pulsing with satisfaction. "There are two trainees hiding in the Ferris wheel."

I concentrated on what mattered, relaying the information to Cyrus as soon as the librarian dematerialized.

With his free hand, Cyrus massaged his nape. "They'll notice how the feeders react to you. We should leave them. As soon as the heat dies down, CURED will send out a van."

Not a typical response from the Cyrus I knew and lo—really liked.

I might be falling for him, as I'd already admitted, but I wasn't there yet. "They'll notice, yes, but they won't know the weirdness is because of me. There could be a million reasons for it. If I maintain a five-foot distance between us, they won't even notice I'm without goggles." I didn't give him a chance to issue another protest. Releasing Cyrus's hand, I followed Domino's path.

We passed a building made of colorful, serrated crystals on one side and concrete on the other. Feeders perched all over it. Other infected rushed about, some carrying or dragging dead bodies.

I stutter-stepped when I noticed Merlot and her cast. She hung over a feeder's shoulder, limp.

Cyrus didn't pause, just reclasped my hand as he passed me, urging me along. "She's dead. We can't help her."

The massive Ferris wheel lay collapsed on its side, its rusted metal frame tangled in a web of snapped cables and splintered gondolas. Once-bright paint was now faded and peeling, streaked with grime and corrosion. Around it, the skeletal remains of other broken rides jutted out at odd angles, their twisted metal structures groaning softly in the wind. Torn banners flapped weakly, their colors drained by time and weather. The air was thick with the scent of damp wood, rust, and disintegrated trash strewn across the cracked pavement. The occasional creak of unstable beams and the distant scurrying of maddened provided an eerie soundtrack for the entire amusement park.

The trainees waited at the center of the Ferris wheel, under an erected pritis pole that projected a small circle of golden light. Winslet.

She huddled together with someone I didn't recognize. They aimed their guns at the feeders collecting around the edges of the ring. Cuts marred both their faces. They quaked with fear.

The feeders clearly conversed with each other, exchanging clicks, calls, and high-pierced screeches.

"Do you know what they're saying?" I whispered to Cyrus.

"They're debating using the trainees as bait for the glowers or eating them alive to build their strength."

At the sound of our voices, the feeders spun, facing us. Cyrus released my hand, and we both palmed a weapon. I'd always assumed feeders were mindless, concerned only with blood and pain. Learning they were intelligent, able to reason out a plan of action—well, I didn't like it.

Another question bubbled to the surface. "When did you learn their language?"

A muscle jumped beneath his eye. "I didn't. I read about it, and suddenly I just knew."

Another reason to visit the Library of Soal as soon as possible.

The guy with Winslet freaked out over the rising noise and fired off a shot in our direction. The bullet missed, thank goodness.

"Hold your fire," I called, knowing he couldn't see past the circle of light. "We're here to help."

"Arden!" Relief failed to crack the anxiety frozen into Winslet's features.

Poor girl. I was so thankful, so grateful, Cyrus had taught me how to combat such fear. "We got stuck out here, too, and we're headed to the base."

"H-Heta told us to wait until reinforcements arrive," she sputtered.

"I *am* reinforcements, and I'm telling you to gather the stones and walk this way." Cyrus issued the rebuke with all the authority his exalted position provided, and the two soldiers snapped to attention. "Do it now."

Though unsteady, the two worked together to detach the pole and appropriate the stones. Holding the lights, they navigated a path over the steel wire ropes and metal stand supports.

The feeders hissed and swiped at the pair, howling with pain and crumbling anytime even a clawtip breached the golden illumination.

As soon as the trainees reached our orbit, the horde drew back. I made sure to stay in the shadows.

"Put the stones in your pockets," Cyrus instructed next.

"What? No," Winslet exclaimed. "The feeders will attack us the moment the lights go out."

"They won't attack," I promised. Having learned from Cyrus, the king of misdirection, I phrased my next words carefully. "The smoke might be confusing them. They're keeping their distance right now."

"O-okay." The shimmering circle shrank, then vanished altogether, as the duo reluctantly obeyed.

"We're going to do this just like your first trial run," Cyrus said. "We'll go in a single-file line. Do not speak without my permission. Hustle as if your life depends on it, because it does. Do nothing unless I tell you. If there's a threat, I'll alert you beforehand. Now tell me you understand."

"I understand," they both said.

I remembered my trial run well, and it was only here, now, that I realized Cyrus had seen in the dark, even then. He'd watched us. Watched me. And I'd had no idea.

"Arden," he said, "you're behind me. Winslet, you're behind her." That put the lord-in-training at the caboose. Cyrus met my gaze, his chest rising with a slow inhale. "Here we go."

"Here we go," I echoed.

As our group started forward, feeders continued gathering ahead of us, some at our left, some at our right, creating a path. They didn't touch us, didn't even swipe at us, but waited.

I swallowed a lump growing in my throat. As soon as the clock ran out, we were in big trouble.

Chapter Thirteen

A good destiny has been planned for you, but you must travel the right roads to live it.

—*The Book of Soal* 1.24.17.10

I knew the exact moment the healing heat ceased holding feeders at bay. It began with the slightest cooling deep inside. As soon as I noticed it, the feeders did as well. They tightened the path, edging closer, their worms slithering so fast it looked as if the tiny creatures danced to the beat of frenzied music.

We'd made it to the heart of a once-magnificent city, its cracked pavement overtaken by more of those creeping thorny vines and tufts of weeds that had pushed through the fissures. Long, fat worms without feeders to host them spiraled around the posts of faded, leaning street signs. Broken glass and scattered debris crunched underfoot, remnants of a once-jubilant time. Beneath the rasp of my panting breaths, I thought I detected echoes of distant laughter and lively conversations. A travesty, considering the circumstances.

More and more infected caged us in, blocking everything but the skeletal remains of mismatched buildings fused with those from Ourland that loomed on either side. Their shattered windows tempted me to herd our group inside, if only for a reprieve from the gnawing hunger projected at us.

"Cyrus," I croaked.

"I know." He dispersed various weapons to me, and I passed them to the others. "Trainees, take the pritis stones from your pockets. Each has a hook. Your armor has little fasteners over your vital organs. Hook the stones there."

He didn't have to say it, but I comprehended things were about to go nuclear. Unease charged the rot-infested air as Winslet and the lord-in-training obeyed, small circles of light appearing here and there.

"W-what about you and Roosa?" Winslet asked.

"I'll be fine without the stones," I piped up, the words springing from my mouth without thought. Uh, I would?

A moment passed. "We'll both be fine," Cyrus concurred, albeit reluctantly.

One feeder stepped closer, almost brushing against me as I passed him. I gulped. Wouldn't be long now.

"On my signal," Cyrus announced, "we fight to kill."

A shudder rocked me. A choked noise left the lord-in-training.

"Y-yes, sir," Winslet said.

Domino appeared from thin air. "There's a problem."

I yelped, causing panic in my fellow trainees. Winslet fired off a shot, nailing a feeder in the shoulder. He didn't fall, but he did jerk and growl, stalking after us as we continued.

"Was that the signal?" she demanded, swinging her gun this way and that, ready to launch another shot.

"No," I said, setting my eyes on the librarian. How I hated his updates. He had yet to arrive with good news.

"I decoded a portion of my book," Domino said. "Without divine intervention, you'll be the only survivor. The glowers who remain in this world can't help. Priority one is dismantling the invisible barrier CURED placed around the fruit field."

So we were on our own. My heart thudded as I motioned for the librarian to tell me the rest. There was more, guaranteed. How would I survive but no one else?

"There's a sole path to victory, keeping you all alive." From his expression to his stride, iron control descended over him. "You must ingest your piece of the Rock."

That didn't sound so bad. Like Cyrus had said, it would give me strength. So why the attitude?

Though I wanted to ask that and a thousand other questions, I stayed silent and dug the piece from my pocket. Unlike the crumbles I'd ingested before, this one was completely solid with no give. Although, in the warmth of my hand, the stone softened, becoming malleable.

More feeders stepped closer to us, growing as gleeful as the laughter I'd heard.

"If you do this, you will alter your fate," the librarian said, solemn. "You'll walk a new path, and there'll be no going back to the old one."

I stiffened. Now *that* sounded ominous, as if I'd been on a great road, and I would suddenly find myself on a route fraught with unimaginable horrors. "Explain," I mouthed.

His gaze darted for a split second. "We will be bound together, you and I."

Okay, what did that even mean? Marriage? I sputtered, trying to form a refusal.

He acted as if he'd heard my thoughts. "Our connection will run deeper than a marriage. To defeat this many feeders, you need the skill of a librarian, and I'm the only one willing to aid you in such a way. The only one with permission, as you heard Ember give me."

A valid explanation, yet I still struggled to understand, especially since his somber tenor revealed his reluctance. He didn't wish to do this, and yet he intended to do it, anyway.

Wants you for his own.

Tremors rocked me on my feet. How would my brand-new boyfriend react to a full-on bond with the librarian he'd asked me to ditch? I couldn't, wouldn't, do that to Cyrus. *We'll find another way.*

"There isn't another way to save him," Domino stated, again reading my thoughts. "The passage in my book was clear. Doing this is the only chance he has. Yes, you might lose him anyway, but that will be his decision, not yours." He canted his head. "Shall we proceed, Arden?"

Yes. No. Indecision tore at me. I needed time to think but so few seconds remained.

"Why?" I mouthed. He risked his own future, and it couldn't be for the reason Cyrus had suggested.

"I've seen ahead." He lifted his chin. "You . . . matter to me."

In a mentor/mentee way, right? Surely. The same way he mattered to me. But if the situation were reversed, I couldn't say I would create a mystical bond with him.

"Get ready," the high prince stated. "As I count down from ten, move away from each other."

We'd run out of time.

Cyrus glanced at me, his resolve severe. "Whatever you must do to survive, do it. I don't care what it is, Lady Pink. Survive," he repeated.

"Same, sugar bear. Same." Very well. Decision made. I glanced at Domino and nodded. *We shall proceed.*

Projecting no emotion, he waved his hand in a bid for me to do what needed doing.

Bottoms up. I hesitated a split second before tossing the piece of the Rock into my mouth and gulping. Only then, after it was done, did I realize I'd maybe kinda sorta, like, consumed part of a god. Did I regret it, though? Not even a little bit.

I waited, uncertain, nervous, and hopeful. One second passed. Two. No change, other than a slight twinge of yearning for what could've been. How long until something happened?

"Sheathe the guns. Withdraw a short sword and the injector," Domino instructed.

Though I trembled, I obeyed, tightening my fingers around the hilts of each weapon.

Cyrus began the countdown. "Ten. Nine. Eight."

With each new number, we increased the distance between us.

Our audience threw back their heads and released a chorus of shrieks and pops bubbling with anticipation.

"Tell me when you feel it," Domino shouted over the noise.

Feel *what*?

"Five. Four. Three," Cyrus continued.

The heat faded completely, leaving me frozen.

"One," the high prince shouted and launched into action.

Perfect timing. The feeders launched into action, too, swarming us. Winslet and the other trainee didn't hesitate. They fired off shot after shot as Cyrus and I struck down anyone within striking distance. In a constant stream of motion, I slashed, stabbed, and swung, pressing the button on my dagger when applicable, causing an explosion inside my victims, ending their lives. Muscles stretched and burned.

When I ran out of CO2, I replaced the dagger with my other short sword. My blades chopped and sliced through necks, shoulders, torsos, and ankles. Wherever I struck, destruction followed. Blood spurted from their severed arteries. War sounds laced the air. But no matter what we did, or how many we felled, the feeders kept coming. More and more and more. An unceasing stream. They swiped at us, snapped their teeth, and crowded us. But, still, I felt no different. Well, other than the eruption of sharp stings and pangs caused by fresh injuries.

The librarian flickered in and out of view, all but pawing at the ground, ready to be tagged into the fight.

Multiple feeders crashed into Cyrus, taking him down.

"No," I screamed, slicing through one combatant after another. Fear overtook me, and there was no stopping it.

Cyrus fought his way free with few injuries and sprang to his feet, leaving dead feeders on the ground. Thank goodness. But . . .

Seeing blood stream down his face did something to me. Cracked something wide open in my chest, releasing . . . not a tide of fury but something like it. Something hotter. Stronger. The fear evaporated. How *dare* they?

It was then. That moment. Sparks ignited, spreading from my heart to my head until an inferno raged. The flames ate up everything in their path, and I no longer had to wonder what Domino had meant. "Now," I called.

In a blink, the librarian whooshed through the horde of opponents and slammed into me. I gasped. He stayed put . . . as if I *hosted* him?

The heat I'd experienced before was nothing compared to what I experienced now. I was enveloped. Engulfed and devoured. And yet, I remained perfectly safe. Because suddenly, Domino and I were connected, not two people, but one super being. His power flowed through my veins, my limbs, not overtaking me but fueling me. His instincts undergirded mine. We moved with perfect synchrony, gliding from cluster to cluster, eliminating multiple feeders at once.

Hot blood wet my clothes and skin as the bodies of my enemies fell, minus their heads or various parts. My speed astounded. My elegance thrilled. I dodged stray shots taken by the trainees, who had forgotten how to work as a team. I, however, predicted their actions and contorted accordingly while simultaneously dodging blows from the feeders.

Cyrus worked seamlessly with me. So smoothly, in fact, it was as if we'd trained together our entire lives. When one struck, the other defended. He tossed victims my way, and I finished them off. And yet, bit by bit, I began to lose sight of the world around me. Just for a fraction of a second at first, then another and another, until I stood inside a bedroom while Domino fought in Theirland.

Confused, I skimmed the room, noting the number of books stacked on the nightstand and desk. Tome upon tome crowded a bench at the foot of a large bed draped with a dark-blue comforter. No photos on the walls. The cutest black-and-white dog sat at my feet, peering up at me with a mix of adoration and confusion. A living, breathing dog rather than a meta.

My hands itched to stroke that soft fur, but a robed man I recognized approached. Not too long ago, I'd watched him protectively gather the unconscious Ember in his arms.

"Dom." He snapped his fingers in front of my face, his brows drawing together. "I need your help."

"I'm not Domino." I frowned. I'd spoken with the librarian's voice. Astonishment conquered new ground as I looked myself over. Gracious. I *was* Domino. At least, I inhabited his body the way he inhabited mine.

"Ah. It's you. The girl. Arden," the newcomer said, his features hardening. "You agreed to the bonding."

I would never be able to articulate the weirdness of knowing I was in the process of killing a feeder while simultaneously conversing with Ember's boyfriend. "How is Ember?" I asked, and it was still Domino's voice I heard.

"Awake, too weak to get out of bed, and trying not to worry about those under her care. Your mother and Mykal Ellison, to name two." The barest twitch of his jaw muscle alerted me to trouble. "Actions have consequences."

I splayed my fingers over my—Domino's—belly. Oh, wow. I shouldn't notice something so trivial at a time like this, but sweet goodness, the muscle definition on this guy. "Please don't hurt them to hurt me."

Twitch, twitch. "Now you insult me. As if I would ever purposely harm the innocent. I meant the women trust Ember. Now we must pair them with someone they've never met and start the process all over. Wasted time, wasted effort."

I cringed. "My apologies. Is there anything I can do?"

"Yes. Listen when Domino speaks."

Ouch. "Okay, I don't mean this in a bad way, but you really know how to cut a girl to the—" A strong suction yanked me back into my own body.

Domino still inhabited me—I felt him. We stood rooted, panting, two swords clutched tight in our blood-soaked grip. Feeders were piled around us. His emotions intertwined with mine, until I could no longer tell them apart. Resolve: We'd done what was necessary. Relief: Cyrus and the trainees survived. Trepidation: What came next? There was a marked absence of satisfaction.

Blood splattered every inch of Cyrus, including his thunderous expression. "We live to fight another day."

Yes, but how was this bonding thing supposed to work? Would Domino remain a presence inside me forever? Would I drift from my body to his, over and over?

"You were amazing, Arden," Winslet praised between heaving breaths. The trainees were injured—the lord more than the lady—but they remained on their feet. "How did you do that?"

What had she seen? "Which part?" I asked, playing innocent as I wiped my blades on my pants and sheathed the weapons.

"Move so swiftly. Work those weapons so flawlessly." Awe coated every word.

"I've given her special training," Cyrus snapped, his patience hanging by a fraying thread. A true if misleading statement. "Let's go before another horde arrives. Line up."

We obeyed and once again started forward, soon running, our boots splashing in pools of scarlet.

The base came into view, stunning in its entirety. Glass hallways connected a series of differently shaped buildings. Some had a domed ceiling, others a flat roof, while a few featured a twisted steeple. Most sections sprawled, but one stretched toward the sky. If walls weren't studded with crystal, they were dotted with windows. Fences formed a barricade around the perimeter.

Cyrus reached back and placed a pair of goggles in my hand. I trembled as I settled the thin metal around my brow and the lens over my eyes. Instant gloom, the precious light gone as if it had never been. I hated it.

I didn't see Domino exit me, but I suddenly noticed his absence. There one moment, gone the next. It wasn't relief that I felt but bereavement. With him, I'd tasted unfettered strength and unbreakable connection. Now, without him, I struggled to remain upright as I followed Cyrus.

The high prince must have sensed my mounting fatigue. He slowed our stride, allowing me to limp along. But I didn't topple, so, win. When we reached the first gate, a buzzer rang. Dead bolts unlatched, and an opening allowed us through. The pounding, racing footsteps of soldiers reached my ears.

"High Prince Mallow is dead." Mr. Vyle's voice came next. He'd ventured outdoors to collect us personally, which meant he'd known of our approach. "Ember Cruz is responsible."

"I know. I saw it happen," Cyrus informed him without revealing a hint of his emotions.

We entered the building, leaving behind the stench of rot in favor of sterile nothingness. From sweaty hot to quaking with cold.

I ripped off the goggles and blinked to clear my vision. Soldiers encircled us. Medics pushed through them to shove various pieces of equipment at us, taking our vitals. Cyrus didn't protest, so I didn't either.

"Lady Roosa, Baron Wildwood will escort you to Dr. Korey." Mr. Vyle motioned to the soldier in question.

"Arden is staying with me." Cyrus's firm tone allowed no argument. "We won't be visiting Dr. Korey."

The executioner darted his gaze to me, pursed his lips, and gave a stiff nod.

Not a single word of rebuttal? No threats? Cyrus had more power than I'd realized.

Perhaps Vyle knew of Astan's interest in the high prince. An awful, sobering thought.

Cyrus took my hand, linking our fingers, and led me into an enclosed decontamination stall.

Though it was just the two of us, I didn't doubt cameras recorded every nuance. We didn't speak as we toed off our shoes and stripped out of our weapons and battle clothes, removing everything but our jewelry. He wore a necklace of his own, five rings, and three bracelets. I was certain each performed a unique duty.

A special enzyme mist sprayed from various spouts, cleaning us. Dried blood and grime evaporated, and Cyrus's ambrosial scent turned the small space into the sweetest dream. At first, I stared down at the floor, exhausted, but temptation drew my gaze up, up. His legs were tattooed with thick, dark slashes representative of a tree trunk, while leaves and branches stretched over his torso and arms. From those branches dangled flowers and fruits.

He was a garden of delights.

Our gazes met, a flutter of keen awareness in my heart. I held his stare, unwavering, even when he lifted his chin and dared me to take a more thorough peek.

I traced my tongue over my lips. He took a step closer.

Need clawed where I ached most. I took a step closer too. So others watched us. So what. In his glittering eyes, everything he felt snapped into crystal-clear focus. Joy. Relief. Confusion. Anger. Confidence. Uncertainty. Anticipation. Hunger.

So. Much. Hunger.

A mirror to the things bubbling in me. I could have lost him tonight. I should have died. Changed destiny or not, I comprehended the preciousness of time, and I wouldn't waste another moment without Cyrus Dolion.

The spray ended and a compartment in the wall opened automatically, revealing a stack of folded clothes and two pairs of boots. We broke our staring contest to dress. Surprise, surprise, both sets of fatigues were a perfect fit.

The stall door opened, and Cyrus once again linked our fingers. Silent, he led me into a hall abuzz with activity. Soldiers rushed trays of food and water to the now-clean lord and lady who'd arrived with us. Felix leaned against a wall, alone, arms crossed, watching us with narrowed eyes. Lolli and Summit huddled together with Mr. Vyle, whispering. Upon spotting us, they ended their conversation.

Looking at them brought a brief pang of sadness. Not fury. Not resentment. Just sadness. An odd emotion at such a time as this. Confusing too. It had no bearing on the situation.

Oops. Spoke too soon. The muscles between my shoulders bunched, fury rolling in, overshadowing the sadness. A wildfire of questions and accusations smoldered in my throat, begging to be released. Somehow, I held my tongue. If I launched accusations now, I'd have to explain events I wasn't ready to explain.

Others spotted us, too, and paused for a beat.

Lolli strode closer, but Cyrus shook his head. A single, jerky shake that stopped her midstride and drained the color from her cheeks.

"A bullet grazed Arden," he told Mr. Vyle. Truth. I had been grazed when the bullet sliced through my stomach. "I rendered aid." Also truth. He was the reason I'd survived long enough for Ember to do her thing. "The teams left us behind. We found two trainees and fought our way back."

Again, all factual, to the point, and verifiable by others, with no frilly details tacked on.

"Now I've briefed you. There's no reason to speak with us until tomorrow." Cyrus paraded me through the gaping crowd, making an explicit statement, putting all rumors to bed. We were together.

Oh, it wasn't our relationship that surprised them. Well, not entirely. His boldness about it might be a contributing factor. Mostly, it was the fact that we'd survived the field of feeders on our own. I held my head high, acting as if such a feat should've been expected.

We glided through security checkpoints, leaving everything and everyone behind. Finally, we soared through his apartment door. Alone. Just the two of us.

In the foyer, he faced me. Our gazes tangled together again, igniting flutters in my belly.

"There's a lot we need to discuss. Much to figure out." Intensity off-the-charts hot, he stepped closer. "But the answers are in our books, and we can't get to those until we return to Ourland. The chat can wait."

I stepped closer too. "Then what will we do?" The huskiness of my voice surprised even me.

Awareness glinted in his eyes. Only a whisper of air separated us. "Why don't I show you?"

"Yes, please." I tilted up my face, ready for his kiss.

"I wouldn't go any further if I were you."

The familiar voice hit my ears, and I stiffened, zooming my gaze beyond Cyrus to the red-robed man now standing only a few feet away. "Domino."

Chapter Fourteen

I declare, "You are a chosen vessel."

—*The Book of Soal* 2.5.9.15

Cyrus eased back and scrubbed a hand over his face. "The librarian is here, I take it."

"Yes," I rasped, looking between the two men. Both projected a mix of irritation, resolve, and determination.

My boyfriend popped his jaw. "You could have waited, Dom."

"No, I couldn't." The librarian jutted his chin. "I've been here the entire time."

Yet not even I had sensed him. Could he hide himself from me, or had he created a block?

Cyrus noticed my reaction and pursed his lips. "How's Ember?"

"Awake and recovering," Domino and I replied in unison. "She sends a message," he added, focused on me. "Use your second life well."

"I will," I whispered, ducking my head.

The high prince steadied himself while my friend pinned me in place with the heaviness of his gaze. "We're bound together now," he reminded me, "our roots connected."

"I know," I responded. But. Um. "What does that mean, exactly?" Clearly he was trying to convey something I hadn't yet comprehended. "That you can never leave my side?"

"In a way. While I can leave your side physically, our lives are tied. We'll never not be aware of each other. Or affected by the other's actions. If you die, I die, and vice versa."

I opened my mouth. Closed it. Opened. Closed. Strode into the living room. The boys trailed me. I stopped at the coffee table. Relocated to the velvet-covered settee before the unlit hearth. Then the couch. None of the switches assisted the processing of what I'd just heard.

A growl rumbled from Cyrus. "What did he say?"

I couldn't tell him. Not until I understood the mechanics of it all. "I need more information first." Sinking on the edge of the couch, I gazed at the librarian and demanded, "Start talking. Explain how this is possible."

The librarian anchored his arms behind his back, adopting a prebattle stance. "Ask Cyrus about the seed he gave you. The one that grew the piece of the Rock you ate."

I gulped and swung my gaze to the high prince. "Tell me about the seed you gave me when I awoke from Shiloh's attack."

Cyrus pursed his lips. "I removed it from a berry I'd found weeks before CURED sent me to retrieve the one I ate. It's the same kind of seed CURED now protects."

Jolt. "My seed matured into the Rock. Are you saying the berries growing in a Theirland field will also mature into the Rock?"

"Yes."

"That is the third requirement for the rise of the gods," Domino stated. "The Rock will reach full maturity in Theirland. It is at that time the chosen man will agree to serve as Astan's host."

My mind whirled at the implications, and I covered my mouth with trembling hands. The final two conditions were being fulfilled in tandem. How long did I have to pluck Cyrus from the god's claws?

"Why would CURED protect a section of the Rock?" It made no sense. They despised the Rock and sought only to destroy and discredit it. *Him.*

"There's a point in the growth that allows us to craft a deeper bond with Tsuri," Domino explained. "We become a doorway into the library."

The same way Domino had become a librarian.

Cyrus paled as I relayed the information, and I probably reacted similarly. If someone infected with Madness became a door to the library, the entire CURED army could march in, burn books, attack residents, and invade the utopia beyond it, bringing the infection with them. The perfect revenge.

"Let's backtrack a sec," I told Domino. Inhale, exhale. "I ate a fragment of the Rock to become Soalian, but I wasn't"—I waved an arm between us in lieu of speaking the word *bonded*—"to anyone else."

"You were." His unease flowed into me. I *felt* it. "The first time, you were planted in Tsuri, who is planted in Soal, who is bound to all who partake. This develops stronger, longer roots in him . . . and in me. When I cloaked you, our roots twined."

Dang. That made all kinds of crazy sense. It was the equivalent of grafting plants. "This isn't ideal." The understatement of the century.

"Believe me, I'm aware." Both his expression and his stance softened the slightest bit. "I've seen a snapshot of my future, and you are included in it. I wanted, *want*, to get there."

That, I understood as well. Look at everything I'd done to *prevent* a certain future. "Tell me what you saw."

"No."

Before I could press, Cyrus spoke up. "You two hammer out the details of whatever this is and let me know where you end up." He pivoted on his heel and stalked toward the kitchen. "I'll make dinner."

I almost ran after him. I longed to. But I remained in the living room, attempting to ground myself in my environment. Pritis stones dangled from a glass ceiling, the lights appearing to fall from the night sky. Polished walls displayed paintings of past gentry and their families. Crystals covered every corner, the uneven edges flecked with gold. Stunning, luxurious, and familiar, but not at all comforting.

"He may not forgive me for this," I whispered, my voice as ragged as my emotions. "Consuming the Rock was supposed to set me on a different path, not barreling toward the one I read about."

"It did both. Before, staying away from Cyrus was temporary."

And now it was permanent? No. Surely not. He must be wrong. "What you're implying . . . You're wrong. Very wrong."

"Rarely. And not about this."

"Victors predicted my marriage to Cyrus." I would never agree to wed someone hosting Astan.

"Are you certain?" Domino slanted his head. "What did he say, exactly?"

I clung to the memory as if it were a lifeline. "He said, and I quote, 'Who wouldn't want to speak with the much-desired wife of the high prince? Though I suppose you are merely his future much-desired wife at this point.' End quote."

The librarian's expression turned pitying. "A much-desired wife doesn't promise marriage but longing, Arden."

Oh. Oooh. Talk about a dagger to the gut! "You should have explained better," I snapped.

"You should have *trusted* me." The gentle rebuke defused the worst of my anger.

He wasn't wrong. "You told me I was still learning you. That you would earn my trust."

"Exactly what I attempted to do." He paused. "Do you wish you'd made a different decision?"

Yes. No. Maybe. Tears singed my eyes and blurred my vision. My chin trembled. "What can I do?" Because I wouldn't abandon Cyrus.

"Exactly what I must do. We will learn from our mistakes and start fresh." He stepped closer. "It's not all bad, Arden." Extending his arm, he said, "Come. Let me show you a benefit."

I hesitated only a moment before pressing my solid hand against his misty one. Somehow, he clasped my fingers and tugged me to a stand. I stood but left my body behind. No longer did I smell the base, feel the brush of air, or contend with the whirl of anxiety. There was only peace and Domino.

"I'm a spirit like you," I stated, awed.

"Yes." He maintained his hold on my hand and led me through the foyer.

I cast a glance toward the kitchen, where Cyrus puttered about, before I followed the librarian, curious. Domino ghosted through the door, and though I stutter-stepped, I slipped through it too, right on his heels. A little laugh escaped me as we traversed the hallway, leaving behind the two men guarding my door.

"Where are we going?" I whispered, and yes, okay, I really dug this perk. No denying it.

"You'll see." Domino offered me a fleeting smile that lit his entire face, the sight momentarily blipping my brain. "Ready?"

We floated down, down, through the floor and into a bedroom.

Spotting Lolli cuddled up next to a contented Roman, who glistened with sweat as he shifted strands of her hair between his fingers, I wheezed a breath. What! First, only, like, ten minutes had passed since I'd seen her. Which meant she'd come straight here after Cyrus and I passed her upon our return to the palace, and Roman had been waiting.

Second, mere hours ago, this woman had attempted to murder me. She would have succeeded, too, if not for my fellow Soalians. Now she enjoyed herself with my friend?

"—find so fascinating?" she was saying, petting his ripped abs. "I get that she's understated and pretty, but pretty doesn't usually inspire such intense devotion."

"According to the guy who dated her before the high prince, it's her eyes. When she looked at him, he saw deep wounds and wanted only to heal and protect her. I don't see it, personally. She's a handful, that's for sure."

"They're discussing me," I cried, then slapped a hand over my mouth. Oops.

"They can't hear you in this form."

Right. Relief flowed into tense muscles, and I lowered my arm. As she questioned him about my fighting style, I muttered, "I'd really like to leave."

"Very well." Domino led me through a wall and into High Prince Summit's room.

The prince reclined naked in a chair, grinning and sipping whiskey as two trainees kissed different parts of his body. "Good little war bunnies," he praised, petting one's hair.

Thankfully, we didn't stick around here, either. We slipped through another wall, entering Felix's suite. He was alone, standing at attention near the foot of his bed, all brawn and burden with his arms anchored behind his back and his feet braced apart. His eyes were closed, as if he were lost in thought.

We went through a series of walls and floors. Honestly, it was one of the weirdest things I'd ever experienced. The journey ended inside a gym where twenty or so young men and women exercised, pumped iron, and stretched. They wore determination like a second skin.

"These are the hosts already chosen by the gods," Domino said.

Sympathy roused a determination of my own. If these people learned the truth, their acceptance would become refusals. Surely.

"Come." My companion led me through other walls and floors, finally stopping inside a temple I'd visited before, with Cyrus's father. Statues of Astan and his pet dragon lined the walls. Bala was her name, the namesake of CURED's central base of operations.

The biggest statue featured a massive Astan behind a human-size golden throne, gripping its curved top. His wings, folded in at his sides, the tips brushing the arms of the royal seat. Before, his horns had curled downward. Today, they perched above the halfway point . . . and might have just risen another inch, right before my eyes.

A shirtless, bleeding Mr. Vyle dropped to his knees before it and began mumbling the same phrase over and over. "Grant me power, my master, and I will accomplish your will."

Revulsion pricked me.

An old man in a gold robe sat upon the throne, cackling with his head thrown back in abandon and his arms spread high and wide. "It's mine, it's mine, it's mine!" A wild, insane sight.

Recognizing him, I blanched. "That's the emperor of Ourland." But the truly shocking part? Slithering shadows twined around every statue, the throne, Bala, and even Mr. Vyle and the emperor. Especially the emperor.

"He celebrates the capture of the berry field," Domino said, determination hardening his voice. "He shouldn't. We'll get it back soon enough."

"I'll help you, however I can," I vowed.

"Thank you." The librarian gave my fingers a soft squeeze.

I unveiled a wry smile. "No need to thank me for doing my duty, Dom."

He snorted, and it was a little too cute for my liking.

The shadows must have sensed us, even if the men did not. They drew together to form a wall in front of the pair, spoiling our view.

"Come." Domino drew me up into the air, through the ceiling. The higher we went, the faster we traveled, until boom, we stopped inside a bedroom I recognized. The one I'd seen before, when I'd spoken with Ember's boyfriend.

I stood beside the librarian, who sat at the foot of the bed with his dog perched at his feet, peering at him with adoration. No longer was Domino's body solid against mine, but mist.

Frowning, I waved my hand *through* him. He wasn't mist. I was.

"You're the solid one, and I'm invisible," I gasped out.

"Yes." He bent over to scratch the adorable and increasingly more excited dog behind the ears. "This is Archive."

"Hello, good boy," I cooed, wishing I could pet the animal too. Cyrus owned cats who hated me. "You have a charming name."

"It's fitting. He helps me shelve books when he isn't eating my shoes." Domino stood and strode to a small area with a hutch, where he prepared a bowl of kibble.

As Archive chowed down, the librarian walked to a wall without decorations—then he walked through it.

Reeling, I followed him. One second I was in his bedroom, the next I was standing in a library. *The* library. A massive three-story room with thousands upon thousands of leather-bound books meticulously stacked along freshly polished shelves.

Shimmering golden sunlight filtered through stained glass windows that bore the same symbols carved into the Rock, spotlighting certain areas with brilliant multicolored lights. Hand-carved tables made from various types of wood displayed the most sublime treasures. Musical instruments I yearned to hear played. Vases overflowing with flowers I longed to sniff. Jewelry glittering with gemstones brighter than any I'd ever seen. Cushioned couches and chairs offered spots of relaxation under flourishing trees that grew from the floor.

Flower-heavy branches extended in every direction. People moved about in harmony with a soft melody that seeped from speakers I'd never seen. Many called greetings to Domino. The scent of clean, worn leather, sweet peaches, and creamy coconut teased my nose. My second-favorite fragrance after Cyrus's, and yes, okay, the librarian's.

"Where is the soil that nourishes the trees?" I'd always wondered.

"Here, everything is a type of soil." Domino started forward, and I quickened my steps to remain at his side. "It is born of Tsuri, and *he* is soil. In him, we are what he is."

A perfect explanation too vast to fully absorb in a mere moment.

Anyone we neared moved out of his way and into mine, but I ghosted right through them. And it was weird. Though I felt only a flash of warmth, I inhaled sharply each time. "May we visit Ember? I'd like to thank her in person and ask about my mom and Mykal."

"Her quarters are restricted, but I'm currently receiving the information you seek."

My brows drew together. "Like a download . . . in your mind?"

"Yes. And no. Revelation flows through our bond to Soal. One day, you'll be able to do the same." He paused, slanted his head in that way of his. "As a precaution, your mother has been assigned undercover Soalian guards who see to her protection. Mykal still roams the streets. She's staying with a group of rebels who reject both CURED and Soal."

Hey, it was progress. "Anything new from Victors?"

"Not at this time." Domino led me into a small, private room with two chairs tucked into a single table, where a lamp in the shape of a swan in flight spotlighted an open tome.

Tremors of reverence slipped over me. "Mine?" I asked, hopeful.

"Mine," he corrected, his tone deeper, almost guttural. He closed and lifted the precious book with a careful grip, then offered me a closer glimpse of the leather binding. After opening to a yellowed page, he asked, "What do you see?"

I eagerly scrutinized . . . "The code." I pursed my lips. "Am I able to decipher it?" Since we were bonded, I supposed it wasn't outside the realm of possibility.

"Arden." Cyrus's voice penetrated my awareness. I heard him, but it sounded as if he called to me from a long, echoing tunnel. A soft snapping wrecked my concentration.

The library vanished. Cyrus was standing before me, and I sat upon the couch once again. He cupped my face, his thumbs grazing over my cheekbones. "Arden?"

My body had stayed behind while my spirit ventured through the library with Domino. "I'm here," I assured him.

Our gazes met, and he searched mine, radiating concern. "What happened? You completely checked out."

Ugh. Best to tell him now, rather than drag out the big reveal. "I'm connected to him. Rooted. To Domino. He pulled my spirit into the library while my body stayed here."

Cyrus blinked twice. A hard, blank mask spread over his expression, reminding me of paint spilling over paper. "Not just linked but rooted," he said with a hollow tone. He straightened, his spine like steel.

I chewed on my bottom lip. "There was no other way to survive the battle," I rushed to explain. "Maybe it was wrong. I would hate it if you bonded with Lolli, especially if you did it without talking it over with me first. There was no other way," I repeated. "No time."

He ran his tongue over his teeth. "I did tell you to do whatever proved necessary to survive, and I meant it."

The note of misery in his tone nearly became my undoing. "I don't deserve to hear your problem with Domino, but I'm asking you to tell me anyway. Help me understand what I'm up against."

A thousand emotions passed over his expression in an instant, but nothing stuck, the blank mask secured. "His parents worked for mine. We grew up together, were as close as brothers. Closer, really, since I have brothers, and we barely speak. After Domino joined Soal, he tried to recruit me. I turned him in. CURED took him to a rehabilitation facility, where doctors carved open his body and used him as a pritis factory until his escape. He produced a higher-wattage pritis than other glowers, so CURED wanted him back." Guilt and shame crept into his expression and pitch. "They vowed to execute every member of his family unless he returned of his own volition. He didn't return, and CURED kept its word."

My chest tightened. I cupped Cyrus's shoulder, offering comfort. "I understand. You know my worst secret. How I turned in my own mother. Rest assured, I'm not judging you," I promised gently.

He ducked his head. "When I became Soalian, Domino ensured I comprehended the pain I had caused him in a multitude of ways."

That . . . hmm. "Revenge doesn't sound like him." Not what I knew of him, anyway.

"People can surprise you." He let his head fall back and stared up at the crystal ceiling, apprehension whipping from him in increasingly agitated waves. "Rooted," he repeated.

"We would've died without his aid," I reminded him.

"I realize that. But this complicates things. You can feel him, and he can feel you, I take it."

"Yes. Kind of." I shifted in my seat. "It's muted. An awareness that he's close if I need him. The bond, um, can't be undone." At least, I didn't think so.

His posture grew stiffer. "Throuples and threesomes aren't my thing."

"Nor are they mine." Until Cyrus, I'd never really been part of a twosome. The thought of being so intimate and vulnerable with someone who could break and harm me had never appealed.

He inhaled deeply, nodded, and handed me a plate he'd set on the coffee table. I eased back on the couch, and he sat beside me with a plate of his own. Side by side, we each ate a sandwich layered with moist, shredded chicken, a creamy pepper-and-fruit spread, and melty cheeses. All the real deal, I'd bet, and none of the lab-grown "meat" and "dairy" ordinary folks were fed when we decided to splurge on something other than a tasteless meal bar made from mystery ingredients.

"How do you want to proceed?" I asked with the barest tremor.

"Give me time to think."

We finished eating in silence. At any other time, I would've moaned over the sublime flavors exploding on my tongue. Tonight, every bite settled like a lead ball in my stomach.

When we finished, we set our plates aside, still silent. I understood his upset, I truly did. Like I'd told him, I'd be super upset if he connected to someone else. The question was, did he want to be with me enough to get past it?

Needing a connection with *him*, I curled myself against his chest, resting my head on his shoulder. He didn't rebuke me but slowly wound an arm around my waist. Slow and distracted, he stroked his fingers along my side, pausing now and then to toy with the ends of my hair.

"It's a complication," he repeated as if the conversation had never paused, assuring me he'd considered nothing but my new relationship with Domino.

"Yes." I offered no more, unwilling to pressure him.

"I don't . . ." He sighed.

I gripped his shirt, crinkling the material between my fingers. *Don't throw me away when you need me most.*

"Throw you away?" he fumed.

Oops. I'd spoken out loud.

He tightened his hold. "Arden, that isn't what I'm considering."

"Then what?"

"How best to proceed with you. Splitting up isn't an option."

Heat washed over me, and I melted, pouring myself over him. "That's a good answer."

"We should take this day by day and learn how the bond between you and the librarian works," he said, and I nodded, eager. "While we do, we will remain together."

"Yes, yes, forever yes."

"As for today, I think I'd like to be wooed," he said, and ran two knuckles along the underside of my chin.

A laugh burst from me, totally spontaneous and utterly unexpected, born from relief and affection. "Wooed? As in, courted?"

"Exactly." He flashed a sly smile. "Give me a compliment."

"You can't just order someone to compliment you," I replied, giggling.

"I can and I did," he insisted, pretending to pout. "I want what I want, and I want it now."

Snickering, I slid into his lap, straddling his thighs. "Do you hear yourself?" *Tsk, tsk, tsk.* "The great and powerful future king of Ourland just *whined.*" Most people were too afraid of his position and cold, distant demeanor to risk speaking to him. Me? I lightly traced the length of his facial brand with a blunt-tipped nail.

"And yet you still deny him." He gripped my backside and squeezed. Just like that, his amusement died, replaced by desperation. "Give me what I want, Pink." He rasped the demand.

I—went—molten. Bracing my hands on his shoulders, I wiggled closer and purred, "I won't give you a compliment, sugar. I'll give you many."

His gaze remained on my mouth. "I'm listening."

"I'm awed by your strength, and I greatly admire your protector's heart. Your ability to walk into a room and assess everyone and thing wows me. And baby, you are gorgeous."

His eyes hooded, his heavy lids sinking low. "I also have a multitude of scars and tattoos. Don't think I've forgotten about your fetish."

"Well, in my defense, those scars and tattoos look incredible on you."

"*You* look incredible on me." He tipped up his face to nip my bottom lip with his teeth. "You are brave and kind and sweet. So sweet. So very, very sweet. I love you, and I like you."

Aah! He'd said those three little words again. And he'd added three more, equally powerful. Heat painted my cheeks even as a smile bloomed. "I lo—like you too." My heart skipped a beat. That had been too close for comfort. "I like you very much."

An answering smile lingered. "You almost said it."

The heat in my cheeks cranked up another thousand degrees. "True," I admitted, leaning closer. We exchanged breaths, every inhalation igniting the most delicious aches and pangs. "I think I'm afraid of my feelings. With Astan determined to use you as his host . . ."

Cyrus gave a clipped shake of his head. "I will never give in to him, I swear it." He caressed my earlobe, and I nuzzled into his touch. "But I understand your hesitation."

"You're not mad?"

"Mad? I want to kiss you more than I've ever wanted anything. But I won't." He growled the statement. "Domino doesn't get to experience your pleasure. That is for me alone."

Inhale. Exhale. "I wish . . ." So many things.

"We cannot go backward," he said, exhaustion settling into his features. Looked like the day had caught up to him. "We start today. You may be bonded to him—at the moment—but you're mine forever."

Breath—gone. "I won't share your pleasure either," I told him, standing. A separation I couldn't bear. "Come on. Let's go to bed." I urged him to his feet and led him to the bedroom, where we stripped to our undergarments and climbed under the covers.

He gathered me close and shut his eyes. "Stay with me," he muttered. "All night."

"I will," I vowed, conforming my body to his and luxuriating in his heat. *I will stay with you always.*

Chapter Fifteen

The same measure you use with others will be measured with you.

—*The Book of Soal* 2.3.6.38

Cyrus and I fell asleep tangled together. I used to wonder why so many couples risked everything simply to spend a few hours together. Now I got it. The warmth. The intimacy. Filling my lungs with Cyrus's incredible scent. The companionship. The sense of safety and belonging. The *aching*.

"No," Cyrus muttered, yanking me from a light, dreamy doze. "No!"

When his entire body jerked, I popped open my eyes. "Cyrus?" We were on our sides, with him behind me, curled around my body. I patted the hand resting on my stomach. "Everything okay?"

"No!" He flopped to his back, allowing me to twist around. His head thrashed over a pillow, the brand on his face much paler than his skin, the puckered flesh pulled taut.

A nightmare? "Hey, hey," I cooed, gentle, so gentle, as I caressed his chest. "I'm here. It's okay. You're okay."

"Born . . . rule." With a roar, he jerked upright and yanked on handfuls of his hair. "Can't lose . . . won't . . . mine!"

Can't lose . . . the crown? "Wake up, Cyrus."

In lieu of a response, he punched his temples, as if he attempted to dislodge his troublesome thoughts.

"Stop it!" *Please.* I latched onto his wrists, taking control of his arms. "Sugar, I need you to wake up, okay?"

He wrenched from my hold and sprang from the mattress to stalk forward. Overhead lights switched on automatically. To my dismay, he tried to walk through the door. When that failed, he punched. *Wham, wham, wham.*

I leaped up and over, putting myself between my sleepwalking boyfriend and the entrance. There was no need to duck or dodge. Even in sleep, he was a protector, striking the door around me. "Cyrus!" I shouted as he drew back his elbow, intending to launch another strike. Blood dripped from torn knuckles. Desperate, I slapped him.

He went still and shook his head. Blinking rapidly, he lowered his arm.

Relief caught me up in a whirlwind. I petted his chest, cooing, "It's okay, it's okay, it's okay."

His eyes found mine and narrowed. "What happened?"

"You had a bad dream and decided the bedroom door was enemy one."

The color drained from his cheeks, and he gripped my shoulders. "Did I hurt you?"

"Not even a little. Come on." I urged him back to the bed and applied pressure to ease him into a sitting position at the edge. "I'll be right back." I darted off to gather the first aid kit.

He said nothing as I cleaned and bandaged his abrasions. Though the medications must sting, he displayed no trace of unease.

"Do you remember anything?" I asked after finishing my task.

"I have a vague memory of fighting Felix and the other royals. Then you were ripped from my arms."

Can't lose . . . My ribs constricted. He'd referenced me, not the crown. "Only a dream," I rasped, moving to clean the mess I'd created.

"Arden." He grasped my wrist and tugged me onto his lap, sideways.

Understanding, I wound my arms around his shoulders. "It's okay, baby."

"Is it? There's a residue of panic inside me." Resting his cheek against my shoulder, he released a shuddering breath. "I don't do panic."

"I know," I said, stroking his silken hair, certain Astan was at work here. The god spearheaded CURED, and this gonna-lose-her fear struck me as a play straight from their handbook. Get him all riled up, then offer him as the lone solution. "Tell me about your brother." Felix not only had a starring role in Cyrus's dream, but the brothers had been in Theirland together during Cyrus's episodes of memory loss. Maybe speaking of him would jar something loose. "You love him, but you don't like him. Why?"

Cyrus heaved a sigh. "He's older by a year. Our mothers hated each other, but our father insisted on spending time with us together. We became friends. Played ball, laughed a lot, and cheered the other as he rose in rank. Then a rogue glower killed his wife, and suddenly everything changed. *He* changed. He puts on a good show in public, but in private it's clear he lives only for revenge."

My brow furrowed. "Rogue glower isn't a term I'd heard."

"A Soalian who no longer follows Soal."

Hmm. I hadn't realized such people existed, though I guess I should have.

Domino materialized a few feet away, snatching my attention. He wore his standard uniform, hood drawn down, and exuded determination and resolve. "Big things are underway. Mr. Vyle is on his way here. He'll ask you about your experience on the battlefield, among other things. You have eleven minutes."

He didn't wait for my response but disappeared, leaving me with frothing curiosity.

Big things? What big things?

"What's wrong?" Cyrus demanded, sensing my upset.

"We have eleven minutes until Mr. Vyle arrives."

He traced his tongue over straight, white teeth. "Domino told you this?"

"Yes." I pressed a swift kiss to the hollow of his throat before bounding to my feet and urging him to his. Having never spent the night with a man, I fumbled for the proper protocols. When in doubt, go with polite. "Thank you for holding me. I had a wonderful time."

He allowed the subject change, the corners of his mouth twitching. "Thank you for allowing me to hold you. I had a wonderful time as well." Turning toward the bathroom, he casually stated, "I love you."

"I lo—like you."

Beyond the door, he called, "You love me."

"Maybe." An idea hit, and I swiped up the first aid kit before stalking to the other suite's bathroom, the one I'd used in the past. I rushed through a shower, brushed my teeth, and braided my hair.

While naked in the stall, I opened the kit and withdrew the scissors. Though I trembled, I did it. I executed my idea, dragging the blade tips across my side, where I'd been shot. The sharp sting sucked, but I persevered, bandaged the wound, and dressed in clean fatigues.

When I emerged from the bedroom, I found a freshly showered, changed Cyrus waiting for me in the kitchen. He offered me a super-delicious fruit smoothie.

I was only halfway done with the tasty concoction when Mr. Vyle marched into the apartment as if he owned the place. He wore a suit and tie, not a single hair out of place, as usual. He was alone.

He took us in, standing side by side at the counter, and the slightest pulse of annoyance crossed his features. He'd hoped to find us asleep and at a disadvantage, I'd bet.

Guess I owed Domino. Again.

"Good morning, Mr. Vyle," I said with a satisfied smile.

His eyelids slitted. "Good morning, Lady Roosa. High Prince Dolion."

Cyrus took a drink of his smoothie before demanding, "Why are you here?"

"We must discuss what happened yesterday." A command, not a suggestion.

"I have questions for you, so yes, we will discuss what happened yesterday." Cyrus ushered me past our uninvited guest and into the living room. We settled on the couch, an obvious team.

Mr. Vyle unbuttoned his jacket and sank into the chair across from us. "I'll start. I've spoken with several soldiers, and many claim they saw someone shoot Arden at close range from behind."

"What are you implying?" Cyrus asked casually. "That she miraculously healed?"

A nervous laugh bubbled up and would have escaped if a comforting tide hadn't swept along my bond with Domino, quashing it. A sensation as welcome as it was disquieting.

"I'm implying nothing." Mr. Vyle waved in my direction. "I'd like to hear Lady Roosa's side of the story."

Here goes. "As Cyrus already told you, a bullet grazed me. Not from behind but from the front." I clicked my tongue. "Before I fell, I spotted High Princess Lolli with a smoking gun aimed straight at me."

Mr. Vyle thought for a moment. "Show me your wound."

"That isn't happening," Cyrus grated. "My girlfriend isn't showing you any part of her body, ever. I have seen the wound. Either the word of a royal is sufficient, or it isn't."

I placed a hand on his and offered him my sweetest smile. "It's fine. I'll show him. I don't mind."

He blinked. Compressed his lips. Threw a thousand curses at me without uttering a word. Nodded stiffly.

I lifted the corner of my shirt, revealing the bloodied bandage, which I removed and tossed on the coffee table between us. "Happy? It opened in the shower, and I cleaned it up as best I could." *Find the lie in that, bud.*

Mr. Vyle couldn't mask his irritation. "You require tending. I'll send a medic—"

"I'll take care of her." Cyrus tapped a finger against the arm of the couch and changed the subject as if nothing more needed to be discussed regarding the shooting. "What's the outcome of last night's excursion?"

Fury flashed in the executioner's eyes, there and gone. "Things went exactly as we hoped. Glowers arrived en masse, but they couldn't bypass our barriers and reclaim the field. They are still trying. Feeders are flooding in from all over the realm to attack, doing our work for us."

The field where fruit—the Rock—grew. "I noticed the barrier but couldn't see it."

Though he didn't look as if he wished to address me, his need to gloat got the better of him, and he said, "That's because it emits a frequency that can be disarmed only one way."

Mr. Vyle said no more, and I barely stopped myself from probing further. I needed to be careful. Already he suspected me of aiding the enemy.

Cyrus drummed his fingers against the arm of the couch. "Explain why I wasn't told of this plan or the creation of this frequency."

"Let me be blunt, Your Highness." Mr. Vyle put his nose in the air. "Your girlfriend has been under investigation as a potential traitor."

"And now?" he demanded.

"We have cleared her."

Surprise intermingled with relief. Though I could guess the reason. I hadn't reacted to the smoke. Gratitude joined my mix of emotions. Another reason I owed Domino.

"Today, we will be—" A buzz blasted over the intercom, quieting Mr. Vyle.

An automated voice repeated the same phrase five times. "All ranks report to the auditorium."

The executioner stood with smooth grace and rebuttoned his jacket. "Dress Lady Roosa's wound. Until we speak again . . ." He strode from the apartment.

"You stabbed yourself?" Cyrus snapped, popping up and rushing to collect the first aid kit.

"I kept it superficial."

"Still unacceptable," he grumbled. As gently as possible, he cleaned and bandaged me as I'd done for him.

"Any idea what's going on?"

"No. But it's not good for us. That much I can guess." He pressed a prolonged kiss to my lips and took my hand. "Do not leave my side."

On the walk to the auditorium, I didn't see Domino, but I sensed his calm confidence, as if he traveled with me. I welcomed the presence of such a strong ally, a fact I kept to myself. No need to complicate an already-complicated situation.

We traversed hallways, elevators, and security points, other soldiers rushing in the same direction. All paused to salute Cyrus as they passed. Aggression powered an electric current in the air.

Shadows slithered over every statue. The essence of Astan—the Madness. But they were thicker than usual, nuzzling small cracks I'd not noticed before. Dismay worked through me.

The closer we came to our destination, the denser the crowd became. But no matter the number of bodies clogging a corridor, people hastened out of the way, soon creating an open path for us. A perk I couldn't lament.

We entered the auditorium, a place I'd never been. Bleachers encircled a center stage, with chairs stretched across a podium. Lolli sat between Felix and Summit. Each of them watched us, unabashed. Summit displayed his usual mocking grin. Mr. Vyle sat among them, but he was busy speaking with a trio of guards.

Cyrus continued forward, as if he intended to take me up there with him. No way, no how. I dug in my heels, forcing him to stop and face me. "I want you with me," he said.

"That isn't wise, and you know it. We'll cause an unnecessary uproar. Go," I said, freeing my hand and waving him on. The soldiers around us did their best to pretend they weren't eavesdropping. "I'll see you after."

Or rather, after I completed my scheduled patrol of the "pritis mines," which should kick off immediately following . . . whatever this was.

Rather than argue in front of others, he nodded stiffly. I pecked his cheek before darting off. Many eyes followed my progress up the bleachers. I claimed a seat near the top, watching as Cyrus stomped up the dais. He went straight to Felix, who held his palms up in a gesture of innocence before switching chairs.

Cyrus sat, leaned in, and snarled something at Lolli. She paled but swiftly pasted on a brittle smile, trying to act as if nothing troubled her.

This was how he "handled" her? I almost shouted, "Not good enough."

Roman and Winslet plopped into the open seats beside me. He took the left, she took the right. Miller joined us, easing beside Winslet. Each addition surprised me.

"What's going on, Ardie?" Roman demanded, acting as if he hadn't ignored me for days.

"I don't know," I replied, unable to stop the flash of memories. Roman, in bed with the woman who had tried to murder me. "I really don't."

"First, we should all take a moment to recall I pegged her relationship with the high prince while she denied it." Miller spread his arms, jubilant. "And let's not forget her dalliance with the emperor and the guards he assigned to her. So? What's it like dating both grandfather and grandson?"

Roman leaned over and punched him in the stomach. "Enough."

"You're setting yourself up for heartache, you get that, right?" Winslet patted my shoulder as Miller gasped for breath. "From rumors I've heard over the years, relationships between royals and common gentry never work."

If I said I wasn't worried, I'd be lying. I'd read my book. But I had no desire to share any of that. All I could do was shrug.

Mr. Vyle approached the podium, and the crowd quieted. "Welcome to the new day. I understand yesterday was tough. We lost forty-three of our best."

A pool of regret and sympathy welled.

"The good news is," he said and grinned, "we also identified twenty-seven glowers hidden among us."

Gasps blended, mine included.

"Behold." Mr. Vyle motioned to someone beyond an exit, and guards marched in, leading a group of bound, battered soldiers. Gashes littered their exposed, soot-streaked skin. I noted swollen eyes, cut lips, and limps. A chain connected one prisoner to another.

Boos rose from the audience, but I remained quiet, my stomach roiling. This. The reason for the drugged smoke. A plan straight from the CURED playbook. Capture the weakest Soalians, parade them before men and women who'd just fought advanced feeders, and frighten anyone who'd been considering switching sides. Maybe CURED even hoped to incite older glowers into revealing themselves with protests.

Diabolical. Even knowing what I knew, the urge to fight for my allies might overpower me. I white-knuckled the arms of my seat, holding on for dear life. *Stand down, Roosa.* I was outgunned, outnumbered, and ill prepared. Maybe Domino and the others had a plan of their own.

Yes, yes. Of course, they did. And if not them, Cyrus.

Despite the distance, I swung my gaze to him. He already watched me. With a single shake of his head, he issued a clear command: Act unaffected.

A tremor worked through me. No doubt Mr. Vyle had spies woven into the crowd, on the hunt for any hint of sympathy.

Withering inside, I nodded.

"Do not allow their lack of worms to sway you. These infected are too far gone for treatment," Mr. Vyle said as the prisoners were lined up behind him. He held out his hand, and a baron marched over to give him a sword.

The roiling in my stomach worsened. "Surely he isn't going to kill them." Because CURED needed them. Would imprison them as they'd done to Victors and use their bodies as pritis factories.

"He's the executioner," Roman said, unconcerned. "What else do you expect?"

No, no, no. As Mr. Vyle moved to stand in front of the first prisoner, tremors invaded my limbs. A team of glowers would swoop in at any moment. Yes, any moment now.

"Any last words?" Mr. Vyle asked. Hoping they would beg for mercy or change their allegiance?

"Soal is the cure," the soldier called to the audience, his head high. "CURED is the dis—"

The executioner struck. A swift swing of his weapon. The soldier's head fell to the floor, his body standing for several seconds longer. Blood sprayed over Mr. Vyle and the royals, none of whom reacted.

A gasp congealed in my throat. Cheers erupted throughout the crowd, Roman one of the loudest.

"Anyone else have anything to say?" Mr. Vyle asked, his fury unmistakable despite his calm demeanor.

Without missing a beat, each Soalian cried, "Soal is the cure!" Their lack of distress erased the veneer of calm from the executioner's face. "CURED is the disease. Open your eyes and—"

With a grunt, he struck again and again. As heads rolled and bodies toppled, Roman and Winslet popped to their feet, clapping excitedly.

I sat frozen, steeped in revulsion and helplessness, choking back horror, fighting my tears, and swallowing a rise of vomit.

Warmth spread from my shoulder, light as a whisper, and I knew. Domino was behind me, offering what comfort he could. I bit the inside of my cheek and held tight to our bond, certain it was the only thing keeping me from falling apart.

"These brave soldiers fought for what they believed was right," he told me. "They did not die in vain."

Do not cry. Don't you dare. I didn't care if they hadn't died in vain; they'd died. That was bad enough. They should be alive and well.

A blood-splattered Mr. Vyle removed a pocket square from the breast pocket of his suit jacket and wiped his face before returning to the podium. A cleanup crew overtook the stage, swiftly removing the remains and mopping up the blood. As they worked, fury sparked wrath, the two twining inside me, leading to a wildfire of hatred. The executioner deserved a taste of his own medicine.

"Now that we've completed that bit of unpleasantness." Mr. Vyle motioned for the cheers to end, and everyone went silent. "There's a second reason for this meeting."

The hatred only spread and deepened.

"Yesterday's excursion also served as a testing ground for your skills, resilience, and aptitude," the executioner continued, sending a wave of agitation through the audience. Usually CURED's tests ended in anguish. "We have selected twenty of the best and brightest for a special training program that will take place here in Theirland."

Wait, wait, wait. I sat up straighter. The last special assignment had led to the death of my teammates. They and others were purposely infected with a nasty strain of Madness and transformed into mindless soldiers.

"When I call your name, come forward." Mr. Vyle wasted no time. "Lord Roman Alexander."

A grinning Roman erupted from his seat. Applause rang out as he jogged down the bleacher steps and onto the dais, where he stood at attention, projecting great satisfaction.

Other names were called, both Winslet and Miller among them. The fact that the "best and brightest" were mostly trainees I'd served with didn't escape my notice. I wondered if CURED had placed us together for this, always this.

"And finally," Mr. Vyle said with a bit of glee, "Arden Roosa."

My heart skipped a beat. No. He hadn't called my name. He just hadn't.

"Stand," Domino said, still behind me.

I met Cyrus's gaze once again. He was scowling, his hands fisted in his lap.

Reluctant, I rose to my feet and with trembling legs made my way forward, unsure what awaited me.

CHAPTER SIXTEEN

I will always be with you; I'll not fail you nor abandon you, so hold tight to your courage.

—*The Book of Soal* 1.5.31.8

I stood on stage, dazed and queasy, peering out at the crowd. Anger and envy peered back at me. Other soldiers wanted to be where I was, and most believed I was only here because of the man I dated.

They didn't know I wanted to be where they were. Not here, a member of a "special" team, meant to become the host of a god, I'd bet.

The royals passed by us, taking time to shake our hands and offer congratulations.

Summit paused to rake his gaze over me. "Not as useless as I first assumed. Good to know."

Felix crooked his head, as if he couldn't decide what to make of me. "Your relationship with Cyrus reminds me of what I shared with my wife." The lack of emotion in his voice turned his sweet words into a threat. "I only hope your end is better than hers."

I believed he loved his brother, but he also vied for king. For Astan?

Lolli squeezed my fingers too hard. "This changes nothing."

Cyrus grazed his thumb over my knuckles and signed a message against my palm. *I love you.*

His silent declaration stuck with me long after the royals exited the stage and disappeared beyond a wall. I stood there, wanting to shout for him. To shout the truth to one and all. The need simmered and boiled within me, ready to spill from my lips at any second . . .

"Do not," Domino said, appearing in my line of sight. Though transparent, he snatched my attention, the confession dying on my tongue. "The majority aren't ready to listen. You'll ruin your life for nothing."

My lids slid closed, just for a moment. Let me go out rescuing innocents and those I loved, not wasting my breath.

Domino wasn't done. "If nothing else, you're safe. You and the others are now officially marked as potential hosts."

Exactly what I'd suspected. A cold weight settled on my chest. I'd understood my connection to Cyrus might lead to my selection, but now that we were in the thick of it, I realized I wasn't prepared.

"Behold, our extraordinary team of lords and ladies." Mr. Vyle clapped, igniting a forced round of applause from the audience. "By the time you see these fine soldiers again, they'll be a new class of warrior led by your new king."

The cheering tapered to silence, unveiling more crackles of envy and disappointment that served as fuel for the pressure building inside me.

"Congratulations," Mr. Vyle said to us before motioning to a baron who stood off to the side. "Go and await the royals, who will join you shortly."

The baron led us from the stage and through a narrow corridor I'd never walked, to an underground garage where a luxurious bus waited. No sign of Cyrus. I guzzled unease fresh from the well. Where, exactly, were we going?

"I should get my stuff," a soldier in front rushed out.

"You have everything you need," the baron interjected, waving to the bus's open door. A clear command.

We boarded single file, most trainees overjoyed. A few of us remained quiet, obviously shell-shocked. Plush leather seats stretched two to a row, stitched with gold thread and spaced wide enough for real legroom. Soft-blue lighting ran in strips overhead, casting a calming glow against polished steel trim. Each seat had a retractable screen on the back. Winslet chose the spot beside Roman, leaving the too-smug and grinning Miller as my seatmate. I wasn't upset by it.

To my surprise, familiar warmth uncoiled, the knowledge that a friend was near filling me. It didn't spring from my bond to Domino. . . but Miller?

"Look at me." He pumped a fist into the air. "I'm at the top of my class without notching my bedpost to get there."

I arched a brow at him. Overcompensating to conceal his true affiliation? "Your talent for sucking the joy from every situation is unparalleled."

He tsked under his breath. "Wow, Roosa. I aimed below the belt, but you just had to go and shoot above it. Wow," he repeated, shaking his head as if greatly disappointed in my cruelty.

Here goes. "I know what you are," I muttered for his ears alone, giving Lolli's line a try.

He didn't take the bait. "And what is that? Handsome? Elite? Perfect? Hate to break it to you, but everyone knows that. Or did you mean I'm not royal enough to crawl into bed with you?"

I gnashed my molars. Maybe he wasn't the Soalian. And yet, the warmth. It only increased. But if he *was* the Soalian, he must be able to turn the telltale signs on and off. But did he do it at will?

Staring him straight in the eye, I replied, "You are my friend and ally, just as I'm yours." Maybe he decoded my message. Maybe he didn't. I'd put the hint out there, and it was now up to him.

If I was wrong, I was wrong. I'd deal with any consequences. Enough playing it safe at every turn. Great risk carried the potential for great reward.

He snorted, but he also searched my eyes, growing serious. Oh, he got it, all right. But what did he think of the notion that we might play for the same team? If he still did. Considering what Cyrus had told me about rogue glowers, people could choose to serve Soal, then later renounce him.

The very reason the high prince had urged me not to pursue this route. But Domino believed the other Soalian could help me. Today, I would trust his judgment, as I had not done on the battlefield. I needed help more than ever.

Finally, Miller twisted in his seat, facing forward, silent.

The royals boarded the bus, cleaned of blood. Unusually sharp determination filled Cyrus's eyes. Though he knew better, he intended to come back here and either move Miller or escort me to the front.

With a shake of my head, I altered his plan. *Don't you dare single me out.* Not here, not now. He paused abruptly, collected himself, then claimed the first available seat. High Princess Lolli took the seat across from his without glancing in my direction.

Interesting. Whatever he'd said to her on that dais had an impact. To my surprise, Miller didn't comment on the obvious interaction.

A voice spilled from an intercom, silencing every conversation. "Buckle up. We're going through some rough terrain, but we'll stop for nothing."

I obeyed as the bus drove up a winding ramp and exited the garage, entering Theirland. I peered out the window, unable to see through the gloom. None of us sported goggles, yet no one suffered from symptoms of RVM.

"The windows must be made of the same stuff as our lenses," Roman observed, tapping the glass.

Well. No wonder I couldn't see past the gloom. A fact I celebrated as we bumped along a path at full speed, eliciting telling thud after thud. We were either running over dead bodies or slamming into feeders.

The vehicle careened left, verging on the tipping point, and I could only hold on for dear life, my heart pounding. True to the driver's word, we didn't stop until we reached our destination.

The royals disembarked first, but trainees weren't far behind them. I gawked as I emerged into a wonderland. A clear dome covered a well-lit lawn and glinted off a rippling moat, extending over the emperor's palace. A home designed in dreams and fairy tales—and forged in nightmares. It was massive, made of glittering crystals edged with gold, but countless shadows danced around the highest points. They all had eyes. Icy fingers of dread skittered over my spine. Madness, Madness, all around.

Just in case non-Soalians shouldn't notice the shadows, I resumed my examination. Lush plants grew in abundance, as heavy with fruit as those in the Library of Soal. The water gleamed with an ominous pinkish tint as ripples spread over the surface. Something big must be swimming beneath.

I had no problem seeing the world beyond the dome's transparent, shimmering veil. A field of dry briars and parasitic weeds, with feeders wandering aimlessly, their heads bowed and their shoulders stooped. Even the worms on their scalps hung limp. Why so lifeless?

"This way." Mr. Vyle ushered us along a long gold-brick bridge dotted with statues of various dragon-type creatures, their eyes studded in rubies. I knew of only one dragon, Bala, Astan's beloved pet, but I should've guessed there were others.

I bit the inside of my cheek. Did they awaken too?

Mr. Vyle reached out to trace a crack in the calf of a statue of Astan. A reverent, affectionate brush that set my nerves on edge.

The beginning of the end.

A countdown kicked off, seconds vanishing, and there was nothing I could do to stop it. *Tick tock. Tick tock.*

The blood in my veins chilled, yet perspiration dotted my hands. I zoomed my gaze to Cyrus. His head was lifted high, his shoulders back, and his stride confident.

We stand in a stalemate, the battlefield between us a nightmare of lifeless bodies and scattered limbs bathed in the unflinching light of Theirland's twin suns. Lavender and gold streak the sky, casting an eerie glow over the blood-soaked earth, where rivers of crimson carve fresh paths through the flatland. Overhead, a restless flock of scavenger birds circles, their shrill cries piercing the thick, heavy silence as they await their feast.

A fresh wave of CURED soldiers floods in, surging from behind the former high prince and hurrying to kill the array of glowers trapped around me. Men and women I admire. Many more will die today if I don't stop Cyrus.

Tension invaded my bones. I now recognized the battlefield of the coming battle—the same one we'd fought on before, where the Rock grew. Were we one step closer to war?

As our group approached an open glass foyer inside the palace, I wanted to run. But I didn't. I was strong. Capable. I could face this challenge head-on or hide, but I couldn't do both, and only one choice offered a path to victory.

Domino appeared out of thin air, walking beside me. "I'm working behind the scenes," he vowed. "Know that. You will never be without my aid."

I took his words to heart, grateful for his encouragement.

We entered a spacious ballroom with ornate white columns stretching toward a vaulted ceiling adorned with intricate gold filigree. More statues along the walls depicted some of the same gods I'd noticed in Bala City, their stone faces frozen in expressions of silent judgment. At the far end of the chamber, a royal dais loomed, its steps polished to a mirror sheen, leading up to a single throne made of interwoven horns, most of them jagged, as if they'd been torn from their owners in battle. The air itself trembled with frantic energy. A hum ignited beneath my skin, setting my nerves on edge.

Mr. Vyle climbed the steps and stood at the right side of the throne. At the same time, the royals formed a row just below the dais, as if they'd practiced this until achieving perfect coordination. They faced the executioner, leaving us with a view of their backs.

The baron who'd accompanied us directed us to form a line behind them, standing in the spaces between their bodies. Domino remained at my side as promised, an endless well of calm.

I wished so badly we were in the library, and I was reading my book. Or his. I needed to learn more about "the end."

A soldier blew a trumpet, the sound scratching more than my ears. My skin crawled, but I forced myself to stay still.

The emperor entered the chamber from a side door, and I blanched. I'd never seen him in person, only in news clips on screens as I jogged to my different jobs, in holograms played on a loop twenty-four seven inside certain buildings, and when Domino had led me through the base as a spirit. Today, shadows slithered all over him, so thick they resembled a voluptuous black robe. Like his son and grandson, he was tall and leanly muscled. He was also steady on his feet.

A crown studded with rubies rested on his full head of hair. Despite his age, the only wrinkles to mar his countenance stretched across his brow. In one hand, he held a scepter. In the other, a sword topped by a globe of the fused worlds.

Upon reaching the throne, he stopped and faced us.

"Bow," Mr. Vyle commanded, and my stomach churned.

The royals dropped to one knee and lowered their heads without hesitation. The trainees did too, including me, though I moved slower than everyone else. This didn't feel right.

Able to take the sensation no longer, I popped back to my feet. Thankfully, Cyrus did as well, and others followed.

"Welcome to my home." Emperor Dolion eased upon the throne. "My utmost congratulations on your accomplishments. From my princes and princesses who vie to become my successor to the candidates who seek positions on my council. I'm told you have excelled in numerous ways, and yesterday's battle was no exception."

I didn't have to wonder if his "council" would consist of godly hosts.

"In the coming days," he continued, "you'll undergo rigorous testing. Some will not survive. I don't say this to scare but to prepare. The end will be worth the means. Those who succeed will enjoy privileges you've only ever dreamed possible." He paused to drum up drama. "This is your chance to change your fate."

No, thank you. Not for this girl, and not for Cyrus. We were made of stronger stuff.

Domino settled his hand on my shoulder. He didn't say anything, but then, he didn't need to. I accepted the gesture of comfort with my chin lifted high.

"Now go," the emperor said, motioning to a door. "Eat. Drink. Celebrate your great accomplishments. Tomorrow we begin."

Tomorrow.

Tick tock.

The royals exited first. The librarian released me and stepped back, disappearing as if he'd slipped behind a curtain. Though I missed the direct contact, peace flowed between us. I might not be able to see him, but he was here, as promised. Grateful, I followed my fellow soldiers out of the ballroom into a wide, empty room with tall ceilings. Cyrus and the others remained in the area.

Miller bumped me with his shoulder and mumbled, "Let's talk later, yeah?"

I nodded, nervous and hopeful. He joined Roman and Merlot, and the trio drew together to whisper, leaving no room for anyone else. No matter. I had my sights set elsewhere.

I closed in on Cyrus, who was speaking with his half brother, neither party particularly happy about it. Their conversation ceased upon my nearing, with a nod from both men. Hmm. Cyrus's expression. I'd never seen such coldness from him.

"Lady Roosa," Felix said, giving a stiff incline of his head before striding off.

Before I could ask what that was about, Lolli sauntered over.

"Congratulations, Arden," she said with a fake smile.

"Thank you, High Princess Lolli," I said, mirroring her expression. "Shot anyone lately?"

"Many anyones." She arched a brow. "Are you referring to someone specific?"

Dang her. I pressed my tongue to the roof of my mouth.

She wasn't done. "One day, I'll be queen, and you'll be punished for your insolence."

"I warned you what would happen if you threatened her." Cyrus whipped out his arm and grabbed her by the neck.

Her eyes widened, her mouth opening and closing with only broken sounds escaping as he squeezed.

All conversations ceased, every eye on us. Shock created a dam in the river of my peace. He exhibited the same unnatural sharpness he'd displayed on the bus.

Something was wrong with him. "Cyrus," I said as gently as I was able, wrapping my fingers around his wrist. "Let her go. Please." This kind of violence wasn't like him. He exuded the same kind of hatred I'd felt for Mr. Vyle, and it helped me realize the danger of such emotions.

Cyrus blinked fast, as if trying to clear his thoughts, and released her abruptly.

As she gasped for oxygen, he popped the bones in his neck and asked me, "Why don't I show you to our room?" He sounded almost pleasant, but strain gave him a harsher edge.

"That would be nice, thank you," I said, eager to get him alone.

"This way." He slung an arm around my waist and led me away from the gaping group.

We passed through a shimmery curtain of air, entering a moving hallway. I gasped as the entire space swung to the left before settling, ending in a winding staircase.

"What just happened?" I squeaked, flattening a palm over my racing heart.

"The palace readjusts when new guests visit, ensuring they can't memorize the layout. For the emperor's trusted few, however, it returns to the original floor plan."

Wow, wow, wow. "It's, like, alive?"

"I honestly don't know."

We traversed a wide hallway with multiple doors, each flanked by armed guards. Meta of various sizes patrolled here and there. They were ferocious up close, with metal teeth and claws.

I cringed as one sniffed at me, only then noticing the portraits on the wall. The emperor, holding a jewel-studded goblet in toast. Tagin, the former king, with a spear. Some high princes. Felix, with two axes. And there was Cyrus. How distinguished he looked, decked out in a royal uniform, holding a bejeweled sword.

"Hey, what were you and Felix discussing?" I asked.

"We agreed to be the last two royals standing."

A secret alliance. *Smart.*

Cyrus led me to the farthest entrance, which opened automatically as we approached. We swept inside an opulent chamber with antique furnishings I'd only ever seen in history books. Polished wood, fine fabrics woven with bold colors, and massive portraits of only Cyrus hanging along papered walls.

As soon as the door shut behind us, he heaved a heavy sigh and scrubbed a hand over his face. "I didn't mean to go so far with Lolli. One moment I intended to respond verbally, the next I held her throat in my hand, whispers of '*kill her*' filling my head."

Only one explanation made sense. "Astan." I took his wrists and guided his arms around me, stepping closer to put us chest to chest. "He's influencing you." Exactly as Domino had said.

"I'll work harder to guard against him." Cyrus tangled his fingers in my hair and angled me to ensure I looked only at him. "Tell me again you'll never leave me."

"I'll never leave you."

A tinge of relief. "I need to kiss you right now, but I would be kissing Domino, too, would I not?" He searched my gaze. "I can almost see him in your eyes."

"He's here with me, yes." I refused to lie to him.

With a huff of resentment, Cyrus released me. "Let me show you what we're up against." He stalked to a set of double doors, opened them, and motioned me through.

I passed him, ignoring my dismay and stepping onto a wide balcony. Our room occupied the top floor on the east side of the palace, allowing us to peer down at the grounds and beyond the dome.

My mouth hung open in disbelief. From this vantage point, I saw the battlefield, the berries now shielded by that protective barrier. A sea of feeders attacked the contingent of glowers assembled there, the two engaged in fierce combat.

"We've got to help them," I said, white-knuckling the railing. "Maybe there's a switch to shut off the frequency. Lolli could have it. Her men set up the equipment needed to create the shield."

"Judging by things I've overheard her say, there's a single doorway, but whoever opens it experiences unmitigated pain."

Chapter Seventeen

I'm looking for people willing to do the necessary work and rise in the ranks of the kingdom; apply within.

—*The Book of Soal* 2.1.4.19

Tick tock. Tick tock.

My internal countdown made itself known, screeching at full volume as I considered our options. Or rather, option. Find that key and sneak to the field. If it hurt to open the door, fine. It hurt. I'd do it and I'd deal.

But first we needed to discover what, exactly, that key was. "Introduce me to your grandfather," I said as wind lifted my hair.

Cyrus arched a brow. "You hope to interrogate the ruler of our world?"

"I do."

To his credit, he didn't blanch. "Will you be subtle with your questions?"

Okay, so, I might have been a tad overzealous during my previous interrogations. The very interrogations Mr. Vyle had referenced during our first interaction. A time I'd rapid-fired forbidden questions at CURED's most illustrious leaders. "I promise I'll try my very best."

He sighed. "I'll set something up."

As other royals and trainees stepped out onto their balconies, Cyrus linked our fingers and backtracked, pulling me into our room. The door shut of its own accord, and his shoulders rolled in.

He released me and muttered, "We are losing this war."

No. No! That was Astan's influence. It must be. "We're still breathing, Cyrus. We haven't lost anything."

He stalked to a wet bar and poured himself a drink. After downing it, he poured another and downed it too. "Would you like one?" he asked with a flat timbre.

"No, thank you." I'd tried a coworker's home brew a year ago, and I'd hated how out of control I'd felt.

Cyrus poured a third glass, lifted it, set it down. Lifted it. Set it down. Gripping the edges of the bar, he bowed his head.

Desperate to give comfort, I closed the distance and wrapped my arms around him from behind. With my palms flat on his torso, I rested my cheek between his shoulders, suddenly overcome with tenderness. His ambrosial scent saturated the air, turning every breath into my favorite dream.

Few people got to witness his vulnerability. Only those he trusted. A small circle that consisted of me, myself, and I. My troubles were forgotten as I sought to absorb his. "Look at me, Cyrus."

For several long moments, he remained as he was, tense and silent.

"Please."

Slowly he turned, as if he couldn't resist my plea. I didn't release him or ease back but pressed closer, letting my weight settle against his powerful body. Our gazes held as I tipped up my face. As we melted into each other. As I conformed my shape to his, enjoying every ache and pang that ignited. The most delicious heat spread to my limbs. Every inhalation came with a side of intoxication. This sensation I liked.

"You aren't in this alone." I traced my fingers up his arms and over his shoulders to rest them upon his nape. "Stop trying to carry everything on your own. It's weighing you down. We aren't without hope. We have each other and Domino. Whether you like him or not, he's an asset. We have our books. Ember and her crew. A purpose and a mission."

A moment passed before he gave me a small but sweet smile. "I like this side of you. The warrior spirit I noticed your first day at Fort Bala."

His husky voice acted as embers and smoke, curling through my senses. "Is there another side of me you like?" There might have been smoke in my voice too. "Perhaps a *softer* side?"

His eyelids sank low. "I very much like your softer side." He set a hand on my hip, between the gap left by my shirt and pants, and the instant sear of skin against skin unraveled me from the inside out. "Do you remember when I said I wouldn't kiss you while you're connected to the librarian?"

My heart raced toward him, no finish line in sight, only the endless pull of his presence. "Mmm. I'm still pouting about it."

He slowly bent his head, stopping when his lips hovered directly over mine. I breathed his air, and he breathed mine, and it was the hottest moment of my life.

"I've changed my mind." He swooped in, pressing his lips against mine.

I opened, greeting his tongue with my own. A moan slipped out. He was pleasure itself, and I sipped at the well, savoring every second. We continued tasting each other, slowly at first, but soon the tempo increased. With it, the pressure inside me intensified, and I strained toward him.

We'd kissed before, but this was different. Something deeper and sweeter. A quiet storm of fire and silk. Intimacy able to steal my breath, with a fierceness that set my skin alight. And yet, beneath the longing, there was something else. A tremor of desperation. A whisper of fear . . . Perhaps a bite of recklessness and ruination.

He spun us both around, pinning me against the bar. A single kick of his foot widened my legs, allowing him to push a leg between mine. Thoughts whirled, soon fragmenting, dissolving, and evaporating.

Threading his fingers in my hair, he tipped me off balance, forcing me to rely on him.

I pulled at his shirt with grasping hands. Barely pausing the kiss, he ripped the material over his head. His tattooed pectorals drew my palms like magnets. I caressed his ribs. His lower stomach.

He hefted me onto the bar, then stepped between my legs again. Still the kiss continued, deepening. I needed more of him. Wanted everything he had to give. But. A tugging sensation. Slight. Noticeable. It erupted in my deepest depths, and for a moment, I was certain I was in the wrong place at the wrong time. That I should be . . . with Domino.

Perplexed and appalled, I wrenched from the kiss. I did *not* just think that.

Expression hardening, Cyrus backed up several steps and blustered his next breath. "You feel him." A hard statement, not a question.

Guilt and shame flared. "I think he needs to tell me something."

Domino appeared beside Cyrus a heartbeat later, ending the conversation. He glanced between us and pressed his lips into a firm line. "Ask him to show you the tome."

My brows drew together. "You have a tome here?" I asked Cyrus. What kind? Soal's books never left the library.

Cyrus's brows drew together too. "No, I—" He blinked, shook his head. "I do. I remember now."

He stalked off and returned a few minutes later, wearing a shirt and holding a thick, ancient-looking book. A small, oily shadow slithered around it, and I recoiled, instantly anxious. But calm washed over me, just as it had done earlier, chasing away the anxiety.

"My grandfather has a library similar to Soal's, and he gave me this," Cyrus said, leading us into the living room. He settled on the couch, and I claimed the chair across from him, allowing Domino to stand at my side. "I think . . . I think this is one of the reasons I lost my memories. I blacked out every time I opened it."

"That is a history told by a Soalian scribe who lived long ago, but as you can see, Astan attempts to distort the story," the librarian said.

"Read it," he instructed me, and I vehemently shook my head in denial. Black out? No, thank you. "You are connected to me, the contents unable to ensnare you as they did Cyrus."

Fine. I reluctantly requested the book, which Cyrus slid across the coffee table between us. The moment I brushed my fingers over the cover, the shadow broke apart, evaporating, as if afraid to face me. Good, that was good. Perhaps I had more power than I'd realized.

The absence of the dark haze revealed striking leather decorated with mesmerizing swirls of gold. I set the heavy tome on my lap, took a calming breath, and cracked the spine.

"You can read it?" Cyrus asked, curious.

"Yes. The title page calls this *The Rise of Harmonies*."

When I gently flipped the thick, yellowed page, I came to a hand-painted picture of a gorgeous, familiar man with a mop of curls and white wings tipped in gold. He wore jewel-studded armor.

"That is Astan," Domino said. "Among the ancients, he's known as Eos. Enemy of Soal."

I'd heard the term before, though not its meaning. I'd been told Eos was the technical name for the Madness.

I examined every detail. Something was diff— "He's without horns!"

"Correct. Those grew after his affair with Briar Rose began."

As he spoke, bowed horns grew over Astan's image on the page. "Why only then?"

"When a heart is changed, the body follows," Domino replied.

Beside me, Cyrus made a frustrated noise, and I gave him a reassuring smile. "I'm only seeing illustrations so far." The next page offered another hand-painted picture. This one of the exquisite woman I'd seen in Ember's class. Flower petals clung to her curves. From her fingertips grew curling vines blooming with lush, green leaves and ruby-red fruit.

"Briar Rose, now Astan's wife." Domino flicked his gaze to Cyrus, who watched me with a hard stare. "She's a grower, able to produce seeds. Flowers. Trees. Fruit."

That statement yanked my attention back to the book. "I'm a grower too," I rasped, dots connecting. I flinched. "She's chosen me, hasn't she?"

Domino didn't respond to my question. "When she aligned with Astan, her seeds became tainted, the same as her heart."

The next series of pages showcased paintings of Bala, Astan's pet dragon, who was far more ferocious than expected, with glittering emerald scales and eyes as bright as rubies. Those teeth . . . that spiked tail . . .

Then came Astan's most trusted council and guards. Finally, I reached text.

There were no symbols, no code. Nervous, I read the first line.

> Once upon a time, there existed a kingdom ruled by the most beautiful and powerful of creatures, where power danced in the air like stardust. Allow me to take you there . . .

Black dots wove through my vision, and I caught myself tilting forward.

"Stop," Domino said, and I immediately rocketed my attention to him. The dots faded, and I righted. "Do not read it while fearful. The emotion opens the door to Astan's essence, allowing it to weave a sticky web through your thoughts."

Yes, I'd felt that. "I understand," I told him, girding myself for the next passages.

"Continue."

I began to read once more, my emotions on lockdown. This time, when images invaded, they didn't take over my mind, and yet I was there. Living in the past, a time before and beyond.

> In this enchanting world of worlds, there lives a radiant woman named Rose. A spirit reminiscent of the wild

woods, and a queen as cherished as she is captivating.

As Rose flutters through the lush gardens, her long, white robe sparkles with diamond dust woven into the fabric. With grace and joy, she visits tree after tree, bringing them to bloom with a captivating song that embodies the very life of the land.

When a dashing figure emerges from the shadows, she startles. His potent presence causes the very atmosphere to vibrate. Despite warnings, she is instantly intrigued. His allure is undeniable, his eyes twin orbs of molten obsidian.

"Hello, sweetness," he calls, his voice as powerful as thunder and yet as gentle as summer rain. He appears carved from magic and stone as he unveils a smile known to make even the bravest of souls falter, for he is Astan, the land's former king, defeated long ago by Rose's beloved husband, Tsuri.

She is not afraid. Tsuri warned her that this being would come. The dispossessed royal cannot harm her in any way unless she steps from their territory. "You shouldn't be here. Nor should you use such an endearment with me," she admonishes. "It's improper."

Astan steps closer to the border of Tsuri's kingdom, his grin coy, mischievous. "You're right." Six golden stars light his irises. "I should wait until I've tasted you."

A blush stains Rose's cheeks, and her lips curve into a smile both smug and firm. "You never will."

Astan's grin deepens, but there's something more in his eyes. A silent promise, a challenge . . . and an invitation. "Don't be so sure. My determination is without equal."

Though Rose stands resolute in her refusal, she cannot deny a hum of attraction between them. He is perfection personified.

"Stay there if you wish, but know I will be ignoring you from here on." And so, as the sun sets on the realm of light and color, Rose continues to dance in the gardens, her song ever sweet, while Astan lingers, his desire for her blooming with fruit of its own. But her awareness of him never fades.

And so, the tale of Astan and his Briar Rose begins.

"Astan craves what belongs to Tsuri," Domino said from beside me.

My fingers tightened on the volume, nearly tearing the pages as I recalled Cyrus's use of the endearment "sweetness" the morning we'd kissed passionately in my cell.

"Read on," Domino said, and once again, I obeyed, eager to learn more.

Though I quaked, I did it. A secret affair unfolded, Astan working to paint Tsuri as a monstrous husband in Rose's eyes. When her husband warred with the other man, she fled and died. Though Tsuri poured his strength into her, bringing her back to life, she worked with Astan to destroy what remained of Tsuri. Soal meted vengeance, imprisoning Astan and those in his care.

Sympathy for Astan and his love stirred within me. He only wished to be with her.

"This is why Soal's books are not allowed to leave the library. Astan infects everything he touches, and that infection works to distort history, making him the savior and Tsuri the monster. The reason Soalians who read this without an anchor can be ensnared." The librarian patted my shoulder. "We must go."

No, no. I needed to stay here. To read on and learn more. Maybe Tsuri *was* a monster. Why not let Rose go? She and Astan clearly loved each other and—

"Close the book, Arden." The firmness of Domino's tone penetrated my awareness. "Do it *now*."

I obeyed, and the world vanished. Breathing deep, I took in my surroundings, grounding myself in the real world. Theirland. The room I shared with Cyrus. He hadn't budged from the couch or ceased observing me. Although, he now glared.

My shallow, panting breaths carried me straight to confusion. "Why did you make me stop?"

"You had begun to welcome Astan's whispers," Domino said. "In this regard, he's a grower like you, planting and watering his lies in the minds of vulnerable humans. Today, you sampled the smallest taste of his allures."

I shifted in the chair and, with trembling hands, placed the book on the coffee table. Domino was right. I *had* allowed the god's whispers. I'd been inside the Rock; Tsuri was no monster.

"We should eat breakfast and prepare for the day." Cyrus stood and strode off.

"Breakfast?" I blurted. I'd been consumed with the book all night? I twisted to glance out the balcony window, and sure enough, morning light streamed into the room.

"He needs to visit the library and read his book," Domino stated.

My brows drew together. "Do you know something we don't?"

"Always."

Frustrating librarian. Rather than press for clarification, I said, "Cyrus isn't the same guy who turned you in. A mistake he made in ignorance. I did the same to my mother, and I have yet to shake the guilt." I paused, giving my words a moment to sink in. "I trust you, Domino, with or without a bond. You are my friend, and I'm glad you're in my life. But if you do anything to hurt him, even withhold information, I'll go nuclear."

"You should learn more about your opponent before you make such a threat," he quipped. "I'm very good with bombs." He flashed a small smile that rattled me to my core, then vanished like smoke in the wind.

Grumbling under my breath, I followed Cyrus's trail. And I was proud of myself. I only cast a longing glance at the book on the coffee table twice before entering a small kitchenette, where the prince was in the process of preparing a feast of toasted sweet bread, fruit jams, and scrambled eggs. All delicacies for an average citizen like me, used to those tasteless nutrition bars. But I was more interested in the chef. He was so close, yet he felt so far away.

"I received a call while you were . . . otherwise occupied," he said, spreading an apple-and-fig mixture over the bread without looking my way. "We've been summoned to the throne room. Twenty minutes."

He didn't ask what I'd read, and I didn't explain, more worried about his distant demeanor than comparing stories. I clasped his wrist, stalling him. "You are my favorite person. That hasn't changed, and it won't. If you believe nothing else," I said, using words he'd once spoken to me, "believe I'm dedicated to you."

He cast me a quick smile that didn't quite reach his eyes. "I know you favor me, Pink."

But he wanted my love. And I wanted to assure him I'd reached that point. Yet, if I spoke the words now, when I wasn't yet certain, we'd both regret it.

We ate in silence, and I hustled to the bathroom, where I brushed my teeth, braided my hair, scrubbed up, and dressed in clean fatigues. Three seconds remained on the timer when I joined him in the foyer.

The moment I was within reach, he cupped my nape and swung me into the wall. My new favorite position. With his face hovering inches from mine, he blazed all kinds of fire at me. "I requested this before, and I'm requesting it again. I'll request it every day forever. Whatever you must do to survive, do it. Promise me."

I licked my lips, my throat going dry. Today, we began the trials, and as the emperor had noted, not everyone would come out alive. "I promise. You too. No dying, Cyrus Dolion. I have plans for you."

"Schedule me for a discussion of these plans. I demand every detail." He swooped down and pressed a swift kiss into my lips, then ushered me into the hall. Two guards jumped to attention, moving into our path.

"I'm here to serve you, High Prince Dolion," one guard said.

The other kept his attention just over my head. "This way, Lady Roosa."

They were odd, these men. Handsome and strong, but as robotic as the meta, evincing no emotion. They reminded me of the soldiers King Tagin had turned into mindless drones who obeyed his every command.

Had the emperor altered them? I couldn't ask Cyrus. He was already on the go. And wouldn't you know it, Lolli sidled up to his side, acting as if being choked by him yesterday was already forgiven and forgotten.

She winked at me over her shoulder before smiling up at him and saying something that made him bark out a laugh.

I bit the inside of my cheek. Either I trusted him, or I didn't. And really, look at everything I was putting him through with Domino.

Sighing, I followed my guard down the hall. Other trainees exited their rooms and rushed over to join us. Any meta we came across, we avoided, moving out of their way.

Only Roman appeared well rested and at ease. He slung his arm around my shoulders. "You ready for this?"

"Let's hope so," I grumbled, missing Cyrus, and yes, Domino too. A fact that filled me with immense guilt. *Anyway.* I'd rather be with the emperor, finding the key to the energy field. But that would come later.

The guard led us through a series of tunnels, archways, and winding staircases. Finally he stopped, stepped aside, and motioned to an open doorway. My knees quaked as we entered . . . a torture chamber? Crumbling stone walls, stained and splattered with dried blood. A rack and other instruments of torture waited here, there, everywhere.

"Yeah, I'm suddenly not so glad I'm here," Miller muttered.

"No one will be upset if you return to the base," Winslet retorted, doing her best to appear unaffected. Impossible, considering she'd turned ashen.

"Excuse me. I see someone I'm soon to know." Roman released me and bounded over to a beauty with the most severe case of perma-scowl I'd ever seen.

The only other female among us, other than Winslet, caught my gaze and winked. "Lolli says hi."

My eyes narrowed.

"Attention," the guard called.

All of us jumped into the correct formation and pose. Mr. Vyle entered the room, wearing his customary suit, looking quite dapper. Chipper, even. He motioned to another guard, who entered with a large box. "Each of you pick a weapon."

When my turn came, I peered into the box. Everything we'd trained with and more. What were we going to do with these?

Nervous sweat beaded my brow as a thousand scenarios dashed through my mind. We'd either act as a team or fight as individuals. Maybe feeders would flood the room, and we'd need to kill or capture as many as possible. Worst case, we'd be forced to interrogate a glower in front of everyone.

I selected the netter, the most familiar to me—and the least damaging to others.

"We have a problem," Mr. Vyle announced. "There are twenty of you, but we need only fifteen."

Tensions rose in an instant.

"You will take care of the problem however you deem best." He adjusted the lapels of his jacket, merciless. "But rest assured, no one leaves this room until five of you are dead."

With a pointed glance at me, he strode from the room. The door closed behind him, sealing us in.

Chapter Eighteen

The road to destruction can be smooth, worn by its many travelers, while the road to victory is fraught with opposition; trust me, and I'll make a way through.

—*The Book of Soal* 1.19.118.8

Shock rippled through the enclosure in a series of lightning strikes. We stood frozen, all of us wide eyed, darting our focus from one face to the next, silently begging someone to tell us we'd misunderstood and didn't really need to do what we were just ordered to do. The order echoed in my skull, too surreal to grasp, too atrocious to obey. This was Madness, plain and simple. The disease in action. CURED's way. *Astan's* way.

Did they hope to prove we'd do anything they commanded, no matter what, or did the reason go deeper?

If we did this, it would be cold-blooded assassination. The mass murder of innocents. I would not, under any circumstances, be part of that. Of course, I might die within the hour.

Whatever the consequences, remember? I jutted my chin and skimmed the weapons chosen by my foes. A dagger. A whip. A sword. A spear. A harbinger. A gun that released pain darts. A mini crossbow. A triwhip. A handheld pritis cannon. A throwing star. Plus things I didn't recognize. I had the only netter, without an extra clip of ammo. Meaning, I had eight shots.

"No one strikes anyone else," Roman announced, taking charge. Something he'd done since the beginning. "One at a time, we'll state our accomplishments and qualifications, then allow others to ask questions. Anyone who attacks another before we conclude our discussion will die."

It wasn't a bad plan, but it failed to de-escalate tensions. On the contrary. The air crackled with anxiety as everyone backed away from everyone else, inadvertently forming a circle.

"No one needs to die," I said, unwilling to hold my tongue. "This has got to be another test." Yes, yes. A pop quiz, different than I'd originally assumed. "Think about it. They're eager to prove we've learned our lesson after the last go around. Never act without certainty." If we stuck together and refused to do this terrible thing, we had a chance. I drove my idea home. "They wouldn't have picked us for this special assignment if they wanted us dead. Anyone who kills innocent people could be kicked out of the program."

Many muttered their agreement.

"You know what I hear? Someone who should be one of the five," the girl who'd spoken for Lolli piped up.

The same soldiers who'd agreed with me now nodded in agreement with her. Icy fingers of dread crawled over me, threatening to steal my good sense.

"She's sleeping with the guy most likely to become king," Miller snapped. "She's exempt from this."

An attempt to help me?

"No one is exempt," the same girl retorted.

Others muttered their agreement. I prepared to respond. Until I noticed shadows slinking into the room, spilling from cracks in the walls. Then I sealed my lips. The gloom split, creating multiple paths, gliding over to check us out. I fought to hide my horror, while no one else reacted.

Revulsion eroded my calm as an obsidian tendril slithered up my leg and back to sniff my nape. It recoiled from me and swooped to

Lolli's acolyte. It must have liked her scent better, because it nuzzled her. As it did so, it faded, as if being absorbed into her skin.

I shuddered. The same disappearing act happened to others as well, each shadow choosing a different soldier to . . . inhabit? No horn had blasted, at least. And no one displayed an outward sign of what had just happened.

"Look," my accuser said, cocking her gun. "For those who don't know, I'm Lady Dollop Atmans, *cousin* to High Princess Lolli, and the identity of your bed partners means nothing to me. I care only about results."

Others nervously readied their weapons.

I forged ahead, anyway. "If cold-blooded murder is what you consider a good result, you aren't someone I'm interested in following."

"And now you insult Mr. Vyle and the emperor himself," she spat.

"Both of you hush," someone interjected. "It's not cold-blooded murder if you're protecting Ourland from a Soalian." She trained the mini crossbow on Winslet. "And you're a Soalian, I'm certain of it."

"How *dare* you?" Winslet exclaimed. She backed up several steps and raised her hands. Considering she'd chosen the dagger, she currently had no defense. "Soalians killed my dad. I want them all dead."

"Exactly what a Soalian trying to cover her tracks would say," Dollop snapped, taking aim with her harbinger. "Fact is, you tried to recruit me last night."

"That's a lie!" Winslet gasped. "You asked me what I thought of all the glowers dying, and I said—"

Boom! Dollop pulled the trigger, a bullet flying. Winslet jerked, a ragged groan escaping. Her eyes rounded, and she dropped her dagger. Looking down, she pressed her hands over a blood-soaked shirt hole near her belly.

Shock blasted me. Shock blasted us all.

"You said it was a shame," Dollop stated, as cold as ice. "Now be a good little Soalian and die."

Winslet's mouth opened and closed, crimson leaking from the corners of her lips. When her knees buckled, she fell, crashing into the floor. It happened so fast there wasn't time to react or offer aid.

"Put her on the rack," Dollop commanded.

In between pained, gasping breaths, Winslet attempted to crawl away. Two trainees advanced. "I said . . . it was . . . a shame because . . . they weren't dying . . . faster."

"Stop!" I shouted, moving to block them. "This isn't right."

They shoved me aside, clasped Winslet by her arms, and dragged her bleeding body to the rack, where they bound her wrists and ankles despite the severity of her injury. Weak as she was, she couldn't fight her way free.

Right now, Winslet's affiliation meant nothing to me. Rushing over, I sheathed the netter and removed my shirt. Cool air kissed newly exposed skin. Bra on display, I pressed the material against the other woman's wound.

"You're gonna be okay," I muttered. "You're gonna be okay."

Dollop scowled at me and raised her gun, aiming at my heart. "Don't worry, Roosa. You're next."

"Actually, you are." The retort came from Roman, who punched her in the head. Her knees buckled, and she fell, slamming into cold stone. The weapon skidded from her grip.

She moaned and curled into herself as he collected the harbinger and aimed.

"You should have listened to me." He fired, shooting her in the temple, ending her life.

Hot blood and brain matter splattered across the room, raining over my face, and I sucked air between my teeth. *Get it off, get it off, get it off.*

A dark shadow rose from her dead body, and my frenzied wiping ceased. The being zipped around the room, going faster and faster until I couldn't keep track. But I felt the moment it rammed itself into me. Cold froze my veins, and fear gobbled me whole. I stood panting, my thoughts whirling as fast as the shadow. *I'm soon to be unmasked. Killed.*

A failure to Cyrus and to Soalians worldswide. To Dom and to Ember, especially, who put their own lives on the line to save mine. My mother will mourn and grieve my loss, inconsolable. I'm going to die. The mantra played on repeat inside my mind, growing louder. Louder still.

"Obviously," Roman stated matter-of-factly as I spiraled, "Lady Dollop blamed someone else to hide her own guilt. Otherwise, she would've taken the time to be certain." He sheathed the extra weapon in the waist of his pants, but that didn't make it—or him—any less of a hazard.

Anchor, Arden!

I frowned, looked around. Domino?

Going to die.

Anchor!

The two voices collided, and realization came. The fear. It was fueled by the shadow.

I held tightly to my bond with the librarian, fury rising and drowning out the fear. The mantra quieted, and out came the gloom, shooting from me as if I'd shoved it.

I ground my teeth. Tricky Astan. His essence had brought those awful feelings.

Roman worked to free Winslet, and no one dared stop him. As he eased the wounded woman to the floor, I followed her down, keeping the pressure on the wound. Her fallen dagger. It was *right there*, beside her arm.

Hiding my actions, I collected the weapon, preventing anyone else from using it.

"There's a Soalian in this room, and it's not Winslet," Roman announced with confidence as he straightened. He took aim with Dollop's gun. "It's Miller."

Miller jostled and stumbled backward, shaking his head. "Why would you say that?"

Nearly everyone else aimed at him too. I floundered for something, anything that removed suspicion from the soldier.

"You attempted to recruit me." Roman lifted his nose in the air. "Always asking me questions and dissecting my responses to find cracks in my allegiance to CURED. I turned you in, and Archduke Heta instructed me to keep tabs on you, which I did. I followed you in Bala City and caught you looking at the Rock." He motioned to two soldiers. "Put him on the rack. Let's find out who's working with him."

The pair converged on Miller, who fought to maintain his freedom, throwing punches while avoiding theirs.

Whoa, whoa, whoa. I couldn't let them interrogate Miller. Not because he might implicate me, though he might. He could be the one Domino had prompted me to find.

"Do you hear yourself?" I shouted at Roman, doing my best not to jostle Winslet. The room went still. Roman had aided me only moments ago. Now, I returned the favor with honesty. "Nothing you've said makes him a traitor. Roman, listen to me. Please. You're making the same mistake as before, only worse."

"Restrain. Him." He glared at the soldiers, and they resumed their fight against Miller.

"I'm cured," the potential Soalian snarled after the pair trapped his arms behind his back. "That's the truth, straight up."

I didn't know why I comprehended the difference between his use of cured and CURED, but I did.

Maybe the other soldiers did as well. They showed him no mercy as they bound him to the wooden rack.

"Let's start with the easiest part. Deny your loyalty to Soal." Roman moved in front of him and crossed his arms. "Say '*I despise the Rock.*'"

Even hearing those words, I cringed inside. The thought of uttering them hurt me in ways I hadn't expected.

"Will you believe anything I say?" Miller snarled, struggling without success for freedom.

"No." Roman motioned to a trainee, who turned the crank on the rack, pulling on Miller's limbs. "But I still want to hear you say it."

Miller spit on him.

Roman wiped away the spittle, casually stating, "Who's helping you?"

Miller was too busy panting and groaning to speak.

"Are you so far gone with bloodlust, you can't grasp the incongruity of your words?" I straightened, my hand on the hilt of my netter. "You won't believe anything Miller says, but you'll still torture anyone he names?"

"Unless you want us to believe you're a conspirator, shut up." Roman pointed at the trainees. "I can't be the only one he's tried to recruit. Maybe he succeeded with one of you. Just tell me who accepted, Mills, and the pain stops."

Okay, I had a decision to make. Take him down, possibly dying in the process, or let the madness continue.

As if there was anything to consider. Still. I tried one more time to reach him. "Miller is our friend, Roman."

He offered me a fleeting smile. "That's your problem, Ardie. You see the best in people who will turn on you at the first opportunity. You failed to realize I'm not anyone's friend. I can't be. I see you all for what you are. Ticking bombs."

More nods of agreement from our spectators, and I had no words to refute him.

He pointed to our bound teammate. "You have ten seconds, Miller. Then the real hurt begins."

Very well. I had a new goal—take Roman down. With eight nets, I could hobble him and his staunchest supporters. Maybe the rest of my challengers would back off. If not, I also had Winslet's knife.

Excellent. I now had a plan. *Let's do it.*

As swift as I was able, I unsheathed the gun, aimed, and squeezed the trigger. *Click, click.*

I scrambled to check the clip, and my heart sank. No ammunition. I'd just assumed it was loaded . . . A fatal mistake I hadn't factored into my equation.

Maybe Roman noted my actions. Maybe he assumed I'd aimed at someone behind him, thinking to protect him. Either way, the attempt to use my weapon drew the notice of others and acted as a starting bell.

"She's Soalian!" someone screeched.

Ding, ding, ding. Chaos erupted all around, no one immune. *Boom! Whoosh! Click!* Grunts, groans, moans. Battle sounds blended, creating a discordant chorus. Arrows soared at me, quick reflexes yanking me out of harm's path at the last second, ensuring none of the missiles landed. Not in me, at least. Winslet, however, took an arrow to the leg and cried out, agonized.

Soldiers toppled throughout the room. Miller struggled to gain his freedom with all his might to no avail. I removed a lace from my boot and used it as a tourniquet on Winslet's leg, then leaped to my feet to cut at Miller's bonds. I didn't care if it painted a target on my back. We were past that.

One wrist freed.

Roman ran out of bullets and kicked a soldier in the face, sending his limp body flopping to the floor. He turned, ready to take on his next opponent. Spying my efforts to aid the prisoner, he confiscated a sword and marched toward me, felling another cadet along the way. Arcs of blood sprayed over a wall, triggering something. A holographic movie played in vivid color, snagging my attention. Roman got busy with someone else, seeming to forget me.

In the feed, Mykal occupied a small, windowless cell, banging her head against a wall. Crimson streaked her brow and leaked from her ears.

A whimper lodged in my throat. Was this happening in real time? Or recorded in the past?

The setting changed, revealing Victors strapped to a bed, fully awake as a man in a white apron cracked open his ribs. He screamed until hoarse and bucked against his bonds.

Suddenly I had a view of his still-beating, glowing heart. I gasped and pressed a hand over my mouth. This was the past. What had happened in captivity.

The monster working on Victors sliced into that heart and extracted a perfect, glowing stone. With a final scream, the Soalian sagged against the gurney and sank into unconsciousness.

I hunched over and emptied the contents of my stomach. By some miracle, I didn't vomit on Winslet but beyond her. The horrors Victors had endured . . .

Tears welled. I wiped them, then the corners of my mouth. Was this feed meant to distract me? Taunt me? Test me, specifically? *What, what?*

"Arden, behind you," Miller barked, working on the other wrist.

I spun just in time, dodging a trainee's swinging spear. Without pause, I drew back my elbow and launched a strike of my own. My fist slammed into his nose, and cartilage snapped. He collapsed, roaring as blood poured down his face. Roman fought two others a short distance away.

Unfortunately, my opponent wasn't out for the count. He kicked my feet out from under me, and I crashed, air exploding from my lungs upon impact. Dizziness nearly overwhelmed me, but Cyrus had trained me well. I didn't wait until my vision cleared to act; I attuned to my other senses. A slight whoosh of air signaled my opponent's approach. I blocked, then threw a punch. Contact. My knuckles rammed into his throat, a quick influx of pain blunted by a fresh tide of adrenaline. The soldier slumped to the floor, gasping for breath he couldn't catch.

Another soldier lunged at me. I leaped from my spot on the floor and punted him in the stomach. He stumbled backward, a cluster of shadows glomming on him. They must've come with a side of empowerment, because he glided to his feet with a skill he hadn't previously displayed, my dagger clutched in his hand.

I scrambled up, and he lunged again, faster. This time he slammed into me, and we fell to the floor, him on top. I twisted to evade the dagger he attempted to thrust into my gut.

Boom! He sagged over me, dead.

A new river of hot blood spilled over me as I wiggled out from under his weight. I saw Miller, holding a pritis cannon.

I offered him a quick smile. "Thank you."

"Soal for one, Soal for all," he muttered.

Confirmation! He *was* Soalian. The one I'd been searching for. The friend I'd felt so many times. We could discuss his insults later. Because he would survive. We both would.

Boom! Miller jerked, his jaw going slack. A portion of his chest was missing. His mouth floundered open and closed as he collapsed, crashing into me, taking me down with him.

I lay there, dazed and shell-shocked, as seconds passed, a light dying in his eyes. Then, suddenly, he ceased moving. I didn't . . . I couldn't . . . he . . . I . . .

Mr. Vyle's voice spilled over the intercom. "Six are dead. You may stop now."

I . . . I . . . I . . .

Medics raced into the room, working on patching up the survivors. While one worked on Winslet, another rolled Miller off me and checked my vitals. Mine, not his. I didn't speak or move. I couldn't. My trembling limbs were as heavy as boulders. He was dead; Miller was dead, and five others with him. Winslet might die too.

Tick tock.

Chapter Nineteen

I shall not die but thrive and share the wisdom of Soal.

—*The Book of Soal* 1.19.118.17

Silence pressed down on me as the survivors stumbled from the chamber, leaving behind walls soaked in blood, gore, and death. Cold air wrapped around me, biting into my bare skin. Dazed and numb, I couldn't bring myself to speak. Whether the shadows I'd glimpsed remained in the others or not, I didn't know. Now, I didn't care. All I could think about was scrubbing every inch of my body with scalding water, then curling up in bed, safe in Cyrus's arms.

Two guards stood at attention. One stepped forward to announce, "I'll escort you to your rooms."

He led us away. Everyone but me.

The second guard barred my path. "You have a meeting, Lady Roosa."

Because of course I did. "With whom?" I asked, voice raw. I wrapped my arms around my middle.

Silent, he marched in the opposite direction. Though unsteady, I followed with a single goal in mind. Maintain my bearings a little while longer. A feat I wasn't sure I could manage.

He escorted me to a frowning Mr. Vyle, who waited in front of a closed door. "Today's performance leaves much to be desired, Lady Roosa."

"I'll accept a failing grade with pride, Mr. Vyle," I replied, my tone flat.

He made no further comment as we traversed the hallway. To my surprise, he removed his jacket and settled the material over my shoulders. His warmth and scent replaced the metallic-tinged cold, but I didn't like it. I didn't remove the jacket either. I'd done enough fighting for the day.

Miller and five others were dead. Winslet might die too. I'd glimpsed some of the torment and torture Mykal and Victors had endured in captivity. The reminder knotted every muscle I possessed.

"Did the group pass your test?" I demanded. "Did we kill the right soldiers?"

"That is to be determined."

Whatever. I would learn the truth through Cyrus or Domino. "Tell me why, at least." An all-encompassing demand meant to cover everything I'd just witnessed and endured.

He didn't pretend not to understand. "There are many reasons. Let's start with the footage of your friend and the former leader of the Tome Society. It was important that you see them. There are indications you'll be with Cyrus long term. Therefore, you must comprehend what occurs to those who betray us."

Us. Meaning CURED. "Last I'd heard, Mykal and the Soalian escaped." Wasn't like no one suspected Cyrus shared behind-the-scenes details with me. "You showed me old feed."

"That doesn't make it any less haunting." A chiding note colored his voice. "She's infected with Madness. Recapturing her would be a mercy for everyone who loves her."

When a meta turned a corner, heading our way, it moved from the path, deferring to Mr. Vyle. A shock I would have explored further any other day. Here, now, I had only the strength to think, *Later.*

We rounded corners and climbed a flight of stairs, and I picked up our conversation where we'd left off. "Cyrus is the one who captured John Victors. In fact, he's the only royal to ever do so. Crown him king and let him do it again." He could dismantle CURED before Astan's horns ever sounded. No "human hosts a god" necessary.

The executioner performed a double take, as if staggered by my words. "Your loyalty to Cyrus is unmistakable, and commendable, but he doesn't need to be king to succeed in such an endeavor."

I wondered . . . Did Mr. Vyle wish to be king himself? I hadn't forgotten what I'd seen when I'd spirit-walked with Domino. Vyle, prostrate, begging Astan for power.

"You asked about my reasons for pitting trainees against each other," he said. "If you are chosen for this . . . special assignment, you'll be expected to do objectionable things without argument. At times, you'll need to invade Soalian strongholds, and when you do, you'll discover that people you trusted are your enemies. What will you do then?" Asked with a leading edge.

"I'll always do what I believe is right," I vowed.

He misunderstood and nodded, as if pleased. "Best to remember a moment of misery is a small price to pay for a lifetime of privilege."

"And what misery do you suffer, Mr. Vyle?" The question left me before I could run it through a filter.

He stopped, forcing me to do the same. Peering at me, almost agonized, he admitted, "The kind you cannot even comprehend, Lady Roosa. I'm not ashamed to admit you are a mystery to me. I know Soal courted—or courts—you, but as I said, your loyalty to Cyrus is unmistakable. And his to you. I have witnessed your resourcefulness firsthand. You are a novice, yet you are skilled enough to shed a trained tail, help a high prince defeat an army of feeders, and beguile multiple men at once. In the beginning, I underestimated you. But no longer. I'm confident you can be a major asset to us. Or a terrible enemy. If that's the case, I will wreck you without hesitation, Lady Roosa. Be assured of that."

He moved on, leaving me floored, and I had to hurry to catch up, his threat clanging between my ears.

We turned another corner, and a familiar tug ignited as if . . . no, no, surely not. But what if?

The tug flourished, as if the Rock loomed nearby. I fought to control my reactions, not wanting to give anything away. Confusion set in. I'd been assured a doorway to Soal's library hadn't yet grown here.

The tugging faded when we snaked around the next corner, but I glanced over my shoulder, mentally photographing the hallway. Multiple entrances, all closed and flanked by armed guards.

We reached another guarded door, this one made of solid gold. Mr. Vyle motioned to the watchmen on duty. They pressed a series of buttons on a wall pad, and the metal opened automatically, unveiling a chamber with high ceilings, massive marble columns, and white floors veined in scarlet.

"Astan will help you, if you'll let him. His methods might be unexpected, but his results are unparalleled." Having said his piece, Vyle strode off.

Unexpected? Unparalleled? Try disastrous.

With no idea what awaited me, I stepped into the space alone. A temple. Silence reigned, not a single sound penetrating the air. Cyrus and the other royals perched upon silver thrones, arranged along the side walls, each chair flanked by towering statues. Those sculptures represented a different god, their forms a medley of ancient power. Among them were Briar Rose and Bala, the pet dragon-thing, as enigmatic as ever.

My gaze lingered on the exquisite Briar Rose, drawn to her by a magnetic force. She wore a gown studded with gemstones and flowers. Unlike the others, she projected otherworldly grace and dignity. I might have stared at her for hours, if shadows hadn't caught my notice. They nestled against the deities as well as royals. Recalling what those shadows had done to me and my fellow trainees, I reared back, repulsed.

Every royal's eyes were closed, including the emperor's. He sat atop the only gold throne. It occupied the space in the center of the back wall, at the feet of Astan's likeness. There were no noticeable cracks in the statue. But his horns . . . I pressed my hands to my protesting stomach. They'd risen another notch.

A pregnant woman in a white gown stood at his side, with ten guards stretched out behind her. Even their eyes were closed. The woman's only piece of jewelry was a thick silver chain with a fancy wrought-iron key hanging between her ample cleavage.

A key. My breath caught. *The* key?

Only the wealth of shadows kept their eyes open. Those that cloaked the emperor, especially. They coiled around him as if they were pieces of jewelry.

Altogether, it was the creepiest thing I'd ever witnessed. Were the royals entranced? Meditating? Pondering the answer to a riddle? What?

I stood immobile, unsure what to do but knowing I needed my boyfriend as the horrors of the day came crashing into my awareness. "Cyrus?" I rasped.

The shadows fell away from him, as if shoved by an invisible force. Suddenly his lids popped open, and his attention swung to me. He frowned, appearing perplexed, and unfolded to his feet, every movement labored as if he was wading through an ocean of water. The struggle lessened the farther he got from the throne until finally he strode with ease. Concern replaced his bewilderment.

He cupped my cheeks in his warm, calloused hands and looked me over. "What's wrong?"

I bucked up, jutting my chin and pretending I wasn't ripped apart at the seams by everything that had happened. "I'll be okay." I whispered the assurance, yet my voice echoed from the walls. But would he? "Get me out of here."

"Come." Cyrus snaked an arm around my waist and ushered me from the room. He walked so swiftly, I almost couldn't keep up.

I cast a glance over my shoulder, to the pregnant woman and her key.

Cyrus and I didn't speak again until we were sealed inside our private bathroom.

"What was that place?" I demanded. "Why were you frozen like that?"

"I don't know." His guttural timbre boiled with frustration, anger, and even a hint of fear. "Let's get the blood off you."

The blood of my teammates. Whatever remained of my shock dissolved, ensuring I experienced in unison reactions I'd previously staved off. Tremors started in the center of my torso and worked their way to the tips of my fingers and toes. New tears welled. A cry lodged in my throat.

"I think we should focus on what happened to you in that temple," I croaked.

"We will. Just not now." Cyrus turned on the water. Soon, hot steam thickened the air.

My tears spilled over as he removed my bloodstained clothes and boots. I let him do it, even raising my arms to help. He shed his own as I brushed my teeth, then entered the waterfall first and drew me in behind him.

"Roman killed Miller, who was Soalian," I said, my tone going flat again. Head bowed, I stared at the black-and-white tiled floor inside the stall. The liquid spray rained over me. "Winslet might be dying. She was shot twice. Five others are already dead. We were pitted against each other in a free-for-all."

He pressed the tenderest of kisses into my brow. "It's awful. It hurts. I can't make it better. But I can clean you up and hold you, and I want to—I *need* to do that. Let me?"

"Please." The cry escaped me, and there was no stopping the heaves that shook my entire body.

Cyrus held me through it all, cooing and petting me, and when I at last quieted, he soaped me up from head to toe. His touch wasn't sexual but reverent and comforting. Loving and tender.

We'd been naked together before, but we'd been in front of others then. Here, now, we were alone, and I was fragile, as naked on the inside as I was on the outside. Never had I felt so exposed and vulnerable. The dueling sensations left me uncomfortable with my comfortability.

"Tell me a happy story about young Cyrus," I begged, desperate to hear something sweet.

He hesitated only a moment. "One of my earliest memories is of my father taking my mother, me, and Felix on a picnic. The king wasn't some big, strong commander of the world's most powerful army to us but a man who played catch and made us laugh. I still smile when I think of that day."

As he washed and conditioned my hair, I imagined him that way. Young and carefree, releasing peals of laughter, and I almost smiled myself.

Every so often, he paused to collect my tears with the pads of his thumbs and kiss the burning tracks left behind. "You will grow through this, I swear it."

"Grow," not "get." The distinction caught my attention, jarring me from my free fall into sorrow and grief. "I wish I'd known you as a little boy."

"I'd rather you know me as an old man." He shut off the water, toweled me off, and offered me clean clothes. "Tell me a happy story about young Arden."

The answer already waited at the edge of my tongue. "My most favorite memories are working on my indoor minigarden while my sister danced around me and my parents snuggled together on the couch, cheering us on." Days long past, never to be repeated.

Sadder now, I donned the T-shirt and panties while Cyrus pulled on a pair of boxer briefs. He twined our fingers and urged me into the bedroom. I didn't protest as he readied the covers and helped me slip underneath.

"Let's do some snuggling of our own." He gathered me close, and mmm, his warmth. His strength. I soaked them up, not sure how I'd ever lived without them.

As he stroked my hair, then my back, I relaxed against him bit by bit. Eventually, my muscles softened until I was molded against him, with my head resting on his shoulder and my upper half draped over his.

Though fatigued to the bone, I failed to drift to sleep. "On my walk to the temple, I thought I sensed the Rock." The raspy confession placed my exhaustion on vivid display.

"No, you sensed a rift between worlds that *leads* to the Rock."

A tidbit we could use to our advantage. "Tell me what you remember about the throne room."

He paused for a moment. Rubbed the center of his chest. "The emperor told us to sit. Obeying is the last thing I remember doing until I opened my eyes and spotted you splattered in blood, wearing Vyle's jacket."

Another blackout. Not good. "Who was the pregnant woman with your grandfather?"

Cyrus worked his jaw. "Giselle. His mistress. He keeps her in a separate wing, near his suite, on the other side of this compound. It's guarded more than any other. She and the child are his pride and joy."

"She has a key." Perhaps the key we needed, perhaps not. But there was only one way to find out. "I want it."

"You'll have an opportunity to take it. We're having dinner with Giselle and my grandfather this evening." A small smile of satisfaction flashed. "You asked for a meeting, and I'm delivering."

"Thank you, Cyrus." Truly. "I lo . . . love . . ." I opened my mouth to finish the declaration. Shut it. Shifted against him, agitated. I tried to say the words. Wanted to. I also wanted to kiss him. To *show* him. But my book. Domino.

The librarian's name whispered through every part of me, guilt and denial vying for supremacy. He was a friend, only a friend.

A friend who had helped me today in ways I didn't yet understand.

"It's okay," Cyrus said, cutting into my thoughts. "I'm a patient man, and soon enough you'll be mine. *Only* mine."

Never mind the "patient" comment. His voice. It had changed ever so slightly, frosted with the briefest hint of malice. It was so unlike him, I froze for a moment. When my mind reactivated, I asked, "You found a way to sever my link to Domino?"

"Yes," he replied, back to his normal self. "No." A growl resounded from him. "Maybe. Instructions were *right there*, at the edge of my mind, but now they're gone."

A shudder rocked me against him. I thought, maybe, Astan might be responsible for those instructions, but I saw no shadows on Cyrus. Didn't mean they weren't *in* him. And did I even *want* to sever my bond with the librarian?

I wasn't sure.

We slipped into silence and lay curled together for an eternity and a single heartbeat, wrapped into one.

He sighed. "We should prepare for dinner." As he set up, he dragged me with him. "Everything you require is in the closet."

A groan of regret seeped from me. As much as I wished to face the emperor and steal his companion's key, I didn't want to leave this bed. But this was war, not business as usual. Time to buck up.

I kissed his cheek and climbed from the bed. In a closet as big as my childhood bedroom, I found more than I needed, including a vanity with different creams, cosmetics, and hairstyling tools. I marveled at the luxurious fabric as I dressed. Tried not to sob, whimper, or go numb as I applied different products to my face and body, hiding a multitude of cuts and bruises. Cobbled together a risky plan as I pinned sections of my hair.

The emotional highs and lows created a daunting challenge, but I persevered.

I examined myself in a full-length mirror. The satiny gown clung to my curves with a scooped neckline, off-the-shoulder straps, and a cinched waist minus a diamond-shaped swatch of material on each side. A scarlet bodice tapered into a jet-black skirt, with a long slit stretching from the top of my thigh to the floor, where the gown's hem pooled.

Black stilettos studded with rubies turned my feet into a work of art. Not bad. Not bad at all.

"You stun me."

Cyrus leaned one shoulder against the closet doorway. He'd tamed his hair, but not his eyes. They glittered like gemstones, a paradox of raging heat and glistening frost. He hadn't shaved, the dark stubble on his strong jaw thicker than usual.

Desire coiled within me as he made his way over, each step slow, deliberate, and impossibly magnetic. Grimed up, he was hot. In a perfectly tailored black tux, he unraveled every thread of reason I had left.

"And you . . ." I glided my palms up the lapels of his soft suit jacket. "You defy description."

"Give it a try," he said, clasping my hips, more relaxed than he'd been since we entered enemy territory. He was an ember of desire and a whisper of devotion. "Tell me how handsome I am."

He'd seized the moment, and I would too. But where to start? "*Handsome* isn't a strong enough word. You are beyond gorgeous. Sexy but dangerous. Powerful and awe inspiring." I gently nipped his bottom lip. "Delicious."

His eyelids hooded. "And I'm yours?"

"All mine. *Only* mine."

"Well, then." He kissed me with raw, unfiltered carnality wrapped in tenderness. "That's a very good description."

"And yet it's not good enough." I toyed with the ends of his hair, holding his gaze, growing serious. "Don't listen to Astan. You won't lose me. As long as you're you, I'm yours."

"Don't worry, kitten. I want nothing to do with him." He gave me another of those sweet kisses.

"I knew this day would come, and I planned accordingly." Cyrus withdrew a velvet box from his pocket and cracked open the lid. A sparkling ruby choker graced the interior.

Delighted, I ghosted my fingertips over the gems. "This beauty doubles as a weapon, I'm assuming."

"It does. Hair up."

Lifting my curls, I held my breath as he stalked behind me and fastened the jewels around my throat, just above the clear beads. His fingers brushed my skin, a prickle of heat against the chill of metal, rousing a storm of goose bumps in their wake.

"This particular weapon slays my good sense." Cyrus advanced, prowling around me, his eyes trailing over my curves. "But that is the extent of its power."

"Then it's my favorite," I said with a grin.

A loud knock came from beyond our hideaway, shattering the moment.

He heaved a sigh. "Our escort is here. I hope you're ready for what's to come."

Deep breath in, out. Was I prepared to meet the leader of our world, who could have me killed with a snap of his fingers? "Yes. Let's do this."

Chapter Twenty

There's no need to seek revenge; let the rotten fruit fall from the tree on its own.

—*The Book of Soal* 2.6.12.19

The strangest woman served as our escort. A large crystal headpiece crowned her hair, while a porcelain mask concealed her face. Slashes of pink rimmed the eyeholes, and a dark, crimson heart stained the mask where her lips should be. Delicate flowers adorned one temple, their vines curling over the other in a mesmerizing pattern. Her flowing black robe, spun from the softest silk, trailed behind her like a shadow, rustling over the ground with every step.

No armed guards stood outside our door, or any door for that matter, as if they'd fled. No meta either.

I glanced at Cyrus, hoping for an explanation, and he delivered.

"I told you the castle rearranges often, but no one, not even those of us who fathom the layout, can find the emperor's wing without the aid of his personal servants. These individuals have been forcibly silenced, yet they are fully authorized to kill anyone who enters without permission."

"By *forcibly silenced*, do you mean they vow not to speak, or . . ."

"It's done surgically, and with their consent."

Yikes. That was hardcore. And soon I would come face-to-face with the guy who demanded such a life-altering action. With a snap of his fingers, he could order my death. I worked on my defenses the entire trek. Or I would have, if I hadn't worried for Domino.

Where was he? Our connection had dulled, and I couldn't feel him as strongly. Or at all. Had something happened to him? No, of course not. He was too powerful. There must be some other explanation.

Focus. I couldn't afford to get lost in apprehension. Shadows covered the walls, shifting as we approached, a reminder of the horrors I'd experienced inside the chamber of death. I cringed away.

"My grandfather collects them," Cyrus said in an effort to distract me, motioning to the many side tables displaying an abundance of goblets, big and small, old and new, decorated and unadorned.

The attempt to distract me worked. "Why?"

"There are rumors Astan owned a goblet made to contain water from a fountain of youth."

How interesting.

We slipped through a shimmery patch of air that filled an archway, and suddenly I spied the emperor. He wore a suit and tie, resembling an older, albeit shorter version of Cyrus. The plain but elegant pregnant woman—Giselle—stood at his side. Diamonds of various size decorated her neck, wrists, and fingers. To my disappointment, she wasn't wearing the key.

The couple waited beneath another archway in front of a large sitting room with high-backed velvet chairs and intricately carved wooden tables, their surfaces gleaming under the soft glow of floating crystal orbs that drifted lazily through the air. A grand fireplace crackled with mesmerizing blue flames that cast flickering shadows upon a mantel sculpted with battle scenes and bookshelves bursting with tomes.

Both the emperor and his companion brightened as we approached.

"Grandfather," Cyrus said, and the two men embraced. "I'm pleased to present to you Lady Arden Roosa." He waved a hand toward me. "Arden, the emperor, Piven Dolion."

"Your Majesty," I said softly, offering my best curtsy. "It's a pleasure to meet you."

"So, you're the infamous Arden Roosa." He looked me over with deep, mysterious eyes. "From everything I've observed, the Dolions either love or hate you. I'm glad Cyrus suggested we do this so I can finally pick my side."

A vague threat issued with an easy smile. I decided to laugh as if he teased me. "Prepare to be won over."

"I shall." He motioned to his companion. "This beauty is Giselle," he said, his tone softening at the same warp speed as his expression. His affection for the woman couldn't be denied. He traced his knuckles along her jawline, beaming adoration at her. "The key to my every happiness."

Jolt! Did he know I'd come for the key and now planned to toy with me?

Giselle wound her arm through his and grinned at me. "Let me set your mind at ease. He adores Cyrus, so he's predisposed to favor you."

I returned her grin, though mine faded fast, lost in a wave of nervousness. How was I supposed to introduce the field of berries, the force field, and its key without her wearing said key? "I appreciate the reassurance."

"I'm not late, am I?"

The familiar voice came from behind me. I twisted, spying Felix as he strode closer. He dazzled in a streamlined tux, his hair artfully styled and his eyes sparkling.

The brothers exchanged a swift hug, not as stiff with each other as usual but not quite friendly either.

"I hope you don't mind, Cyrus, but I invited your brother. And now that we're all here, come, come. I had Chef prepare a veritable feast." The emperor and Giselle led us into the dining room.

The vaulted ceiling was a stunner, adorned with intricate frescoes of celestial scenes and draped with shimmering silken banners that shifted color with the changing light. Gilded columns reinforced the walls. A long, polished table of dark mahogany occupied the room's center, set with silver goblets and plates resting atop brocade place mats woven with the imperial crests. Each piece of dishware reflected the warm, golden glow of an elaborate chandelier made of intertwined branches that held a glowing pritis rather than a bulb. Stained glass windows dominated the far end of the room, depicting mythical creatures in vibrant hues, their forms seeming to alter subtly as I neared. A faint aroma of exotic spices hinted at the lavish feast soon to be served, while the air carried a faint melody as refined as the decor.

The emperor claimed the head of the table, with Giselle at his right. Cyrus offered me the seat at his left, a place of honor. Felix took the spot at Giselle's right, across from him.

Immediately, masked servants glided over to fill our goblets with white wine. Others followed with the first course, which I could not identify.

"Caviar on blini with crème fraîche," Cyrus whispered, as if I knew what any of those words meant.

Felix toasted his grandfather with a sardonic smile. "Only the best for us, isn't that right, Grandfather?"

"Indeed." The emperor bit into the circular . . . toasted bread? Pancake? It was covered by a white glob sprinkled with black globules.

The others mimicked him, so I did the same, tasting salt, cream, and tang with a light crunch. Mistake! I tried not to gag before gulping a little too much wine to wipe out the awful flavors.

Careful. Intoxication could blow this entire operation.

Emperor Dolion looked my way, and I schooled my expression into polite interest. "I know my son, Tagin, spoke to you about the gods before his death," he said as servants removed our plates and left us with small bowls of warm amber soup.

"He did, yes." No reason to deny it. But where was the emperor headed with this?

As if he needed a moment to prepare himself for the conversation to come, Cyrus interrupted, leaning toward me once again to clarify what I'd be eating. "Butternut squash with sage and brown butter."

Sounded delightful, and I couldn't spoon in a bite fast enough. So good. My taste buds welcomed the rich, decadent flavors.

"I'm curious what you think of this revelation," the emperor said. "It must've been a shock to learn the gods live."

"It was for me," Giselle piped up, stirring her soup. "Personally, I find Astan's fight to reclaim his world, and his woman, deliciously romantic. Overcoming eternal slumber to be together."

"That's because your heart is so pure, my darling." He kissed the center of her palm.

"I agree with Giselle." Felix's low bass gave the words added weight. "Love is worth fighting for."

Compassion rose within me. The guy had lost his wife. His beloved.

"I'm still dealing with shock," I admitted. Perfect opening. "From gods I'd once considered a myth to toxic berries to invisible force fields, everything is new to me."

The emperor didn't take the bait before a third course was delivered. Tuna tartare with avocado and sesame soy dressing, according to Cyrus, which was better than the soup.

"Earlier, when Mr. Vyle ushered me to the temple to meet with Cyrus," I said, trying again, "I noticed your necklace, Giselle. Such a lovely key."

Cyrus settled a hand on my thigh and squeezed ever so lightly. Oops. Guess I'd bypassed subtle again.

"Isn't it?" She grinned ear to ear. "Piven gave it to me."

I waited, hopeful for another tidbit, but she lapsed into silence when a servant rushed over and bent down, seeming to whisper in the emperor's ear. Though the masked woman made not a sound, unable to speak, he understood the message.

"Excuse me," he told us. "There's something in need of my attention."

Another servant hurried to pull out his chair, allowing him to stand with ease. As he strode off, an idea sprouted.

I gripped Cyrus's thigh, hoping he understood *my* message: *Cover for me.*

His brow wrinkled with puzzlement, but this wasn't the place to explain. I pulled my attention inward. If Domino could pull my spirit from my body, I should be able to shove it out on my own.

I expected a battle, but it was as easy as slipping a hand free of a glove. One moment I was seated beside my boyfriend, the next I stood within the table.

Cyrus must have recognized the change in me, because he occupied Giselle with talk about baby names. Grateful for him, I whisked along the same path the emperor had taken. It was a relief to discover he hadn't gone far. I could only be separated and unresponsive for so long before others noticed, despite Cyrus's best efforts.

The emperor and Mr. Vyle conversed in the sitting room.

"The boy. Miller," Mr. Vyle said without a speck of emotion. "He was a Soalian. The only one of the bunch. His pritis was much smaller than expected. He must have teetered on the brink of reinfection."

I pressed a hand over my aching heart. So I'd been right. Miller was the one. I wondered if a smaller pritis explained why I'd sometimes sensed his connection and sometimes hadn't.

"And the girl?" the emperor prompted, as unconcerned as his executioner. "Winslet."

"She accepted Astan's deal."

Curiosity grabbed and shook me. What deal?

"Excellent. She'll accompany us tomorrow. Astan wishes the royals to behold the Rock's progress," Emperor Dolion said. "We'll leave the trainees here. Call it a day of mourning or a time of refreshing. Whatever you feel is best."

Mr. Vyle blinked with surprise. "You'll be forced to use your key."

"Yes." The emperor cast a pining glance toward the dining room. "But I won't deny our great god his request."

Well, well. No need to try to steal Giselle's key this evening, risking everything. I'd just accompany the royals in spirit and witness the key in action. Learn how to use it. *Then* I could steal it.

"Soalians still fight to bypass the shield," Mr. Vyle pointed out.

"Good. Let them. Before the trip, we'll set up an array of pritis poles near the base. Glowers can never resist saving the lights that belong to their precious fallen."

"I'll see to it personally." Mr. Vyle took a step backward, intending to leave, only to pause. "Shall I cancel tonight's gathering?"

What gathering?

I didn't hear the emperor's response. My bond to Domino buzzed, as if coming back online, snatching my concentration. Between one blink and the next, I found myself sitting in a chair, peering at Ember, who lay in a soft, comfy bed, propped up by a mound of lace-covered pillows, with a quilt draped over her legs. The bright glow of a bedside lamp chased shadows to floral wallpaper and heavy velvet curtains. Her hair was tangled, her cheeks newly hollow, and her skin ashen, but she was awake. A book rested on her lap, its pages slightly curled, as if it had been held too tightly for too long.

How in the world had I gotten here?

"—judging time correctly," she was saying, "he'll become Astan's host within the next three days."

"Word is spreading among the rogues."

Domino's voice hit my ears. I was inhabiting his body, as before? But how? He didn't currently inhabit mine.

"They've learned odds are high that Cyrus is the chosen one," he continued, unaware of my arrival, "and they're considering executing him before it happens."

Both denial and protective instincts bristled within me. Cyrus was in danger. I must return to him. Must warn him. Now! But though I tried, I couldn't exit the librarian.

"We can't let that happen," Ember said, and I settled down enough to listen to Domino's response.

"I know. I'll guard him with my life, you have my word."

Always willing to die for the cause. A trait as admirable as it was disconcerting.

"Hold on. I sense . . ." He rubbed the spot between his pectorals. "Arden?"

"Surprise!" I must have spoken inside his head, because the words didn't come out of his mouth. "I honestly didn't mean to intrude. I was in spirit form, spying on the emperor, and boom, the next thing I knew, I was here. And before you command me to leave, don't bother," I hurried to add. "I've tried. Also, you should know the emperor plans to open the force field tomorrow. He's going to use the only key while distracting glowers with pritis poles."

A growl vibrated in my ears. "She's here with us," he told Ember before conveying my message.

So he could hear me. "Please tell her I appreciate all she's done on my behalf, and I deeply regret the pain she's endured. At the first opportunity, I intend to make it up to her."

"She's apologetic and thankful," he said, offering no more.

Men were so frustrating sometimes.

He stood, saying, "I'll instruct our army to back off the shield and others to hide near the base and wait."

"Before you go," Ember replied. "Several of my soldiers believe they spotted Victors in Theirland. As for Mykal, she remains with the exiles, but I think she's close to accepting her invitation into the Tome Society."

Excellent news.

Domino strode from the room and entered a heavily guarded hallway, the soldiers bowing their heads in deference. "You did well today, Arden," he said under his breath.

Did I, though? "Miller is dead. Winslet is fighting for her life." Speaking of . . . "The emperor told Mr. Vyle she accepted a deal with Astan."

"She's as good as dead, then."

Domino's flat statement hit like a concrete slab and must have knocked me out of his body. Suddenly I was seated at the table, panting, unable to ask the librarian about the temporary dulling of our connection. Cyrus was in the middle of a speech describing our current course.

"—pan-seared scallops with a harmony of sweet and savory. The golden-brown crust is the perfect complement to the tender, buttery interior. As you'll notice, the lemon beurre blanc is rich and velvety, adding a creaminess that elevates the flavor profile, while the tangy citrus tinge provides a pleasant contrast. The asparagus is both light and indulgent. Elegant, some might say."

Honestly, it was the most I'd ever heard him talk in one setting, and I wanted to laugh and hug him. I tucked Domino's prediction away. Now wasn't the time to consider Winslet's fate.

The emperor had returned, and both he and Giselle peered at the high prince with glazed eyes.

"You've motivated me to try it," I interjected, digging in.

Relief flashed over Cyrus's features, but so did irritation and a promise for retribution. He knew I'd been with Domino; that much was clear. There was nothing I could say to console him while we were in the presence of others.

"I don't think I've heard anyone describe a plate of food so eloquently," Giselle offered with a genuine smile, revealing a kindness I hadn't expected from someone so close to the man responsible for today's massacre.

The meal dragged on with only small talk. Nonsense chatter that meant nothing and revealed less. By the time we were served beef tenderloin with truffle mashed potatoes and roasted root vegetables—my favorite dish of the evening—followed by an assortment of soft cheeses with honey, nuts, and fruit jams, which was then followed by chocolate fondant with vanilla bean ice cream and raspberry coulis, I didn't want to speak ever again, only groan. So full! At any moment, my stomach might burst.

"I have a surprise for you, Arden." The emperor folded his napkin and placed it on his empty dessert bowl. "A surprise for all trainees. Tonight, we celebrate your accomplishments with a party."

Guess it hadn't been canceled. "How exciting."

"It is, yes. A true honor." He motioned to servants, who swooped over to pull out our chairs. "The festivities kick off in an hour, and there are things I must do beforehand."

A clear dismissal. Good. I hadn't done what I'd come here to do, but I'd accomplished far more than expected. Now, I wished to have a word in private with Cyrus.

He stood and helped me to my feet. I curtsied to Emperor Dolion and smiled at Giselle and Felix. She smiled in return. To my surprise, he did as well, but with bite. Cyrus and his grandfather hugged again, this one a bit longer than before, with the emperor whispering in Cyrus's ear.

They parted but peered at each other for several heartbeats before Cyrus nodded and stalked to me, clearly fuming. "Felix," he acknowledged in lieu of a goodbye.

"Cy-rus," his brother replied, overarticulating the syllables of his name.

We linked fingers as a masked servant led us to our room. Still no guards or dogs present. Once we were sealed inside the chamber, Cyrus stalked to the couch, sat, and bowed his head with his elbows resting on his knees, a picture of frustration, concern, and dwindling hope.

He didn't ask me what happened with Domino, as I expected, but said, "My grandfather offered me his blessing for our relationship. And the title of king."

My heart soared. It was everything we'd hoped for, served on a silver platter. "Then why are you—"

"I must first accept Astan. If I refuse, he vows to award the title—and you—to Felix."

Whoa, whoa, whoa. "He can't just award me to another man," I sputtered.

"I assure you, he can do anything he desires."

"Not to this Soalian. And honestly, sugar, that isn't even the most pressing issue." I replayed the conversation between Ember and Domino. The rogue Soalians plotting the execution of the man I loved.

Blink. I did. I loved him. I'd loved him from the beginning, but fear had cloaked the vibrancy of my feelings. Now, the knowledge sang within every cell.

"Whatever you learned from Domino," he intoned, "just tell me."

I strolled over and lifted his chin with two fingers, bringing his gaze to mine. The resolve in his heartbreaking eyes nearly broke me.

"I learned Mykal is well, and Victors might be in Theirland. Rogue Soalians suspect you are Astan's chosen, and they hope to kill you, but Domino guards you with his life." I opted not to mention the field trip. Not right now. It could wait as the other info sank in. My next confession couldn't.

He flinched ever so slightly.

"Most importantly, I realized I love you. I love you, Cyrus," I confessed, my voice a low, husky promise. Our entire relationship had been a whirlwind of training, battles, interrealm trips, tragedies, and triumphs. But this eclipsed everything. I traced the handprint brand, my favorite privilege. "Every part of me loves every part of you."

He bolted to his feet, a mere whisper away, towering over me. At first, neither of us did more than study the other. In the heels, I was taller than usual. Still not at eye level, but my lips were closer to his. Each of his heated breaths acted as a caress, igniting new flutters in my belly.

When I'd first met him, I'd grown nervous any time he'd neared. Now, he inspired so much more. Warmth and aches and desires and need. So much need.

"You said it," he croaked.

"And I meant it."

His eyelids sank low, and his mouth softened. He settled his hands on my hips and spread his fingers to cover more ground. "Marry me.

With or without the emperor's approval, with or without the title of king, I'll have you and no other."

I smiled and ran my palms up his powerful body. "You choose me over Astan?"

He fortified his grip, holding me tight. "I will *always* choose you."

A slow, burning warmth spread through my veins as I melted against him. "What about the prophecies in our books?"

"Either we're misunderstanding what we've read, haven't read far enough to see our happy ending, or we'll find a way to overcome."

His confidence fueled mine, and I nodded. "Yes, Cyrus Dolion. I'll marry you."

Chapter Twenty-One

There is a time to plant, a time to water, and a time to harvest.

—*The Book of Soal* 1.21.3.2

Awe broke over Cyrus as if he glowed from the inside out. "You said yes."

"I did," I confirmed, my grin widening.

Motions fluid, he gripped my nape and yanked me higher, closer, while swooping down and claiming my lips with his own. There was no easing me into a gentle seduction. No soft exploration. He ravaged my mouth, and I ravaged his right back.

His fingers fisted a handful of my hair, creating a pressure and pull I relished. Pins dislodged.

He spun us both around, cupped my backside, and picked me up, then tossed me onto the couch. Lips puffed, expression fierce, he tore at his jacket and dropped the garment on the floor. But soon after he began ripping at the buttons on his shirt, he paused, huffed, and scrubbed a hand over his face. "I might hate myself for saying this, but I think we should stop."

Wait. What? I sat up, panting my breaths. "Is this about Domino?"

"I don't care about your connection to the librarian anymore. We'll deal with that." He collected the jacket and stabbed his arms into the proper sleeves. Bending down, he braced one hand against the top of the couch and cupped my cheek with the other, stroking the pad of his thumb over the rise. "The party. There isn't time to love you properly. And . . ." He scrubbed a hand over his face. "There was a pre–Fall of Nations custom. From what I've read, it serves as a way to honor the one you love."

Oookay. "I'm listening."

"I can't believe I'm saying this," he muttered. "But I think we should wait to be together until the marriage vows are spoken." He arched a brow. "I'm assuming you've never been with a man."

I chewed my bottom lip. "I, um. No, I haven't."

The tenderness he beamed at me would've knocked me to the floor if I'd been standing. Slowly he lowered his face to mine and kissed my lips with gentle reverence. "Let me make your—our—first time special, as husband and wife."

His husky words burned a blush of pleasure into my cheeks. "All right. Yes."

"The wait is going to be torture." As he straightened, he pulled me to my feet. Smiling at me, he glided his strong hands over my dress, smoothing the material. He even tidied my hair, heart-wrenchingly gentle. "But I swear I'll make it worth every second."

Standing there, drinking in his gorgeous, branded face, I could finally see a path to overcome the prophecies written in our books. Tomorrow, I would help acquire Emperor Dolion's key and reclaim the field of berries. Then, whenever the horn blasted and Astan officially selected Cyrus as a host, Cyrus would refuse, no matter the consequences. He would become king of Theirland, despite this. He didn't even require the emperor's blessing. All he had to do? Publicly out himself as a Soalian, lead an army, and *take* the crown.

But would he agree? I thought he might. There was no other way to get everything we wanted without compromising our futures. Once we'd accomplished our goals, we could wed.

Think of it. Me, Arden Dawn Dolion. Cyrus, my husband. Flutters teased my belly. "Let's not tell people about our engagement just yet. We have enough on our plates."

Though he appeared disappointed, he said, "We'll do this at your pace, however you are comfortable."

"Thank you." I was about to snake my arms around his shoulders when I caught sight of Domino, his features etched with pain. Except, no. The librarian wasn't there. Our bond had dulled again.

A knock at the door ended the conversation and my musings. Time to attend the emperor's "gathering."

Cyrus and I walked hand in hand to a temple that featured a statue of Astan, midair, with massive diamond-encrusted wings outstretched, casting shadows across the room. I tried to wrap my mind around the architecture. Nothing held him in the air. Not a cord nor a base. The stone was just *there*, centered between the ceiling and the floor. More shocking, his horns had risen yet again and were now almost at full height.

I pressed my free hand over the pulse pounding in my throat. *Closer to the end than ever.*

There were other statues as well: Bala and ten hybrids. The pet dragon crouched behind Astan to watch over him, roaring at the world, ready to leap at one and all. To the right of her was a couple wrapped together in a highly suggestive lover's pose. Both beings possessed four arms each, and those arms covered a lot of ground.

To the left, two men reached for a large, round orb that hovered several inches above them, and like Astan, it had no anchor. One of the males looked to have daggers rather than fingers, while the other's fingernails coiled like whips.

A female with three legs, each from a different animal, appeared to dance in flames, while the hem of her gauzy, transparent dress rippled at her feet.

Some kind of lizard man stretched across a dais in the back, his expression projecting boredom, anger, and glee all at once.

A catlike man raised a goblet as if toasting the others, while crystal tears glistened on his cheeks.

The being next to him possessed the lower half of a warhorse and the upper body of a man. He held two swords in the air, the tips crossed.

A man with four faces rode him, looking everywhere at once. One face was that of a human with thorny protrusions, the second some kind of goat, the third what might be a prehistoric lion with two sets of razor-sharp teeth, and the fourth that of a snake-monster-thing.

In the very center of the room posed a beauty I recognized: Briar Rose. My breath faltered. Flowers coiled around her throat, while vines covered her arms and legs. Leaves and petals created a dazzling gown. Roses bloomed in her hands.

Unlike the other statues, these were made with shiny obsidian. Shadows slithered around them all, flowing in and out of cracks.

All of it left me disquieted. *Tick tock.*

"Astan's council of gods," Cyrus muttered. "Prophecy tells us Astan, Briar Rose, and two of the others will be the first to gain their freedom in the coming waves, but it won't be long before the others follow."

"Are the gods inside these specific casings? *Here?*"

"Yes and no." He lifted our joined hands and kissed mine. "These stones contain their essence, which seeps from a different dimensional plane than ours."

Like Domino and me when one of us was spirit and the other flesh, the two of us one?

Shudders rocked me on my feet. Did the statues in Ourland contain the essence of actual beings as well? Entities determined to rule our world as their own?

Deep breath in. "Let's get this over with."

Cyrus led me forward with his arm around my waist. The emperor and Mr. Vyle had yet to arrive, but everyone else was present, the royals dressed in formal attire. The trainees wore clean fatigues.

I swallowed a groan. As if I'd needed another reason to alienate them. Although, when they discovered my engagement—and my allegiance to Soal—true separation would come.

Lolli especially stunned in a slinky black gown with less material than mine and a higher-wattage sparkle. A headpiece made of obsidian created a fan of spikes. Beads dangled over her brow, resembling bangs. Rubies arranged to resemble roses circled her neck and climbed both of her arms from wrist to elbow. They also wound around her calves from ankle to knee, glittering with her every step.

Masked waitstaff flittered about, carrying trays with the most delicious-looking delicacies. Desserts, meats, and fruits never served to commoners. Still full from dinner, I wasn't even tempted to partake. Some kind of pale, sparkling beverage flowed from a fountain, and judging by the laughter coming from the trainees as they imbibed, they loved it.

Roman wobbled on his feet as he saluted Cyrus. None of the others bothered to salute at all.

Lolli spotted us and, with a grin teasing the corners of her mouth, sauntered over, selecting a drink along the way.

"Hello, Cy." She kissed his unscarred cheek and brushed her fingers over his broad shoulders, seemingly unconcerned when he stiffened. "Send your favorite accessory to play with her friends. There's something we should discuss."

I rolled my eyes. This high princess had no power over me, and we both knew it. "They aren't my friends." Roman had assured me of that.

"She stays with me," Cyrus said, tightening his hold on my waist.

I could've gloated and remained, but I wanted her to understand I no longer viewed her as a threat. More than that, I trusted Cyrus, my fiancé. "Go ahead, have your chat. You can tell me all about it later." I grazed my nails lightly over his brand in a mimic of her, and he leaned into my touch. "I love you."

"I love you too," he told me, unashamed for others to hear.

Lolli conveyed only boredom.

I sashayed off, expecting Cyrus to release my hand. To my amusement, he gave a little yank and spun me back into him. Impact pushed a laugh from my parted lips.

Expression fierce enough to startle, he commanded, "Stay where I can see you." He used a hard tone I'd never heard before, and it took the fun out of the exchange.

I gave a terse nod. "Sir, yes, sir."

He released me, and I pivoted, striding off. My heels clacked against the hard floor as I worked to school my troubled expression. The center statue drew my gaze. Those flowers. The petals appeared as soft as velvet, and my hands itched to touch.

Roman noticed my approach and did his best to sober up as he elbowed the two trainees standing with him. Acting as though we were bosom buddies and he hadn't ended a man's life mere hours ago, he looked me up and down and wiggled his brows. "If I had realized you cleaned up this nicely, I would've won you over before the HP had a chance."

His words inspired my second eye roll of the evening. "You could've tried," I retorted, and his companions scoffed.

Unoffended, he blew me a kiss and winked. "It's easy for you to dismiss my prowess when you've yet to experience its potency."

His boast earned fresh snickers from our audience.

I couldn't quite pin down how I felt about these guys, especially Roman. But. The bed-hopper was an expert at acquiring information. "Have you heard anything about Winslet's condition?"

He waved a hand through the air, dismissing my concerns. "She's fine. Only had a few scratches."

Um, had we not participated in the same blood battle? She'd had far more than scratches, thanks to a bullet and an arrow. "I got an up-close view of her injuries. If they weren't kill shots, they were the next best thing." And yes, I believed in instant healing. Look at what Ember had done for me. But she was a conduit for Soal. Those aligned with CURED were not.

"Either way, Emperor Dolion has access to special medications and treatments." Roman hiked his shoulders, the incongruity of his words escaping him once again. "I don't know the nitty-gritty details, but I did see Winslet walking around. Hey, look at this guy and tell me if you see a resemblance." He hiked his thumb at the statue of a man reaching for the orb.

I frowned as the statue's features maybe kinda sorta shifted before my eyes, molding into a profile similar to Roman's. One of the creepiest things I've ever seen.

"I'd like a word with you, Arden."

The familiar enunciation came from behind me, just as it had done before dinner with the emperor. Roman and the other trainees backed off in a hurry as I faced Felix.

I inclined my head in greeting. "May I inquire about the subject?"

"You may not." He offered me his elbow. "Come." An undeniable command.

Great. I glanced at Cyrus, or tried to. He and Lolli were gone. So much for remaining in his line of sight. Clinging to my fraying calm, I accepted the high prince's arm. "I'm glad you and Cyrus set aside your differences to aid each other."

"I've always loved my brother. I have no wish to harm him." He guided me forward, snagging a glass from a tray and passing it to me. "This is a special kind of champagne. Taste it."

Trying to unpack his words for any hidden meaning, I accepted the beverage and took the smallest sip, marveling at the effervescence. I told myself I'd had enough, that I should consume no more, yet I took another sip. And another.

"Good, yes?" he asked with a hint of satisfaction.

"Beyond." Before I knew it, I'd finished the entire glass. A huge mistake. In seconds, the bubbles migrated to my brain, and my head swam in an ocean of silliness.

"I've always loved my brother," Felix repeated, then dipped his head closer to mine and lowered his volume. "You, I'm not so enamored of."

Rude. "Thankfully, I'm not dating you." Maybe a second glass of champagne wouldn't be amiss.

"Vyle believes you might be Soalian, but I disagree. I know a CURED handler when I see one."

Me, a handler for CURED? I snorted. "You think I'm with Cyrus to spy for the emperor." I wanted so badly to build my defense and list all the reasons the prince was mistaken. The champagne said, "A fabulous idea!" But I didn't do it. I bit my tongue instead, refusing to elaborate and explain I loved Cyrus and would never betray him.

"I wanted you to know that I know." Felix stopped before Briar Rose's statue, acting as if he hadn't just insulted me. "Tell me what you've heard about her."

Wobbling on my feet, I looked up, up and took in her familiar delicate bone structure. Her high cheeks and elegant nose. Her full, heart-shaped lips and slender jaw.

"Not much," I admitted. "Only that she is Astan's wife and a grower." And the ex-wife of Tsuri.

"To the people of Theirland, she was the equivalent of Mother Nature. A beloved caretaker of the earth and its blooms. Kind to many but savage when provoked. Astan touts her as the treasure of all treasures. The prize of all prizes."

"You speak as if you've spoken with him directly."

Felix continued, ignoring my attempt to steer the conversation. "Before wedding Astan, she was married to Soal's son, Tsuri. Are you familiar with the story?"

"Hmm," I muttered, noncommittal. My heart pounded.

"Soalians tout Tsuri as a being of love and light, but if that's true, why did his wife have a torrid affair with Astan? Why did she choose Astan even after Tsuri died from healing her?"

Questions I'd asked myself. And yet, in that moment, the answer seemed so clear. "Your argument is skewed."

Felix blinked with surprise. "Is that so? Please, elaborate."

"You lay the blame for Briar Rose's unfaithfulness on the husband she betrayed." I walked a tightrope here. By defending Tsuri, I could get myself into big trouble. But I couldn't not point out the obvious, now that I saw it. "Whether he is love and light or not, she had a free will, the choice hers. From what you've described, it sounds like she had a duplicitous heart. Why not condemn *her* for the affair?"

Like me, Felix muttered, "Hmm."

A trumpet blasted, startling me and everyone else. I stiffened, thinking Astan's horns were responsible, but I breathed a sigh of relief as the reason presented itself via masked servants who opened a set of double doors to welcome the emperor. He strode into the room with Giselle at his right, Winslet at his left, and Mr. Vyle on his heels. What a sight. They each wore a voluptuous black robe, with shadows draped over their shoulders like fur cloaks.

They said nothing, and thanks to the champagne, I almost laughed at the spectacle.

They stopped at the statue of Bala and stepped onto one of her paws, which now faced up with its claws flared, providing the perfect protective railing. That paw raised until the foursome looked down upon us. While others oohed and aahed, I vacillated between shock and horror.

Though silence reigned throughout the chamber, everyone reverential, the emperor raised his fist in the air in a demand for quiet. "Many in this room will soon be presented with the honor of a lifetime. The possibility of hosting a god, their power ours. Those of you selected will have a seat at my table and wield abilities beyond imagining. I know, I know," he said. "Many of you have only just discovered these gods are real and that they wake."

Astonishment charged the air. A single phrase snared me. *Their power will become ours. Ours,* he'd said, not theirs. He meant to accept a god, as well, but which one? Not Astan, the leader, since that "honor" (currently) belonged to Cyrus.

"Look past your shock," he said. "Listen for the call . . ."

My ears twitched, and my brow wrinkled. There was nothing, no sound.

Wrong. A soft melody drifted over the airwaves. A familiar, haunting song hummed by . . .

"Arden Dawn Roosa . . ."

My gaze zoomed back to Briar Rose. The sound had come from her, her vocal cords trembling the slightest bit.

"Arden." She angled her head toward me and blinked. Her stony gaze peered into my soul. "Not as lovely as the high princess, but able to do what she never has: inspire loyalty in a king. Well, a future king."

"You're speaking. You're a statue, and you're speaking."

"Yes, but only in your mind, just as you are speaking in mine."

I shook my head, attempting to dislodge her. Had to be the alcohol.

My gaze swept the room, landing on Roman. He stood in front of his look-alike statue, staring up, quiet, utterly entranced. In fact, everyone stood in front of a statue, staring up. Trainees and royals alike. Cyrus had returned, and he, Felix, and Summit stood in front of Astan. High Princess Lolli now pressed at my side, focused on Briar Rose.

What was even happening right now?

"Let me know you," the goddess said. She shifted her position and extended a flower down to me, as if in offering.

Queasy, I rasped, "You think to choose between the high princess and me."

"I do. The problem is, Soal seeks to recruit you." The barest tendril of hatred slipped into her tone. "He's erected a hedge of energy around you, preventing me from performing a proper read."

The queasiness worsened. She sensed Soal. How long until she and the others realized he protected me not because he desired to work with me but because he already did? "Let me make your decision easier. I refuse to host you." Perhaps the wrong thing to admit to her face.

Her chuckle tinkled like bells, the amused sound seemingly genuine, telling me she was unoffended by my refusal. "That's because you haven't yet realized the truth about Soal. How dangerous and deceitful he is. How we are the only line of defense capable of defeating him."

"And yet you didn't defeat him," I reminded her. "Even now, you're trapped in stone because he bound you."

"And you think we learned nothing from our failure?" Bitterness hardened her voice, making the words as sharp as blades.

I rapidly blinked. Okay, so, I'd touched on a sore subject. Got it. "Why would you pick me?" She'd already hinted, but I wanted the reason(s) stated in full detail.

Her lips quirked. "Two reasons. You are Cyrus's chosen, and Astan is mine. But right now, the only thing that matters is stopping Soal before he ends us all, your people included. So I'll make a deal with you. Accept me, and we will reign beside Cyrus. His agreement is already secured."

Already secured?! "No," I snapped. "That's a lie."

"Refuse me," she continued, "and I'll merge with Lolli. She'll be the one at his side, and you'll be dead."

CHAPTER TWENTY-TWO

Guard your thoughts, for they pilot your heart and decide your life.

—*The Book of Soal* 1.20.4.23

I didn't recall walking away from Briar Rose or falling asleep, and yet, the next thing I knew, I opened my eyes to find myself in bed with Cyrus. We lay side by side, facing each other and still dressed in our formal wear.

Cyrus's eyes were closed. He remained so still.

His agreement is already assured.

Anger sparked and swiftly escalated into fury. On top of everything else, Briar Rose was a liar. But what was that prickling sensation on my cheek? I craned my head.

A scowling Domino stood beside the bed, his ghostly hand tapping my face. He dropped his arm to his side. "There's a problem."

Instant sobriety achieved. Heart racing, I jolted upright. "What happened? How'd I get here?" The bedroom I shared with Cyrus.

"Use the rift inside this castle and be at the Rock in nine minutes," the librarian commanded, speeding past my questions. "Both of you. It's a matter of life and death."

His harsh demeanor and stark warning sent my nervous system into a tizzy. "How are we supposed to get past the—" I pressed my lips together, going quiet. The librarian was already gone.

Argh! Did the matter involve the plot against Cyrus? I patted his cheek, frantic. He reacted not at all. "Cyrus. Sugar bear. Focus on me." The words "a matter of life and death" echoed inside my head.

When he failed to respond, I patted with more force. "Cyrus."

Nothing.

I bent my head to press my lips to his once, twice. I mean, it worked in fairy tales.

Well, well, it worked in real life too. As he blinked open his eyes, I did it again and again. Kiss, kiss, kiss. "Wake up faster," I commanded. "We're on the clock."

"Arden?" he rasped, and relief washed over me. He eased upright and looked around. "We're in our room." Confusion drenched his words. "The last thing I remember, I was speaking with Lolli."

"And I'd like to hear all about the chat while we're walking. I'm not sure how we got here either, but we've got to be at the Rock in roughly eight minutes. Domino said it's a matter of life and death."

Cyrus's eyelids narrowed, but he nodded. "All right." He kicked his legs over the side of the bed and stood.

I did the same, my skirt falling around my ankles. My knees quaked, the reality of our situation growing heavier as a chime sounded from somewhere in the palace. Anyone could have done anything to us, and we wouldn't have known. At least we hadn't lost much time, night's darkness evident through the windows.

We exited the suite. Still no guards in the hall, not ours or anyone else's, but the meta dogs were back, patrolling in pairs.

My heart nearly stopped when one looked directly at us. It gave no reaction, however, and moved on. Oookay. Had Domino hidden us from cameras?

As Cyrus and I made our way through the winding walkways, avoiding the dogs, I kept time, counting the seconds.

"Circling back to your visit with Lolli," I muttered, tracing the curve of the voice scrambler I might not ever remove.

He breathed deep as we turned a corner. "Lolli claims she isn't the one who shot you. That it was a royal behind you. A high prince."

That . . . no. I'd seen her. "She lied." Right? Sure, I'd felt pain in my back as well as my belly, but that was only because the bullet had gone all the way through me. "Let me guess. She blamed Mallow. Whose death was announced just before the shot rang out, by the way. But it's not like he can swoop in and defend himself."

"She says she didn't see the prince's face, only the emblem on his clothing."

"Do you believe her?"

"In this, I don't not believe her," he muttered, and I stiffened. "She said the emperor tasked her with freezing as many glowers as possible. That every gun she carried contained the green bullets you noticed, and if she'd shot you, you would've been unable to move until an antidote was injected."

"She lied," I repeated. Down a flight of steps we went. And yet . . . "That would mean Summit or Felix did the deed." Not unfathomable, honestly.

"It could've been a civilian who picked up Mallow's vest."

Fair point. "It could be anyone, then."

"There's more. Lolli has heard whispers about the shooter finishing what he started."

That, too, could explain Domino's "life and death" urgency. But no. Just no. "She's sending us on a wild goose chase, knowing she's responsible. Why tell you this, helping me, her competition?" And I *was* her competition, more so than I'd ever realized. "She doesn't want me accepting Briar Rose."

A muscle jumped in his jaw. "Lolli claimed she's Soalian. We left the temple last night so she could prove it. She let me see her glow."

I'd once wondered if she were Soalian, but I had discarded the notion. Discovering she was indeed my ally threw a wrench in my case against her. "She risked her life to confess, which means she suspects you're Soalian too. The fact that you didn't turn her in only verifies her suspicions."

"I did turn her in, right before my grandfather entered the temple," he said, shocking me to the bone. "There was something off about her glow. A subtle difference that left me uneasy. My suspicion proved true when Emperor Piven congratulated me on passing his test."

An excellent turn for us. "So you don't believe Lolli is Soalian, but you do believe she's innocent of my attempted murder?"

"My grandfather showed me a clip from her body cam. The trajectory of your fall says the shot did in fact come from behind you."

That shut me up. So murderous, duplicitous Lolli wasn't the culprit. Then who?

We grew quiet as we turned another corner. Soon, we would reach the proper wing. A development that deserved my full attention. How in the world were we supposed to bypass—

A thick, white cloud rounded the corner before we did, and we stumbled together. Cyrus drew me backward a step. Detecting a note of rain and earth—Domino's scent—I exhaled, peace washing over me. Help had arrived.

Cyrus placed himself between me and the perceived threat, then backed us up another step. "I don't know what this is."

"It's okay, I do." As the warmth of the fog collected around us, I clasped Cyrus's hand, weaving our fingers. "We're safe. No one can see or hear us. They don't notice the fog either. Come on."

I drew him forward, and we turned a couple more corners, finally coming to the hallway where I'd first sensed the Rock. Guards stood at the entrance, unaware of anything untoward. Except. I gently rotated the doorknob, but dang it! Secured. I guess I'd expected Domino to handle this aspect of the mission too.

Onward and upward. An ID pad was adhered to the wall, but if we dared use it, our identities would be flagged immediately. And what if we didn't qualify to open it?

"Do you have the tools needed to remove the hinges?" I asked, and it was weird, talking to him while standing between two armed guards, knowing without being told Domino would hide the opening of the door as well.

"No need." Cyrus slid the large gemstone on one of his rings aside to reveal a small cubby. He pressed the tip of his index finger inside and when he withdrew it, a thin, round . . . paper? Whatever it was, he adhered it over his ID chip.

The fog began to break apart, and my heart sped up, urgency becoming a whip at my back. "Hurry."

Footsteps sounded in the distance. A changing of the guard? Or had we been spotted?

Cyrus twisted to avoid brushing against a guard and pressed the heel of his palm into the right spot. The door opened without a problem.

"A skeleton key that logs nothing," he muttered as we entered the empty, well-lit room.

The door shut behind us without issue. I would've marveled at the rift now before me, but we'd run out of time.

We sailed through the slit of darkness that cut through the air, leaving Theirland behind. Again, there was no pain or disorientation. One moment we were in the small chamber, the next we stood in another room, this one large enough to contain an eight-by-eight section of the Rock. Though the room was enclosed, with no windows or sunshine, lush flowers bloomed from the top, scenting the atmosphere with a soft, floral fragrance. I breathed deep.

Welcome home. Relief shimmered through me, weightless and infinite, as if stardust were dissolving in the first light of dawn. Hand in hand with Cyrus again, I glanced at an engraved symbol, just glanced, yet the wall thinned into mist. The transformation had never occurred so quickly.

Together we entered a small conference room with a polished mahogany floor, a rectangular table, and cushioned chairs. Bookshelves lined the walls. A sense of rightness engulfed me, sparkling with all the love and light Felix had mentioned.

The librarian sat at the head of the table, his forearms resting on the surface, his fingers linked. Seeing him in person proved as monumental as usual. More so. The heaviness of his intensity sucked all the air from the room.

He waved to the shelves. "Pick a book. Both of you. The one that calls."

I shared a glance with Cyrus. The muscle in his jaw started jumping again.

We strode to the shelves. One side featured volumes of *The Book of Arden*. The other side featured volumes of *The Book of Cyrus*. I didn't fail to notice I had double the number of editions. A fact we would address at the right time.

"Any news about Mykal or Victors?" I asked while perusing the covers.

"Little has changed for either of them."

Well, that wasn't great, but it wasn't the worst either. I traced my fingertips over the letters etched into a tome, gasping when it zinged me. A call? Must be. In that moment, I wanted to learn what information waited inside its pages more than I wanted to do anything ever.

I lifted it with gentle hands and hugged it close.

"That one?" Domino asked. "You're sure?"

"Yes. This one." The same volume I'd read from before.

He waved to the spot beside him. "Very well. Read."

As Cyrus continued perusing his titles, I sat at the table, on Domino's right, and got to work, peering at the symbol on the cover. Like the symbol on the wall, this one opened fast and easy. Excitement speared me.

Trembling a little, I flipped through the pages. Code, code, code. One section captured my gaze for a second, third, and fourth time until I caught myself staring at the symbols. I probed every line and swirl, willing the words to open to me . . .

Nope.

Come on, come on. I stared and probed harder. Still nothing. Frustration set in, and even the code began to vanish, until the page was blank. But . . .

"Focus on our bond," Domino commanded, and I flipped my gaze to his.

Snap. A magnetic force secured me in the quiet gravity of his presence.

"Better." He nodded with satisfaction.

Wait. "Where's Cyrus?" I was alone with Domino.

"Ember requested the pleasure of his company." He leaned back in his seat and folded his hands over his middle. "It was never my intention to cause problems between the two of you."

"My relationship with Cyrus is solid," I stated. "But there's a glitch in my connection to you. Sometimes I don't feel you as strongly as other times. Or at all."

Behind him, the emperor, Mr. Vyle, and Winslet approached the wall, and I stiffened.

"Pay them no heed." Domino waved in dismissal. "You see through the Rock, which sees through the rift. The emperor senses my visit through the remnants of the fog, and he hopes to catch me coming through the doorway. He cannot see or hear us."

I relaxed, but only a little. "The woman beside him." I pointed to Winslet. "CURED healed her, the way Soal healed me."

"No, not the same way. Her body currently hosts several shadows. Within minutes of their departure, she'll acquire her injury again, only worse because the wound will be festered. She'll die in a matter of seconds."

His words whirled inside my head, flinging sorrow and anger. Dead without the essence of Astan. "Can a conduit of Soal heal her?"

"Only if she allowed it, and most Astanians will not."

Astanians. I'd known that was a word.

"About our connection," he said. "It weakens when you are entertaining Astan's thoughts. They produce a frequency."

"I haven't entertained Astan's thoughts," I retorted, offended by the very idea.

Domino didn't argue, just motioned to my book. "Fear is a lock, not a key."

"I'm not afraid," I growled. But wasn't I? Riotous thoughts churned at the fringes of my mind. I was now engaged to Cyrus, even though I'd read a snippet suggesting we would soon become enemies. What if I read something *worse*?

"The pain you experience following the right path will never compare to what you endure when you don't."

Okay, so, he obviously knew about the engagement. "You're not helping matters." I shoved the words through clenched teeth. "This is life and death, and you are spouting pearls of wisdom rather than answers."

"You will never advance to victory if you cling to the defeat. Is that plain enough for you?"

I licked my lips, the hesitation a bittersweet tinge on my tongue. Victory meant trusting Soal, no matter what. Could I really break things off with Cyrus if the god demanded it? Love for the prince roared inside me, a savage, untamed force unwilling to surrender to time or reason. But . . .

To save his life, yes, I could break things off. Forever, if necessary. So. I did it. I pulled the trigger and made the decision. Whatever I read, whatever the book told me to do, I would do, even if I must part with the man I loved. His life mattered more than anything else. Better to have loved and parted than be the reason for his eternal undoing.

Determined, I refocused on my book and gave a little squeal. The code had returned. Guess I'd made the correct choice.

After drawing in a resigned breath, I concentrated on the symbols. They morphed into letters and words, no struggle required. Excitement came rushing back, twice as intense. I set the book on the table and read. And read. Page after page opened to me, recounting a scene from my past, filled with details I'd missed in the moment and threaded with hints of what the future held.

The more I read, the wider dread opened its jaws, preparing to gobble me whole.

When I came to the end, I sat frozen, blinking at Domino, my mind like a shattered mirror, with jagged pieces just out of reach, reflecting too much and too little all at once. However much time had passed, he hadn't budged.

"You know what I read," I croaked.

He didn't attempt to deny it. "Yes."

"Felix shot me."

"Yes," he repeated.

Tears seared my eyes as I read the passage again.

> High Prince Summit shouts, "A high prince is dead, fall back, fall back." His voice cracks with panic as he herds soldiers toward CURED's vans.
>
> My heart threatens to seize. Not Cyrus. Please, not Cyrus. The very idea nearly paralyzes me.
>
> Domino finishes calling for more elites and charges back to the field, wind flaring his robe as he waves the newcomers to their assigned positions.
>
> High Prince Felix spots me. He may be behind me, but his thoughts curdle the air between us. He raises his harbinger. Hesitates. And squeezes the trigger.
>
> Agony sears my midsection. I crumple, the world tilting sideways. As I hit the ground, my blurred gaze snags on High Princess Lolli. In that moment, I'm certain. It had to be her.

"Why?" I croaked. I'd had an enemy, and I hadn't known it.

"Felix's reasons are his own, but I have permission to tell you he's a Soalian who verges on reinfection. A rogue."

"Felix is Soalian," I echoed, shocked to my core. "And he decided to *murder* me."

A tender sorrow crept into the librarian's eyes. "Every human faction has those who are good and those who are bad. We are no different."

But. Cyrus's brother wanted me dead.

I swiped at my burning eyes and jumped to the end of the passage, where the true horror lurked.

> As I stalk through the base, my focus remains on Lolli. I fail to notice the fury in Felix's eyes as he reclines against the wall. He's certain his bullet hit its mark. Knows I was healed supernaturally. But by Soal or Astan?
>
> Felix shifts his concentration to my companion, his decision clear. If he cannot kill me, he must take out his brother before the coronation.
>
> He doesn't know Cyrus's end is already set, and I'll be the one to wield the blade.

Hands quaking, I pushed the book away. No more. "Is this tidbit about the future assured, written in stone as part of my new destiny? Can it be changed?"

"Your story can always be changed, but what you cannot do is go back and alter the decisions you made in the past. Wheels have been set into motion, and they'll drag us down a certain path. But you are looking at this wrong. The passage shows you *thinking* about running Cyrus through with your sword, not actually running him through. The right question to ask yourself is this. What will I do if *he* doesn't change course?"

I stiffened my spine. Cyrus would. And so would I. "I won't kill him." I shook my head for emphasis and got slapped by my own hair. "I won't. Not ever. Not for any reason."

All gentleness, Domino told me, "Then you won't. So why worry about it?"

Frustrating man. "I joined this team to save lives, not destroy them." Especially that of someone I loved.

"You're worrying," Domino pointed out.

"But this can't be right. I didn't know I would one day stab Cyrus, so I couldn't have entertained such a thought before this moment. Therefore, this passage isn't an accurate representation of what happened."

"Your heart discerns more than you realize, especially when you read a passage of your book, which you had done before this event occurred. Far more was contained in the words than you can possibly fathom in one setting. It always takes a bit of chewing for your mind to digest everything. In that regard, you knew, and know, what's to come."

I thought back, recalling the blip of sadness I'd experienced when I'd spotted the royals speaking with Mr. Vyle, Felix among them. As if I had, indeed, known what was to come.

"Why did Soal show me this?" Why?

As proud as he was grim, Domino told me, "You were finally ready."

Chapter Twenty-Three

Foolishness is revealed with a quick temper; it is when you control your emotions that you master the circumstances too.

—*The Book of Soal* 1.20.12.16

The door opened with a whoosh. Cyrus stomped inside, glowering. But he took one look at me and evinced only concern. "What's wrong?" He stalked over, crouched in front of my chair, and cupped my cheeks, searching my eyes.

"I might stab you," I admitted, miserable. "And also, Lolli and your grandfather told the truth." The raggedness of my voice scraped my ears. "Felix shot me. He's a Soalian whose motives are still unknown."

Rage iced every inch of Cyrus, and he jerked to his full height. "I'll kill him."

"You don't have permission from the emperor." Or Soal. "You'll be disqualified and never become king. And did you miss the part about me possibly stabbing you?"

He ran his tongue over his teeth. "I have permission. And I'm not worried about what you'll do."

Okay, I'd definitely be asking more about that permission. But first, I clasped his hand and peered up at him through my thick fan of lashes. "Felix has decided to end your life instead of mine."

Cyrus worked his jaw. "He won't succeed. But he *will* pay." The rage deepened as he helped me stand. "We should go back."

"Yes." We'd go back and think. Plan. "What did you read in your book? Anything about agreeing to pretend to be stabbed by me?"

"Nothing." Flat tone, flatter expression. "The text remained coded."

Because he'd feared what he would read? Seeking confirmation, I darted my gaze to and from Domino, who watched us with obvious pity.

"Tell me Ember is racer ready, at least," I requested with a tremor.

"She's better every day and almost operating at full strength." A muscle beneath his eye jumped. "We discussed what I'd read in my book previously." Turning his palm into mine, Cyrus moved his grip to my wrist, squeezing tight, as if he suspected I might bolt.

"You mean the part about losing me?" Unease settled between us, an invisible blockade neither of us could breach.

Lids lowered to slits, he offered a clipped incline of his chin.

I wondered . . . Did Ember and Soal attempt to protect him from what I might do? Did they fight to save his life? Maybe at some point I was driven to insanity?

Domino unfolded to his feet.

Cyrus scowled at him. "Don't even think about telling me to let this go. And I don't want to hear knowledge of the ages from *The Book of Soal*, either. We're leaving."

"I have no intention of offering you advice. Wisdom isn't for fools."

The librarian's gentle rebuke told me three things. He'd expected this, had prepared for it, and could not be intimidated. He wasn't afraid of what was to come, his trust in Soal unshakable.

Strung taut, Cyrus opened his mouth, as if he meant to shout or snarl, only to go quiet.

I looked between the two men. The ferocious pull from both made me feel as if I were a knotted rope trapped in a brutal game of tug-of-war.

In the end, I allowed Cyrus to usher me to the transparent wall. I cast a glance over my shoulder. The librarian watched me, his quiet demeanor inviting me back into his orbit of peace.

Words rushed along my tongue, but they died before being spoken. I had a thousand things to say, yet I understood none of them. Better to remain quiet.

The emperor and Winslet were no longer visible through the rift. Unfortunately, a meta now patrolled in the room.

"Are you able to provide us with cover again?" I asked Domino, not letting myself steal a second glance.

"I am." He strode over and flattened his palms against the wall. "Go."

My eyes widened as his body turned to white mist, which absorbed into the wall, went through the rift, and filled the palace room. I'd known the fog came from him, but I hadn't known the fog *was* him. That *he* was the one who enveloped me. But how . . . ?

Cyrus urged me through the wall, the rift, and into the room. The fog wrapped around us, a warm embrace in a cold world.

He opened the door, the dog unaware. Though the number of guards had tripled in the hallway, we exited without notice. As we strode along the hallways, Domino remained with us. The closer we came to our suite, the faster Cyrus walked, until he stormed forward. I almost couldn't keep up.

When we reached the sitting area connected to the royals' suites, Domino's fog released us and drew back. A chill infiltrated my very being, magnifying when a meta approached us, its red eyes flickering.

"G-good boy," I said when it stopped nearby, watching me specifically.

"Go to our room and stay there." Cyrus released my hand and stalked to Felix's door. He didn't bother knocking, just shouldered his way in.

Stay here? Ha! I raced after him, skirting the meta and catching up as Cyrus yanked a sleeping, suit-clad Felix from bed and tossed him across the room. The high prince crashed into the wall, waking as he slid to the floor.

A warrior to his core, Felix scrambled to his feet, two daggers already in hand. "Well, I don't have to wonder what this is about," he quipped, not the least bit repentant. "Only how you found out."

The dog stopped at my side, recording the interaction. I froze.

"You shot Arden," Cyrus said anyway. Slow and measured, he removed his jacket and draped the material from a knob on the dresser. He rolled up his sleeves, revealing the tattoos on his forearms, utterly unbothered by the other man's weapons and his lack thereof.

"I tried to do you a favor, brother. She's ruination with a pretty face. Paid by Grandfather, commanded by Astan. Reporting your every move. You're too enamored to see it." Bitterness coated the statement. "Trust me, I've been there, and I was forced to take care of the problem in a way I will never forget."

Puzzle pieces clicked. His wife must have been a CURED plant, and *he* was the rogue glower who'd killed her. Probably after he'd discovered the truth. To cover his actions, he blamed another. Truth that wasn't the truth. Maybe before her death his wife had turned him in for being Soalian, and he'd gone through some kind of "treatment." Maybe not. But I'd bet his thirst for revenge wasn't directed at Soal but CURED.

"Arden is mine and of no concern to you," Cyrus stated.

"But *you* are a concern to me, brother. I have a goal, you see, and you play a part in it," Felix said, twirling his daggers. "Anyone who gets in my way will suffer, even you."

"Hey! There's no reason for violence," I interjected. "Sounds like you both want the same thing. And neither of you wish to be disqualified from becoming king, right?"

Cyrus jutted his chin. "I told you. I have permission to take out *anyone* who threatens my life."

"As do I," Felix grated.

A heartbeat later, it was too late to intercede. They launched at each other, the battle savage. Felix slashed at Cyrus, who parried and confiscated a dagger, then followed the disarming with a vicious punch to the face.

The high prince grunted as blood spurted from his nose, but the injury didn't slow him down. Between slashing at each other, they punched, kicked, and elbowed, grappling over the bed, throughout the space, and into the living room. No part of their bodies was excluded from the abuse.

The dog watched, never intervening.

Wounds abounded and furniture broke. Neither man showed mercy. At this rate, they would both die.

Unsure of what else to do, I went low and swiped my leg out, sweeping Felix off his feet. As he fell, I threw myself between the combatants, holding Cyrus back with an arm extended. He could've easily knocked me aside and resumed the battle, but he stood in place, glaring down at his opponent, a predator with his sights on tasty prey.

He was panting. So was I. Blood leaked from a gash on his brow, bruises already forming along his jaw.

A bleeding Felix vaulted to his feet as Lolli and Summit rushed into the room. Like us, they still wore their formal wear. They were rumpled, as if they'd just woken up.

She looked between the fighters and smiled, as if she'd just won an award. "You struck at each other. You're disqualified."

I fisted my hands, tempted to take a swing. Wasn't like *I* was in the running for king.

"I have permission," the brothers snapped in unison, and Lolli paled.

The high princess sputtered, unable to form words. When she collected herself, she faced Summit, demanding, "Do you have permission to strike at us?"

The usually amused good-time guy bared his teeth and shook his head. "I have the opposite."

So. Only Felix and Cyrus. Had the emperor expected the pair to come to blows? Did he know more than we'd realized?

"I'm not finished with you," Cyrus snapped at Felix before clasping my hand and leading me out.

"Same, brother," Felix called.

The meta followed us as we marched out, but Cyrus shut our bedroom door in its face, keeping it out. I led the high prince to the living room couch and rushed to collect the first aid kit. When I returned, I found him reclined where I'd left him, staring up at the ceiling. He stopped me as I began cleaning the gash on his brow.

"I'll do this," he said, his tone deadened. "You should prepare for the day. We spent most of the night in the library."

Pang. "We should talk about what happened."

"And we will. Later."

"Let me hold you, then." *Please.* He'd never needed comfort more.

"Later," he repeated. "I'm not currently at my best." He kissed my cheek, rose, and strode off, closing himself inside one of two sleeping units designed for couples who preferred to sleep alone in case the other broke with Madness.

I sat there for a long while, feeling more and more hollowed out from the inside. Which didn't do anyone any good. There were passages from my books to unravel.

Determined, I headed to the other room, stripped in the private bathroom, and stepped into the shower stall. Warm water rained over me, and I moaned. I'd needed this.

As I washed up, I set aside thoughts of Felix and pondered my predicted future with Cyrus. The bigger problem. How Astan intended to claim him . . . how it looked like the god was succeeding. How Cyrus and I would one day face off on a battlefield.

Forget what I might do to him. What happened to my allies before the face-off?

According to the passage: *More will die today if I don't stop Cyrus.*

In a blink, my world merged with another. I remained in the shower, but I also stood on a body-littered battlefield, with a blood-streaked Cyrus across the distance.

Shock bowed my body. This was a vision, the book passage I'd read seeming to unfold outside of time, part of the past, present, and future all at once.

"It doesn't have to end this way, Arden," a grinning Cyrus called, his taunt as shocking as his appearance. The suns highlighted his missing facial brand. The handprint was just . . . gone.

In the present, I reeled. Though I didn't move my mouth, I heard myself retort, "You're right. Walk away, and I'll spare you."

His grin turned wry even as he spread his arms and thin, snakelike shadows seeped from his fingertips, coiled up, and banded around his neck. I could only watch, dumbfounded. He'd done it. In this version of the future, he'd accepted Astan.

"I admit, your new confidence is adorable," he said.

"Isn't it?" Vision me rocked on her heels and white-knuckled her sword hilt.

Just as suddenly as the scene appeared, it evaporated, leaving me alone in the shower, quaking and nauseous. I flattened my palms against the stall wall and bowed my head, dread an oppressive weight on my shoulders.

If Cyrus accepted Astan, we would become enemies, no two ways about it. There'd be no relationship, no marriage. Only war. *Of course* I would stab him, exactly as I'd read in the passage.

A spiral of trepidation uncoiled, a barbed vine eager to pierce and poison every part of me. Why would Cyrus ever accept Astan?

Knock, knock, knock. Through the bathroom door, Cyrus called, "I've been summoned by the emperor."

I jolted. The trip to the force field. Or maybe an interrogation concerning the fight with Felix? Either way . . . "I'll be right out."

Mind whirling, I shut off the water, stepped from the stall, and patted myself dry with a fluffy blue towel. I'd envisioned discussing the trip with him, but I was glad I hadn't. Cyrus may not realize he was being influenced by Astan. I hadn't, not fully. Yes, we'd perceived some of it. But all of it?

If he'd already inadvertently accepted any part of Astan, he wasn't in his right mind. And if he wasn't in his right mind, he wasn't the Cyrus I trusted. He needed help.

Rushing, trembling, I dressed in a clean T-shirt and fatigues and tugged on a pair of socks and combat boots.

Bracing, unsure how I'd react knowing what I now knew, I exited with a cloud of fragrant steam, head high. Cyrus sat at the edge of the bed with his elbows on his knees, but he stood upon my exit. He'd showered and changed, too, and now wore a uniform like mine. His cuts had been cleaned and tended.

He was both a knife to my heart and a balm to my soul, but I met his gaze without fear, letting my love shine unguarded. Now wasn't the time to put up emotional shields. Not when I hoped to reach the core of his being, where it was pure Cyrus with no hint of the god. "Do you know what's going on?"

"No, but you get the day off." He strode over and rested his hand on my nape, brushing the ridges of my spine with his thumb. "What will you do?"

Ignore the thrill of his action. "Mmm. I think I'll lay down." My body would, at least. I still intended to accompany him; he just wouldn't know it.

"Miss me," he said, low and husky.

"Stay safe." I rose on my tiptoes to kiss his lips, then strolled to the bed, calling, "I love you. Please remember that."

He observed me as I settled beneath the covers, an odd expression on his face, as if he suspected something more was going on. "Everything will be all right, Pink, I promise." After hesitating a moment more, he strode from the bedroom.

I worked fast, shoving my spirit from my body and chasing after him. He shut the main door behind him and whistled as I slipped through. An action I didn't understand. He drew his brows together, as if confused as well.

Clacking sounded in the distance, quickly getting louder until a meta cleared a corner and took a post at the door between the two guards stationed there. With some type of gun strapped to each side, it looked as if it had wings. The number 999 was painted along its dagger-sharp tail.

"No one goes in," Cyrus told the dog. "No one nears the woman inside. I want her undisturbed. Understood." A command, not a question.

I smiled. He was taking care of me.

"Yes, High Prince Dolion," the guards said in unison. The meta said nothing, but it didn't need to. It engaged its weapons.

The other royals gathered at the end of the hallway, where they whispered among themselves. They went quiet as Cyrus approached. He and a patched-up Felix exchanged glares.

"Where'd you get the dog?" his brother demanded.

"That isn't any of your concern. *Nothing* in my life is your concern."

A nonanswer. Because he didn't know? I didn't like this. No, I *hated* this.

"You're always putting the girl's safety above everyone else's. What's so special about her, anyway?" the high princess muttered.

"Everything," he responded and motioned in the direction he intended to walk. "Shall we?"

Chapter Twenty-Four

You are a treasure beyond measure.

—*The Book of Soal* 2.3.12.7

The royals armed up and loaded onto a bus much fancier than the others. It possessed a clear roof and body, offering a full view of the outside world. No doubt the glass, or whatever it was, was maddened proof. Plush seats offered a comfortable place to rest.

Giselle occupied the vehicle already, seated up front, directly behind the driver. If she wore the key necklace, I couldn't tell. She smiled and waved at Cyrus and Felix, as happy as could be.

Confusion speared me. The emperor adored this woman. Why take her to a battlefield teeming with feeders and glowers, his greatest enemy? Especially while she was pregnant with their child.

Cyrus chose a spot in the middle, but I kept going, opting to stand in the back to observe everyone at once.

A festering, silent Lolli took the seat in front of Cyrus. A bold decision. The bruised Felix and a sullen Summit picked the seats directly across from them. The air popped with malice even I could feel. Everyone buckled in.

Mr. Vyle and the emperor entered behind an armed, blank-eyed Winslet, and I cringed. *Not the same girl.* She took the spot next to Giselle, who immediately launched into a conversation about the baby, bubbling over with excitement. Mr. Vyle sat directly behind them while the emperor remained standing, facing the royals.

"Welcome, everyone." He pressed his fingers together, creating a steeple. He wore a tunic and trousers, and other than the shadows clinging to him, he looked so average. If I'd met him on the streets, I never would have guessed his title. "This marks an important occasion for us all. Our gods are soon to make their final selection, and what happens today will play a vital role in their decisions.

"You'll need your goggles," the emperor added, motioning to the driver before claiming the seat across from Giselle and Winslet.

As everyone donned and activated their lenses, the vehicle started forward. We exited the garage and sailed along a paved road, an electrified fence on both sides of us, shutting out the world beyond. As soon as we cleared it, the road became littered with bones, articles of clothing, and shoes.

Wide-open plains stretched on one side, and mountains loomed on the other. Though there'd been a handful of zombielike maddened on the day of my arrival, none were present this morning.

Lolli repositioned, leaning against the glass to face everyone on the bus. "Briar Rose has chosen me. I've been assured."

I didn't miss the note of smugness in her voice.

Disgust twisted Felix's features, and there was no masking it. I wondered how I'd ever missed his utter contempt for CURED. He was a rogue Soalian focused only on vengeance, willing to destroy anyone who got in his way. "You can't even tempt Cyrus to forget a lowborn lady for a single hour, *Lollipop*. What makes you think a goddess wants to spend an eternity with you?"

Temper flashed over Lolli's features, but when she next spoke, she sounded as confident and carefree as before. "When I take the throne, you'll be my first casualty."

"Your threats are as fake as your orgasms," he clapped back.

Summit said nothing, just stared straight ahead, his expression set in stone, his mind elsewhere.

Cyrus remained silent as well, his emotions on lockdown. Knowing him, he'd begun to prepare for whatever trial awaited him.

The bus approached the statue of Astan, and I did a double take, my heart pumping with a sudden burst of adrenaline. The horns had risen. They were almost fully erect now, with tips a mere inch from pointing to the sky.

Urgency swept me into a whirlwind. I was running out of time, but—I—refused—to—panic. Even if Cyrus accepted Astan for whatever reason, even if we became enemies, even if I stabbed him, we could prevail. The horn blast wasn't the end, merely the *beginning* of the end.

"Glowers incoming," Summit shouted. "An entire horde."

All eyes followed the line of the high prince's pointing finger. A large shimmering blur preceded a loud *boom!*

The vehicle lurched to its side and rolled. Initial impact caused no cracks in the glass, but momentum tossed the occupants about. Only I remained unaffected, the vehicle spinning around me. I watched as Giselle clutched her stomach, terrified, unaware a muted bubble of light encased her, acting as a sort of cushion. As Cyrus bounced and jerked in his seat, buckled in. As the others were thrown about.

Even before the vehicle skidded to a halt, glowers glommed on to it, slamming their fists into the glass. No, not with their fists. Each wielded a vibrating hammer. Cracks formed and grew until the glass shattered, spraying in every direction.

Cyrus unfastened the belt and sprang to his feet, a dagger in each hand. The other royals, Winslet, and Mr. Vyle did the same as they recovered, choosing different weapons. Together, the group scrambled from the remains of the vehicle to defend the emperor and a frightened Giselle from glowers doing everything in their power to reach them. Gunshots boomed, the vibrations scattering an abundance of clouds that had cloaked two suns.

I ghosted from the wreckage, slipping into the morning light as Cyrus threw himself into the cluster of Soalians nearest Giselle, knocking several down. The fallen came up swinging swords of fire. Brutal combat ensued all around.

We were so close to the force field, to seeing the key in action. Why do this?

Once Cyrus and the others maneuvered Giselle and the emperor to solid ground, they worked to form a hedge of protection around them. The battled raged on. Emperor Piven clutched his chest, muttering, "This wasn't in the book, this wasn't in the book."

I might not understand what was going on, but I trusted Domino, Ember, and yes, Soal. They helped innocents; they didn't harm them. Cyrus knew this too. But as a double agent, he had a part to play. He couldn't give away his true allegiance, and yet, he fought back with utter savagery, ferocious with every blow, never pulling his strikes.

As he swung his daggers, they elongated, slashing more than his immediate challengers. To his credit, however, he never delivered a death blow.

I spotted Domino among the attackers. A master swordsman with expert-level skill most people couldn't wield after three lifetimes of training, and I marveled. He fought his way through the circle, reaching Giselle. She resisted as he liberated her from the emperor's clinch.

"Let me help you," he pleaded, attempting to flee with her. "You don't have to die today."

"He'll help you," I shouted, but no one heard.

"Piven! Piven!" Her struggles grew more pronounced until Domino released her. She raced back to the emperor, swallowed up in the circle of protection.

Domino ducked, avoiding Summit's swinging sword, and met my gaze, able to see my spirit despite being in his physical body. He radiated resignation and sadness.

Oops. Cyrus tripped over Mr. Vyle, who had stumbled over debris in the road. He went down, but he did it with grace, swiftly rolling to his feet and coming face-to-face with Domino.

They didn't hesitate to attack the other without a shred of mercy.

"This is your last chance," Domino snarled at him. A sudden burst of desperation arced across the connection between us. "What you're considering doing won't end well for you. Or her!"

"You seek only my misery," Cyrus shouted, deflecting a strike.

"That is a lie fed to you from the spoon of Astan."

What did Cyrus consider doing? Accepting the god?

"Leave," my fiancé commanded. "You and your kind aren't wanted here."

Just as suddenly as the battle started, it ended. The glowers leaped into the air and whizzed across the sky, disappearing.

The royals didn't relax but tightened the circle around the emperor and a sobbing Giselle, all panting, bleeding, and on alert.

"You were awfully chummy with that glower, Cy," Lolli said, ready to stab anyone who approached.

"He's being courted," Felix growled. "Same as the rest of us."

No one denied it.

"None of this matters right now," the emperor snarled, and the royals went quiet.

Rather than stick around, I whooshed to the force field. The shimmery dome pulsed with electrical power. Dead glowers and feeders circled the perimeter, in various stages of decomposition.

The sight turned my stomach, and I was glad I couldn't smell their stench. What would happen if I attempted to bypass the wall of energy without a key?

Let's find out. I reached out, stretching out my arm . . .

"Do not!" Domino's voice rang out, an intractable command.

I glanced over my shoulder, finding him mere inches away, no longer in bodily form but spirit. My chest tightened with relief. "You work fast."

"Those who come into contact with the wall die without exception, even as spirits."

Cringing, I drew my arm away. "Why did you go after Giselle? She's an innocent."

"We wished to save her from what's to come." Anguish contorted his features. "I warned her. Thrice, I warned her. She made her choice."

So many questions, no time to ask. The emperor marched his entourage our way. Everyone exuded anger, including Cyrus.

"This," the emperor said with an unmistakable growl brewing inside the word, waving to the dome, "is a defense like no other. There is only one key to enter. For Soalians, and for us." He raised his chin and squared his shoulders, then held out his hand. "This key creates a ten-minute doorway."

Winslet slapped the hilt of a dagger in his palm. With a crook of a finger, he motioned Giselle over.

She obeyed, hesitant, wiping her tears along the way. Tremors rocked her on her feet. "I . . . I know I said I wished to do this. I know it's an honor. I just . . . maybe we shouldn't. . ."

"Shh, shh, my darling." Emperor Piven gently stroked the side of her cheek. "It will be okay."

My stomach turned again. "What's he going to do?"

Domino said nothing, but then, his increasing anguish spoke for him.

"No," I said, shaking my head. "You can't let him."

"Sir," Cyrus said, taking a single step forward.

"Not another word," the emperor snapped, silencing him.

Everyone stiffened, including Giselle. Fresh tears rolled down her cheeks.

"Behold, the key." The emperor struck, driving the dagger deep into her carotid. "The sacrifice of someone you dearly love."

Giselle's blood spurted, arcs of crimson spraying.

"As you are aware," he continued, his tone educational even as a tear slid down his cheek, "feeders experience no love, and Soalians are bound by their rules." He let the body of his pregnant lover collapse to the ground, where she writhed, gasping for breath she couldn't catch, pressing her hands against her open throat. "There's no better defense for our Rock. No guards for the enemy to recruit or buy off."

Winslet grabbed the dying Giselle by the hair and dragged her to the dome.

Righteous fury brought a new wave of strength, helping me shuck off my shock and rush over. Though I did everything in my power to free the innocent woman, I failed.

Helpless, I could only observe as Winslet flung her into the dome. Upon contact, Giselle jolted, hit by volts of electricity. She shook for several seconds before sliding into the dirt, leaving a crimson trail smeared on the dome.

Each of the royals had blanked their faces, revealing nothing of their emotions. But I knew Cyrus, and I sensed the shock, disgust, and wrath churning inside him.

Smoke curled from the smears, and in that small area, the shimmer faded.

"Each of you is allowed to bring a single dagger inside. Discard everything else." The emperor walked through the opening, head high as he stepped over his lover's fresh corpse.

Everyone shed their guns, swords, whips, and bows. Lolli followed the emperor first, with Summit directly behind her. A pallid Cyrus and Felix remained behind for several beats, peering at each other before striding forward.

I entered, too, certain hot tears poured over my cheeks. I felt their sear, even in my spirit. Domino remained at my side.

"This," the emperor said, stretching out his arms with pride, "will be the new king's legacy."

My jaw went slack. The berries had begun their transformation. They'd grown together and darkened, creating a twelve-inch barrier, eight feet long. The insides still pulsed with radiant colors. More astonishing, John Victors perched at one end, tending the soil and muttering, "The end is here, the end is here."

No one else but Domino noticed him, and I realized Victors was a spirit, like us.

"Victors," I called, but he never glanced up.

"Isn't it lovely?" the emperor asked, beaming as though he'd grown it himself.

Lolli twittered with delight, drumming her fingers together evil villain–style.

"One day, I will burn the library to the ground," Summit swore.

"And you, Cyrus?" The emperor faced the group. "What will you do to the library?"

One of my hands fluttered to my throat as silence stretched.

Finally, he said, "I will formulate a plan after I've gathered every bit of information available, not spout the first whim that pops into my head." This earned scowls from all his peers but Felix, who had reverted to a blank expression. "Those books can be used against Soal and all of his followers."

My fiancé wasn't a liar. He didn't lie to anyone, ever, for any reason. Lies had teeth, and when you freed them, they came back to bite you, always. But he did know how to misdirect. This was a misdirection, only a misdirection.

The emperor smiled. "The time has come for Astan to make his final decision. War is soon to erupt in both worlds. We must be ready." He sashayed toward the opening, Winslet and Mr. Vyle behind him. When the royals attempted to follow, he held up his hand, telling them without words to remain where they were. "The gods wish to learn the truth of your mettle. Who is strongest. Who is wisest and the most resilient. Who is willing to do whatever it takes to complete a job. Today, we will find out."

"If you want to open the door and leave," Mr. Vyle announced, "you know what you must do."

The dome closed behind the threesome, sealing the royals inside.

As they darted their gazes at each other, readying their daggers, a piercing blast of a horn cut through the daylight.

CHAPTER TWENTY-FIVE

Though the field seems barren and the battle lost, do not let your hope wither, for I shall carve a path where none yet exists.

—*The Book of Soal* 1.23.43.19

The horn blast filled the enclosure, rough and raw. A bold, primal screech of rage, hate, and violence. Even in my spirit form, nerve endings screamed in protest; the pain of each wild note reverberated throughout my entire being. Ripples of agony nearly buckled my knees.

The royals smashed their hands over their ears and screamed. Domino stood in battle position, his eyes glittering with challenge as though he'd waited for this his entire life. Victors had vanished.

The nightmare lasted forever or mere seconds, I wasn't sure. My brain was currently the consistency of soup. The moment the sound tapered to quiet, realization dawned. The last sign. It had happened.

The end was here.

Astan would select his host.

The royals squared off, facing each other.

"I don't love any of you, and you don't love me," Lolli said, a quiver in her voice.

"Same," Summit proclaimed, backing up. "But I know who does." Both he and Lolli eyed Cyrus and Felix.

The brothers hadn't recovered from the horn blast as quickly as their peers. Ashen and unsteady, each held the other's bleak stare.

Horror suffused me, a merciless flood filling my throat. The emperor—Astan—had planned this. Had wanted the brothers, his grandchildren, to battle to the death. The final test, winner take all.

"You desired a go at me, brother." Felix smiled without humor. "This is your only chance. But understand this. I won't go down easy. This is my sole opportunity to dismantle the Tome Society and CURED from top to bottom. It's the only reason I live."

"CURED?" Summit gaped as Lolli bellowed, "Traitor!" Both bristled and bowed up, gearing for attack.

"Don't you dare touch him," Cyrus snarled at the pair. His exhalations grew choppier, verging on growls.

Felix jutted his chin. "Grandfather paid Tabby to spy on me, did you know that? I gave her the world, and she betrayed me as soon as I gave my life to Soal. I was forced into treatment. You cannot comprehend what they did to me in there," he shouted, spittle spraying from the corners of his mouth. "I would have forgiven my Tabby Cat. I loved her and understood she was as brainwashed as the rest of us. But to gain my release from the facility, I had to prove I'd turned my back on Soal. I didn't, not at first. I waited for his help. But days of torture passed, and he did *nothing*. Finally, I had to accept the truth. I can trust only myself. The emperor watched, beaming with pride as I did what he demanded." Agony contorted his features. "I killed her. I murdered the woman I loved." Tears streamed down his cheeks. "She begged for my help. Pleaded for my forgiveness. I struck anyway."

Sympathy and resolve flittered over Cyrus's features. "The emperor will be dealt with, but so will you. I won't be dying today. I was born to rule, and that's what I'll do. I'll wield a power not even Grandfather can subdue."

No. He wouldn't do this terrible deed. He hated CURED. Hated Astan and everything the god stood for. Cyrus wouldn't murder his own brother. He was smart; he would find another way. "We have to stop this."

"We cannot," Domino replied. "We offered each a way out. Like Giselle, they made their choice. Now they reap the consequences."

No. I didn't accept that. "Cyrus," I shouted, racing to him. Panic and fear overtook me. "Cyrus. Listen to me. Please." I jumped in front of him. Waved my arms. Nothing. No response as he and Felix braced, preparing to attack. "Cyrus!"

"You cannot stop this." Domino's sad assurance buzzed across our bond, sending me into a new tizzy of movement.

"Please, Cyrus. Whatever Astan offers, say no."

"Arden Dawn Roosa."

The familiar feminine whisper hit my ears, halting my activities. Briar Rose. Confused, I turned and scanned my surroundings. She'd sounded so close, yet she hadn't entered the dome.

Then, I felt a tug. A tug so strong it yanked my spirit backward several stumbling steps. What the—*yank*. I stumbled back another three feet. "Domino," I shrieked, digging in my heels.

He bounded over and clasped my wrists in his intractable grip, but the next tug proved strongest, dragging him with me. Closing in on the dome . . .

If I touched it, I would die. So would Domino, via our connection. I fought for our lives. Fought so hard.

It did no good.

Tug. Another several feet. Mere inches away. The next haul could be my last. "Try to save yourself," I pleaded, accepting my fate. "Help Cyrus. Don't give up on him. Look out for my mom and Mykal. Thank you for everything."

"I'm here for *you*," the librarian snapped. "Always you."

"Survive," I commanded him, wrenching free of his hold, hoping against hope. Momentum carried me to the finish line. Maybe he could recover. I braced—

And slipped through the dome without difficulty.

Astonished, I whooshed across the land, moving so quickly the terrain blurred. Then I was inside the castle, going through ceilings and walls. Into my suite. My eyelids popped open, and I gasped, jolting upright in bed. The thudding of my heart filled every inch of my body. *Buh-bum. Buh-bum. Buh-bum.* A war drum.

Though I threw myself against the pillows and squeezed my eyes shut, I didn't return to Cyrus and Domino. The librarian didn't follow me or appear.

"Arden Dawn Roosa." Briar Rose called to me once more, a clear summons.

I jolted upright again. Panting from exertion, I wrestled with the compulsion to visit her. If I could get to the garage, I could steal a vehicle and return to the dome in my physical form.

And do what?

Tears seared my eyes.

"Arden Dawn Roosa. Come to me. Now."

No more whispers or kind requests. The goddess shouted a directive that reverberated through my cells.

My limbs acted of their own accord, propelling me onto my feet. Though I resisted from the inside, my outside paid me no heed, padding into the hall, just as I was.

The guards hadn't abandoned their post. Nor had 999, the meta Cyrus had summoned before the field trip. At my appearance, the men snapped to attention, one rushing ahead to lead the way, the other following me. As we motored onward, the meta kept pace at my side.

I'd always secretly longed for a pet of my own, but I had barely been able to afford cheap, awful meal bars for my mother and myself. This meta, I'd never have to feed, yet I couldn't ditch it soon enough. Its metal frame and multitude of weapons were anything but adorable.

No one had to be told where to go; somehow, they already knew. Along the way, other trainees exited their rooms, heading in the same direction. We didn't speak. In fact, everyone else appeared entranced, staring straight ahead.

Dread pricked my nape as we navigated the maze of hallways, taking an unfamiliar-to-me route. And yet, we ended up in a very familiar place: the temple of gods. Guards stationed at the open doors allowed us to sail inside without issue. I tripped over myself when the statues came into view. They looked to be flesh and blood now, full of color and life, the stone gone as if it had never been. Yet, none had moved from their perches.

I pressed a fist against my thudding heart. Trainees spread out without prompting, approaching different deities. No one neared Astan, I noted with a shudder. The king of gods was a stunner in multicolored detail, his horns the deepest black, his wings the whitest white.

As his glittering eyes tracked my every move, he smiled, his teeth as sharp as blades. I shuddered.

"Finally, the day has come." Glee emanated from Briar Rose as she shifted, slowly extending her arm toward me. Vibrant-green vines coiled around her fingers, spreading to her elbow. Flowers of varying colors bloomed with lovely petals, unleashing a sweet floral bouquet.

A berry grew from the center of one of the flowers, reminding me of those produced by Tsuri. It glowed, though not with the same brightness. I witnessed the progression of it all, astonished.

"Go ahead. Taste," she urged. "Let me make all your dreams come true."

My chest clenched. For as long as I could remember, I'd yearned to be a grower, working alongside Ourland's agricultural giants. I'd taken special gardening courses, took extra jobs to afford the proper tools, and poured all my energy into learning my craft. I'd done my part, paying taxes on the money I made, while also paying taxes on the money I spent, while also paying taxes on everything I supposedly owned, which I'd purchased with already taxed money. Yet CURED had other plans for me and demanded more. Demanded everything, including my life.

When I was recruited for military service to pay off my mother's back taxes—money she shouldn't have owed—my aspirations died. It was then that I'd begun to wake to the truth that CURED wasn't a remedy but a disease, corrupt at its very core. So join them once again?

"No," I grated.

The berry evaporated. "My casing is gone, but I require a host to shed what remains of my prison. I choose you, Arden," she grated back.

My legs threatened to buckle under the weight of her tone. "I don't care."

"Say yes," she continued, "and I will grant you a power beyond imagining. You'll own this world and the other. Create a garden oasis as you've always yearned. Feed the entire population. Live a life you've only dared crave in secret, with Cyrus at your side. He is Astan, and Astan is Cyrus. It's already done."

Lies and bribery. It was such a human thing to do. In fact, she struck me as a woman desperate to live again, willing to promise anything to get it done. But I knew better than to accept a deal with a lying cheater.

"No," I repeated, shaking my head for emphasis. "I'm not interested in sharing my future with you." Maybe I couldn't grow flowers and berries with supernatural ability, but so what. "The emperor, Astan's number one man, murdered a pregnant woman. I want nothing to do with any of you."

"Your only other option is Soal, a horror you cannot yet fathom. Let me show you what life will be like, once he is defeated . . ."

Images invaded my mind in tightly coiled spheres, wrenching a moan from me as they unraveled. One scene after another consumed my attention, each stripping away a layer of calm.

A throne room of glitz and glamour took shape, bright sunlight streaming through stained glass, causing colorful globes to dance within the crystal walls. Precious gemstones glittered in a floor as clear and blue as an ocean. Flowers bloomed from above, raining a petal here, a petal there. A chandelier of vines hung from the center, as big as a house and dripping with pritis stones. Knowing I was the one who'd created the beauty and splendor in this dream world left my heart fluttering.

A massive dragon-like creature perched at the edge of an inner balcony. Bala, more ferocious than even visions of her promised. She awaited my command, ready to do anything I desired.

Beyond the windows stretched a garden teeming with flowers, trees, fruits, and vegetables. Happy people tended the soil, conversing and laughing as they pulled weeds. Warmth spread through me. They appeared well fed thanks to my skills.

When I spotted Cyrus, my entire being lurched. Shaded by leaves and limbs, we worked alongside people who adored us, pulling bright-orange carrots from the dirt. A dream come true, exactly as Briar Rose had promised. Me, gardening and growing. Belonging. Loved. Helping others.

A gentle breeze lifted a lock of my hair, and Cyrus tenderly smoothed it from my cheek, leaving a small streak of dirt. He snickered and playfully kissed me, spurring laughter from me. We exuded utter joy.

This couldn't be real. It was too perfect, too special. Too attuned to my deepest desires.

Cyrus was supposedly the host of Astan, yet in this vision he was nothing like the merciless brute who'd instructed an emperor to pit his grandsons against each other.

I closed my eyes, but the action only shifted the scene, unveiling a moonlit field of dewy flowers, where Cyrus and I danced, the rest of the world forgotten. We gazed at each other with intense longing but also an air of playfulness. I wore a loose, pale-pink gown encrusted with diamonds, the hem swaying over a lush plain of grass.

"You, sweetness, are my everything," he rasped in my ear.

"Am I?" I replied, a husky tease. "Prove it."

"You mean my adoring gaze, the two worlds I gifted you, and the things I did to your body this morning weren't enough?" He tsk-tsked, six gold stars flashing in his irises, there and gone.

"Excellent. You understand," I quipped, and he barked out a laugh.

"You are perfection itself. Never change."

"Never," I vowed with a smile.

He returned the smile. "You do recall those things I did to your body earlier, yes?"

"Mm-hmm." My eyelids turned heavy, sinking low as I poured myself into him. "I don't think I'll ever forget."

"I'm about to do everything all over again." He lowered his head, pressing his lips into mine.

The scene changed. No, only the woman in his arms altered. No longer was she me . . . but Lolli.

Cyrus twirled her around the ballroom, gazing at her with the same adoration.

Real me bucked up, eyes open, ready to rumble. *That is not happening!*

"It will," Briar Rose said, pulling me from the vision, "if you refuse me."

In an instant, the ballroom vanished, and the throne room reappeared, now devoid of gemstones and flowers. A cry of denial parted my lips as I took in the barren tundra beyond the window, the colorful garden gone.

A loud bang startled a gasp from me, and I craned my neck to see what had caused the noise.

Summit and Lolli stumbled into the temple, bloody and bruised, their clothing torn. My heart kicked into a wild sprint.

The door to the dome had been opened. Either Cyrus or Felix had died.

"Where is Cyrus?" I breathed out.

The royals didn't hear me. Summit knelt at the statue next to the one Roman conversed with and ducked his head. Lolli came straight to Briar Rose, dropping to her knees at my side.

"I offer myself to you, goddess," she muttered. "If you accept me, I will serve you however you see fit and work to ensure you never regret your decision."

I stumbled backward several steps, fighting a tide of sickness. Where was Cyrus? He should appear any moment . . .

Any second now . . .

"Arden," Briar Rose called, but I ignored her.

Hot tears welled, and I pressed my fingers against my quivering lips. He wasn't dead. I would know it. Sense it.

Maybe he needed help. Yes, yes. I'd gear up, go out there, and find him.

I hurried toward the entrance just as Cyrus stomped in. Oh, thank goodness! He was alive.

His gaze found me and narrowed, his lashes nearly twining. He was bloodier than the others, the brand on his face taut, his eyes stark. Grim. A wound on his throat still leaked crimson. Gashes marred his blood-coated hands. His clothing was torn in multiple places.

"Cyrus!" I rushed to him and threw my arms around his shoulders. "You survived."

"I did." For the first time in our association, he didn't hug me back. His arms remained at his sides, his hands fisted. He huffed every breath.

I cut off a cry. "Felix is dead?"

"He is." His expression didn't change, but his tenor flattened, becoming deadened. "He fought hard to kill me, but I took the necessary steps to prevail."

Domino's words echoed inside my head. *Fate forever changed.*

I patted his arm. "I'm so sorry, Cyrus." The words failed to express the depths of my sympathy.

"Come with me. There's much we must discuss." He pried me off, leaving smears of blood to cool on my skin, then turned on his heel and stalked away, expecting me to follow.

I hurried after him, countless questions pawing for release. It was a miracle I kept them under lock and key, saying nothing. Not here, not now. I couldn't turn off my mind, however. Had he rejected Astan's offer? He must have. Except, I wasn't so sure . . .

Necessary steps.

As we turned a corner, we came upon the emperor. He waited at the end of the hall, chin up, his arms behind his back. He hadn't cleaned Giselle's blood from his skin, and I shuddered.

"I knew it would be you," he said with a proud grin. "I always knew."

"Bow," Cyrus commanded without slowing a step.

The emperor lost his pride, his joy, and blanched. Though clearly grinding his teeth and stiff, he obeyed, bowing. "We'll work together, you and I, and bring Soal to his knees."

"No. *We* won't." Cyrus stopped mere inches from him and, without hesitation, palmed a dagger and slammed it into the emperor's belly. Not once, not twice, but three times.

I pressed a hand over my mouth and stumbled away from the violence, my eyes going wide with shock.

The old man gasped and toppled, twitching on the floor. Cyrus stepped over him and continued.

My brain blipped. Had that just happened? Was it another vision? It must be. Because my Cyrus wouldn't murder a man in cold blood, even someone as cold and callous as his grandfather.

"Arden," he snapped.

Floundering, I gave chase. He led me to the catacombs of the palace, into a library. Not Soal's but similar, with freshly polished wood, artifacts from eons past displayed in glass and a tree growing from the floor, blooming with shiny golden fruit.

"C-Cyrus?" I asked, uncertain, drawing my arms around my middle. "Why did you do that? Why did you kill your grandfather?"

He shot me a look, his brazen grin unfolding slowly. "Because I'll share my throne with no one."

Six golden stars flashed in his eyes.

Chapter Twenty-Six

You will find me when you seek me.

—*The Book of Soal* 1.24.29.13

"You host Astan," I gasped out, shock waves crashing through me. Astan, creator of the Madness and leader of CURED, now abided in Cyrus, who had agreed to house him. They were together, two now made one.

A new swell of horror choked me, threatening to consume my entire being.

"Yes. And no." He massaged his nape. "I agreed to do it, and I can sense him. I even know his thoughts, except they are my thoughts. That makes no sense, I know, but there's no other way to explain it. I'm still me, just better." His expression softened. "Accept Briar Rose, and I'll give you the worlds, Arden. I swear it." He cupped my cheeks as he'd done so many times before. "Be my wife. My everything. Help me destroy Soal, as we have dreamed for so long."

The more he spoke, the more it felt as if someone had scooped out my insides and salted the wounds. "Do you even hear yourself?" Destroy Soal *as we'd dreamed*?

He pursed his lips. "I suggest you watch your tone with me, sweetness."

Sweetness. Not Pink, or kitten, or even Bubble Gum, the very first nickname he'd bestowed upon me. But sweetness, the same endearment

Astan had used with Briar Rose. An endearment Cyrus had used with me before this, and in the passage of my book. More proof Astan was at the helm.

"Or what?" I snapped, uncaring about the consequences. This was my worst nightmare come to life. There was more of Astan influencing Cyrus than we'd realized. I loved this man, but he wasn't my devoted, protective, tender fiancé anymore. This man killed without remorse.

"Or I'll be displeased." Before my eyes, he schooled his expression into adoration. He traced the pads of his thumbs over the rise of my cheeks, saying, "Everything I've done, I've done for you."

A lie. The first he'd ever told me. "You did it for yourself. I begged you not to."

He forged ahead, unaffected by my declaration. "You told me to survive, so I did. I love you, and I want a life with you. That hasn't and won't change. Don't you want a life with me?"

"With you, yes." Desperately. I clasped his wrists, clinging to him, hoping to make him understand. "But I don't want a life with you *and* Astan. I told you that. Warned you. I meant it then, and I mean it now."

"You don't understand. Not yet." Leaning down, unwaveringly confident, he pressed his lips into mine. A soft, gentle act of affection. "But I'm assured you will."

A flash of those golden stars sent a chilling rush through me. "Are you even Soalian?" He couldn't be, not with Soal's enemy—our enemy—cohabiting in his body.

Another flare of irritation. "That doesn't matter." He tightened his grip. "You'll host Briar Rose, and you'll see. We were destined to rule together."

More scooping, more salt, the burn in the center of my chest almost unbearable. Destined, he'd said. My path was altered the day I bonded with Domino. Was this to be the result: a life at war with Cyrus? The very result I'd feared.

The very result my book predicted.

"Why did you accept him?" I rasped. There was no reason good enough. "Why?"

"I saw my future with and without him." He gave my cheekbones another caress, then hiked his shoulders. "I liked 'with him' better. It was the only way to keep you."

I screamed internally. "He's a liar, Cyrus. You know that. You *hate* that. Why would you believe him? I'd already agreed to marry you. I would have stayed with you forever." Now . . .

A muscle jumped beneath his eye. "His visions corroborate what I read in Soal's books."

"That's because you're missing a puzzle piece. But it's not too late to undo this." *Please, don't let it be too late.* "Renounce Astan. Refuse to host him a minute more." Could he? If all things were possible, then yes. *"Please."*

"I have no desire to do so." Cyrus released me and stepped back. His head tilted up, and his eyes closed, as if he were savoring something sweet. "The power bubbling inside me . . . I've tasted only a fraction of what's there. As soon as my body is used to it, I'll have access to the full measure. The things I'll be able to do . . ."

My hope began to wither, but still I clung to what remained. If he'd tasted only a fraction of the god's power, it absolutely *wasn't* too late to free him. The problem was, he loved this. The power-hungry man before me would never willingly relinquish an ounce of the god's ability.

Cyrus strode to a table in the back, lifted a tome, and read the spine before setting it aside. "Briar Rose requires an answer, sweetness. She's eager to enjoy her freedom, and she won't wait much longer." As he stretched his arms high in the air, the hem of his shirt rose, revealing the patch of tattooed skin between the garment and his fatigues. A never-before-seen scar, thick and raised, extended from one hip to the other.

"What happened out there?" I asked, sick to my stomach. "With Felix, I mean."

Voice harder than stone, he said, "It's not worth discussing."

As if only then noticing the blood on his hands, he frowned. With a wave at a far wall, he somehow transformed that portion of the room before my eyes. From wood panels to an open bathroom with a shelf of towels, a sink, a mirror framed in gold, and a matching shower stall, water already raining.

A bold display of the very power he praised, and a blow to what little remained of my optimism.

Cyrus gripped the neckline of his shirt from behind and pulled the material over his head. One glimpse of his familiar torso usually sent my heart skittering into a wild rhythm. Today, I looked upon a stranger. Oh, I knew those rock-solid muscles cut by years of training and battle intimately. Knew the treetop tattoo, with its branches riding the length of his arms, displaying flower buds that appeared to bloom before my eyes.

He stripped completely, utterly unabashed, and walked into the spray. Winking at me, he all but purred, "Join me. I'll make you glad you did."

My nails cut into my palms. "Only yesterday, you preferred to wait until our marriage."

"We can be married today, if you'll agree to host Briar Rose. There's no reason to wait."

There was no reason to reiterate my refusal of Briar Rose either.

"You should clean up, if nothing else," he said, undisturbed by my silence. "We have much to do."

Remembering I was streaked with blood, I stalked to the sink, where the mirror hung. I flinched. Oh, yes. Scarlet smeared my cheeks.

Mouth dry, I swiped and wet a rag, then soaped my face. "Worth discussing or not, I'd like to hear the details of what happened inside the energy field."

"Very well." His indulgent tone suggested he did this solely to please me. He shut off the water and snatched a towel. Drying off, he grated, "As I grappled with Felix, I couldn't bring myself to deliver the killing blow. My reluctance allowed him to gain the upper hand, and he injured me. I was dying, we both knew it. He bragged that the first thing he would do as king is make you an example and take your head. That was when Astan showed me your future if I let myself die."

My insides flash froze. Cyrus, dying. How close I'd come to losing him. "Go on," I croaked.

He tossed the towel to the floor, withdrew clean clothing from a rack that suddenly replaced a wall, and dressed with stiff, forceful jerks. "He showed me you would escape death at Felix's hand . . . and marry Domino."

In other words, the god had used another lie to bait him. I growled internally. "My relationship with Domino isn't like that." I'd given Cyrus my heart. My loyalty. Faithfulness wasn't an option but a certainty.

"Your relationship with Domino will *never* be like that. You are mine." Cyrus swooped in, cupping my cheeks again. The golden stars lit up his eyes and stayed put as he studied me. "I am yours. Say it. Say those words."

I meant to pull away. To protest. I leaned closer, studying him in turn. Those stars. They spun, slowly at first, then faster and faster until becoming rings. *Mesmerizing.* Warmth cascaded through me, relaxing tense muscles.

"Say it." The husky entreaty tickled my ears.

Yes. There was nothing I yearned to do more. I loved and adored this man. Our future was now and forever. "You are . . . I . . ." A buzzing sensation in the center of my chest seized my attention, halting my affirmation. What in the world?

In the ensuing pause, I saw past the spinning and into an endless pool of writhing shadows. My horror returned, a sudden revelation shocking me to the core. This. This was how he'd won Rose. *She's under his spell.*

"Say it, Arden." An unmistakable command this time, anger frothing within the words.

And what would come next, hmm? Giving Briar Rose permission to inhabit me? "No," I stated. "I will never be Astan's."

His eyelids slitted. "You want the librarian."

I opened and closed my mouth, saying nothing, thinking nothing.

"Perhaps you require a peek into Domino's future." Again, Cyrus waved a hand toward a wall. A hard jerk of his arm. In a mimic of the Rock, that wall became a screen that showcased something happening beyond it.

We peered into a dungeon cell, with windowless rocky walls stained with splatters of crimson. Gasping, I pressed my fingers over my mouth. Mr. Vyle perched on the velvet-covered cushion of an antique chair, drinking whiskey as the librarian hung upside down from a chain anchored to the ceiling. Blood poured from multiple wounds into a bucket.

Bile seared my throat. "Th-this isn't the future. It's a distortion." It must be. Astan could only lie. "You're trying to scare me into complying."

"I wasn't, but I can." He waved to the wall, and the screen suddenly peered into our suite.

Holding my hand in a firm grip, he led me forward. In the span of a blink, we stood inside the bedroom we shared.

When next he faced me, he was almost gleeful. "Let me show you what happens when I'm without Astan." His pupils pulsed, eclipsing his irises for a single beat. They retracted, those six glowing stars gone.

Dare I hope?

Cyrus frowned, his brows drawing together. His inhalations quickened, becoming labored. Sweat beaded over his upper lip, and the color drained from his cheeks. "Arden?" A second later, he issued an agonized grunt. Wounds broke out all over his body, blood leaking from each. The scar I'd seen on his abdomen? It gaped open.

"What happened? What's wrong?" I rushed to him, flinging my arm around his waist just as his knees buckled. Acting as his crutch, I dragged him to the bed, and he toppled onto the mattress.

"I don't understand," he said between labored breaths. "I should be in the field with . . . with . . ." Misery contorted his features.

"It will be okay, it will be okay." I rushed to the bathroom to gather the first aid kit, then rushed back to his side. After I cut away his new clothing, I tended to his wounds, cleaning and administering the proper medications. I explained everything I'd learned to the best of my ability.

As his physical pain dulled, he should have relaxed. He only grew more agitated. "I must have healed when Astan inhabited me, then returned to my injured state when he left."

Goodness gracious, some of the wounds were deep. The curative gels and sealants I applied would aid in his recovery, but would they work fast enough? "You don't need him to thrive or even survive. Soal will send a conduit." I would make sure of it. "Or I will be a conduit." Yes, yes.

Domino! I shouted his name across our bond.

No response came, and I gulped. He'd said the bond weakened when I entertained Astan's thoughts. But I wasn't. Was I?

"I love you," Cyrus croaked, resolved.

Resolved . . . to die? No, no, no. "I know you do. So listen to me. You will live. Okay? But you can't host him again. Promise me. We'll find another way."

"I promise." When I finished tending his injuries, he mumbled, "Stay with me. Need you."

Hot air lashed my lungs, a stinging whip I couldn't escape. I settled in at his side, careful not to jostle him. I luxuriated in his warmth, his scent. His eyelids sank, and he drifted to sleep.

My mind whirled. Cyrus needed help—a plan essential. Astan would attempt to join with him again, which meant I better read my book. Which meant I must get to the Rock. Which meant I should speak with Domino, who still hadn't responded.

I sent another SOS along our connection and waited . . . waited. No return message. I frowned, worry attempting to creep in. Had something happened to him?

Heart drumming, I eased from Cyrus's embrace and stood. I'd have to get to the Rock without Domino's help. If I got caught, I got caught. The payout exceeded the risk.

I shifted to peer down at his sleeping form, pleasure and heartbreak colliding inside me. If he accepted Astan a second time, he would set off a chain reaction of events leading to our war. I sensed it.

But I wasn't going there. Not now. Better to be mission minded.

Determined, I carefully eased a specific ring from his finger. The one with the skeleton key. I also confiscated some of his other jewelry, checking them out before I donned them. Another ring, filled with a fine, white powder. Probably a sedative, maybe a toxin. An array of metal wristbands that opened and locked into daggers when shaken.

Deep breath in. Out. With a final glance at the man who had changed the trajectory of my life, teaching me to see past fear and fight for what I wanted, I tiptoed to the door. Now it was my turn to help him. And I would. Determination turned my bones to steel. I wouldn't fail.

Chapter Twenty-Seven

I will do what I say, and nothing and no one can stop me.

—*The Book of Soal* 1.24.1.12

There was only one way to reach my destination alive: with unflinching confidence. No hesitation. No backing down. Anything else would set off alarms.

Head high, I opened the suite door and marched into the hall as if I had somewhere important to be, because I'd been summoned by someone important. Honestly, I had. In Soal's welcome letter to me, he'd instructed me to read my books. So. A summons. By a god.

The guards were gone, replaced by the meta. 999 again. It walked at my side, its steps smooth and light despite its significant weight.

"Lead me to the temple," I demanded. The Rock was on the way.

The creature accelerated, pulling ahead.

"I'm gonna call you Nine," I muttered.

It provided zero feedback, robot-dog speak for *don't care.*

As we traveled the corridors, I removed my weapon of choice. Two bracelets I would shake into daggers at the right moment. If I could shred the meta's circuits, it couldn't follow me into the rift room.

My heart thundered harder with every hallway closer. I hoped Domino's fog would sweep toward us, confusing my metal companion. Alas.

I held my breath as we rounded the final corner. Two armed guards waited at every door. Eight in total. Very well. I cobbled together a plan. Rip out Nine's wires, blow powder at everyone else.

Someone exited the temple beyond the hallway and strode in our direction. My spirit sank. Mr. Vyle. He wore a pristine, tailored suit and whistled under his breath, nothing like his blood-splattered future version.

My skin flushed hot with fury at the reminder. This man, this executioner, had sat, utterly unmoved, as Domino swung from the rafters toes up, bleeding to death.

Mr. Vyle's gaze lit on me, and his gait slowed. Clearly he intended to have a conversation. I performed a quick calculation. If I proceeded full steam ahead, all of CURED would learn of my allegiance to Soal. Cyrus already knew, which meant Astan must know, though so far he'd chosen not to reveal it. Which didn't seem like the god's MO. Maybe he couldn't tell? But also, maybe he could. Either way, if I did this, I would be labeled a worldswide traitor, and rightfully so. I'd be hunted. If I managed to survive the ensuing battle with the executioner, of course. And there would be a battle.

If I didn't fight to reach Soal, Cyrus would wake up before I read my book and received instruction. Astan would seek a bond before I had a chance to help him. All could be lost.

Very well. So be it. Today, I stopped hiding. For Cyrus, I would do anything, even this.

Nine slowed and moved to the side, offering me a straight shot to Mr. Vyle.

"Hello, Lady Roosa." The executioner adjusted his wrist cuff. "Might I inquire why you're visiting the temple without Emperor Cyrus?"

Well, well. Mr. Vyle already considered Cyrus his leader.

"You may do so, yes." Forget starting my opening strike with Nine. Mr. Vyle was the bigger threat. For all I knew, Cyrus had commanded the dog not to harm me for any reason. "I politely decline to answer."

A flash of surprise crossed Mr. Vyle's face. My cue. As Cyrus taught me, if battle is inevitable, strike first, strike hard, and strike fast. Up first, taking out as many opponents as possible.

I launched into action, sweeping the jewel of a ring aside and spinning, blowing powder in every direction. Multiple guards collapsed. Mr. Vyle stumbled several steps, but he didn't fall.

With a flick of my wrists, the bracelets clicked into blades. I lunged and slashed. Contact. The tip sliced through the midsection of a guard, Mr. Vyle, then another guard. The soldiers crumbled, clutching gushing wounds, but again Mr. Vyle remained on his feet. His wound bled for a moment, but the flow ceased within seconds.

He drew back his arm, intending to punch me. A growling Nine jumped between us. Good boy.

Mr. Vyle paused. Comprehension lit his eyes a split second before his entire countenance changed. His features sharpened, and his pupils slitted with a glowing golden outline. Smoke curled from his nostrils, and black claws grew from his nail beds.

"Soalian," he hissed, revealing a forked tongue.

Nine attacked, but Vyle shredded the metal beast in seconds. Realization and horror collided. Vyle hosted Bala, Astan's pet.

With an inhuman roar, he launched at me. We slammed together, flying to the floor. Impact shoved air from my lungs. Pain and dizziness welled, but they dulled in a storm of adrenaline.

When Vyle swung a hard fist at my face, I rolled to the side. More stings flared and dulled as I twisted and kicked, punting him in the nose. Cartilage snapped, and blood spurted.

I clambered to my feet, and new guards swooped in, imprisoning me. Fingers pulled my hair, squeezed my biceps, and shackled my wrists.

Through some miracle, I fought free and dove for the door to the rift room. But Vyle spun in front of it and slapped me, raking thick, black claws across my cheek. Searing agony, faltering vision. He kicked and I flew into a wall, cracking stone. My brain rattled against my skull, and my lungs emptied again. Dizziness roared back in a thunderous whirlwind as adrenaline dwindled. How much longer could I hold him off?

As long as it takes. I was Soalian. I could do anything.

A sudden, unexpected tide of strength swept through my limbs, flowing from my bond to Domino. Power up, baby! I recovered quickly, stopping a subsequent strike. But Vyle was faster and stronger than feeders. It wasn't long before his fist collided with my forearm, shattering bone.

Agony not even my bond to the librarian could dull. Black dots winked through my vision. Vomit readied.

Vyle drew back his elbow to deliver another strike. I moved to parry when a scowling robed man ghosted through him.

Domino whooshed inside me. *Click.* Instantly healed and running on pure, undiluted octane, I shot off like a rocket, attacking everyone within reach with a skill I'd never learned.

Unlike before, when I jumped between bodies, we remained connected, the librarian's mind open to me and mine to him. Vyle must have sensed his presence; he backed off, giving the guards a chance to subdue us.

Where have you been? I bellowed inside my head.

Through the bond, he heard.

If you knew half the things I had to do to get here . . . His growly words filled my head, an all-consuming tide drowning my anger.

We hobbled the remaining guards, our expert teamwork heralding the screech of an alarm. Dang it! Other soldiers would arrive any second, yet we had a final obstacle: Vyle.

With his patented almost grin, he trained his harbinger on us. "You can't beat me," he stated, smug.

"We don't have to. You're already defeated." Domino pushed the words from my tongue. I soaked up his confidence and swagger, gulping straight from the tap. "Tsuri comes. You are soon to drink the cup of his wrath."

I didn't know the specifics of the threat, but what a threat it was. My skin bristled with goose bumps, as if the air itself electrified. Vyle turned ashen.

Flawlessly in sync, the librarian and I stepped forward, unafraid.

Our challenger reacted with a flurry of urgency, hammering at the gun's trigger. Bullets zoomed our way. Perhaps I was seeing through Domino's eyes. I watched those little missiles approach in slow motion. I could have moved aside but didn't bother; there was no need. My body flickered in and out of intangibility, going from solid to mist and back to solid all within a heartbeat. The bullets flew through different sections of my torso, spraying the soldiers who had entered the hallway behind me. Down they fell.

Shock glittered in Vyle's eyes. He ejected the clip, shoved in an extra, and fired anew. As Domino and I walked . . . jogged . . . sprinted forward, we twirled the makeshift daggers made from the bracelets and misted as necessary. Almost within striking distance . . .

With one swing, we would remove the executioner's head.

We lifted the blades.

Boom!

A new shot rang out from behind us. A white-hot pang stung my side, and I jerked as Domino was shoved out of my body. Anguish pulsed in every inch of me. Blood poured down my side. Panting, I craned my head to glance over my shoulder.

Roman held a smoking gun. He sighed with displeasure. "I told you we weren't friends, Ardie."

"From behind?" I spat as my knees buckled. "Coward."

"That wasn't a kill shot," he told me, unabashed. "Just a little trim to ensure you stay put."

New guards poured into the hall. They bypassed the lord-in-training and came straight to me, binding my wrists with metal cuffs and hauling me roughly to my feet. My gaze remained on Domino, my sole source of comfort.

"They won't kill you," he stated, panting as if he, too, experienced pain. "Briar Rose hasn't rendered her final decision, which means you're still in the running. Cyrus, even as Astan, won't let anyone end you—yet. I'll return, and we'll get you out of here. Survive, Arden. That's all you must do."

He vanished before I could respond. Good thing. I only gurgled a series of incomprehensible noises. I'd lost. I'd taken a gamble, and I'd lost. Now, all of CURED knew what I was, and there was no going back.

Sickness churned in my belly as a grinning Vyle approached. "You almost had me convinced you'd chosen CURED." He sheathed his gun. "You were a much worthier opponent than I'd expected."

Were. Past tense. As if he no longer saw me as a threat.

As the alarm died, a new voice rang out. "Explain."

A single-word command Mr. Vyle heeded without delay as Cyrus marched our way. "Lady Roosa attempted to sneak to the Rock. When I sought to apprehend her, she fought. This is the result of her capture. She is Soalian, Majesty. A powerful glower, judging by her movements."

"Her affiliation isn't your concern." He looked between us, lingering on me several beats longer, his fury growing.

What little hope I'd retained withered to ash the second I noted the golden stars in his irises. He'd agreed to host Astan again. Or perhaps Astan never really left him.

Yes. That. Fury sparked. I'd bet my savings I'd been tricked. Now, there was no going back—for either of us.

"Why is she injured?" The fury graduated to a rage icy enough to freeze my cells.

"The lord-in-training, Roman, is responsible," Vyle stated. "He is Mercurio's chosen, and he prevented her from leaving."

Behind Cyrus, the guards parted, providing a clear path to the guy I'd once admired.

"Majesty." Roman bowed in deference. "I will serve you faithfully for—"

Cyrus palmed a gun, twirled it in his grip, and fired a shot without ever turning around, nailing Roman between the eyes. "Mercurio can select someone else."

The trainee fell forward, already dead.

I gasped at the speed and violence of everything, horrified all over again.

"What would you like me to do with the girl, Majesty?" Vyle asked, undisturbed.

Cyrus didn't miss a beat. "Lock her in the dungeon for now." He shot out his arm, capturing the other man by the chin to ensure he listened well. "Have her tended, and make sure there's not another scratch on her, or I'll be . . . perturbed."

Vyle paled, as if there were no greater threat, and inclined his head. "I'll see to her recovery personally."

Cyrus flicked his tongue over his teeth, holding my stare as I panted through my pain. "I suggest you behave, sweetness. My patience with you grows thin." As he spoke, he lifted a finger and mimed a spin, which turned out to be a command Vyle heeded.

The executioner picked me up and forced me to stand.

Cyrus slid the rings from my fingers, adding, "You won't like what happens if you attempt another escape."

"I don't like *you*," I spat at him, my knees nearly buckling. But fall? No. "That's the problem."

"You don't know me." Eyes narrowed, he erased the gap between us, butting up against me. "But you will."

Though I hurt, I didn't let myself back down. Here I was, peering at a face I cherished, breathing in a scent I treasured—although, yes, I noted a slight difference now. A tad sharper. But I digressed. In any other situation, I would've been confident of Cyrus's desire to protect me. Today, I couldn't trust him, and it sucked, especially because I knew what was coming. The battle. My sword slicking through his flesh.

"So beautiful." He grazed his knuckles along one side of my cheek. A corner of his mouth twitched, a reaction Cyrus often had with me as well. He was in there, aware. He must be. "You value the truth, so here is an unvarnished fact, nothing hidden. You will host Briar Rose or die. As always, the choice will be yours."

He turned on his heel and stalked off.

Vyle gave me a shove in the opposite direction, forcing me to walk over slain soldiers. Blood wet the soles of my boots, a squeak sounding with every ensuing step. I even left little crimson prints in my wake.

When I didn't move quick enough for his liking, he gripped my bicep. It hurt, but to be fair, everything did.

"Don't think I won't tattle about your treatment of me," I muttered.

"Don't think he'll always care," he replied, smug. "You'll refuse him, and he'll kill you. I'll be his favorite again."

So much for Briar Rose's vision of a happily ever after—the dragon as enamored of me as Cyrus.

We descended a staircase and passed through a shimmery veil. Between one step and the next, we exited a narrow hallway and entered the dungeon with bloodstained walls and barred cells lining both sides. Most were filled with moaning, groaning maddened. Some contained glowers. All were trapped in various stages of starvation and torment.

"I think you'll be pleased with your cellmate," Vyle said, leading me toward a cage smaller than the others and occupied by only one glower.

Another shock. Victors, here. He sat in the far corner, one leg bent at the knee, with an elbow resting at the crest. His bored expression never wavered. He wore torn, dirty clothing, his hair sticking out in spikes. The injuries he'd sustained in captivity hadn't fully healed, his skin bordering on sallow.

"So good to see you again, Lady Roosa." His voice lacked substance, but his joy was true. "You're right on time."

Vyle unlocked the door and hauled me inside. He pushed me at the cot pressed against a wall. My knees gave out, and I plopped onto the stretched cloth, doing my best to appear bored as well.

A guard rushed in with a medical kit. Vyle claimed it, then tossed it on the cot beside me. "Don't die," he commanded before stalking out and confining me inside. "Ask your friend what he's endured. Soon, you'll experience the same firsthand."

He stalked off, and I deflated, air leaking from a part in my lips. "I'm both thrilled and sad to see you again, Victors. Wish it had been under better circumstances."

"But, my girl," he said, as brazen as I remembered him. "The real fun is just getting started."

Chapter Twenty-Eight

Your war isn't with flesh and blood but with the spirits within them.

—*The Book of Soal* 2.8.10.3

"Real fun," I echoed hollowly. "We're prisoners, Victors."

He frowned, as if disappointed. "Don't be ridiculous, Miss Roosa. We're nothing of the sort."

I didn't have the strength to match wits with him. I tried to catch my breath as I examined my wound. Not a kill shot, exactly as Roman had claimed, but it hurt. Still, his death hurt more. I hated what he'd done, but I hadn't wanted him dead.

"I'd offer to help you with the doctoring, but my vivisection says no." With a sunny smile, Victors motioned to the bandage peeking out from the neckline of his shirt. The lightness in his eyes provided a shocking contrast to our miserable dungeon, our abysmal situation, and the barbarity inflicted upon him.

"How were you recaptured?" I asked, opening the first aid kit.

"Oh. That. I turned myself in again."

You've got to be kidding me. "Why would you do such a thing?" Especially after all he'd already suffered.

"For starters, I didn't want to miss the big finale. Also, I thought it might be nice to take a beat and prepare you. The worst is still to come, my dear."

I flinched and muttered, "We are living in a horror novel." I needed as much strength as I could muster, as fast as I could muster it. Hands shaking, I withdrew the disinfectant. No painkiller. Better to maintain my wits right now. As I squirted the cold liquid directly into my wound, I struggled to silence my scream. The sting! I could only breathe through it, waiting for black dots to stop flashing. When I could see again, I applied the healing gel, then a butterfly bandage to seal the sides of broken skin together.

Deep breath in. Out. In, out. Okay, the worst was over, at least.

"Have you forgotten *The Book of Arden* is a romance?" Victors asked. "Give it time."

"Romances are supposed to end with the bad guys defeated and the couple headed for a bright future. It's science. Look it up." My shoulders rolled in. "I can't see a way we can recover from this."

"That's too bad. The you I see has learned from her mistakes and is making better decisions, heading for a better destination."

Well, he wasn't wrong about that. I *had* learned from my mistakes. If I could go back, I would avoid Cyrus on the battlefield, exactly as ordered, trusting my fellow glowers to aid him.

Where would we be today if I'd listened? Here, now, we'd accomplished our goal, yes. Cyrus wasn't just king; he was emperor. But at what cost?

Bonding to Domino had been the beginning of the end for my relationship with the high prince. I'd helped save our lives, but I'd also changed *both* our destinies. While part of me wanted to resent the librarian, I couldn't bring myself to regret our dealings. But now, we were all on a train speeding along the tracks, no longer able to brake.

"I'd argue the use of the word *better*," I muttered.

"And that's your problem," Victors said. "You are focusing on the moment rather than the end."

"This *is* the end."

"So shortsighted," he tsked. "Do you really think I'd be here without a foolproof plan to save you?"

"Why do you even care?" I muttered. "I'm one person."

"Ah, but you're *our* person."

Anger flared. "Cyrus is—was—our person, too, yet here we are," I griped. "He's possessed, and the war is raging."

"I hear blame in your voice. You know nothing of what we've done for him," Victors snapped with an unexpected anger of his own. "Nothing *I've* done. Did he share with you the messages I brought? The warnings Ember and others delivered? Tell you of his meeting with Soal? Explain the whole story he read?"

I pressed my tongue to the roof of my mouth and shook my head. I'd had no idea Victors visited him. No idea Cyrus met with Soal himself.

"No one but Cyrus is responsible for his choices. Not even you, Arden. You accept *that*, I hope."

"I do," I said and sighed. The new emperor of Ourland was as much a free moral agent as I was. "And I don't."

Victors tsked again. "Careful, my dear. A little drop of doubt poisons the entire glass of water."

I pursed my lips. "How very Victors of you. Cryptic responses have always been your specialty."

"Thank you," he said and grinned.

"That wasn't a compliment." Frustration uncoiled, wrapping around me. My chin trembled. The shock of it all was fading, leaving me with emotions I wasn't ready to deal with and certainties I didn't like or have any idea how to change. "Soal imprisoned Astan before. He should be able to do it again." Thereby freeing Cyrus.

"Tsuri imprisoned the gods."

Hold up. "Tsuri became the Rock after bringing Briar Rose back to life. How did he create the prisons?"

Victors didn't explain. "Reimprisonment isn't the way forward. Total annihilation is. The time has come. We're finally ready."

I closed my eyes for a moment. Where did this leave Cyrus?

"Good news is, Astan isn't all powerful. None of them are. Though they abide in their hosts, they require constant anchors and total agreement."

"Say more. Please," I added.

"Emotions act as a sealant. Astan specializes in fear, greed, and pride, as you've noted. Root those from Cyrus, and the god will lose his stronghold. Cyrus can eject him."

His words reverberated. Before I'd come into his life, Cyrus had been fear-free. What if I'd shared the fruit of my anxiety with him?

I thought back to the moment trepidation had first reared its ugly head. The train car ride to Fort Bala. It had overwhelmed me, almost palpable and worse than any other distress I'd ever felt, almost as if I'd tapped into a rushing vein. Rather than fight it, I'd buried it for study later, allowing it to grow.

I leaned forward, closing my eyes and resting my head in my upraised palms. Had Astan targeted me even then, his sights set on using me to bring down Cyrus?

Flash. I saw the shadow that had risen from the body of Tagin Dolion seconds after his death. How we'd stared each other down for several beats. Maybe the plan to win Cyrus over was born in that moment. Maybe even before it. Either way, I'd played right into his hands, sticking my head in the sands of "later" rather than facing my enemy head-on right from the start, giving him time to establish roots.

"Now, now. None of that," Victors said, guessing my thoughts. "No need to get down. Even when you make a wrong turn, there's always a way to get where you need to be."

I really, really hoped so. "How far in the future have you read?"

Another grin spread, there and gone. "Past the climax, all the way to the ending celebration of victory. It's glorious, I promise you. The comeback story of all comeback stories. That's the theme, in case you were wondering."

Good to know. "Do we all survive?"

"There will be casualties. In war, there always are."

Figured. "So what are the tropes of this comeback story, hmm?"

His eyes glittered with humor. "Those are up to you."

Fair enough.

Footsteps rose above the moans and groans echoing all around us, reaching my ears. An ambrosial scent hit next, sparking as much dread as anticipation. Cyrus.

I sat up straighter as he and an army of armed guards entered my vantage point. His intense, star-studded stare promised the worst had yet to come. Before, I might have withered. But this was Astan, not Cyrus, and I wouldn't cow to my enemy, giving him what he craved.

He'd changed again, now sporting a sleek black suit and tie. He looked good, but I recognized a weapon when I spied one.

I didn't bother rising when he stopped at the barred door. "Guess you figured out what to do with me."

"I have," he confirmed. He dropped his gaze to my side, where the bloodstained hem of my shirt had gotten trapped in the corner of the bandage. Though he stiffened, he commented not. Rather, he turned his attention to Victors. "Enjoying your stay, old friend?"

"Honestly? Yes. I didn't turn myself in for nothing." Victors flashed his most guileless grin. "The more you swagger about, the closer we come to the final chapter in *The Book of Astan*. It's a tragedy."

Cyrus brushed invisible lint from his sleeve. "Soal made a mistake, basing his victory upon the integrity of his word. His precious truth. If only one detail in his book is altered, he loses everything."

I tried to make sense of what I'd just heard. Was he implying the crux of the entire war between CURED and Soal boiled down to Astan making Soal a liar? But that made no sense. Unless there was something at play I wasn't seeing.

Victors laughed so hard, he coughed. Though he clutched at his wound, he didn't stop laughing. "You think . . . mistake . . . you . . ."

He was still chortling when a glowering Cyrus dragged his narrowed gaze to me. "Come." He shoved the command past clenched teeth. "There's something we must do."

My heart blipped, but I masked it with a smile as irreverent as Victors's merriment. "Sure thing. I'd love another opportunity to defy you."

He worked his jaw, clearly not used to such insubordination from me.

A guard rushed over and opened the cage. I could have resisted when Cyrus closed in and hauled me to my feet, but why risk opening my wound? Also, I was determined. And curious. What did he have in store for me?

"I suggest you behave and walk behind me like a good little girl." He smoothed the wrinkles from my clothes before striding from the cell.

With a final glance at Victors, who winked, buoying my spirits, I followed Cyrus through multiple corridors, up two staircases, and into a large, opulent chamber.

"The emperor's chamber," Cyrus stated without emotion. "Mine now."

I came to an abrupt halt as the door shut—and sealed—behind me. A sheen of sweat glazed my brow when I spotted the massive bed, with its covers pulled down, ready for someone to slide underneath. Nervousness fizzed in my veins. "Why are we here?"

He opened the door to an equally luxurious bathroom with gold everything. Faucets, sinks, counters. Even the toilet. *Grotesque.* After he opened the shower stall and pressed a series of buttons on a wall panel, hot, steamy water rained from an overhead spout. Only then did he face me straight on and command, "Strip."

A protest burst from my mouth, spurring a smile from him.

"Don't worry, sweetness. I have no plans to force you to bed me."

I bit my tongue, tasting blood. The sound of Astan's preferred endearment coming out of Cyrus's mouth was more disgusting than that gold toilet. "You intend to watch me bathe."

He gave a negligent shrug. "You'll clean up and dress on your own, or I'll help you."

An act clearly meant to intimidate and shame me. Well, he'd miscalculated. There was no better way than this to reach the heart of Cyrus, a man who had no desire to share me with another.

Holding his gaze, I shed my shirt. When his breath caught, I grinned inside. *Ding, ding, ding.* Head high, I shimmied out of my pants.

He swallowed and fisted his hands. I removed my undergarments sloooowly, sliding off the straps of my bra . . . unhooking the clasp . . . letting the material whoosh to the floor . . . pinching the sides of my underwear and wiggling free. Naked, I rolled back my shoulders.

Panting a little, he roved his gaze over me. His pupils spread over his irises, snuffing out the stars, and I knew I'd succeeded.

"See something you like?" Triumphant, I traced a fingernail between my breasts.

He took a step toward me, stopped abruptly, and scowled. "I comprehend your play, but again, you forget I am Cyrus and Cyrus is me. I can do nothing he doesn't allow."

Well, well. He'd just copped to a big weakness. I mean, he and Victors had already explained it, but the far-encompassing consequences hadn't dawned on me until this moment. Cyrus could, indeed, be saved.

I smiled with glee.

Realizing his mistake, he stomped from the room. "You have ten minutes. If you choose not to wash and change, I'll carry you out naked," he snapped before slamming the door shut, leaving me alone.

Reeling, I scrubbed from head to toe and donned the clothing he'd provided, opting to play the game to its conclusion. A sheer, gauzy gown of pale pink that clung to my curves like a second skin, with a hem that floated around my ankles, revealing barely-there sandals.

I steeled myself for what was to come. Another meeting with Briar Rose, probably. She had yet to choose her host. Since there were still two contestants in the running, and Lolli had already granted her consent, I must logically conclude the goddess was desperate to have me.

I'd get the hard sell again, cranked to level maximum, guaranteed. But no matter. My determination solidified.

A soft tugging on the inside drew my attention inward. Determination fizzed along my connection to Domino. The most potent determination I'd ever encountered, tinged with excitement. He must have discovered something in his book.

The librarian's emotions fed my own. We would get through this, whatever was thrown at us. We'd do what was needed, when it was needed. If Cyrus and I ended up on a battlefield, as I'd read, so be it. Maybe I would even stab him. Heck, at this rate, I would *absolutely* stab him. But I wasn't afraid of the notion anymore. All we had to do was survive the battle. Everything else could be fixed.

If I lost his love, I lost his love. "It will hurt," I muttered, needing to hear myself say it, "but I. Am. Not. Afraid." Hearts could mend. I nodded with confident assurance, dulling the *doubts*. "I'm not afraid." I repeated the mantra again and again, until I was screaming it. "I am not afraid!"

In the ensuing silence, my heart rate slowed. A heavy weight I hadn't known I carried lifted from my shoulders, and a little laugh escaped me, all hint of fear gone.

"You are stronger than I anticipated."

Cyrus's voice pulled me from my head, and I twisted to face him. He stood in the open doorway, one shoulder leaning against the frame. Though he did his best to appear completely at ease, he couldn't mask the sharp energy seething beneath his skin.

He held a glass of what looked to be champagne.

"Vyle said the same. But I'm stronger, period," I replied and grinned. He might host a god, but I served *the* god. The one who'd defeated Astan before, who would do it again. A fact that I'd lost sight of at some point. I had consumed the Rock. Tsuri himself. Son to Soal. I could do anything. "I believe you mentioned we had a place to be."

His gaze slid over me—and iced. "There's something I wish to do first." He gulped back what remained of the champagne, set the glass on the counter, and closed the distance.

My pulse fluttered. Whatever he intended . . .

He didn't utter another word. Just lowered his head and slammed his lips to mine. I reacted on instinct, opening for him as I'd done countless times before. Using my culpability to his advantage, he poured the champagne down my throat, ensuring I swallowed it before he thrust his tongue against mine once, twice, three times. He lifted his head and smiled coldly. "Now we're ready."

Chapter Twenty-Nine

> This day, don your armor and take up your weapons, for the battle is upon us.
>
> —*The Book of Soal* 2.10.6.10

As my former fiancé led me through the castle, I felt as if I floated in a dream. Clouds somehow both light as spun sugar and as dense as fog swept me up in the most delicious, effervescent dizziness. Thoughts loosened, desires unmoored, and inhibitions drifted into the ether.

"You drugged me," I said, and a little laugh bubbled up.

"Just a bit." He pinched his fingers, all sheepishness and charm.

My sweet prince. I could almost pretend he was Cyrus again and all was well. "I'm going to defeat you," I told him, beaming a sunny smile and batting my lashes at him.

He snorted and flashed an indulgent smile I'd missed. "I like you like this. Soft and silly."

"Wrong. You don't like me at all." He couldn't. "Someone who likes me doesn't drug or threaten me. You're more Astan than Cyrus."

"Impossible. I told you, sweetness. We are one and the same, equal parts of each other."

"Repeating a lie doesn't make it true."

"I can't dip into his memories without permission, and he can't dip into mine." He performed a little spin to gently bop my nose without missing a beat, as playful as Cyrus. "We know only what we think together."

That couldn't be right, but okay. "If any part of Astan is mixed into any part of you, that means you are no longer one hundred percent grade-A Cyrus Dolion, and that's who I love." My Cyrus was strong and brave, protective and playful. Integrity lived and breathed in his veins. He didn't murder, lie, or cajole.

"Now, now. I don't hate you for being bonded to Domino, do I?" he asked, ever reasonable. "Just give me a chance to prove my affection for you is as genuine as always."

A sliver of me wanted to say yes, but deep down, I knew that choice would open a door I'd never be able to close. "What was in that champagne, anyway?" I tried to force myself to concentrate on what mattered. I had a plan to execute . . . probably?

"Nothing dangerous. Just a little something to whisk all your troubles away. The same substance Felix used." How amused he sounded. Smug too. "You enjoyed it then, and you are enjoying it now. Admit it."

"Enjoying something doesn't make it enjoyable." No, that wasn't what I'd meant to say. Or even the crux of the problem. *Focus.* "You violated my trust." Yes. That. And how did he know what Felix had done?

"I helped you, and you didn't even have to ask. You're welcome."

Great. He made it sound as if I was ridiculous to question him. "You're being deliberately confusing. Stop it."

"Certainly, but only because you asked so sweetly." He caught my hand, giving my knuckles a soft kiss, sending warm tingles skimming up my arm. Still holding on, he paused at the threshold of a vast chamber and spread his free arm. "Welcome to paradise, Lady Pink."

Paradise. A previously unvisited yet not unfamiliar ballroom I'd seen in Briar Rose's vision. The beauty stole what remained of my wits. A veritable garden of delights for more than my eyes. That floral scent. I breathed deep. Like olfactory champagne, sweet but effervescent.

Colorful blossoms flourished around every statue. Light tinted with shades of azure and emerald streamed in from the domed ceiling, flowing between vines that created a flowery canopy. Petals of pink, blue, yellow, and red twirled down, down to line the floor. I ached to roll among them, covering myself in their perfume.

"The suns shine again," Cyrus said, clearly pleased. "How could that happen, if I were as evil as you've been led to believe?" He didn't give me a chance to process the question but led me forward. "Look. See."

The open balcony doors welcomed a warm breeze that rippled through the curtains and vines as we stepped outside. Gripping the swirling metal railing, I peered out at the world beyond. Two suns glistened upon the smooth moat below, spotlighting an empire of marble bridges and drowned citadels. Remnants of another city?

Awed, I pulled my gaze to the horizon, where the domed force field glittered. Lovely. *Appalling.* Memories attempted to break free. This wasn't the "paradise" he promised. I just couldn't remember why.

"Say yes to Briar Rose, Arden," he urged, his voice a caress. Cyrus twirled me in front of him, wrapped his arms around my waist, and eased us into a slow dance, evoking a yearning I'd too often suppressed. The stars blazed to life in his eyes, inviting me to stare. "I'll give you peace, safety, and security. More than that, I'll love and adore you."

As I peered up at his sunslit face and drank in his adoring expression, the strength of his embrace provided a welcome respite from the constant barrage of battles I'd faced. It was difficult to care that he was the host of Astan, the worst of humanity. He just . . . he looked and felt and smelled like my Cyrus.

I leaned closer . . .

On the inside of me, a little voice whispered, *Anchor.*

"Say yes to Briar Rose," Cyrus repeated, dancing me back into the ballroom. "Becoming her host will eradicate your bond to Domino, making it a problem for us no more. Experience her power. Grow your gardens. Rule the worlds at my side." He released me and stepped back to extend a hand in my direction. "Be mine."

Anchor.

I stilled and sobered, the effects of the drug fading fast. In that moment, I knew I could reach for Cyrus or Domino, but not both.

I smiled, a little sad. "You can't give me peace, safety, or security. You aren't Cyrus." No need to change my argument. And no need to elaborate. My mindset hadn't changed.

I reached for Domino, and strength poured through me.

Cyrus dropped his arm and calmly stated, "If you refuse, you'll be a liability to me. I don't think you need to be told again what happens to liabilities."

"Oooh. A threat." I clicked my tongue to the roof of my mouth. "It's not a lure. It's not even original."

"We're past threats. I simply tell you the truth. That *is* what you prefer, yes? I cannot allow you to run around, wreaking havoc on my plans. With or without you, I will continue to build my army and take what rightfully belongs to me." Resentment dripped from his words. "One way or another, I will claim Soal's library. I will take the power of his pen, and I will rewrite my story."

"Why do you need his pen?" This was the first I'd heard of it. "Why can't you edit your own?"

He breezed past the questions, sweeping me back into his arms and twirling me over the dance floor. In the background, leaves rustled in the breeze, creating a soft, romantic song. "Look into my eyes. See my sincerity. Hear my certainty. You will enjoy being empress. A goddess." His eyelids hooded. "Mostly, you'll enjoy being mine. I'll make sure of it."

"Under your rule, everyone else will suffer." Eventually, I would too. A liar lied. A killer killed. A thief stole. No exceptions. "See *my* sincerity. Hear *my* certainty. I will never be yours unless you reject Astan." I clutched the lapels of his jacket and held him close, letting him feel my softness. "Reject Astan," I repeated.

"Reject Domino," he snapped, and guilt seared me. Deep breath in. Out. "Do you truly believe Soal is the better leader?"

"I judge a tree by its fruit. Your people are maddened, his aren't. So yes." I plowed my fingers into Cyrus's silken hair and peered into his eyes, hoping to reach his heart. "Please, sugar. Time is running out." At the first opportunity, I intended to bolt. "Reject the god or lose me."

His irritation intensified. He looked over my shoulder and nodded. "I'll give you one last chance to make the right decision."

A whisper rolled through my head. *With me comes more than power. You'll be loved and adored by all. And the abilities you'll have. Never again will you be helpless. My power will flow through your veins, becoming our power. We'll use it to save both worlds. Seeds and soil will be ours to nurture and command.*

Briar Rose, here to deliver the final blow. More persuasive than Cyrus and Astan, seducing with my wildest dreams.

To resist, I had to scrape fragments of strength from the bottom of a barrel. If I did it, if I said yes, it meant *helping* the very beings who were responsible for twenty years of misery for me.

I pressed my fists into my temples. "Enough."

But she wasn't done. *At least this way, you'll have influence over Cyrus. You can steer his decisions the direction you prefer. All you must do is say yes to me . . .*

A logic more tempting than any threat. It battered at my resolve. Because she wasn't wrong. I could influence him for good. Keep tabs on him. Weaken Astan's influence. Help people. So why not do it? Wasn't the future more important than the present?

Ugh. Here I was, doing exactly what Cyrus must have done: rationalizing. Flirting with monsters and their agenda. Briar Rose played on my emotions, nothing more, eliciting a lethal mix of hopelessness and helplessness. An expert manipulation tactic.

Anger bubbled up, and I intoned, "No. I reject Briar Rose. I reject Astan. I reject . . . you."

He pinched my chin between his fingers and lowered his other hand to my injury, squeezing the freshly patched gash. "Is this really the end you want for us?"

Sharp, searing pain rocketed through me. "Hurting me isn't helping your cause," I grated through panting breaths.

"You think you know hurt? I assure you, you don't. None of you do. But everyone will learn, if Soal wins. How do you think I won over your precious fiancé? By proving the depths of Soal's evil." He squeezed harder. "I'll do anything, even destroy those closest to me, to oversee his defeat."

I waited, desperate for Cyrus to push to the fore and take over, not daring to breathe. But seconds passed . . .

His fingers clamped tighter.

Air hitched in my throat. "No."

Briar Rose huffed with indignation, her presence lifting from me in a rush.

Cyrus must have sensed it. "Very well," he stated, easing the pressure. Disgust and irritation glowing in his eyes, he shoved me from him. "You'll live only until I rid myself of this irksome desire for you."

I stumbled, tripping and falling when the hem of my dress caught beneath my sandal. Pain reverberated in my wound, and a fresh wave of dizziness filled my head.

The clack of high heels hit my ears. Agony exploded through my body as Lolli walked over me, stabbing my hand with a shoe.

Cyrus smiled without humor and stiffly offered his arm as she approached. "Ready to decimate Soal, sweetness?"

"Beyond," she replied with an airy little laugh. She was decked out in a gown as sheer, gauzy, and pink as mine. "I was born for this."

A statement Cyrus had made, as well.

"Let's get this done, then. Pour yourself into her. Glowers are advancing on the gate, and your first order of business is catching them." A cold laugh. "They'll fuel us for centuries."

Interesting choice of words.

The pair forgot all about me, as if I weren't any kind of concern. But then, I *wasn't* a concern. I could only watch, powerless, as they drew together, peering deep into each other's eyes.

Lolli clutched at his shirt and gritted out, "Briar Rose is afraid you won't want her in my body."

He cupped her cheeks as he'd so often done to mine. "She is my sweetness. I want her, whichever body she inhabits." He traced his fingertips over her face, so tender, and I imagined he mesmerized her with those starry eyes. "It's time. You are our opening act in the new war. We've waited long enough."

Lolli smiled, pausing to savor the moment. "Yes, Briar Rose, I accept. I am yours, always."

A moment passed, but nothing happened. Not outwardly.

From somewhere in the castle, a crash sounded. Vibrations shook the floor, lights flickered, and dread licked up my spine.

Something big had just toppled.

The pair weren't surprised or upset by whatever had happened. The opposite, in fact. He grinned, and she twittered. Their delight amplified as a cold wind swept through the room, carrying whispers so loud they were a scream. A horde of shadows swooped in next, glommed onto Lolli, and absorbed into her skin.

Appalled, I scrambled backward.

An invisible force lifted her off the floor, and she screamed without making a sound. Her head fell back, her arms spread, and her body arched. Vines coiled from the ends of her fingertips, around each of her limbs, and budded with flowers.

Cyrus's admission reverberated in my head, rallying a new strength I hadn't known I possessed. My teammates were currently headed for a trap. Maybe they'd read their books and knew it. Maybe they hadn't and didn't. Either way, I must warn them. I'd overstayed my welcome in this palace.

I couldn't help Cyrus, Victors, or Soal here, as I'd already proven. If I didn't act now, I might not have another chance. I scanned the room, weighing my options. Armed guards at the door. But the balcony remained unguarded . . . and a moat waited beneath.

It was dangerous. I'd get hurt. But allow fear to stop me? No. Never again. I wasn't hopeless, and I wasn't helpless.

Unnoticed, I clambered to my feet. Before the ritual or whatever finished, I should be gone.

Ready. . .

Set . . . I braced.

Go! I sprinted for the balcony. Faster, faster, ignoring every pang of pain.

A shout of denial behind me. "Arden!" Fast, pounding footsteps drowned mine.

I pumped my arms with more force, passed the entryway, and clutched a fistful of both curtains. Up the ledge. Leap!

As I fell, I spun myself, still clutching the cloth. Cyrus stopped at the rail. Fury glinted in his eyes.

The material jerked taut, swinging me into the side of the castle. Stone met bone, and I was certain the bones lost and cracked.

I hung there a moment, fighting to regain my bearings.

Cyrus began to pull me up as the fabric tore. I scrambled to grab protrusions in the wall and released the curtains. As I scaled down, my fragmented thoughts aligned with a single purpose: Succeed or die trying.

Chapter Thirty

Hatred is a blade turned inward, and in striking, it is struck, but love, ever patient, ever enduring, conquers with its unyielding truth.

—*The Book of Soal* 2.6.8.37

I scaled down the wall at warp speed. Well, my version of warp speed. Guards rushed to different balconies, attempting to grab me as I passed. Thankfully, they couldn't meet me on the ground. The mountain was too steep, with a churning body of water below.

At the lowest point, I had no choice but to jump. Which I did. Down I fell, hurtling toward the water. When I hit, I hit hard. Icy cold emptied my lungs, and muscles from top to bottom seized.

With the last of my strength, I swam to the surface. Or attempted to. Dark spots flashed as I failed to work my limbs, sinking fast. Panic pushed a whimper from my throat. *Going to die?*

A brawny arm banded around me, and a powerful man glided me up, up through the water. We breached the surface together, and I sucked in a gulp of oxygen.

Domino! I'd never been so happy to see another person.

Resolve dominated his water-dotted features. "You're okay. Say it."

"I'm okay, I'm okay," I repeated, fighting past layers of shock deposited by everything that had happened.

As he swam us forward, fish darted. From this angle, the glint of two suns obscured the city that lurked beneath. One day, I'd learn more about it. Now? More feeders than I could count gathered upon the shore. They watched us, all but sharpening mental forks and knives.

"We'll deal with them when we get closer," Domino said. First, we had what might be half a mile to swim.

"How did you get here?" I asked between panting breaths.

"My book provided exact instructions."

I spit out a mouthful of not-so-tasty water, highly aware of a pebble of envy beneath the tide of gratefulness. "I could have used those kinds of details a few minutes ago."

"You had a private meeting with Victors, the exact same thing." He glanced back, catching my eye. Light hit his sharp, rugged features, showcasing the strength inhabiting every hollow and rise. He'd trimmed his beard, the dark hair now cut close to his skin. "You ended things with Cyrus." A statement without emotion.

"Yes." He'd accepted Astan. Preferred the god above our relationship. Had even accepted Lolli, his now wife, considering she hosted Briar Rose. I deserved better. "I don't want to discuss it," I said before Domino asked any follow-ups.

"That's fine. To survive what's coming, you need to create your sword of fire. Let's focus on that. And don't tell me you can't. You are a glower." He glided through the water. "You can."

The severity of his tone chilled me. "How?" I'd never even tried.

"The flames are already inside you. Look past your emotions to the pritis. Soal's fire burns inside it. Then, release it. The flames will run down your arm and produce a blade able to cut through both the spirit and the physical realms."

"You make it sound so easy," I grumbled.

"Because it is, especially now that you're bonded to me. Don't make it difficult. Get out of your head," he instructed. Then, with wry humor, he added, "There's nothing you need there right now."

"Ha ha," I replied with a smidge of humor, splashing water on him. We were almost to the shore, making it do-or-die time.

As instructed, I focused inward and hacked through frustration, heartache, grief, guilt, shame, and dismay. Hey! As soon as I cleared the smog, heat wafted from a glowing orb, trapping me in its orbit and drawing me closer.

A cold film around my heart began to melt, revealing flames.

The feeders grew agitated, ready for their next meal.

Trepidation sparked, dulled by the orb's entrancement. Each flame was fueled by something. That one drew from an emotional bond to Cyrus. That one, the supernatural bond to Domino. That one, a desire to protect and defend the people who had worked so hard to protect and defend me. Another, a need to enlighten the masses with the truth about Soal. There were others. More than I could count.

Before my eyes, the one powered by my feelings for Cyrus changed from glorious gold to putrid green. Worse, it started to chill, dousing the flames around it.

"Sever it," Domino urged . . . and I did, reaching out to pinch it off at the base before giving myself a chance to reason.

Pain like I'd never known burst through me, shoving a scream from my throat.

"You're all right, you're all right." The librarian treaded water, holding me up as my body ceased working properly. "Most people do this in stages, the pain trickling in. There wasn't time for that. Now, at least, you have a chance to save him. And yourself. I've seen it."

"I still love him," I said and sniffled.

"Use your pain to your advantage." Domino swam us forward again, and the feeders started drooling. "Fight. Return your focus to your flames."

Okay, yes. Domino was right. I needed to fight. I couldn't help Cyrus if I died, and I *would* help him. I must. Letting Astan win wasn't even an option.

The flames burned hotter, one growing brighter, calling to me. The tie to Soal at the heart of them all. I reached for it.

Suddenly, flames leaped from the orb. Heat spread over my arm, tugging my consciousness outward. From my shoulder to my fingers, those flames crackled. Just as easy as Domino had promised.

Though the flames brushed him, he remained uninjured. A smile of pleasure lit his face, inspiring a return grin despite the awfulness of our circumstances.

"How many other things do I not know I can do?" I asked.

"Many," he said, and I sighed. Figured.

My feet grazed the ground, and I stood.

"Get ready."

Anticipation among the feeders turned frenzied.

We sloshed forward, coming out of the water. The librarian swung his arm as feeders rushed us, a flaming sword appearing in his grip. Heads dropped without their bodies.

As other feeders approached, I did some swinging of my own. To my shock, a sword of fire appeared in my grip, an extension of my hand. The blade sliced through everyone within reach, body parts plopping to the sand.

Best. Weapon. Ever.

I stayed on the move. Working with Domino, I sliced and diced through the masses. I ignored the chilly wind beating against my wet skin. The weight of my waterlogged gown. The squish of my soaked sandals. Swing, swing, swing. More feeders fell.

Beyond us, an engine roared, the volume cranking fast. Bodies went flying amid a series of thuds before a huge truck came to a screeching halt. Armed guards poured out, Winslet among them. Exactly what we didn't need.

Each soldier carried a harbinger and peppered the area with bullets. Domino maneuvered in front of me, spinning his fiery sword with such speed he created a shield of heat more powerful than metal. The bullets melted, dripping to the ground, never reaching us.

I watched the masterful defense with my mouth agape. Between the ebb and flow of gunfire, when our challengers paused to reload, Domino dipped and turned, moving forward, tossing flaming daggers. Different guards fell until only a handful remained.

"You won't make it on foot," Winslet called. "Cyrus and Lolli are almost battle ready. Time is running out."

"You die today, unless you give your life to Soal," Domino called back. "Did Cyrus tell you that? In order for all of Astan's essence to fill him, you must lose what you were given. The moment you do, you'll bleed out. Don't spend your final moments wounding the only people who can stop him from doing to others what he's done to you."

Compassion welled. She'd reached the end of her story, the final scene set. "Winslet." It was all I could say. I didn't know her well, but I liked her. Her life had meaning. "You can be healed, if you'll let—"

"Shut up," she snarled.

Domino dipped, tossing another dagger. Winslet screeched, and a thud rang out. Injured. I darted around the librarian and charged the remaining guards. He didn't stay behind me long but moved forward, keeping pace at my side.

One, two, three shots rang out. My heart pounded in time, the beats so hard they felt like a hammer against my ribs.

"Lesah," Domino shouted, a command unlike any I'd ever heard, as if he spoke with many voices, all of them from a different rushing stream.

In a flash, the world decelerated to a crawl—but I didn't. Nor did Domino. We blazed. "Lesah?" I asked, having never heard the word.

"Through Soal, we can slip outside of time for short bursts," he explained, mowing down a cluster of feeders. "It takes discipline and strength. Don't try it on your own yet."

"Yes, sir." We twisted this way and that as we ran, able to see the missiles and avoid contact.

New gunfire rang out. I attempted to dodge it, too, but I misjudged the distance and tripped. Domino noticed and bumped me, pushing me out of the strike zone. The bullet sliced through his bicep, and his sword of fire vanished.

"Keep going," he demanded.

I righted and obeyed, slaying the final handful of soldiers. When the last dropped, I froze, panting hard. Time whooshed to a frenzy, seeming to go faster than before the slowdown.

"Are you okay?" I called to Domino. My adrenaline crashed to deeper depths, heralding a tide of tremors in my limbs.

"I'm fine. I'll be fine." His determination and confidence inspired mine. "Help her."

Very well. I stumbled to Winslet. She lay on the ground, panting shallowly through pain. The dagger had ripped through her shoulder and left a gaping hole with singed edges. Color had drained from her skin.

I kicked her fallen harbinger away and crouched at her side to further assess the damage.

"You're not going to win this," she grated, pushing the words out through pain-filled breaths. "Backup . . . coming. More soldiers. More weapons. Orders to capture librarian . . . even if we must . . . injure you."

Cyrus had given an order to physically harm me. I swallowed and, ignoring her warning, cut the shirt from an unconscious guard and returned to Winslet. Though she cursed and hissed, I forced her to sit up, then rigged the shirt as a sling, securing her arm to her body.

"You're coming with us," I informed her.

"Just leave," she spat at me.

Domino came up to her other side and met my gaze. I saw the question in his eyes. *Are you sure?*

I gave a clipped nod. He worked his jaw but slung an arm around her waist and carried her to the truck.

"I hope you know how to drive, Dom," I said, "because I've never learned."

"Welcome to your first lesson. Watch me and prepare to practice."

He must be kidding.

We settled in the cab, with the librarian behind the wheel. Tires squealed, and we peeled out. The landscape whizzed at our sides. An abandoned city with crumbling buildings and statues beginning to bloom with trees and flowers.

"She wasn't exaggerating," Domino said, his gaze cutting to the rearview mirror. "We've got three vans on our tail."

I twisted to peer out the back windshield and groaned. Despite the dirt flinging from our tires, the vehicles came into view. One had a large machine gun attached to its roof, with a shooter behind it.

"Once the gun is within range, it can blow this car to rubble," Winslet bragged.

The shooter took an experimental shot. At least, I figured it was experimental, since it didn't land. Or maybe it didn't land because Domino turned the wheel and we careened to the side, out of the strike zone.

"You won't be able to outrun them," Winslet added, panting. "Their vehicles are faster than mine. I just happened to be out on patrol when Cyrus's order came in."

"Okay, time to take the wheel, Arden." Domino waved me over. "The left pedal is for stopping, the right for going fast. Keep heading west, but zigzag without tipping us over whenever possible."

"Are you kidding? This wasn't any kind of lesson," I squeaked as I shifted closer, assuming control of our very lives. "What are you going to do?"

"What must be done." The second my feet replaced his, he went lax, still, and quiet, not even breathing.

I didn't understand until a familiar rain-and-earth-scented fog filled the cab. Just for a moment, I experienced the warm embrace I'd missed. Then the fog slipped through a crack in the window, engulfing everything behind us.

More shots popped off. I got nervous and jerked the wheel, attempting to avoid a statue. Our truck fishtailed.

"No fear, no fear, no fear." By a miracle, I maintained my composure, kept up our speed, and straightened us out. A few times, bullets landed, but other than some bumps, we continued sailing forward without problem.

"This is foolish," Winslet rasped. "You can't open the barrier without killing someone you love. You've already lost."

Dang it. I'd forgotten about the key to opening a doorway. We must get in. Must stop Cyrus from executing Astan's plan to gain entrance into the library.

I could think of only one way to do it.

Dread gripped me, but I disregarded it. Better this than handing Astan the victory.

Winslet slid a dagger from an ankle sheath.

Heat flared down my arm, pooling in my hand, and, by instinct, I swung my arm at her, my fiery sword appearing against her throat. "Let's call it a draw for now, hmm?" I suggested.

"Fine," she snapped, dropping her weapon.

I opened my hand, and the sword vanished. "You're on the wrong team, anyway. Soal is our only weapon against Astan, his Madness, and the total destruction of our world. That's why CURED fights so hard to make us hate him."

"Just because you *think* it's true, doesn't make it true." Pain and anger drenched her voice.

"Ah. But you've been dealing with Astan for days. You saw him work his agenda through the emperor, and now Cyrus. Is the god who urges a man to murder his pregnant lover really the one you believe should rule our lives?"

A pause. Then: "Shut up," she grumbled.

Determined to put my own plan into action, I pressed the pedal to the floor.

Chapter Thirty-One

Do not throw away my words, and understanding will come.

—*The Book of Soal* 2.16.2.7

A sea of feeders congested every path leading to the field, with more coming. I didn't slow or attempt to avoid them, giving CURED an easier target and jeopardizing my fellow passengers. Instead, I plowed through anyone in our way.

This was war, not business as usual.

We approached our destination without further incident, only to come upon our next problem: an army of glowers midbattle with feeders were outnumbered five to one. At least. Fiery swords glowed, growing brighter every time a feeder fell, as if strengthened by the victory, but not enough feeders fell.

I caught sight of Ember, who fought at the helm. Good to see her up and recharged.

Brakes squealed as I stomped on the pedal. Dirt kicked up behind the truck's tires. The second we stopped, Domino came alive again. I was currently perched on his lap. Not a big deal while he'd been out there, unaware of me, but here, now, it was kind of awkward.

Didn't matter. Feeders walled the vehicle, banging on bulletproof glass windows.

"We need a plan." Domino shifted to park and clasped my waist to lift me off. Or so I thought. He held me tight. "I slowed CURED down, but I didn't stop them. They'll arrive any minute."

I craned my neck, meeting his gaze. Determination flooded our bond. "I'm a step ahead of you for once." I looked over at Winslet. She slumped in the seat, eyes closed, sweating buckets. She'd reclaimed the dagger and now clutched it and her injured arm close. Apparently carrying Astan's essence didn't heal new wounds the way it had temporarily healed the old one. How much time did she have left? "Get me to the force field," I told Domino, "and I'll get you safely inside it." Sacrifice someone I loved? So be it.

I could die without killing him. Cyrus had suspected there was a way to sever my bond with the librarian, and I believed he was right. Snuff out the flame, and boom. Problem solved. The loss of such a deep connection would destroy Domino and me in a thousand different ways, I was certain of it, but he was gonna live, and I was gonna die anyway, so I couldn't regret it.

Suspicions flashed in his eyes. "How will you do it?"

"Better to show you rather than explain."

"But you will survive it?" he insisted.

"Dom, I'm not going to endanger your life," I assured him. "Watch me work my magic."

"Let me guess." He arched a brow. "You plan to snuff out our flame and sacrifice yourself."

"Well, I meet the only qualification. I love myself," I stated. "It'll work. You won't die with me."

"I don't care about that," he snapped.

"There's no other way." Determination mounting, I leaned over, plucked the dagger from Winslet's grip, and sheathed it at my waist. Her eyes opened and met mine. "Don't die believing a lie," I told her. I had one last chance to reach her. Might as well give it my all, nothing held back. "The Madness came from Astan. He tortures innocent people to hide the truth and trains us to do the same. His only goal is the destruction of Soal, who helps us."

The feeders applied enough pressure to crack the glass. Small lines appeared, but they grew longer and wider at a faster clip as the beatings continued.

"I won't let you sacrifice yourself," Domino vowed.

As if he could stop me. I'd made up my mind. "You should cheer me on. You'll finally be free of our unwanted connection."

"It was never unwanted, Arden." He said nothing else, throwing open the door and jumping out. Swing. The sword of fire appeared, and feeders closest to him fell, making room for me.

I stuffed his words, and whatever they meant, to a hidden corner of my mind and followed him out, then shut the door behind me to seal Winslet inside alone and safe. Well, safer.

Side by side, Domino and I made our way forward. Through the bond, I knew when to duck and when to swing my own sword.

"Arden!" Cyrus's voice cut through the grunts, groans, and thuds.

My heart leaped, as usual, but I didn't let myself become distracted. I continued pressing on with Domino, fighting, fighting. Adrenaline pumped through my veins, heating me up. A welcome development. My damp gown offered little protection against the biting wind and swiping nails.

A massive number of glowers rushed past us, attacking the feeders before us head-on, creating a path. Domino yanked me forward. Together, we ran for the gate.

"I won't let you sacrifice yourself," he repeated.

Domino spun, ending a trio of feeders who slipped free of the fray.

Nearby, Ember called out orders. "Bark, shield Talon. Murphy, boost Brenna."

Different glowers paired up, focusing on the force field, attempting different methods to get through it—and failing.

Almost there . . .

The ground. It shook so violently even glowers began to fall. What was happening? Feeders stumbled backward, losing their balance.

Thick, thorny vines broke through the surface, snatching feeders and glowers within tightening coils that slithered around them. Fire-swords snuffed out and vanished as those sharp thorns stabbed anyone who wiggled for freedom.

Inside me, dread mimicked the vines, winding and tightening. This was Briar Rose via Lolli, and these glowers were meant to be "fuel."

I spun, ready to grab Domino and run. Too late. He roared with pain as a vine grabbed him. The sword vanished. Like the others, he couldn't get free. I was the only glower left standing.

A path opened, and Cyrus appeared at the end of it, holding two bloody daggers. My heart lurched. He still wore the suit, but it was no longer pristine. Scarlet-stained rips littered the material.

I readjusted my pose, putting my sword of flames at the ready.

"I told you. You can't win," he said, as calm and smug as could be. "I've planned for every contingency."

Lolli stood at his side, her head thrown back and her arms outstretched, her fingers twitching.

Lolli isn't all powerful. Especially now. Her connection to Briar Rose is too new. Domino's voice filled my head. His spirit might not be joined to my body, but our bond was stronger than ever. *She can only funnel in what her body can tolerate. Soon, she'll tire. All you must do is stall until we get free.*

That, I could do. "Why not kill me while you've got the chance, hmm?" I demanded of Cyrus. "Or snatch me up with vines like all the others?"

He merely rocked back on his heels, silent. But then, he didn't need to say anything. We both knew the answer. Cyrus was still in there, and he loved me.

Right now, Lolli was the bigger threat. I didn't bother tossing a dagger at her. He'd only catch it. I was dealing with the host for a god, after all.

I looked at her. The vines. Lolli, the root. I followed the bark-heavy protrusions to the trapped glowers and swung. The tip of my sword sliced through dirt, severing a thick green coil. The high princess whimpered.

Exactly as I'd suspected. Take her out, and all the glowers would be freed. But I'd have to go through Cyrus to reach her.

"Don't even try," he snapped.

Two buses reached us, soldiers pouring from them, my former instructors at the helm.

Cyrus grinned. "Looks like you've run out of time, sweetness."

"Wrong." I jutted my chin. "I'm still breathing."

We stood in a stalemate, the battlefield between us a nightmare of lifeless bodies and scattered limbs bathed in the unflinching light of Theirland's twin suns. Lavender and gold streaked the sky, casting an eerie glow over the blood-soaked earth, where rivers of crimson carved fresh paths through the flatland. Overhead, a restless flock of scavenger birds circled, their shrill cries piercing the thick, heavy silence as they awaited their feast.

The fresh wave of CURED soldiers flooded the scene, surging from behind the former high prince and hurrying to kill the array of glowers trapped around me. Men and women I admired. Many more would die today if I didn't stop Cyrus. But how could I strike down the man I loved?

Was he still the man I loved, though?

In the morning's brightness, I noticed his missing facial brand. No sign of it remained, and my guts twisted. More evidence of the monster he'd become.

What other changes had Astan made to his body? To his mind? His *heart*?

"It doesn't have to end this way, Arden," he called, grin widening.

"You're right." I huffed and puffed my breaths. "Walk away, and I'll spare you."

His grin turned wry. Thin, snakelike shadows coiled up his arms and banded around his neck before absorbing into his skin. "I admit, your new confidence is adorable."

"Isn't it?" I rocked on my heels and gripped my sword with more force. Cyrus was a god of a man in more ways than one. Beautiful, tall, and powerfully built, with features somehow both surprisingly soft and far too harsh. The contradictions fit. He'd always been a paradox. Demanding yet indulgent. Mysterious but open. Perfect in his imperfections. An opponent feared by the world and yet my greatest ally. From the moment I'd first laid eyes on him, he'd fascinated me. And now, here we were, soldiers on opposite sides of a war I'd only just learned I'd been fighting my entire life.

A chorus of grunts and groans and clinking metal accompanied pops of gunfire.

"You won't kill me." Urgency whipped at my back, propelling me on. Soal claimed I would stab the new emperor and live a romance. The comeback story of all comeback stories. Very well. I would do what I didn't do before and trust him. "But I will hurt you if you continue on this path."

He tsked. "You give me too little credit and yourself too much. I will do whatever proves necessary to secure my rule." A promise he'd made at the start of this journey. "Join my team. Merciful leader that I am, I'll give you one more chance. Refuse, and my desire for you will no longer factor into my decisions."

There was no reason to ponder my response. I lifted my sword. "I will never help you destroy Soal."

Cyrus hiked his broad shoulders. "That's disappointing but not shocking. Just know you chose this, sweetness."

Lie! "No, sweetie. *You* chose it."

He drew in a deep breath, then released a short, sharp exhalation. "Let's get to it, then."

"Yes. Let's." Heart a war drum, I ran at him.

He ran at me.

We met in the middle . . .

I swung my sword of fire. He blocked with ease, as I expected—and hoped.

"Come now, Lady Pink," he said, grinning as he deflected my next strikes. "Your jealousy is cute but tardy. You had your chance."

I knew I couldn't get past him in a physical fight. He'd trained me, and this student hadn't yet surpassed her teacher. But overcoming him with my skill wasn't Plan A. As I thrust and parried, I confessed, "I love you, Cyrus."

He lost the grin. "Not as before. I can tell."

"I need your help one last time."

"I don't care. My desire for you has already faded." He snapped the words at me. "You are alive only as a backup host for Briar Rose. Soon, someone else will be found."

Astan was a liar, incapable of speaking the truth. I could no longer trust anything Cyrus said, even this. Not desire me? Ha!

I took my next strike a little slower, hoping he'd take the bait.

He caught my wrist. I almost grinned as I opened my fingers, ensuring the sword of fire vanished. Rather than launch another strike, I heaved my body against him, flung my arms around his shoulders, and pressed my mouth into his, kissing him with all the love and passion I contained.

He wrenched his face from mine, pressed the tip of the dagger to my throat, and glared down at me, panting.

I licked my lips, imploring him with my gaze. "Don't let me die without a goodbye kiss, Cyrus. Please."

He huffed his next breath. Growled. Scowled. And . . .

With another curse, he dropped the dagger, swooped down, and kissed me. Kissed me hard and fast and thoroughly, until I knew I'd reached the heart of him. I kissed him back while combing my fingers through his hair.

Tears seared my eyes when I encountered horn buds. But I didn't stop feeding him the passion I'd harbored for so long . . . didn't stop pouring my love into him as I snapped off the last bracelet I'd taken from him, flicked it into a blade, and thrust it through his abdomen.

Grunting, he shoved me away and peered down at his gushing wound. Blood leaked from the corners of his mouth.

I wasted no time, sprinting to Lolli, exchanging the bloody blade for my sword of fire. Her eyes popped open upon my approach; she twisted to hit me with a vine, but I swung, removing her head. Her knees buckled. Down she fell, her vines falling with her, freeing the captives. Glowers sprang from the tangle while fending off their opponents. Thousands of shadows shot from her body, screaming as they filled the sky.

Without hesitation, I ran for the force field. At the same time, I dove inward, centering on the flame that empowered my bond to Domino. The brightest and strongest of them. I reached for it, preparing to snuff it out.

A terrible roar drew my gaze to the shadow-filled sky, and my jaw nearly unhinged. Vyle flew toward us, flapping wings of smoke. Wisps of fire sparked from the corners of his mouth, as if he was attempting to spew flames.

Bala had come to aid her master.

Heart thudding, I quickened my velocity. Problem: Winslet stood in front of the force field, hunched over and gasping for breath, even as she stretched out her arms with a dagger in hand, as if she intended to stop me.

If I had to fight her . . .

Her gaze found mine. "Don't let CURED win," she rasped—and stabbed herself, slicing into her own carotid.

I skidded to a halt and gasped. Like Lolli, she toppled. Crimson spurted from her wound, coating the force field. The glittery air shimmered, and a doorway appeared. I stood there, floundering in disbelief.

She was dead. Had sacrificed herself, letting me live. Tears sprang free, streaking hotly over my cheeks.

"Arden!" Domino's voice yanked me out of my shell shock.

The mission. Right. I kicked into motion, slipping through the new door. He ran at my side. I wanted to stop and thank Winslet, but that would have to come later.

Cyrus must have sent in an army as soon as he welcomed Astan, because soldiers waited near the growing Rock, their harbingers trained on us. *Boom, boom, boom.*

Domino twirled his sword, using it as a shield. Forget the army. The difference a single night had made in the structure boggled my mind. The Rock now reached my midsection. And it was still growing, right before my eyes.

A contingent of glowers followed us in, some hanging back to keep out feeders.

The guards continued to hammer at the triggers of their guns. I mimicked Domino, swirling my sword faster and faster until I, too, produced a shield. A conversation we'd once had echoed.

How did you become a librarian?

I bonded to the Rock on a deeper level, becoming part of the doorway itself.

The process required a sole individual. Domino couldn't do it, I'd bet. He was already a doorway.

But I wasn't, despite our bond.

As more roars pierced the air, smoke and flames billowed on the breeze. Vyle must be gaining strength.

"Get me to the Rock," I told Domino. "I'll do the rest."

He cast me a glance teeming with admiration. "See you on the other side, Arden." With the speed of a bullet, he launched at the guards and called, "Ember! Kenneth!"

Both glowers fought their way over, and together we fought our way forward. The countdown in my head morphed into chimes, signaling the last seconds on the clock.

Ding. Cyrus recovered from his injuries and joined the fray.

Ding. Vyle spewed a stream of fire into the throng as he flew through the door.

Ding. War sounds crowded in my ears. More clanging metal. Sharper grunts and groans. Piercing screams. Thuds as soldiers fell.

Ding. The Rock grew another inch.

Ding. The Rock widened.

Ding. An opening between the guards appeared, thanks to Domino. I dove through it. The soldiers noticed. One lunged for me, dragging his blade through my middle and over my thigh.

Searing agony consumed me as I collided into the Rock.

Ding.

The stony fragments grew another inch, their pointy spindles digging into my wounds—growing through them. I screamed as my world went dark.

Chapter Thirty-Two

Not every story has a happy ending.

—*The Book of Soal* 2.1.25.46

I floated in a space without time, where the past, present, and future all transpired at once, everything I'd ever done or would do happening simultaneously, always, and forever. As I slipped in and out of consciousness, I knew everything and nothing.

Awareness came with pinpricks of strength. A prick here, a prick there. Heat spread from the punctures, infiltrating muscles and bones, activating my mind.

I blinked open my eyes and gasped. I stood rooted in place, but I also somehow remained in motion, drifting through the skies of Theirland, peering over the entire expanse all at once. It was bigger than I'd ever realized, with four castles hidden in the far corners of the realm. They each topped a mountain.

The dual sensations I experienced mystified me as much as the worldview.

"Am I dead?" I asked, my voice echoing in the void.

"Far from it. You're more alive than you've ever been." Domino approached me and suddenly I—we—occupied a private room in the library. And yet, I maintained my awareness of the Rock. "You are officially a librarian."

Me, one of the elites. Just imagine!

I scanned the unfamiliar areas and frowned. A lovely room with glass displays of weapons, a mystery tree growing in a corner, and a hologram projecting snippets from my life at Fort Bala.

"I don't understand," I said, spotting the sign that hung over the door. It read **Arden Dawn Roosa**. "What is this place?" *Why* was this place? Stretching out my arms to graze the flowers carved into the wood doorframe, I realized I wore a buttery-soft red cloak. I looked myself over and marveled. A robe like Domino's.

"This," he said, "is your memorial."

"But you just said I wasn't dead."

He held up his hand, requesting quiet, which I happily gave. "When we do special things for Soal, memorials like these are erected. Members of the Tome Society can come, read about our exploits, and learn from our mistakes and successes." As he spoke, he walked around, motioning to symbols carved into the wall. Just like the symbols on the Rock.

Oh, wow. "You have a memorial?"

He nodded. "I do."

So badly I wanted to see it. Read it. But first, I would read my own. Easy to do. The symbols became text, the story of my life there for the taking.

Heart fluttering, I walked about, drinking in my tale. How I didn't trust what I read and traveled down a wrong road. How I'd ultimately corrected my path. How I sacrificed my life for the Rock. How, in return, I gained a new life with a bright future ahead . . . after a series of turbulent times. The symbols that told of those turbulent times, I couldn't yet decode. But I didn't grow nervous by what was to come. I knew what I was fighting for now. Not just Cyrus and me but others. As many people as possible. The world!

My world.

"How much time has passed since I bonded to the Rock?" I asked.

"A few hours."

Goodness. I would have guessed days or weeks or years had come and gone.

"You have much more to learn, and now your true training can begin." Domino took the spot at my side, standing shoulder to shoulder with me. "You're soon to see things you never dreamed possible. Do things that will baffle you even years later and discover a truth you will need eons to comprehend."

"You aren't helping ease the turbulence of my transition," I muttered, tracing my fingertips over a circle with smaller circles inside it.

"Perhaps this will. Your first assignment will be recruiting Mykal Ellison."

Truly? "Consider it done."

He smiled at me. "I thought you'd like that. Now, then. You'll be based inside the library, but you'll be responsible for your domain in Theirland. You can access both worlds through any section of the Rock at any time, but your light will only grow brighter to feeders, and there will be no hiding it. You'll be a lure for them, and they will want only to eat you. Among other things."

"Wait. Back up. My domain?"

"The area adjoining your portion of the Rock." He waved his hand, and the wall became a screen, peering out at the field in Theirland, where I'd offered my life for a cause greater than myself.

I saw both in the physical realm and the spiritual, the perimeter line of "my domain" highlighted by a soft golden glow. That border circled the entire structure and ten feet of flat, barren field.

Guess I'd have to figure out how I felt about all this. What did my responsibilities entail, exactly?

Domino nudged my shoulder with his own. "No worries. I'll help and train you."

"Thank you," I rasped. He was a good man. Wonderful in more ways than I could list. And honestly? I was beginning to see him as an extension of myself, just like my sword. "For everything."

He nodded to acknowledge my words. "When next you fight Cyrus, you'll be ready. I vow it."

Another battle with Cyrus. I flinched. He was my ex, now the emperor, king, and leader of CURED, Ourland, and Theirland. Once my dream, now my nightmare. Worse, he might be Lolli's husband.

I curled my hands into fists. Cyrus was a god and my greatest enemy. Would I ever really be ready to go head-to-head with him?

"For now," Domino said, stalking toward the exit, "I'll let you say goodbye to your past."

He vanished through the doorway, and an approaching presence caught my notice. But the intruder didn't come into the room. My attention zeroed in on the Rock.

Cyrus stood just outside my domain in Theirland. He was shirtless and shoeless, clad only in a pair of black leathers. He peered at me, but also not at me, because I somehow occupied every square inch of the Rock. Slowly walking from one end to the other, he examined every inch of the structure—of me.

"Looks like we have ourselves a dilemma, sweetness," he said, and the huskiness of his voice rippled all over me. "You have something that's mine."

I cringed inwardly, seeing him in a way I never had. The shadows he'd absorbed to host Astan filled his veins, a slight tracery visible beneath his skin. And his eyes . . . A wild glint dominated his irises. Greed clung to him. Evil—there was no other word for it—seeped from his pores.

This wasn't my Cyrus. I'd comprehended that, but I really understood it now.

"The war is only beginning, you know," he said. "Briar Rose will choose another host. The other gods are already rising. Humans are ill prepared for what's coming. They'll crumple as I enforce my rule, and Soal will follow."

Persuasion saturated his tone. He was utterly convinced of his own words.

I admit, his words roused anger. He spoke of murdering my friends, my allies, and those I intended to help. "What part do you expect me to play in this?" My voice imbued every inch of my domain, a whisper and a bellow rolled into one.

"There you are." He stopped in the center and smiled. "Hello, Lady Pink."

"Hello, Cyrus."

"Not sugar bear?"

"Not at this time." Head high, I stepped from the stone, and it felt like walking from the middle of a wave. My robe refit itself to my body, hardening into armor. It happened in an instant and automatically, with no conscious thought on my part. Like a computer running in the background.

The picture of indulgence, he slid his hands into his pockets and rocked back on his heels. "The Rock becomes you, but you'll look even better wrapped in me."

I allowed no reaction. "You said you no longer desire me."

"I've said many things."

"True. You also said you were born to rule. But *I'm* saying not like this. Not with Astan."

He waved away my words. "Too late."

"Then we are enemies."

"We are. The worst has yet to come, you know."

"For you? Yes. I know." And I did. I would show him no mercy in my quest to win him. Once, he'd brought me into the Rock. Now I returned the favor.

Cyrus smiled. "I'll come after you with everything I've got."

"Good. I look forward to your surrender." I tilted my head and returned the smile with one of my own, more confident than I'd been in a long time. I hadn't read more of my book yet, but here, now, I had an ingrained knowledge of what I'd find at the end: victory. "I meant it when I said I love you."

"Loving me will kill you," he warned.

"But you'll live again, so I'm okay with that."

He went still, as if surprised.

"I'm going to free you, Cyrus Dolion. Consider yourself a mansel in distress. I'm the foe you can't shake, even in your wildest dreams. I won't give you up, won't back down, won't capitulate."

Unbridled amusement flashed over his features. "I don't need freeing, sweetness. But you will. I have plans for you . . ."

I lifted my chin. "Whatever you attempt will fail."

He hiked his shoulders, shrugging again. "We shall see."

Yes. We would. "You once loved Soal," I reminded him.

"I supposed I loved you more." He smiled again. "Soal's book told me to give you up. I refused then, and I refuse now. That became clear to me when you branded me with your kiss." He rubbed his fingers over his once-scarred cheek. "This one you cannot see. But I'll win you, just give me time. What I'll do when I have you, for however long I decide you may keep breathing, well, we'll find out together." He strode off, whistling as he vanished.

My heart thudded as I eased back, sinking into the Rock.

Domino waited for me, his presence a much-needed comfort. His dog, Archive, sat at his feet.

Uh . . . We weren't in my memorial but a small, plain chamber with a bed, desk, and private bathroom.

"Your new quarters," he said, spreading his arms. "Decorate it however you please."

I bent down to pet the little cutie. Such soft fur. Maybe he sensed my bond to Domino. Archive leaned into my touch, eager for more, as if he sensed my bond to his dad.

"Come." A picture of power and security, the librarian offered me his hand. "Let's prepare you for what's to come."

Without hesitation, I slid my fingers into his as I stood. "Yes. Let's." Nothing would stop me now.

About the Author

Photo © 2024 Sara's Photo Creations

Gena Showalter is the *New York Times* and *USA Today* bestselling author of over one hundred wildly addictive novels. Known for weaving heart-racing romance into paranormal, fantasy, contemporary, and young adult tales, she's also ventured into the world of cowriting quirky, cozy mysteries and a guide for writing a novel in a year. When she's not plotting epic love stories or slaying deadlines, she wears the titles of mom, grandma, and fur mom. There's a high possibility she's currently working on her next swoon-worthy book and already has a serious crush on the hero.